From Ymir's flesh the earth was formed...
from his bones the mountains...
the heavens from the skull of that ice-cold giant...
from his blood the seas...from his brains the clouds.

The wise jötunn, Vafþrúðnir
(from the Old Norse *Poetic Edda*)

ROBERT L RUSSELL

THOR'S
CRAFTSMEN

BOHANNON HALL PRESS

Library of Congress Control Number: 2024924159

Publisher's Cataloging-in-Publication Data

Russell, Robert L, 1963-
    Thor's Craftsmen / by Robert L Russell ; illustrated by Emelia Ann Designs.
    Niceville, FL: Bohannon Hall Press, 2025.
    330 p.: illustrated ; 23 cm.
    First edition.

1. Science Fiction, American. 2. Weather Control—Fiction 3. Meteorologist—Fiction.
I. Title. II. Russell, Emelia Ann, 1977- III. Mcleod, Bob (fictitious character)
PS3618.U77T464 2025   2024924159

ISBN 978-1-962995-10-8 (softcover)

Published by Bohannon Hall Press

Thank you to all the family, friends and fans who invested some of their precious time and treasure to support me by taking a chance on Thor's Apprentice. Your investment in me is what inspired my commitment to following that effort with Thor's Journeymen and now, Thor's Craftsmen. I truly hope you enjoy this work because it was done for you.

TABLE OF CONTENTS

CHAPTER ONE

RAINBOWS AND DECISIONS

To the world watching in or via the press assembled in Australia, the first on-demand weather modification demonstration by the United Nations with the Chinese facilitating the Thor's Hammer technology was an outstanding success. Within just a few days of the Secretary General's personal announcement of the demonstration his newly regrouped team with his personal participation just pulled off a seemingly flawless operation halfway around the world to restore global confidence in this new technology after the mixed results in India. The UN's disaster which resulted in numerous fatalities and injuries was followed quickly by an impressive second event led by the CCP team who claimed to have more experience with the emerging technology. Their own demonstration, which included a rainbow over the spectator's area was both impressive and inspiring.

After accepting the CCP's help into the existing UN team the encore performance down under in Darwin, which also included a rainbow promised in advance, had renewed the hope of many around the world. News cycles and their video coverage tend to determine how slowly, or quickly large groups forgive and forget, or don't. In this instance, the flames of hope and optimism for what this new technology could do to improve the lives of many were fanned with the encore success in Australia.

The images and videos of the rainbows and those who produced them adorned the news websites, social media, television, podcasts, memes and every other communication medium. This quickly fueled the desires of many to forget the tragedy related to this same technology a mere week or so prior. That was fine for everyone involved, in fact it was the objective, and that objective was achieved.

This was being celebrated by the UN team as they were packing up what they could in preparation for their departure from Australia to the surprise new destination of New York. They were to do a demonstration on their home field at the UN Headquarters. For some this would be a welcome homecoming back to the United States, but for most of the UN team this would be their first time in the US. This was especially true for the new team members from the CCP component who were now ostensibly providing the technical oversight for the employment of Thor's Hammers. While the majority of the team was reveling in their Australian success and the announcement of their next demonstration location, there were a few members of the UN team who had a very different outlook on the day's events as well as those in their near future.

Major General Chen who was the CCP's military lead for the UN effort and their lead *technical advisor*, Mr. Wu, were chief among those who were in that minority state of mind. In fact, both men were currently sitting silently in a small meeting room with their UN counterparts US Air Force Brigadier General Frank Lincoln and Professor Robert Mcleod as they waited for the US National Security Advisor to join them. As they sat waiting, Frank considered the pros and cons of having this discussion with both Chinese team leaders but he had come to trust Tom's judgement especially on politically sensitive matters of this kind. He knew from the limited small talk they had engaged in that these men had families and he was confident that would weigh heavily in what they decided to do next.

While the world focused on yet another very successful and inspiring UN demonstration culminating with cheers and happy snaps of the programmed conditions that produced a rainbow for the crowd, they were intentionally unaware of some additional successes transpiring at the same time. While the weather was being modified and new conditions appeared as described for the spectators and media to observe, some of those observations had been altered for internal use by the technology team. This intentional data manipulation created a false sense of concern that was deliberately escalated to generate fear among a targeted set of the demonstration team, specifically Mr. Wu and his remote clandestine regional weather modification airborne system operators. The false data gave him the impression things were not going as planned, as he was getting conflicting information from his UN and CCP teammates which triggered a series of radio and computer system calls to provide both clarity and confidence in one version of the truth over the other. He had in fact confirmed through a series of contacts that the expected CCP regional on-demand weather capability had performed as expected and the UN team's data was flawed. Those urgent contacts were what was needed.

In doing so, the host nation military and other US national technical teams were able to identify and *acquire* these unsanctioned CCP systems operating in Australian sovereign territory without coordination or approval. And for that, Major General Chen and Mr. Wu would be held accountable by both their home and their host nations. For now, they sat quietly pondering what that might look like in either instance. After what seemed like an eternity plus one year, Tom, the US Ambassador to Australia and a man who only identified himself as a Senior Australian Government Official speaking on behalf of the Prime Minister entered the room each taking a seat as they surveyed the others in the room before beginning what could only be described as an uncomfortable conversation.

The Australian Government official began the conversation with a simple statement. "Major General Chen, what we observed and have now confirmed can only be described as a deliberate, hostile and unsanctioned operation against the Australian people conducted within our sovereign lands and airspace. This is an act of war, clearly was deliberate and conducted by those under your command. As such, you are being held as a Prisoner of War not a criminal. And Mr. Wu despite your civilian attire, given your role in this unsanctioned action, you are clearly an enemy combatant in this operation are also being held in the same status as a prisoner of war. Do you both understand my government's position as I have explained it to you?" The man paused and waited for each to respond.

General Chen shook his head left then right in reluctant agreement as he spoke, "That is your view from what you know, and I understand there is little I can say or do to change that. I understand your position, Sir."

Mr. Wu took his lead from the General, but appeared confused as to what this meant for him and how that might differ since he was not a military member. As they were similar in status within their governing party, Mr. Wu always considered the uniformed members as a workforce assigned to meet the stated objectives for the weather modification effort. "I understand what you said, but I am not sure I know what that means for me. I am not a military man; I am a scientist and not a warrior like my friend General Chen." Mr. Wu quibbled without surrendering his peer status with his colleague. He was a party loyalist and knew that whatever happened he would need the Major General on his side whether that was here or at home, if they ever made it back home.

"Why is it there are no UN seniors here for this discussion? I see the Australian and US governments are represented but I don't see my UN colleagues. Why is that?" Major General Chen asked and Tom took the opportunity to enter the conversation to provide the needed clarity for all those in the room.

"War is not a UN interest. Peacekeeping, yes, and we may get to a point where that is our topic, at which time, we will expand the participants. Right now, our ally Australia has asked for US assistance in addressing this unprovoked act of aggression against their homeland. And we are more than happy to oblige in this situation. So, let's cut right to it. Shall we get to the heart of the matter General, or do you want to spend time posturing or testing our resolve? I have the time and position to do either but you and Mr. Wu sadly do not. In a very short time, you will have no options because your weather modification systems are not only offline, they are off to somewhere other than where you intended them to go. You won't get them back. The stories you tell your superiors will either get you dead or keep you from getting dead. I imagine they will also significantly impact the health and well-being of your families, but you would know much more about that than we could.

"So that you have complete situational clarity, I will confirm for you some things you may suspect but not know for sure. We have each of the remotely piloted vehicles and their airborne weather modification systems that you used in today's operation, as well as, the airborne spares. We have the command-and-control vehicle, the input distribution communications modules and their operators. We also have Zach and the both of you. What we don't have yet is the final decision on what to do with all of this. That is where you get a limited say in your own fate." Tom paused to let this sink in, as he decided to take the awkward silence as long as needed until one of the two CCP men broke the silence. That would be the indicator for where this discussion would likely end up.

"Why should we believe such a story?" Mr. Wu challenged Tom's summarized version of today's events but was surprised to hear Major General Chen responding to his question instead.

"Because you panicked, broke our established protocols and, in the process, pointed them to every operational asset we had down here. You made it as easy as taking candy from a baby, Mr. Wu. It's as if you had planned it with them, and that is how it will look to those who were monitoring the events from our homeland. You and Zach both doubled your billing and turned over our most sensitive capabilities to your new partners who have deeper pockets to fund a bigger piece of the pie for you than the party at home would ever consider. It doesn't have to be true; it only has to appear to be true and Tom here has made sure that is what it looks like."

He paused, then looked at Mr. Wu as he continued, "And for your actions I will pay dearly. I am accountable for the success of this operation, and any failure. Today's failure was spectacular, and it happened under my command. I will be held accountable for your failure, actual or perceived.

The US, or Australia, has our RPV systems. It doesn't matter for us if it's one, the other or both because, at the end of the day, we don't have them. You and I, Wu, will be blamed for losing or giving away this crown jewel of CCP global technological influence. Instead of adding to our own nation's power, we handed it over to our peer nation-states. No coming back from that Mr. Wu. There is no choice of which story to pursue here, Tom. The price for failure if we return to our homes is certain. The choice for Wu and me is simply life, or death. That is our decision today. There is only one outcome if we return to China; there are perhaps alternatives to choose from for us, if we do not.

"My decision is already made but, Mr. Wu, you must choose for yourself, either life outside of China or death back in China. There is no guarantee they won't find you wherever you go. Likely they will search for us and, just as likely, they will find us and kill us anyway. But returning to China guarantees it."

Tom was impressed at how calmly General Chen communicated the situation to the man who put him in it in the first place. And he did it with the appropriate candor and severity the situation warranted. In fact, Tom was curious what decision he had already made, more so than he cared about the decision Mr. Wu had not yet made.

"I have a wife and child at my home. A sister with a husband and child, and our parents," Wu paused as he considered what fate they may endure because of his actions. "How can I be assured of their well-being?"

"You can't but we could try. We will need to get them all to one spot, then we can bring them all to join you. That said, the more people, the more likely they are to be caught. That is an all or nothing game for them if we agree to that course of action," Tom began. "Listen, I like both of you guys, but I won't bullshit you. We aren't the ones who are going to be trying to make your families pay for what you did; that gift is coming from your countrymen. We will do our best to get your families out but, at the end of the day, whatever happens to them is largely, almost exclusively, on them." He paused to give Mr. Wu a chance to re-engage which he quickly took.

"To get my family out. To have them meet with me, live safely somewhere else. What will that require of me, to get that for them?" Mr. Wu had seen the light that Major General Chen had shined brightly on the face of his countryman who was uniquely responsible for the predicament in which both men found themselves. Tom's response was short and measured.

"You work for us now. You explain and train us in detail how to use these airborne units. We get whatever we need to understand and safely operate these systems. Just as importantly, you provide us a roadmap to everything that is already operational. All the regional systems already out there, those that are planned, and what is beyond those. You gotta give us everything. Both of you. Either you are both all in or you are both out. Candidly, my preference is you are both in, but I don't always get what I want as you can appreciate seeing how I am stuck out here with you all," Tom concluded and his attempt at humor was not at all appreciated.

"That is a lot to ask of us Mr. Tom." Wu protested, but Tom popped off with a ready response.

"How much is your family worth to you, Mr. Wu? Less than we have asked you to provide, is that more valuable to you than your family? Really?" Tom pushed back.

"No, that is not what I was saying, I mean what I was going to say..." Wu argued with Tom as he struggled to fully comprehend his situation.

Major General Chen quickly tired of Wu's struggling to come to terms with the situation. "Wu, they will own us. We will do what they say when they say. We will give them what they want; tell them what they want to know. It's little different than our current situation in China, except the Americans won't eliminate our families if we fail or fail to deliver in our mission like we have done here. In return, they will unite us to the extent they can with those family members who are willing to relocate to the US to be with us. Those who do not will likely pay a heavy price. A selfish death for us and our family is not a luxury we can choose when the alternative includes a life with our families...wherever that might be. I choose my family and a new beginning. There is no other option," he paused and looked somberly at the man who was about to make his life easier or harder.

"Then, General, I accept your choice and will do the same. Mr. Tom, it looks like we will be wanting some assurances about our family members before we get much further into what our next steps here might include," Wu summarized as it appeared they were entering a new phase of the UN fielding of Thor's Hammers.

"Very well then," Tom agreed. "You will provide me the names and locations of your immediate family members. Those will be our priority. You will also provide the names and locations of others, family friends, peers whom you believe your authorities may use to try to leverage you to do something other than what we have agreed to. This list is important but the names on this list will be opportune and not our priority. Do you understand the important distinction I am making here? We cannot promise anything with respect to their safety but, if there is something we can do during our approved operations, we will include those people if it presents little or no additional risk." Tom paused to make sure that they clearly understood that help was conditional. It had to be beneficial to the US. It was not because these people were important to Chen or Wu.

"Yes, Tom," Chen agreed. "I understand, you will help them only if it helps your government's objective. We are quite familiar with that concept."

"I suppose you are," Tom agreed. "We will begin getting your people out immediately. But they will need to come voluntarily. We will not kidnap anyone, and we will make all our contacts at the same time to prevent any reaction. They will have one opportunity only. That is how these things work. This will all happen while we are en route back to New York. We will know who is joining you by the time you arrive in the States. You won't be going back to your country. Neither will those who choose to join you. That will be our focus for the next few hours. Making your lists and helping us determine where they will be and how best to communicate with them. Most important in this process is you helping craft the short message for each family member because it will need to be convincing if you want them to walk off with the person delivering it on your behalf. Shall we begin now?" Tom asked already knowing the answer.

As both men nodded in agreement, he addressed the rest of the group, "All right then. General Chen and Mr. Wu will come with me so we can begin our tasks. The rest of you will need to continue business as usual, packing things up and loading out for our next scheduled demonstration in New York. This looks, smells, tastes just like we have done in the past. We have eyes and ears much closer and watching from everywhere now. So, be mindful of what you do and say. You are not to discuss, even among yourselves, anything about any of the operations or events outside of the demonstration that we put on for the public. It's all overt operations or it's not discussed until our next get together which will be stateside. So, take some time and be as normal as any of us can be with what we are here to do for the UN. Except you, Frank, I need a word. The rest of you, thank you and see you back stateside."

With that the few key players in the room cleared out with their minds working hard to digest the events they just witnessed and their significant impacts on those families. Tom walked toward Frank and they had a short but intense conversation not for the ears of the other two who remained.

"Frank, I need you to take this circus back to New York, but I need a *Charlie Foxtrot* arrival that takes a couple of days to sort out. Airplanes diverted to alternate airfields...ground transportation and hotels all spread out...cargo unaccounted for. I mean a real shit show in the Big Apple. We need as much time and confusion as we can between right now and them being able to confirm what they likely already suspect. I know that may tarnish the Air Force's, maybe even the US's, otherwise stellar reputation on such things, but the irony will play well with the press. UN on-demand weather modification team's arrival and schedule impacted by bad weather in New York. Have Bob gin up something with Thor's Hammer if you guys can't think of something better. However you do it, you need to make it believable enough to buy me a couple of days to pull off the rest of this stuff. If we don't have their families in the states, these two will have no reason to help us and I don't intend to bullshit them if we come up empty. The alternative for us and them is not a pleasant one. I need this one Frank; they need it; we all need it," he ended.

"OK Tom, I will make it happen," Frank assured him.

"Thanks Frank. We probably should have made you a two star but you'll see that soon enough," Tom said as he turned toward Chen and Wu and gestured for them to follow him.

As word from the Secretary General's announcement of New York as the next demonstration location spread, Betty first heard it from the news coverage of his speech. While she was excited at the prospect of rejoining the group, she was unsure if that would happen or what her role might be in this newly integrated UN-CCP team. At this point that really didn't matter too much to her as long as she had the opportunity to help where she could. She was proud of what she and Steve and Miloc had uncovered since their return, but the lack of information since then proved frustrating for her and Steve, as they waited for word from across the world on what their next task would entail.

That was one side of the coin, the other side of the coin was just as interesting but not at all frustrating. For the last several days Steve and Betty spent time together exploring New York, eating and drinking their way from one site to another all the while getting to know each other. They had more in common than either expected when they met and spending time on whatever they decided in this new place proved to be quite an adventure for both. Without ever using the word date, the two widowed colleagues found themselves doing exactly what most people would describe as being on a series of dates while on vacation in New York. They were very much enjoying themselves and getting to know each other in the process.

As they sat in a small Italian deli having lunch, Steve's cell phone rang and, surprised at the clarity of the connection, he put the call on speaker for Betty to hear Ann's words. "Hi Dad, how are you?"

"Great, doing great but, more importantly, how are you?" Steve asked.

"Fine. I suppose you saw the demonstration down under went great. It was amazing. I can't wait to see you and tell you all about it in person," Ann gushed, knowing the story was going to be a two-drink event.

"And I suppose you also saw the Secretary General's announcement that the next one will now be in New York? We are packing up now to head back. I can't wait to see you."

"Yes, we heard. We are excited to see you, too. Can't wait for you to get back. How's Bob?"

"*WE*...can't wait?" Ann asked through her smile.

"Hi Ann; it's Betty. Your dad and I are having lunch together. He put you on speaker; that's great to hear you will be back soon. I don't know how much more of this sight-seeing and tourist adventures we can handle without a little real work to balance it out just a little bit."

"How much more *WE* can handle? You too, Betty? OK then, get your vacationing while you can, we will have some work to do when we get back. And he's fine by the way, Bob, he's fine. See you both in a couple of days, I will send the details when we have them. Or maybe we will just surprise you when we get back. Love you, love you both." Ann hung up and smiled as she looked over at Bob who was looking a bit puzzled at her.

"We might just have to consider a double wedding," she joked as she walked toward him. "Seems Betty and my dad are getting along pretty well by the sounds of that call. They are out having lunch...again, and I can just hear the smiles in both of their voices. Maybe we should give them a few extra days," Ann smiled as she hugged Bob, not realizing that Tom and Frank had already set that little favor into motion.

CHAPTER TWO

STARTS AND RESTARTS

As they were waved aboard by the young Airman standing on the ramp of the large cargo jet, Bob and Ann joined the group who walked toward and then climbed into its cavernous cargo bay. They made their way past the pallets and the tie-down straps securing them to the floor and took a couple of seats for a full day of flying to New York. The long flight would allow them time to consider all that waited for them as they entered a very new phase of this saga. While Bob and Ann had chosen to continue their current roles supporting the UN's effort to first demonstrate and then field Thor's Hammer technology, they had a new context and timeline in which they needed to do these things. The revelations of the past few days were still difficult to fathom for Bob and he appreciated the relative downtime he expected to have on the flight to process it all.

He could not shake the fear of missing out on the development efforts already underway to understand the advanced airborne versions of Thor's Hammers they had just liberated from the CCP in Australia. Knowing there were more of these covertly operating in many regions including in the US both excited and infuriated the atmospheric scientist. Here he was now embracing the task of bringing a new technology to the world that was not new at all. His job now included describing what the capability could do for the greater good, but doing so without exposing what it has already been doing for years to advance the interests of a few. All this needed to be done while also contributing to, but not exposing, the ongoing efforts of the US and UN who were the unlikeliest of partners given the UN's history. They now had to leapfrog the existing CCP regional capabilities by putting their own systems on orbit to neutralize the existing clandestine networks. What could be simpler?

It made him wonder what Doc would have done in this situation, and that made him think some more about what happened to him and why. Doc paid the ultimate price for discovering their secret, and Bob still needed justice for what they did to him. Intellectually it was clearly a technology the CCP deemed worth killing for and would likely have been viewed the same way by any other government who secretly possessed it. Bob could see that from a political perspective, but every one of those decisions impacts real people and that makes each action personal. At least it's personal for the people on the receiving end of those decisions. Doc, Betty, Father Gannon, Bob, Ann and now all those in their orbits were still being impacted by a decision to eliminate the person who could and did reveal that secret. And to what end when instead of keeping that secret, the results of that decision further exposed it, so they failed?

And now, very similarly, Tom had Major General Chen and Mr. Wu were making similar decisions. While under different circumstances, their decisions would likely have the same results for some of their family members and colleagues. Once again, some would likely perish in a seemingly futile effort to keep some version of this technology a secret to gain an advantage, or at least to mitigate the risk from an advantage that already existed. It seemed to Bob this was a never ending back and forth and, whether it was this technology, the one before it, or the ones to come after it, the story seemed to change very little except for the names of the technology, their locations and, most importantly, the names of the people who had to pay the price for their version of the same basic story.

To support that line of reasoning, Bob considered Chen and Wu, the decisions they made and the outcomes each expected. But their comrades, the two Senior Colonels who clearly were there to run the clandestine network of advanced sensors, were not given the same opportunity to decide their own fate. Quite the opposite. They would shoulder the blame for not only losing the hardware that was captured, but also for the mysterious disappearance of their two important colleagues. Someone would need to pay the price for these losses, for the embarrassment, and for not seeing the treachery of Chen and Wu who would clearly be considered traitors. Those sins would surely fall on the shoulders of the two senior military men who were left behind to fill the important roles of both distraction and scapegoat for all that just occurred. Bob reasoned there were few alternatives to them meeting a fate similar to Doc's and, while that was not personal for Bob, he understood that the two Senior Colonels would have a very different view from his own. Bob considered what he might do to ensure that he and those around him were not put in a similar position in retaliation for what was unfolding now.

As he was deep in thought, Ann was drifting in and out of a nap that never really took hold on the loud, jostling and generally too warm aircraft. She could see Bob was wrestling with something in his head and thought better than to interrupt whatever he was pondering. So, she yawned, stretched and tried to force herself back into her mediocre nap. There were still a lot of flight hours to log before they reached their destination.

Zach had also endured a very long flight out of Australia but his was much more comfortable than the military cargo jet carrying the UN team back to New York. While he was not sure precisely where in Florida he was being held, Zach was confident he was on a military installation with heavy security and little else in the way of staff or facilities. He correctly reasoned that he was on a large range, auxiliary airfield, or other remote spot that was convenient by air to any number of important and accessible government installations and technology centers. Having time to consider both his situation and what value he might bring to whatever the next thing would turn into had put him in a foul mood.

The US military, and the UN by extension, had their own Thor's Hammers and now also possessed the most advanced airborne versions in the CCP inventory. The version of this technology that Doc and Bob had turned over were among the earliest and most limited range systems. The ones captured in Darwin were the most advanced and capable in the CCP program. They did not have an overall program name, but instead had names for each of the regions the systems were operating. The Thor's theme was unique to the area of operations that included the University.

The recent celebrity Bob initiated and the UN attained for Thor's Hammer unknowingly served as a great source of embarrassment for the CCP members assigned to their still-operating regional network of the same name. Every headline or video that referred to that name unwittingly rubbed just a little salt in the wound for those affiliated with the current program. Those affiliated with the earlier program were very few and far between as the loss of their namesake device to Doc was more than many assigned to it were able to survive. While considering this amused Zach a little, he understood the embarrassment of getting outside the lines of acceptable outcomes and being consumed by an entity that had little tolerance for failure or treachery. And, while he appreciated being liberated from his unexpected stint with the CCP, he recognized that would come at a high cost. His day of reckoning with the leadership of the nation whom he had recently betrayed was now imminent as he was back on US soil. It was ironic because, for Zach, the CCP captivity was his temporary freedom from US consequences. He correctly reasoned it would not take long to see which was going to be worse, US or CCP captivity.

For now, anyway, the accommodations had been quite pleasant. A small but comfortable jet with plenty of food and beverages to choose from had brought him here. He was allowed to watch some movies to pass the time on the long flight and, although nobody was talking to him, he was treated as professionally as his prisoner status allowed. Similarly, once they landed, he was transported in a large SUV and allowed to see where they were and where he was being taken. Now, he sat comfortably in what looked like a ready room for mission planning or deployment preparation.

It was a large room with tables, maps and a good number of large computer monitors mounted on the walls. One of them had a news broadcast. The other had a ballgame but neither had the sound up. While he was comfortable, the handcuffs and leggings reminded him that was likely to be temporary despite his last instructions several hours ago when he was told by the security team leader outside the room to hang out. It was gonna be a while before they got to him. True to their word, it was nearly four hours of waiting before the door opened and a man walked into the large room with a pizza box and a six pack of beer.

He addressed Zach as he waived him over to the table closest to the entrance, "Come on, it's time," Tom began as he put the pizza box and beers on the table. "If I take the handcuffs off, are we going to have a problem? Before you answer that, know that I hold your fate in my hands. I want to get off on the right foot, if we can, but I am a realist and I am tired and hungry. So, there is no misunderstanding, if you say no but do cause a problem you will be saving me a lot of time. It's pepperoni with extra cheese. I am told you prefer wine over beer but tonight beer is all there is."

As Zach walked toward the table, he looked Tom up and down, considering his response as he pulled out a chair and took a seat. He then took a deep breath and looked intently at the man standing behind the pizza box as he stretched out both of his hands towards him and said, "Pepperoni and extra cheese sounds good. A beer sounds good, too. If we have problems, let's save them for later. I can see you have had a long day, too. Shall we get to know each other a little and talk about what comes next?" Zach asked as Tom nodded and moved forward to unlock the handcuffs, remove them and drop them into one of his cargo pockets where they would remain readily accessible.

He opened the box that would double for their plates and then Tom opened two beers and handed one to Zach and introduced himself, "Zach, my name is Tom. Please go ahead and dig in; we're gonna eat as we chat. I am the reason you are here and I am the only way you get out. There is no good cop or bad cop; there is only me. There are no cops.

"This is not a game. It's as real as anything will ever get for you. You are in deep shit and you might not get out of it. You have us and the CCP both ready to dig a hole and plant you in it. That's not a threat. That's just the facts." Tom paused as he took a bite from the slice in his hand and watched Zach waiting for a reply.

"Thanks for the pizza and beer, Tom. I don't know yet if it's a pleasure to finally meet you or not, but you certainly have my attention. Let's say, for discussions sake, that I do want to get out of this *deep shit* you say I am in. And, say, I'd like to avoid everyone who might be looking to put me in a hole. What might that look like from where you sit, Tom?" Zach said as he took another bite and began to chew.

"That depends on you. You see Zach, I need something that you may or not be able to give me. It's a little complicated, actually. You see, what I need is *enough*. And right now, neither of us know what *enough* is. That's the hard part about this new relationship we have, Zach. You see, right now we both need *enough*." Tom paused and took another bite, as he wanted to keep the cadence of the conversation going.

"That's a pretty vague request, Tom...I guess technically it's not a request; it's still a statement. That is quite the complication but let's say I do get you this *enough* that you are needing. What is my motivation? What do I get once you get enough? *Enough* of what? These are two important things for us to consider, if we are to come to an understanding. I gotta know what I'm getting into, if I'm to gauge whether or not it's better or worse than the position I am in right now." Zach took a drink from his brown bottle and then another bite of pizza as Tom nodded his head.

"Yes, those are two important things for us both to understand. So, let's get to the bottom line here so we can enjoy our mealtime together. I need everything you know about the CCP weather modification program; everything you saw, heard, or smelled. I also need everything you think they did or think they can do, where they are doing it, or are planning to. I need you to collaborate with a lot of people on a lot of things in a very short period of time and I need you to be part of our solutions without holding anything back. I need you on *our* team for our current effort one hundred percent. For that, I promise you will disappear. If we get enough, you will disappear to a faraway place where nobody knows you and you can sit on a beach or a mountain top and grow old and spend your money however you see fit. If we don't get *enough*, you will also disappear, but you won't be caring about the location or the view." Tom took a drink of his beer and took another bite of pizza as he gave Zach time to consider the choice before him.

"This team of yours, do I know any of them?" Zach asked.

"Yes. In fact, I believe you used to work directly for our team leader. The President of the United States. To be candid, he didn't even want us to bring you back after what you did in India. So, do understand that he is not a fan. I almost had to ask you to step out of the airplane on your way back from Australia., while it was still airborne," Tom said, only half joking.

"For the record, I was just a bit player in that wind event. They had me believe something different. They didn't need me or use me for that. They didn't need to," Zach said truthfully as Tom casually clarified for him.

"Not the wind event he is upset about. We know that was them. The flooding and crop damage shortly after you split the research facility with the President's Thor's Hammers. That was why he ended up bending the knee to the UN Secretary General. He doesn't like that guy and he sure didn't like you putting him in a position where he needed to do that," Tom continued while eating.

"Nope, that wasn't me. Now, to be totally transparent, I was there considering how I might make some money on futures like Bob Mcleod and I had talked about in our chats, but that disaster in India was a CCP solo. I know this because it freaked me out when it was happening. I thought my devices might have malfunctioned or there might be some other microchip or code I didn't understand and, maybe, I told it to do something I didn't know about. As I was struggling with all this and wondering what happened and why, that's when they picked me up, I mean the CCP...in India. It was them. They have a regional operation in place there and they used it. They made a lot of money but I did not. I got a long bus ride to their secret underground facility and you all got to focus on blaming me for what they did. That one is not on me, but I was an unwitting part of their plan as I was their perfect scapegoat. Well, that was then and this is now. I will help you flip the script, Tom; I will help you get up and running," Zach assured him.

"Well, that is progress, now isn't it?" Tom asked. "I will let the President know that was the case when we talk next. In the meantime, Zach, we have a lot of debriefing to do and a lot of planning to cover for what you will be doing the next few weeks. Right now, I am ready for another beer and some more pizza. How about you?"

"I can do with some more. How about you give me some idea what I need to do so I disappear the right way," Zach agreed.

It seemed like Zach was ready to get started, so Tom continued, "OK. You are going to do something we already know you can do. You are going to help our research and development team understand and reverse engineer the systems we took from you and your friends in Australia. As we are doing that, we are going to find a way to exploit or neutralize the CCP's existing networks. And, if that isn't enough fun, you are also going to help us leapfrog their current versions and get a US variant on-orbit so we can cover any place on the globe at any time. We are going past their regional abilities with our own global ability. Your job is to get us *enough* to do all that. The good news is we have everything we need to succeed. That is, we have a plan but not enough time," Tom confided the truth. While he left out a few important parts and details, he was shooting straight about what they were doing and what Zach would be helping them accomplish. He now had some idea of what success needed to look like.

"Well, I was hoping for a little bit of a challenge but, if that's all you want, when do we start?" Zach said with such a straight face that Tom was not sure whether he was being sarcastic or not.

Being one to leave little to chance, Tom pressed for clarity. "So, you think you are going to be able to deliver on your end of our deal?" he asked as Zach drained the beer from the bottle.

"I can if you give me the right people to work with. I am going to need some very specific information and I am afraid only a few members of the CCP have the knowledge we will need," Zach conceded as Tom cracked a smile and slowly responded.

"I anticipated that and am working on assembling the rest of the team as we speak. Will you be able to get what you need from your UN cohorts General Chen and Mr. Wu?" Tom asked.

"Those are two of the names I would have given you if you asked me who I would want to have working on this," Zach answered.

"But will you be able to work with them? I imagine there may be a little bad blood among you from your recent histories," Tom stated more than asking Zach.

"I can work with them. It's professional not personal with those two. My assumption is they will be just as motivated to collaborate on your objectives as I am? I would hate being the only one squeezed to take this from crazy idea to an actual on-orbit reality. They will need to help me— help us—as much as I am needing to help you? You seem to be the type that can be particularly talented in motivating people, Tom." He waited patiently for Tom's response.

"Again, yes. I am confident they are as motivated as you are to see this work. In fact, I am very interested in how the three of you are going to adapt to your new reality. You know...where everyone has a reason or several reasons to see that we are successful. In fact, you should be seeing them in the very near future as they are en route as we speak," Tom revealed as he finished his beer and policed up the remnants of his food and empty bottles and headed for the door. "Enjoy the rest; you don't need to save me any. Thanks for keeping your word, please keep doing that. I don't want to put these handcuffs back on you. Bad for morale all around."

Several hours later, Zach and Tom were reunited in the briefing room with a large group all clad in civilian clothes. But some were clearly in the military despite their casual attire. Zach recognized a few of the faces but could not precisely place them, that is until he saw the three men standing together. He recognized them from the UN demonstration team in Australia. Those three were all Air Force or, at least, that's what the uniforms they wore communicated, whether factual or a cover remained to be seen. Not being bashful, especially not now, Zach strode over to the three men and addressed them as he approached.

"Hello General Lincoln, nice to see you again and glad it is under much better, more appropriate, circumstances than our last meeting," Zach smiled and extended his hand which Frank grasped and shook in true professional military form.

"Hello Zach. You remember Captain Lessur and Sergeant Andies from our Australian adventure together?" Tom greeted and questioned him.

"Of course, I never forget a face. Names yes, faces no. It's a pleasure to see you again. I trust my escapades to date have not caused you any negative consequences?" Zach was sincere in his hope.

"Hey..." was all either of the two could muster in response. Their instructions were to be neither adversarial nor cordial. Neither was sure what that looked like in real life. They hoped they hit the mark with this response and Zach did not take their mediocre greeting personally...well, not yet anyway.

Tom began to get everyone's attention as it appeared he was leading this briefing as well. "Listen up, everyone. I need your attention so please wrap it up and listen up. I need you all in receive mode for the next several minutes." He then proceeded to explain to the group the same plan he had previously described to Zach. As he wrapped up the briefing, he added another update for some of them in the room, "So, advancing the Thor's Hammer technology by exploiting the systems that we recently acquired in the *Thor's Journeymen* operations in Australia and getting an operational space-borne version on orbit, as soon as possible, is the *Thor's Craftsmen* mission. And you, *this team*, you are all now read in. Let's make this happen; now get to it," Tom concluded as he headed straight for the two casually dressed men who had arrived shortly after the discussion began.

"Major General Chen, Mr. Wu—Gentlemen, welcome to *Thor's Craftsmen*." Tom smiled, "I trust your flights were OK? We have a lot of work to do and a very short amount of time to get it done."

CHAPTER THREE

STRAP IN

D rifting in and out of naps, conversations and bumpy patches of air for the better part of a day, those aboard the large military transport were pleased to be descending into their stateside destination. Ann was particularly excited to be back to see her dad and get an update on how things were going with him and Betty. Although she had not known her long, the time they spent together demonstrated all the qualities Bob had described time after time when he talked about his long-time colleague. As she sat next to Bob discussing how they hoped their next day at the UN would go, the aircraft began a sweeping left turn and began to level off from its slow descent. It was clear to everyone aboard that for some, yet to be announced, reason their flight had just gotten a little longer than they expected.

A few minutes later the aircraft commander put the word out that they were diverting from LaGuardia to McGuire Air Force Base in New Jersey to address an aircraft issue. They could not risk landing at the busy commercial New York airport and not be able to take off due to some technical thing that seemed to make sense to most of the people discussing the reason for the diversion. This would impact both Ann's ability to catch up on news about the budding romance as well as the UN team's ability to get things rolling back in New York. The upside, she thought, was she would get to spend a little hurry-up-and-wait time with Bob while the next leg of their journey was readied for the group who, by UN protocol, traveled as a unit.

Once they were on the ground and assembled in a passenger holding area, several busses rolled up outside and the next steps were becoming more apparent. The team leader for their aircraft announced that the busses were there to take them to lodging where they would be spending the night while the work on the aircraft was performed. They would have the opportunity to get some food, shower and sleep in a bed before the busses returned in the morning to bring them back for the short flight, assuming the aircraft was ready or a replacement was available. Bob was frustrated by the delay but Ann seemed to welcome the break it would provide the two of them. "I believe we will be able to find a way to pass the time while we wait for them to fix this thing," she assured the Professor who was smart enough to read between the lines of his fiancée's statement.

As they loaded onto the bus, Ann pulled out her phone and listened to the ringing from the other end until it went to voicemail, "Hey Dad, it's Ann. We have been delayed and will be spending the night at an airbase in Jersey. We won't be back until tomorrow at the earliest. You guys will have to make the best of it without us for at least one more day, maybe more, if they don't get this plane fixed. I am sure they will make some arrangements to get us back to New York if it's going to be a while but, in the meantime, my cell and Bob's are both working. Call if you need anything, and I will pass along any updates when we get them. Give our love to Betty; see you both soon I hope," she concluded, hung up, and then looked at Bob who was giving her a look of his own.

"You don't seem to think it necessary to call Betty to update her too? A little presumptuous to expect your dad to keep her updated don't you think?" Bob asked.

"Nope. I am pretty sure she was either listening with him or, just as likely, she will hear the message when he plays it. My dad is pretty good about answering the phone when I call. He knows my number and the phone tells him who it is. If he didn't pick up my call, he really doesn't want to be disturbed and that can only mean one of a couple of things. My money is on *they* didn't want to be disturbed. At least that is what I am hoping," she smiled.

The bus rolled out and it wasn't long before they completed the relatively short drive from the flight line to the lodging office to get their keys. It does take a while to check in two busloads of people, especially when they are unexpected, but the staff worked politely and diligently to accommodate the weary travelers. Bob and Ann closed the door behind them after entering the small but comfortable room and, without missing a beat, Ann put her things down while walking towards the bathroom as she said, "I am getting in the shower and I could use a hand...or two." As she turned on the water. Bob smiled, put down what he was carrying and walked toward the sound of the running water and replied, "I have two hands and I'm bringing them both."

Meanwhile, Steve pressed play on his phone and he and Betty listened to the voicemail from Ann informing them of the delayed arrival plan. That did not seem to bother either of them because one more day of playing tourists seemed like a win for everyone involved, except maybe the UN team that was falling further behind their already aggressive schedule.

Mr. Dau had been put in an awkward position as they left Australia. He had to keep the UN effort on track while also navigating the delayed and seemingly random arrivals of the now fractured demonstration team and its cargo. While he understood the necessity of the delays and the need to persevere despite them, he could not help but wonder how much good they would actually do for the family members of Chen and Wu. While he may never know if the extra efforts going on right now would make a difference for them, he knew with near certainty that he would want others to try their best for him if it was his family on the line. For Mr. Dau, it was that simple. *Do for others as you would have them do for you.* Words to live by and he was one of the few at the UN who walked the talk. It was as rare as it was refreshing to see his level of professionalism and dedication to help people who he had never met. Too bad that was so uncommon across the leadership of this organization.

"And the last item on the agenda today is *Thor's Craftsmen*." The Secretary of Defense looked around the room as he continued, "If you aren't already briefed into that program, this is your que to leave the room please. That would be most of you. Thank you all."

He paused to allow most of the straphangers and self-important bureaucrats to depart and once the door was closed began the discussion, "Mr. President, our efforts to get Major General Chen's and Mr. Wu's designated family members out of China and into the US have been mostly successful. I say mostly because several of Mr. Wu's family who were contacted chose to stay behind. As is our protocol, we made a video of the exchange to ensure Mr. Wu has proof that we tried but the decision to leave them behind was not ours. We fulfilled our end of the agreement and his obligations are the same. His wife and daughter are safely on US soil. So, he does have much to be appreciative for despite the others, whose whereabouts are currently unknown."

Fitz paused to give his boss a chance to ask any questions and, with none forthcoming, he continued, "We now have Chen, Wu and Zach all on site with the rest of the team. The equipment has all been processed and is also on site. They have begun the exploitation and decomposition of the CCP systems and the weather modification modules from the airborne systems. Tom reports that Zach appears to be willing to do what it takes to keep himself in the asset column and out of the liability column. He also wanted me to let you know that Zach was adamant about not being the one who did the India crop flood disaster. He claims that was an operational CCP regional system that pulled that one off. They have been using it for a while, and it is still operational."

"Doesn't sound like Tom believes him. Did he give you a confidence number on that?" the President asked.

"He does believe him, with 95 % confidence. That's Tom's number and you know as well as I do that 95 % from Tom is 110 % confidence. Tom believes Zach, and Tom is human lie detector," the Secretary reminded the President.

"If that is true, then we have underestimated the Chinese technical ability, the extent of their offensive use of these systems and the risk they pose with their existing regional networks. Especially the ones here in CONUS," General Charles stated flatly. "I am not sure the entire arsenal of US military weaponry would have any impact on a prolonged environmental attack. We can't shoot down a hurricane or a drenching rainstorm. Nuking something like that is just as likely to make it worse as it is to stop it. And, even if we did, they could just keep them coming as long as they had devices. This is a fight fire with fire type of capability and right now we are at quite a disadvantage. The best option for us in the near term is to go after their networks or whatever or whomever is controlling them. They have what we don't. So, we need to either take or take out what they have."

"That is not a good place to be. Get Tom on the line. I want to hear his assessment firsthand. Not that I don't believe the two of you but, by now, he should know more about the timeline for what he thinks they can do," the President directed as he looked at his two most senior military advisors. Within a few seconds they could hear a phone ringing across the speaker and then Tom's voice came on. "Go for Tom," he barked.

"Tom, it's me. You are on speaker, and I have Fitz, Dutch and a few more of our science guys from the agency and the labs in the room. We are talking about Thor's Craftsmen, and I want your input." He paused briefly and Tom filled the silence with a simple, "OK, Sir."

"First of all, Fitz tells us you are confident the CCP did the India floods and not Zach. Convince me," he challenged, Tom stood tall never being one to shy from speaking truth to power. It was never clear who enjoyed that more, Tom or the man challenging him.

"I went eyeball to eyeball with him. He screwed us when he left but the CCP snatched him up in India and then had him by the shorthairs. Set him up and it worked great. We bought it; I bought it and they didn't even have to sell it. Just let him be him...let us see it and draw our own conclusions. They got exactly what they wanted and made a ton of money in the process. Zach got blamed and we got played. He's more afraid of the CCP than he is of you...well, of us. It checks out. My guys are doing some more forensics and they found an operational network in that region in India just like he claimed. They confirmed at least six systems and they aren't done yet. Devices are the same as the ones we scooped up in Australia. They've been in place at least two years...maybe longer. I'd bet Fitz's next paycheck Zach didn't do India like we thought he did. That's my input," Tom concluded.

"Damn. I know you don't make bets; you make investments by only betting on a sure thing. Well, that's an unfortunate revelation, but I am glad we know so we can recalibrate our efforts," the President conceded. "Do you have everyone you need yet?"

Tom responded a bit hesitantly, "I believe so. We have all the principles, but we did not get all their family members on the list. A few of Wu's would not come out with our teams. That said, we have everyone we could get from the list. That will have to be enough. So, I have Chen, Wu, Zach and Frank Lincoln plus his two Air Force weather guys Lessur and Andies and more engineers and rocket surgeons than I know what to do with. We go full bore in the morning."

"How long do you think you need to get something put together and working?" the President asked.

"Define working, Sir," Tom pressed.

"A working capability on orbit that can make the weather we want and counter all their regional systems at the same time if they use them in a way we don't like. I need both," he clarified.

"I will know more once we roll up our sleeves but right now I'd say a few months would be a stretch goal. I don't know yet what kind of lift we will need for this because I don't know how many or how big the system needs to be. Also, we don't know how many we need, or where they need to be positioned on orbit. We may need to bump some of the scheduled space launches to get whatever it turns out to be up there," Tom postulated with what he expected to be possible but very challenging.

"Good, you have a plan so that means you believe you can do it. That's good. That's the first thing you need. Now I'm giving you the second thing you need for success…not enough time. You have three weeks Tom. That's all I can give you. Make it happen. If you need something, you'll get it," the President said flatly.

"I need to take you up on that right now then, Sir. Need another star on Lincoln's shoulder, Lessur needs an oak leaf and Andies needs Chief's stripes. They will still be way under-gunned for this, but it will help." Tom paused long enough for the Commander in Chief to get a nod from the SecDef.

"Done. What else?" he waited for Tom's next demand poorly disguised as a request.

"I need to be able to roll in and out of the UN effort and bring Mcleod in and out of what we are doing, too," Tom said.

"I thought he made his choice, and that it was the UN effort?" the President asked.

"Yes, but they must be synchronized and I need him for that. Mr. Dau is a good resource for us inside but I need Bob for both that end and our end. He can't be in two places at once but I can ping pong him enough to make it feel like he is," Tom assured.

"OK, we already paid him enough to do that without feeling an ounce of guilt. But that means I am gonna have to placate that asshat UN Secretary General again doesn't it, Tom?" the President rolled his eyes.

"Yes Sir. Of course, you could change our timeline, and…" the President cut him off midsentence.

"I could change it to two weeks if you push this, Tom," he said without the slightest bit of humor in his tone.

"No Sir, this will already be hard enough. But I will need authority to put some numbers on the deals still to be made with Chen, Wu and Zach when the time comes. And that will need to be sooner rather than later given your deadline, Sir." Tom knew what he was asking was a stretch, but he also knew he was being asked to do the *nearly* impossible.

"OK Tom. You have it but remember where that offer comes from and who you are speaking for," the President cautioned.

"Of course, Sir, that is clear and I appreciate it. Anything else you need from me?" Tom asked politely. On the other end of the call the President was surveying the room for any additional inputs.

"Two things, Tom," General Charles added. "Go ahead and have those three Airmen start wearing their new rank. The paperwork and the rest of it will catch up with them. Don't sweat them too much. They have each already earned a promotion. This just gets it there a little sooner and expect to see me soon. I have to be in Tampa for a couple of days and I will check in to make sure you guys are getting what you need. I will roll over any roadblocks that might pop up in front of you between now and then," he assured Tom.

"Sounds great; looking forward to seeing you. Thank you all. Now I have work to do. Good day, Mr. President," Tom said sincerely as he closed out the line. He knew General Charles was legend among the Services, respected by officers and enlisted alike. It was good to be on the same team and Tom knew there would be staff and turf battles that no DC government civilian was going to win without the right endorsement or ink. There was none better in DoD to have backing you than Chairman Dutch Charles.

As he was walking toward the main building where the captured devices were stored, Tom was playing the call back in his head and wondering who else was in the room besides the three primaries who had each spoken. It was an understatement to call the massive hangar a building, but the metal sided structure shielded the contents from both curious passersby and those intent on seeing what secrets were hidden within. Once inside, Tom spotted the man he was looking for and shouted for his attention. "Brigadier General Lincoln! Sir, may I have a word please?" he said loudly as he walked toward him.

Frank quickly finished the instructions he was giving to the small group of Airmen and turned toward the voice calling for him walking briskly to close the gap between them. "Hi Tom, what can I do for you now?"

"How about you buy me a beer? We're celebrating," Tom remarked proudly.

"It's a little early, but I'll bite. What are we celebrating?" Frank asked.

"Promotion list came out. We need to find Captain Lessur and let him know he just made Major and, if that wasn't enough reason to celebrate, Sergeant Andies also just made Chief!" Tom paused and smiled.

"What's going on, Tom? Major's list is not due out for another several months and the Chief's list is later than that?" Frank called the man out.

"Well, we have our own lists, approved by the President and SECDEF. The paperwork will catch up. Come on, don't spoil my fun. Where are they? We need to let them know so they aren't out of uniform any longer than need be," Tom said with a big grin, which was uncommon for him.

"Fine, yeah that's worthy of celebration. They are both still in with the exploitation team examining the weather business end of these drones. Been at it all night due to the tight schedule so it will be a welcome break regardless of what the clock says," Frank acquiesced as they approached the groups huddled over the spread-out pieces that earlier was an RPV-equipped to generate prescribed weather conditions on-demand.

The typical military protocols are generally relaxed a bit in these types of settings where civilians, contractors and active-duty military professionals worked collaboratively on a special project with tight deadlines. This was not to be one of those moments.

"Captain Lessur! Sergeant Andies! Get your asses over here, DAMMIT! RIGHT NOW!" Brigadier General Lincoln shouted so out of character and so loud that everyone stopped what they were doing to see what had the even-keeled senior leader so bent out of shape. The two summoned Airmen hustled over to Tom and Frank who were standing together, each with their arms crossed and looking like they had just seen something that was an absolute no-go.

"Yes Sir, what do you need?" Captain Lessur asked for both men. Andies didn't need anyone to fight his battles for him, but it was customary for the senior member to take responsibility and accountability for whatever may have been screwed up, regardless of who did the screwing up.

"I need you two chowder-heads to be in the proper uniform. I know we have some relaxed standards, but being in the right uniform is pretty basic stuff, or at least it should be. I know you've been up all night, but do you think you can make that happen for me sometime this morning? Damn, I thought you two were well past stupid stuff like this," Frank shook his head as he looked in disbelief at the confused look on both their faces.

"Sir? With all due respect, I believe we are both in the proper uniform. It's our utility uniform, same as the rest of the active-duty members who are here...yourself included. What am I missing Sir?" Captain Lessur asked, wanting to resolve the General's concern but not knowing how to do that.

"If you two can't pin the right rank on your uniforms, then I suppose I will have to do it for you. Want something done right, do it yourself Frank...I am so tired of hearing that. Hold still!" Frank commanded as he turned over his hand and revealed the Oakleaf and the E-9 insignia.

"Congratulations gentlemen, you have been promoted. Now let's pin these on, have a beer and then give you a chance to put these into action." He smiled at the shocked look on both their faces as Tom began clapping and the rest of those watching joined in, relieved but also just a little disappointed there weren't more fireworks coming. As both men stood proudly, adorned with their newly pinned on rank, Tom got everyone's attention with a booming version of his generally measured voice.

"Hold on everyone, just one minute longer. While these two fine Airmen certainly earned their promotions, it seems a bit hypocritical to me that Brigadier General Lincoln is perfectly willing to chastise his troops for doing something he is guilty of himself. I'm sorry, but come on, we can't have everyone working on the *Thor's Craftsmen* program answering to a BG, can we? They deserve better—a more seasoned operator and more senior officer. And while we have all enjoyed working with, and for Brigadier General Lincoln, it's time for a change. I would like to introduce you to your new boss. Ladies and Gentlemen, I give you *Major* General Lincoln." Tom paused, tossed Frank a two-star insignia and began the round of applause and shouts before he continued.

"I would love to hand out more of these but, while I don't have any more promotions, I can assure you all that I appreciate all you are doing in service for your President and your Nation. Congratulations, Frank," Tom said loudly and deliberately so those who heard it now knew he was the civilian equivalent of at least a two star if he was now *first-naming* a Major General. You could tell Frank wanted to use the opportunity to crack wise on Tom, but he was a class act and showed that once again by carefully choosing his words.

"Thank you, Tom, and thank you all," he said to those within earshot. "I may be wearing another star, but it is all of you who earned it for me and I will wear it on your behalf. If you need something you don't have, make sure I know about it. Don't forget, I work for you not the other way around. Now how about that beer? Looks like I'm buying and these other two are off the hook. We don't have time for more than one today but the one we do have time for is on me! Thank you all!" he concluded and led the way to a couple of coolers full of ice and cold beers. Small victories pave the way to great ones.

The festivities were short-lived and within an hour everyone had congratulated the three newly promoted Airmen and were back to the tasks at hand. They needed to put something they hadn't even built yet on orbit in less than three weeks. *No pressure, no diamonds...once again.*

CHAPTER FOUR

NOT AT ALL WHAT IT SEEMS

The UN team was fragmented and spread across three states due to logistics, aircraft and weather-related delays. Most people just accept this as an unfortunate reality of life which happens despite our best plans. The US Air Force, however, is not *most people* and the unscheduled delays with thin excuses from maintainers, schedulers and command centers supporting such a high-profile mission were not playing well with the mid-level brass who struggled to understand why it was so hard to get a few airplanes full of people and stuff into New York. So be it. They should be upset about it. No one bothered to let them know that General Charles had his thumb on the scales for these missions and their unfortunate challenges. The problems would soon be cleared up and the various planes would find their way to their stated destinations, albeit almost forty hours later than they expected to arrive. Tom got the time he needed.

Betty and Steve anxiously waited for Bob and Ann to emerge from the arriving passenger's doorway where the UN team was finally converging with their cargo and comrades from the other flights. Now that they were in New York, they could begin the briefings and preparations for the next demonstration which would be held in their own backyard. After what seemed like hours—because it was—Ann came through the doorway and was immediately greeted by a loud and distinctive whistle from her father. She recognized the familiar sound immediately, looked in the direction from which it came, spotted Steve and Betty and made a beeline for them.

After long hugs, greetings and smiles Steve asked about Bob. "Where is your fiancé? Did you finally wise up and leave him somewhere? Do I need to help hide the body?" The questions drew a smirk from Betty, who was pretty sure he was kidding but wasn't certain. So she, too, waited to hear Ann's response.

"He got tied up with the equipment and Mr. Dau. He said we should head back to the hotel. He'll meet us there once he wraps up here. Not sure how long that will be but it is what it is. I'm starving, so what do you say we stop somewhere on the way to get something to eat? You can fill me in on what you all have been doing. You pick where we eat; I don't care as long as they have food. Let's go before one of these guys decides they want or need something from me." And, with that, she was leading the way toward the exit without knowing or caring how the two elders had gotten there or how they were getting to their new destination. Bob was on his own but that was not new to either of them.

As the three headed to the ground transportation exit, Bob was still struggling with accountability of a large and unorganized technology team comprised of UN and CCP technicians, the majority of whom were in New York for the first time. As Bob looked around at the lack of coordination and the confused looks, it gave him a new appreciation for the behind-the-scenes magic his friend Frank had spoiled them with thus far. Now that Frank was focused on the other side of this technology effort, it was more obvious than ever to Bob that things had changed and perhaps not for the best from his current perspective.

After what seemed like in inordinately long time, the last of the cargo and team were on their way to their destinations and Bob headed back to the hotel. He was hours behind Ann and hoped that she had a chance to catch up with Steve and Betty because, at this point in the day, Bob didn't have the strength or frame of mind to go into the past. The present was all he could handle. As he exited the elevator and walked toward the suite, he could hear Ann laughing and telling a story. He smiled as he walked through the door and saw the familiar faces that he was quickly identifying as his new family. He was good with that and it made him happy seeing them. Just seeing them happy was the best of all things.

After hugs and welcomes and being handed a plate to hold his choice of leftovers from their trip back from the airport, Betty asked Bob what he thought was in store next for her.

"Well, that depends," Bob smiled uncomfortably. "First, I must thank you and Steve for everything you found out back here while we were in Australia. You two found the code and broke this whole thing wide open. For that I will be forever grateful. That said, I don't know what you know or what I can tell you about what comes next. We will probably need to talk with Tom to figure that out formally, but *for family* and *formally* don't mean the same thing. Tell me where you think we are so I can get myself oriented. We have a lot of things happening. I'm tired and not quite sure where you guys are right now in all of this."

Betty started, "Well, we're pretty sure Miloc and his team working with Tom have connected a bunch of the money and companies with the University and the grant you and Doc were working on. Miloc says they killed Doc and that young man who was accused of driving the car. Turns out that he was not behind the wheel. The FBI has been here going through again and again the records we brought. They have a security detail on Steve and me all the time and one on Father Gannon, too. We haven't had any contact with him just like Tom asked. I don't want them to get away with what they did to Doc Auster. If I can help in some way to make them pay for that, I want you to promise that you will let me help. No looking out for me by keeping me in the dark. You let me decide for myself and treat me like the adult that I am and not someone you feel the need to protect. We've already crossed that bridge once. That's where I am in all of this."

"OK, thanks Betty. I can do that for you. It might not be easy but I will do just like you asked," he smiled and gave her a hug. It did not appear that anyone had shared any details of capturing the RPVs, the split team or the ongoing effort to leapfrog to an on-orbit capability that was the new *Thor's Craftsmen* program. He wasn't ready to dump all of that on them tonight and, while he knew it was not his place to brief them into that effort, Bob also knew that he was not going keep any details from Betty or Steve no matter who classified it and at what level. That immunity deal was feeling pretty good right about now.

Zach considered all that *enough* might mean for an on-orbit capability even with Mr. Wu and some other brilliant minds. Was this even feasible and, if so, how? As he struggled with the basic concept of a global system, two familiar faces appeared at the end of the room. It seems that Mr. Wu and Major General Chen had indeed found themselves positions on this new team Tom was forming. That might be very good for Zach as it would take the pressure off him to describe and convey the state of the technology and the CCP program for which they were produced. That would indeed reduce the details he needed to reach *enough* for Tom. Beer, pizza and good news with these two—he was off to a pretty good start he reasoned as he continued further into the briefing room behind his security escort. It seemed that was a common role for many in the room, which kept getting fuller until there were no more empty seats and people lined the walls to make sure they could hear the coming briefing.

Tom appeared at the podium, and began speaking, "Thank you all for being here, regardless of the route that brought you. You are all here by your own choice. If you are having second thoughts, now is the time to head for the door because once we get started there will be no going back. No mulligans; no changing your mind; no do-overs. Clear? Go now, if you're going."

He paused and nobody moved from their spots except to look around to see if anyone else was leaving. "Seeing none, we will begin. Some of you have been here for a couple of days and some have just arrived. We are all working on a project called *Thor's Craftsmen* and the common purpose we share is to put a global on-demand weather capability on orbit. We need to do that in *two* weeks." The murmurs, moans and even some quiet laughter began almost before he was finished saying the word *two*.

But that did not phase Tom and he continued, "We have gained some powerful and knowledgeable teammates that I would like to introduce to those who do not know them already. All three have direct operational knowledge of the RPV systems we are examining. The skill and information they bring to our effort is substantial and we will be relying on them heavily to expedite our efforts and shore up our own capabilities. In our work, they will be addressed as General Chen, Mr. Wu and Mr. Zach. Gentlemen would you please stand and be recognized by your new teammates?" Tom asked. As each of the three stood uncomfortably before the assembled group and nodded in acknowledgement of their new teammates.

"These men are fresh from the UN on-demand weather-modification demonstration team. They directly participated in the planning and execution of the weather modification effort in Australia that utilized the very systems we are currently exploiting for this effort. They will provide all the information you need but we can't all talk with them at the same time. To expedite our communications, the three will take positions at the table up front and will provide a short briefing about their backgrounds and their recent roles within the CCP program. Then we'll take as many questions as we can cram into two hours," he concluded.

And, with that, Major General Chen began followed by Mr. Wu then Mr. Zach. The candor of each speaker's synopsis of their past roles provided a high degree of confidence in their commitment to the new effort as their new teammates listened intently. As Zach finished his statement, the questions began immediately and from a face familiar to each of the three speakers.

Major General Lincoln seized the moment to set the tone of the discussion and the direction of the conversation, "Hello gentlemen. It is good to see that your recent experiences have brought you to this place at this time. I know it has not been an easy road for each of you, nor will the next few weeks likely be much different. We have much to do and very little time to get it done. Let me be very clear about our purpose. We are here to completely undo the work you and your government have done in on-demand weather modification. Any financial or strategic advantage your previous employers enjoyed from this technology ends today. Your individual fates, that of your families as well as our own, depend on our success. For those we care about and their future, that is our incentive and we cannot fail. We have every tool imaginable at our disposal. This is not a question of whether or not we can do this, it is merely a question of how we will choose to get it done.

"We are not here to replicate the systems we have. We are here to use the insights we have gained to do three things. First and foremost, we need to effectively neutralize the CCP's remaining fielded systems from doing any additional directed weather modification operations. Second, we need to develop and create a counter capability that is an efficient and effective global-scale system which ensures that we are no longer at a disadvantage. Finally, we need to employ and operate that on-orbit capability in a manner consistent with a yet-to-be-agreed-upon set of operating rules. So, let's begin."

As the three tasks began to sink in for the group, Mr. Wu was the first to speak in response to Frank's comments.

"General Lincoln. The systems we have fielded work on a grid system that is based on proximity to the devices. So, their placement is an important consideration in achieving the conditions in a specified area. The relatively small devices, various versions of what you call Thor's Hammers, limits their effective range but also ensures the changes don't become so widespread and overlapping that they impair the performance of the other devices in the region. They work in tandem, instead of competing with each other to produce the desired impacts. That strength is also an organic weakness of the overall system. Synchronized systems enable predictable beginnings to assist in producing the desired outcomes across an area. Disrupt that and things may not go as planned. That will frustrate the existing systems and their operations, which helps meet one of your objectives, but it will also put many people at risk if these systems do not perform as the input was intended."

"Thank you, Mr. Wu. How could we reduce the risk in that approach or do you have another idea in mind?" Frank proceeded to encourage the discussion and thought sharing.

Mr. Wu continued, "We can manage all the control sequences in the communications modules. Each of the devices is a node in a grid but the devices are all controlled by a network command module. This typically resides in the vehicle for mobile operations. I am told you already have the one we used in Australia. The fixed regional networks also use mobile control nodes as part of the security plan. It keeps the critical control nodes both compartmented and protected from single-point detection. But they are all accessed and updated via mobile web applications. They are designed so they can all be accessed remotely for routine operations, maintenance and security. Control them or neutralize them and you do the same for the devices they control."

Sergeant Andies took the opportunity to both pursue that line of thinking and to try to mend the fence with his old teammate from the UN effort. "Mr. Wu, I hope we can put past events behind us. We had different jobs to do in Darwin, Sir, but now we have the same job. Are you suggesting we could intercept the input at the controller node and send back a spoof response to the sender? They would think the system received and was doing what was sent to it but we actually tell the devices to do nothing or something different, but the regional operator will see or think they see what they programmed it to do?"

"Yes, Sergeant. That is a direct path in and out. Very similar to what you were able to do at the technology team table in Darwin. But that will be the most obvious path for us so those operating these systems will likely be looking for you to try that again. They will likely be defending against such an effort because they'll know their systems are at risk." Mr. Wu paused wondering if he should have said *we* instead of *you* in his response.

"Thank you that is helpful. Maybe we give them exactly what they expect so they focus on that instead of what we are really doing? That was a pretty successful strategy early on when it was employed against us." Andies hoped the compliment for the CCP effort would be both accepted and considered moving forward with the alternatives being considered. "I am also curious about the range, power and scale issues that we will be taking on for a planetary-scale effort, especially one on-orbit. What does that even look like from a design perspective? A few big somethings or a whole lot of little somethings?"

"Sergeant Andies, your mind works well. I think we will work well together and I will do my best to move on from Darwin. You did well to get me where you wanted me to go. But now my family depends on us *both* getting where we need to go. I have considered this problem many times but have not found a good answer. I think it could be done both ways depending on the amount of risk one is willing to accept and the number of resources one is willing to commit," Mr. Wu conceded.

At this point, General Chen chimed in with some insights, "The party spent a fair amount of time and money researching ideas but none were mature enough to prototype and test. There was also the consideration of a reasonable cover story for whatever was being evaluated. If we remove the need for anything more than simple plausible denial, then our options increase substantially. It was our previous assessment that the most likely success for next generation systems would be a fleet of micro-satellites with substantially overlapping and redundant coverage. This would enable lower power systems, which means they can be much smaller and simpler to build. It also reduces the risk from a single system failure or destruction. Plus, the lift needed for a few big systems is far more expensive and easier to track, especially if we need a covert payload. I think our priority should go to quantity first. If we are successful with those, we can put up some larger more powerful ones for redundancy and to improve the conditions for the smaller systems to work."

Frank pressed this line of thinking, "Thank you, General. Whether on orbit or in the regional systems, how do these systems integrate or pass tasks between them? You said the regional systems work on a grid or a nested grid. So, how do the controllers actually control what each of the devices is doing and when it does it?"

"I will let Mr. Wu take that one. I know the concept, but he can speak to the details so we might as well get into them, too. And, while we are learning how to proceed, I will take this opportunity to ask you to please forego the formality of title. I don't think my rank will follow me to my new beginnings here but, while I still can, I would prefer to keep my surname. Please just call me Chen."

"Of course," Frank obliged, "and you all know I go by Frank. I hope you will feel free to call me by that name as well."

"Thank you, Frank," Mr. Wu began his response following up on Chen's recommendation. "They talk to each other based on conditions. The sensor is told what conditions to produce by input that we call recipes. The conditions begin to occur and then ripple out like a stone thrown into a pond. Once the ripple—or set parameter—comes into the outer range of the next sensor it triggers the next phase in the progression to the desired conditions. Timing comes into play, and the number of parameters being impacted over the time steps also help determine the distance in placement. The systems grids are omnidirectional from the point-source of the device. So, they can ping-pong back and forth to get or produce the desired starting or ending conditions. This makes sure there are no hard or fixed boundaries that are rough or linear like those on a map grid. The atmosphere is a closed system controlled by laws of fluid dynamics, so it behaves like water not like wood or metal. Meteorological parameters interact with each other at blended boundaries rather than stacking next to each other at a fixed boundary."

"That explanation lends itself to the earlier discussion about overlapping orbital coverage of many geosynchronous systems versus large areas from a few polar orbiting assets," Frank both stated and questioned.

"Precisely. But, on a regional basis, we concerned ourselves with sufficient surface observations of specific parameters to make sure the weather was what we expected, as well as, to trigger the handoffs from one system to the next. That density of coverage does not exist globally," Mr. Wu cautioned.

Captain Lessur had been listening intently and took this opportunity to contribute, "We can still use all the existing surface observations. Everyone does that already. But we can also use the ton of imagery and other sensors and do some data fusion from every satellite that is already flying. It's not being done right now but add a little artificial intelligence—or AI programming—and we'd have a constant state of weather conditions to use to inform and direct everything from surface temperatures and winds, cloud conditions, lightning, etc. We know how to do it; we just need the resources to be able to do it."

"I can make that happen," Tom assured them. So, it continued for the next hour or so as the scientists, space-operations folks, strategists, and computer programmers all became deeply engaged in discussions that were helping discount and elevate various ideas and options on what to do and what to avoid. To this point, there was a lot of variety in topics and depth of discussion. Absent from the conversation was Zach. He had deliberately been *all-receive* and *no-transmit* thus far, as he tried to gauge the various faces and personalities in the room.

When he thought he had established a personal baseline of information for each of those gathered for Thor's Craftsmen he finally spoke, "How do we control what we don't want anyone to be able to control?" he asked nobody in particular as he looked around to see who was thinking deeply enough to understand his question and who was confident enough to offer an opinion on the matter.

"Right now, the CCP has their systems, and we are to counter them. The UN team is aiming to get the same technology proliferated so everyone has it. Therefore, nobody has any real advantage as long as they can react to whatever is happening in time to make it *unhappen*. Dueling capabilities on a bad day—temporary agreements on a good day. That means uncertainty every day. The US has us assembled here to take away the CCP advantage, which is regional, and replace it with our own advantage in the form of a global capability. So, where does that put the UN and CCP? What do they do to counter the new US global system and the advantages that provides? What is the end game?"

"I suppose that is for others to decide, and it's also beyond the scope of what we are here to do. Frank outlined our objectives and that is what our team needs to focus on right now," Tom tried to put a cap on Zach's questioning but it was clearly too late for the minds in the room to unhear what was already said and he had a point, "...but we need to consider all the possibilities because we are only going to get one shot at this. Where are you going with this, Zach?"

"We will succeed in putting a global capability on orbit. I see that already, and I see how it will work, and I see how it will fail. If we are successful in our assigned tasks, we will fail to meet our objective. No offense Frank, but it's a paradox albeit not of your making. No, to succeed in removing the relative advantage of on-demand weather for someone we have to get rid of it completely. We need to put the genie back in the bottle. But that is not why we are here. There is no way to have both," Zach concluded with a challenge, "Tell me how, and I am on board."

As the assembled brain power in the room strained in search for the one who would knock the chip off Zach's shoulder, the ongoing silence in the room served only to signal that, for now, he was right.

A man true to his word, General Charles found himself wondering how the team was faring in their efforts to understand the captured weather modification RPVs as the helicopter carried him and his executive officer from Tampa towards the isolated compound where the *Thor's Craftsmen* effort was already underway. He hoped their progress was substantial but understood the likelihood of a speedy outcome was unlikely. As they made their approach and landed exceedingly close to the entrance of the large windowless concrete building, a lone individual made his way to the aircraft and led the two passengers back to the entrance and inside.

"Good afternoon, General. It's good to see you, Sir. I understand I owe you a big thank you," Frank smiled and shook the man's hand.

"Shit Frank, it's us who owe you thanks. That second star looks good on you. I just hope there are still more to come," he only half joked. "Where are you guys with all this? How's it going?"

"We are down here," Frank continued as he pointed and led the Chairman down the hall to show him who and what was assembled and operating. "We've made good progress. We have the right people and they are fleshing out the right information and concepts. Chen, Wu and Zach are all doing the right things and exceeding our expectations. That is both good and bad. Meaning that we now have much better insights to what they have, how it works, its vulnerabilities, etc. That is all good. We have decided on our space-based option and are putting together the requirements and architectures we need so we can develop an orbital system. We're now working on how many, what power, comms and mission sensors, etc. Then we can figure out the onboard power and the lift it will take to get them all in place. The ground stations, downlinks, processing and control nodes, etc. will all get specked out next. We might need to commandeer some existing nodes or centers in the short term while we build out the rest of it, but we will only plan on using off-the-shelf stuff to keep to our timeline. That should minimize the impact to any other systems we might have to borrow."

"That all sounds good. I like it. Well done," Dutch smiled, sincerely impressed and pleased with the update and all that had already been done in such a short amount of time. "Now what are you *not* telling me yet Frank? You led with your chin but I haven't heard that part yet."

"No, Sir, you haven't. We have one impasse that we haven't broken through and it's a big one. It will have an effect on the overall system design, but I don't know what that effect is yet. Haven't gotten to the point where we need to tap the brakes on anything, but I don't think that is more than a day or two away and we will need a vector check," he paused.

"Still haven't told me what it is, Frank," he said patiently.

"Thinking the design through to keep it safe from tampering and counter attacks…once we have a global capability on orbit, not sure how we protect it and who we are protecting it from. That's all still TBD?" Frank was in the unfamiliar position of wondering how best to say what was on his mind.

"You mean, once we mitigate the CCP's advantage by being the only ones with a global capability how do we keep that advantage? The answer to that question is, we can't. We won't."

Frank was a little surprised that the Chairman had come to the same conclusion they had, and then was embarrassed at how much he had underestimated the highest-ranking military advisor to the President. "With all due respect, Sir, then what are we doing here?"

"Come on, Frank! I know you are under a lot of pressure but *no pressure no diamonds* right? We gotta get here to get there." The Chairman waited patiently for the team leader to process the line of thinking and, as if he were wished into existence to buy Frank some more time, Tom appeared in the hallway walking in their direction at a brisk pace.

"Good afternoon, Dutch, how are you?" Tom greeted the man who technically outranked him on the pay scale. Each considered the other a peer in their very positive working relationship.

"I'm good, Tom. Frank was just filling me in. Sounds like you guys are on a good path and making good progress on everything but the endgame?" He hoped Tom had some insight to share with them.

"Yeah, this group renewed my faith in my fellow man. Making good progress on everything except how to save us from ourselves. That's the treadmill issue for us, we keep going round and round," Tom summarized with a different metaphor than the two generals.

"Yeah, that's the problem. And deconflicting in order to align with the UN effort which so far seems incompatible. Giving it to everyone but keeping everyone safe from it seems paradoxical. Not sure we can do both," Tom confessed.

"Trading scales and capabilities lead back and forth between nation states. This is just another arms race with a new weapon. And who is to say this problem stays just between the US and China? The Aussies helped us get it from the CCP when we were in Darwin. They already have a piece of this and then some from that effort. You know NATO and others aren't going to sit by without making a play while the UN hands this out like candy. Fitz and the President have not aligned their thinking on this yet either. If I'm picking sides on this, my thinking aligns with Fitz but he's not the Commander in Chief. I haven't figured out a way to do all this myself but I am pretty sure, if anyone can, it's you guys. That's why you're here and have all this cool shit to make it happen. It's also why I am here checking up on and checking in with you. Let me know what you need and how I can help, because right now that's all I got for you," General Charles confided in the two men.

CHAPTER FIVE

SHIFTING SANDS

They had been working in focus groups through the night on various pieces of their gameplan and were now assembling once again to discuss their successes and challenges. It was rather impressive progress given the relatively small number of people and the short time they had been collaborating. General Charles had departed for DC shortly after his discussion with Tom and Frank. The counterproliferation group had come up with a simple but elegant program that would be employed on the communications server in the CCP command vehicle. This provided the ability to spoof the control console operators with command-received messages sent back to them without their systems actually sending the real command codes and recipes to the remote Thor's Hammers. This affirmed the system control and performance messages that went to the operators indicating the systems were both responding as expected and producing the desired results.

The team, with Wu's help, worked out the exact wording, symbology and syntax and were deservedly proud of their progress as well as their concept. The only big rock they had not removed from their rucksack of challenges was how to get their program onto the regional node's command server so it could do its magic. While that might be the best problem to have at this stage, it was still a problem that needed a solution.

That was a large step in the direction of solving the first and foremost task on Frank's list. It seemed a very solvable problem for a skilled hacker or a direct-action option, either overt or covert. The good news was they had options that could be selected based on the timing and the location of each regional system being targeted. Having viable options is the best position one can find themselves in when solving problems with so many variables. This situation was dynamic, so it was nice to see the solution space was also broad and malleable.

The space operations team had also come up with a good number of options for the group to consider. These centered around existing space-lift that was already scheduled or in the inventory because, with or without their planned payload, some or all of these were going to be needed in order to meet the timeline imposed by the President. The team that had the least good news to report also happened to be the team wrestling with the largest and most complex issues. The operations team was still doing the math and struggling with how to get these systems to both operate in space and operate from space. It was Zach who started the line of thinking that led to the breakthrough that had been eluding them.

"We are looking for the devices to produce the desired conditions on the ground: rain, heat, wind, etc. Low Earth Orbit (LEO) satellites orbit somewhere between 100 and 1,200 miles above the earth's surface. At the lowest orbit, which won't be ideal for what we are doing, that is still a lot of miles between the devices and their intended effects areas which are typically on the surface. That poses us some systems problems with the existing devices and their operation. The Kármán line, where space begins, is about 62 miles above the surface of the earth, right? That cuts the distance between the surface and the devices in half if we look at working from the top down. Weather forecasts and observations focus on the surface because that is where the people are. But don't you also make observations and forecasts all the way up through the atmosphere to get the data you use to forecast surface conditions? Why not just do it upside down? Why not use the devices on an inverted profile from space down instead of from the surface up? Why can't we just stand them on their heads?" Zach challenged the meteorologists in the room.

Captain Lessur and the other scientists were still trying to wrap their heads around what was being proposed when Chief Andies began to run with this unorthodox concept, "Mr. Zach, the primary data used in numerical weather prediction models is very surface and low-level atmospheric centric. But there are over 8,000 satellites on orbit that are looking down with a huge variety of sensors and profilers. We could use the same processes to produce the conditions in the upper atmosphere that are happening when the surface conditions are what we want them to be. We don't have the recipes for the upper atmosphere and I doubt we have the speed to create them in time. There is also the porosity of the observations, a disparity in data types and sources, and the fact that the surface area at the Kármán interface is exponentially larger than the surface of the planet. Forecasting on the surface is hard enough, let alone at the boundary of the atmosphere and space."

But it was Mr. Wu who cracked the door open, "Why are we forecasting, why don't we simply calculate it? Then we would know, not guess? Mr. Tom said tell him what we need and we will get it. We need a lot of computer power to calculate the same equations over and over again across the globe. But we do it from the top down. Run it repeatedly to correlate the conditions up high with the conditions down low. Same processes, just upside down so the sensors can create within their current range. This can be done, but there needs to be code written. And some serious computer clock time."

"We have a very extensive year-round climatological data base that contains specific data for countless points and sites around the world. Our data alone, once you combine it with all the satellite data, could be enough. Pile in the Air Force and civilian climatology data and this might just be doable," Tom added. "But I don't want to give up on the effective ranges, maybe a power booster or some other good idea to use what we already have."

"We may not have that luxury, Tom," Frank added. "Either way, we are gonna need more computing power than we have on campus here. How much can you get us and how fast can you get it?"

As Bob and Ann walked toward the UN building, they could not help but feel a tinge of both pride and nostalgia about the first weather modification event they did together at this very spot. While it was not long ago at all when they and Father Gannon created the thunder snowstorm right here to get the attention of the UN, their whole world had changed in many ways since. Steve and Betty had joined them today in hopes of learning if and how their assistance might help the coming demonstration. They were already behind the compressed timelines due to the very fragmented arrival of the team members traveling from Australia.

Once through the security area, the foursome headed toward the elevator that would take them up to the primary offices. They were scheduled to meet Mr. Dau to discuss milestones and timelines before the primary team meeting still several hours away. He met them shortly after they exited the elevator and walked them to his spacious office where they settled in around a comfortable table adorned with service items and padded leather chairs. The UN of this era was big on pomposity. Style and image seemed more important than integrity and results. What they said and where they said it seemed to matter far more than what they did and the results of those actions. It was nice to be working with one of the exceptions to this culture. Mr. Dau was a man of his word who believed deeply in what the organization he represented actually did as opposed to what it was supposed to be doing.

"We are off to a pretty rocky start. This fragmented arrival has put us at least two days behind and likely more. While the Secretary General is not happy about these delays, he understands that logistics are dependent on many things outside of our control. He is not aware that these delays were by design and, candidly, I didn't want to explain the what and why about it to him. So, if you will please indulge me the courtesy of not revealing to him that it was intentional, then I will be owing you a favor," he began. The look of both surprise and confusion on Steve and Betty's faces was hard to miss but it was just about the same look on Bob and Ann's faces and so the rough starts continued with their meeting.

"So," he continued before they asked him, "I see by your faces that you weren't aware of these intentional but privately needed delays. Frank and Tom needed some time to get several actions completed and this is how we got that time for them. Sorry that word did not get to you and I hope it did not cause you any undue stress. My last forty-eight hours have been remarkable, as a result, and I am happy to see you all. Hoping that feeling is mutual, but I am pretty sure we need to so some updating to ensure that is the case."

"What did they need the time for?" Ann asked.

As Mr. Dau considered how to respond, he went with the one thing he was known for, honesty, "I really don't know what I am supposed to be able to share with whom anymore now that we have split our efforts. No offense intended to Betty and Steve. But since the intent of our compartmentalization is to prevent our efforts from being leaked and or compromised by actions or inadvertent disclosures, I will assume the *more* I tell you the less likely we are to accidentally mess this up. That is, if you are all OK with that assumption. We have already been through a lot together and, in my business, it is often difficult to tell who warrants trust and information. I have no such reservation with any of you."

They all nodded and smiled as they recognized the position Mr. Dau found himself in and appreciated that it was not of his own doing. "No hard feelings, we are just trying to get caught up and help," Bob added.

"Good then," Mr. Dau continued, "They needed the extra time to generate doubt amongst the CCP leadership regarding what happened to their RPV fleet in Australia. That confusion and doubt, combined with not really knowing who was where or being able to get to them for a formal debrief was the window they would use to get whomever they could of

Chen and Wu's families out to join them in the states. We were the scapegoat because we could afford to be and now we will need to make up the time."

"What is an RPV and why do Chen and Wu need their families in the states?" Betty asked. Bob decided he should help get Mr. Dau off the hot seat because he was, in part, responsible for Betty's question.

"Glad you asked. So, I will cover this portion if you don't mind?" He looked at Mr. Dau and Betty who both nodded approvingly. "An RPV is a remotely piloted vehicle. A big remote-controlled drone. The CCP uses a group of them working together with some ground stations and the newest version of Thor's Hammers aboard them to control the weather on a regional scale. They secretly deployed a bunch of them to Australia to use for our demonstration and we snatched them. Now the CCP has lost an entire fleet of their most current version of Thor's Hammers. What we only understood to exist as a device is actually an entire network of them. They have a lot of regional networks already in operations around the world. But now they have one less and we have one more. Frank and Tom and some of the others from our UN team are working on exploiting that technology so we can leapfrog and counter what they have. Our UN team mission is still the same but the context has changed. On-demand weather modification is not a new technology nor is it limited to a local affect. It's real and it's already being used on a regional scale. Turns out we are bringing to the world some-thing that was already out there for years but was not known about."

Steve rolled his eyes and then shifted in his seat without finding a comfortable sitting position, "Damn. You guys keep surprising and scaring the shit out of me. This all sounds like some craziness out of some book Bob Russell wrote. It's hard for me to believe but I know it must be true considering the source."

"Well, I don't know who Bob Russell is but I can promise you, *this is real*," Ann assured her dad and turned to ask Mr. Dau what else he knew. "So, do we know if Tom was successful in getting their families out?

Do we have General Chen and Mr. Wu on our side for what Frank and Tom are working on? And what about Zach?"

He sighed, as he began to answer each of her questions, "Sorry, but I don't know any more than what Bob has shared. That is the other side of this effort and Tom is the common denominator between the two. Right now, my concern is getting the Secretary General off my back and scheduling our demonstration now that the UN and CCP teams have been successful in Australia. Our problem is we don't know what we don't know yet. I don't know what the CCP team is comprised of at this point. I have not seen nor heard from Chen, Wu or Zach or the two Senior Colonels. I do know that we don't have Frank, Major Lessur or Chief Andies. So, we have some big holes in our operation, and I don't know what gaps will be filled or by whom. We will have to wait to see who shows up at the all-hands meeting early this evening. In the meantime, I have a couple of calls already to Tom, but he has returned none of them. We are flying a little blind. So, that is what I think we need to spend our time on right now. Let's decide what we *should* do and then we will figure out what we *can* do once we have an update. I guess flexibility is the key for now."

Bob considered their situation as he listened and proposed the following course of action to the small group, "Following our original script is what we need to do for all the eyes and ears that are focused on us. Our demonstrations have been successful and the Secretary General put us back in New York for the next one. But he didn't say who our audience was supposed to be...did he?"

"Not specifically, that I can recall. He wanted the next demo to be here on our home turf to help restore our brand credibility," Dau agreed. "Where are you going with this?"

"Our mission is two parts. Demonstrate the capability to establish confidence in this emerging technology *and* field it safely and equitably for the benefit of all. Do I have that right?" Bob waited for assurance from Mr. Dau who nodded in agreement.

"So, we are already a couple of days behind. We don't know who we have or don't have yet for our demo and, as such, we don't know how much time we need for a successful demonstration. What if we combine our two objectives into one event? Would the Secretary General bite if he could take credit for capitalizing on the demonstration which will be delayed by a couple of days already, by calling for a coalition-of-the-willing to come to UN Headquarters to discuss how to field this capability *and* see the demonstration firsthand? That buys us more time before the demo, as well as, helping us see who wants a seat at the table—and at what level—for the discussions on how to roll this out? After all, that is the same task we embarked upon when we were here the first time, if you recall?" Bob smiled.

"How could I forget what you did to us all that day?" Mr. Dau nodded as he pondered the idea. "I think the Secretary General would bite on it as long as he announced the meeting, and he got to do it before we cleared it with your President. It would be the kind of needling those two. For whatever reason, powerful people seem to need to exert their independence from other powerful people. We would have to do this without coordinating it with Tom since he is not in contact right now."

"Not so," Steve asserted. "You can announce it without his approval and still coordinate it with him after the Secretary General announces it. Decide on your verbs. Do you need his approval or his coordination?"

"Your point is on point Steve, thank you." Mr. Dau liked how he thought. "So, we heard the upside of this line of thinking, what are the downsides and potential unintended consequences of doing this?"

Betty, quiet until now, decided she needed some answers, "First, the Chinese could pull their team out, tell the world they already have this and then use it on us and we start World War III, or World War Weather or whatever they call it in the history books after the floods and tornadoes wipe out all the good guys—I don't want to be dramatic. Or, maybe just as likely, the US President decides he is tired of the UN and CCP playing both sides and pulls out and decides to go fisticuffs with what they have and hope for the best. When you put big boys in a corner and block their way out, they generally don't sit down and wait for you to provide them instructions on what you want them to do next."

"All true; all possible; all not good for us," Ann agreed. "So, let's make sure the room is big enough. It's filled with other people and there are lots of doors and windows for anyone who wants to leave. We can do that and control the narrative. Keep enough doubt in the CCP so that maybe this works without all the doomsday scenarios? Can we still do all that after we announce the summit or do we need to do it all before we announce it? I mean, in coordination with Tom, whenever he pops up from wherever he is?"

Mr. Dau smiled and nodded, as if very pleased with himself as he spoke, "Yes Ann, we can do all of that after we announce the summit. In fact, I think I can leverage the big kids in the room to play nice at the beginning of these discussions to keep our advantage and help decide both how and when this gets used. International politics is a fickle business to be sure, but I haven't survived this long in this jungle without knowing the trails and watering holes. I think we can do this, and the more I think about it the more I like the flexibility it gives us to not only meet our stated objectives but also to keep them aligned with Frank's efforts."

With those thoughts in mind, the group settled onto the path and prepared their action plans for the upcoming team meeting and their update to the Secretary General. Deciding on the timing and synchronization was vital, and the final touches all hinged on who *was* and who *was not* present for the fast-approaching all-hands meeting.

As if he was monitoring their meeting, progress and ideas, Tom appeared in the UN Headquarters at Mr. Dau's office about half an hour after the group had finished updating the Secretary General and about an hour before their all-hands meeting was scheduled to begin. They quickly regrouped for a discussion and updates so they would all go into the pending meeting as close to being on the same page as they could, given the time constraints. Tom let the group know they had Chen, Wu and

Zach and that they were working feverishly with Frank's team so they would not be at the meeting coming up. He also knew—however he knew things—that neither of the Chinese senior colonels who were in Australia made the trip to the US, nor would they be attending this meeting or any other meetings, for that matter. So, the known was that it remained unknown who would be leading the CCP delegation of the UN demonstration team. Then Mr. Dau briefed Tom on the results of their just-completed update to the Secretary General.

"I must hand it to you guys...and gals...sorry. To you all, that is a very creative solution to this predicament. While I am not sure how I feel about it just yet, the more I consider it the more I think I like the options it leaves open for everyone later. Sorry I have not been in communications but, as I am sure you can imagine, there's been a lot to address these past few days. That said, it's in the past. You have at least one of my phone numbers. I am very curious how the all-hands meeting will be attended by the CCP and equally curious about how they will respond to the Secretary General's announcement. When did you say he was holding the presser?"

"It should be about the same time we are in the meeting. Now that we know who won't be there, I will get that information to him so that he announces and thanks them all by name for the success in Australia and their upcoming efforts in New York. This will give him some outs and will put pressure and doubt into the CCP about the UN complicity with whatever happened to their RPVs. After all, it did happen in Australia not in the US." Mr. Dau smiled at Steve and continued, "Appreciate the coordination, Tom!" He then left the room to make sure he had time to get to the all-hands meeting after he provided the Secretary General the latest information for his press conference.

As the rest of the group made their way from the executive suite office area to the largest of several large meeting rooms it was surprising how little the décor and accommodations changed. At the UN, everyone was treated like a DV. The cost of the niceties was never an object of discussion because they spent money to get money. There never seemed to be a shortage of money at the UN and most of it was in dollars.

It was a few minutes before start time and the room was filling up, but it was absent many of the familiar and key faces that had previously adorned the front row seating. There were some new Air Force officers wearing pilot's wings and looking around for whomever appeared to be in charge. These seemed to be Frank's replacements. Bob smiled outwardly as their presence confirmed that it did take more than one person to replace Frank. Some more new faces wearing the Air Force meteorologist weather badge on their uniforms would be those filling in behind Lessur and Andies. There were a few others, as well, but Bob couldn't tell what they were here for just yet. But what was the most interesting and telling was the Chinese team members. There weren't any.

The start time came and went and still none of the CCP delegation had departed their accommodations. None had cleared the security screening areas nor been granted entry into the UN building. The only person in attendance at the briefing was the Chinese Ambassador to the UN and he had very little to offer the group once Mr. Dau took the podium to open the meeting and address those present.

"Mr. Ambassador, it is a pleasure to see you sir, but I must say it is disappointing that no members of the UN demonstration team are here with you. We were hoping to begin laying the groundwork for our upcoming demonstration."

"Thank you, Mr. Dau, but I am afraid we were unable to assemble the group. We have some work to do to get the appropriate expertise in place to provide the assistance we have committed for this effort." The Ambassador addressed the man at the podium, as well as, those in attendance. "Our apologies, as several of our key members have been recalled for family emergencies and we are assembling their replacements as we speak. It will unfortunately take a few days to make new travel arrangements. I am afraid your options at this point will be to either delay until their arrival or proceed without CCP participation. I am prepared to make that announcement myself, if need be, but am hoping the UN could provide the schedule modification and of course would expect the CCP to accept being the cause for the unexpected delay."

Mr. Dau seized the opportunity to keep peace, so to speak, with his UN colleague and assured him that the delay could be accommodated...and without pointing fingers at any one teammate. He failed to mention to the small group that the Secretary General was at this very moment holding a press conference announcing the delay as well as the expanded scope of their upcoming efforts here in New York. The group wrapped up the business at hand, that is, the next event's locations and timelines and who was responsible for what in the meantime.

As they adjourned, it was interesting to see who bolted out of the room, who stuck around and who they stuck around with to discuss what had just happened, and what did not. After the majority of the straphangers got the answers to their questions and moved along, the same small group who gathered in Mr. Dau's office prior to the meeting were assembled there once again now that it was over.

"Well, that went better than I thought it would," Betty broke the silence as Mr. Dau was fumbling with the TV remote to get the sound up on the breaking news story that featured a picture of the Secretary General and a running banner beneath it that read:

> UN ANNOUNCES WEATHER MODIFICATION SUMMIT IN NY TO COINCIDE WITH THEIR UPCOMING ON-DEMAND WEATHER DEMONSTRATION WHICH WILL BE DELAYED TO ACCOMMODATE THOSE ATTENDING THE SUMMIT NEXT WEEK.

"More time to do the work we have and more work to do in that same time. Are we gaining ground or losing ground?" Steve asked the group.

It was Tom who responded, "Yes."

CHAPTER SIX

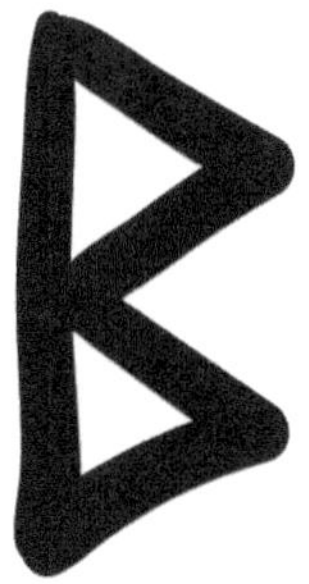

SOLUTION SPACE

T hey did what?" the President asked Tom to repeat what he just said to make sure he heard it right.

"Yes Sir, the UN Secretary General has delayed the demonstration in New York until next week, in part to have it coincide with a global summit on how to best field the technology." Tom paused then answered the question he knew was coming, before it was asked, "The other reasons they did this was to buy some grace and space for the Chinese Ambo to the UN to replace some of his key demonstration team experts who were dealing with unforeseen family emergencies. And it gives us some more time to coordinate our own efforts while also figuring out the best demo Mcleod can do without the CCP covert programs doing rainbows for them."

"This is a report on what happened, Tom. Where was the part where we discussed what we wanted to happen and when? Yes, I'm a busy man but I don't remember that part. Pretty sure I would remember that part, *if* it had happened. Why don't I remember that happening, Tom?" It was more than uncomfortable for Tom when he responded with his assessment, which he knew would likely not be appreciated by the Chief Executive, "UN called an audible. I hadn't returned Dau's calls for a host of reasons, not the least of which was I didn't want a digital trail of what I knew he wanted to talk about. They wanted to apply pressure on the CCP to buy themselves and our team some more time."

"And put that same pressure on *me*! And maybe buy themselves some more time by making me walk back the timeline I put them on?" the President asked as he leaned into his National Security Advisor.

"I suppose you could view it that way Sir, but..." and, with that, he cut Tom off midsentence.

"Well, I damn well do view it that way. I am starting to think you are fanboy'ing Professor Mcleod. I need you to stay out in front of this guy, Tom, not chasing around behind him trying to catch up. If you need help reigning him in, then you better be talking to me about when and how. I don't like being made to eat humble pie from the UN Secretary General or any of his weather demonstration team. Fitz, I need you and Tom to get on the same page with whatever computer stuff and weather data they need for the guys down in Florida. Get them what they need but make damn sure we don't draw a lot of attention on these guys while they monopolize roughly half of all the computing power in the Department of Defense!"

"Yes Mr. President immediately after this conversation, Tom, Dutch and I will get together and make sure what is needed is either ready to go or soon will be. Is there anything else you want to cover while we have everyone here, Sir?" Secretary Fitzgerald asked trying to deflect a little of the heat coming from the President.

"Yes Fitz, in fact there is. Where are we with the Chinese? What do we know—or what do we think they think—about their systems and their people disappearing? Surely, they have reacted in some way by now. I know my phone isn't ringing. What about the rest of you?" the President polled the participants on the call but nobody offered a response, in either the affirmative or the negative, so Fitz continued to break the awkward silence.

"Sir, they have been *cold-mic*, as far as, I am aware. They even pulled their entire UN demonstration team out of play and had their ambassador attend the first meeting in New York solo. They appear to still be assessing what happened and who did what. I must believe they suspect our involvement. They certainly have to suspect the Aussies because it all happened on their turf, but they are not discussing it in any of the intercepts that we have. It's a temporary reprieve to be certain but, for now, they are not engaging or openly discussing any of this that we can see. I don't know if that is good, bad, both or neither," Fitz reported.

"Frustrating but not surprising. For now, it's neither but that will change," stated the President. "That is all for now. Keep the pedal to the metal on our efforts and run over anything that gets in the way until we have something on orbit. Anything else is a half measure and, while it might be helpful or even necessary, we aren't done until that happens. Am I clear?"

"Crystal clear!" Fitz answered for the group, and the call ended. Within seconds Tom's phone rang and when he picked up it was apparent to him that the SECDEF was not finished with whatever was on his mind as he asked more questions and made more requests of Tom until their call ended abruptly with Tom rolling his eyes and punching more numbers into his phone. After a few exchanges he was heading back toward the groups working on the various portions of the solution the President had referenced. He was met in the small room by Major General Chen and newly-promoted Major General Lincoln.

"Sorry to pull you both away from your main effort, but I need to chase another solution for some folks who are helping us get where we need to be," Tom began. "Sir, I need you to tell me where and how the decision makers discuss and decide what happens with these weather modifications. We need to better understand who decides what, how it is tasked, what the preferred communications are and where can we lean in and listen? We need to know more about how the CCP is viewing this and what responses and timelines they are considering or deciding. We need something more than we have, and we think that comes from you."

"Tom, that is simple, but you won't like the answer. As you know keeping this technology a secret is vital. To do that for nearly a decade was quite challenging and compartmentalization was key to that success. That is both the good news and the bad. I have been the top of that compartment for the military for several years now—three years...almost four. I had very specific, hand-picked senior colonels, one for each network in my command. Two of them you met on the UN effort. They each had a small team who knew some but not all of what we were doing and how to do it. There was depth but no breadth to it. Very much what you would call a vertical structure; like a thin chain.

"The part you won't like is when I tell you I got my instructions, training and everything else that I needed to know about these missions—orders, all of it—from Wu. He was my only point of contact on this since I came on board. If I needed clarifications, replacements, funding, or equipment, I went to Wu and nobody else. So, to help those trying to help us, we need Mr. Wu to share what he knows," Chen concluded but Frank chimed in first.

"If that is the case and we have both of you, then right now they have a broken link between the military capability and the body politic of decision makers. Sir, I want to make sure I heard you correctly. Each regional network has its own senior colonel running it, it's completely decentralized? Besides you, who knows who all these people are? And their subordinates, operating locations and the like? What records are there and where are they kept?"

"I don't know if there are any centralized records. I kept a set of records in my safe but I coded the names of the commanders and their locations. It's not a brilliant cypher but it is coded. The rest is in my head, Frank. This was *the* most covert program in our history. When I say compartmented, I mean, unless you were actively in it, you'd never know it was real," Chen paused for Frank to consider his next question.

"That being so, we may have inadvertently broken the chain hard when we got both you and Wu. We got two links that were still connected and we got key links. They may not even know yet. Maybe there is no chatter because they don't know yet. The demonstration went as planned, right? The senior colonels know their commander is not in contact, and the politicians know their Mr. Wu is not in contact but they must still consider that you are lost in the mess in New York. If not, they really don't know what to think. They may not even know we have their assets *or* their people. Is that possible?" Frank pursued.

"From my perspective yes, it's possible. We need Mr. Wu to help us assess if it is possible or even probable from his knowledge," Chen suggested. A few moments later, after Tom posed the same questions to Wu, Chen sat silently through the entire discussion. They all nodded as Wu confirmed that he too had only one contact for all his interactions. That person was the same Provisional Governor who had attended the demonstrations in India. It was indeed possible that key people had some concerns, but they had not yet reached the level of those who could do something about it.

"This is something I did not anticipate," Tom confessed to the three men in the room. "We can't assume they don't know. But it is now perhaps an equally bad assumption that they do know their RPVs are missing and for that matter that Chen, Wu and Zach are also gone versus just out of communications for far too long. I will give this to Fitz and let them decide what they want to do with their assessment teams. We have enough to do here. Thank you all; now get back to your efforts. This doesn't change our tasks or our timelines."

"Tom, could this mean there might be another opportunity to get our remaining family members out? If they don't know yet, might there be another opportunity?" Wu asked hoping against hope.

"No, it doesn't. If they don't know yet, it won't be long before they do. We cannot put our people in harm's way again because, if we're wrong and they do know, then they will be watching your remaining families. They get our guys, we have you…guess how we get our guys back? Trading you for them is a lose-lose for all of us. That risk is not one we can take. I told you that was a one-time-only shot. This is one of many reasons why. Sorry my friend, but that's a hard, no," Tom explained.

"I understand. And I am sure you understand why I had to ask. If you will excuse me, please, as you said I have a lot to get done in a short amount of time so I will return to my tasks." With that, Wu exited the room followed by Chen and then Frank. Tom punched some more numbers into his phone, "Fitz, it's me. Yeah, I have an update for you." Then he proceeded to explain what he had learned to the SECDEF so he could take that for consideration and action in his efforts to support the ongoing *Thor's Craftsmen* operations and prepare for a potential war he hoped to never have to fight.

"No offense Tom, but you don't look very good. You OK?" Ann asked the now-familiar face as she gave him a welcome hug. "What brings you to New York?"

"Thanks, Ann. It's good to see you. And that is why I am here...well, to see *both* you and Bob. Is he around; I am on a pretty tight timeline?" he got straight to the point.

"Yeah, seems it's been that way since I met you. Does it ever change for you? The pace I mean, has it always been like this or is it worse with all this weather stuff?" she asked.

"Yes," he smiled politely, "Bob?"

"He is up in Mr. Dau's office. That is where I am supposed to meet him anyway. Walk with me, unless you think I will slow you down," she said as she strode into the UN headquarters building where they were scheduled to meet to discuss how to integrate the demonstration and the summit. She continued the conversation as she left without looking back to see if Tom was following, "How much coffee do you drink in a day, Tom?"

"From your earlier comment, I am going to say either not enough or too much," he tried to lighten his tone and enjoy the company as they made their way deeper into the UN building.

"Seriously, how much?" she persisted.

"Depends on where I am and what I am doing. Traveling like I have been doing lately, I grab a cup whenever I can," he confided.

"Good, because I need some and as soon as we are through security that is our first stop. There is a shop in the lobby. They know what they are doing when it comes to coffee. All kinds, from all over. Do you have a favorite?" She was both telling and asking, using one of Tom's techniques on him to see how he liked it.

"Hot...black...strong. Don't care where it's from as long as it's not bitter or burnt. And, as long as you're buying, I am fine with a brief pit stop along the way. Since I will be crashing your party unannounced, we might want to bring a couple extras for Bob and Dau. How's Betty?" Tom asked as he cleared the metal detector and collected his items from the X-ray belt.

"Glad you are fine with it because I wasn't asking, and Betty is pretty good. I must tell you, Betty and my dad have really hit it off. I think they were both entrenched in their daily work, so they didn't have to think much about what they were missing. Plucking them from that showed them there was more to do and more that they were missing. This whole thing has actually been good for them. Hope there is more *good* to come for all of us. Is that why you are here, Tom? Please tell me you are bringing some good news with you."

"Some of it will be good. We'll have to see about the rest of it," he smiled as they approached the coffee counter where the attendant recognized Ann and greeted her by name. She ordered four large coffees, two with cream and two without then handed the attendant a hundred-dollar bill.

"Thank you, the rest is for you and I will see you next time," she said, as she took the two with cream while Tom took the two without. Then they headed for the elevator. After a series of pressing buttons and security codes they finally stopped on the floor where Mr. Dau's office was located. They walked down the hall and were lucky enough to find Bob and Dau alone and preparing for the upcoming discussion with the Secretary General and his key staff.

"Look who I found wandering around the streets of New York looking for someone to let him in the UN building," she joked as Tom entered the office right behind her, put the coffees down and extended his hand to his two friends who each would not settle for less than a manly hug.

"It's good to see you both," Tom said.

"I bet. From the looks of you, it would appear that the company you have been keeping has been harder on you than we were. It's not too late to come back to the UN team. I am sure we can find something you might be good at should you need a break from all that national security stuff," Mr. Dau offered and considered for a moment what he might do if Tom accepted his offer.

"As enticing as that sounds, I'm right in the middle of something that will follow me here if I jump ship. I would not want to put that on you. In fact, that is exactly why I am here. Can we talk, just us for a while?" Tom was tired but his intensity never seemed to wane. As Dau closed his office door, the four picked up their coffees and settled in to give Tom their undivided and uninterrupted attention.

"I would apologize for just showing up unannounced but seems like that is more common than not so, yeah, sorry *a little*. I need to cover a lot of topics, so please bear with me. First, I need your thoughts on whether or not you can tell if the Chinese reps on your teams know anything about their systems being missing or if they know where Chen, Wu and Zach are or are not?"

"Well, we got the CCP team members settled into their billets, but haven't seen them here beyond that. Their UN Ambassador showed up at our briefing...not them. He has been the only one we've seen so far. We have another meeting in a couple hours. He should be there but it's a principals' meeting so, if any of the CCP demonstration team shows up, it should not be more than about seven of them. That would include Chen and Wu's replacements," Bob explained. "Why Tom? What's the context?"

"You have been paying attention Professor…good!" Tom smiled. "Not to be repeated but we think—due to their security protocols—they may not yet know their systems have been captured. They do know they haven't heard from Wu or Chen and that is concerning, but they may very well not know the extent of the problem just yet. If you were to put what you've seen since you've been here in that scenario would it make sense of or would it refute that possibility?"

"I can't think of anything that would make it not possible. I figured they were buying themselves time to decide on and prepare their response. But it could be they bought themselves time to try to understand what was happening and why Chen and Wu had quit responding. I suppose that could look the same to us whichever was true," Bob concluded. Ann and Dau both nodded in agreement with nothing to add that would thwart the working theory.

"Are you suggesting we put Chen or Wu back in the lineup?" Ann asked.

"No, we don't have that level of confidence nor would we, even if we did. It is really helpful to keep them out of sight. If they don't know what happened, then they don't know who is—or is not—involved. It could be the Aussies, could be the UN, could be the US…could be anyone else. But it might be helpful to plant some seeds of doubt and give them some red herrings to chase. Especially if the UN Ambo is the one bringing them. Do you think the Secretary General would be on board with some high-level misinformation operations, or do you think we should stay south of that level?" Tom asked.

"Depends," Dau assured him. "The man has a conscience but he only uses it when it is convenient to him."

"Good to know. Can I sit in on your upcoming meeting; get a sense of where they are and who shows up?" Tom asked. "Based on that, we can call an audible for what I take back with me to the SECDEF and the team."

"I think that is a good idea. It will also demonstrate that the US is still engaged and serious about this effort. You guys took a credibility hit with the whole arrival disaster. I am sure the Secretary General would accept your apologies for the poor performance of your Air Force after General Lincoln departed. It seems Frank set the bar very high and the poor chaps they sent in behind him have struggled to fill his shoes," Dau said knowingly. "I have not told him that was by design, so do not throw me under the bus on this one, Tom."

"Of course. That will work for me. Next topic if we are ready?" Tom asked. "Gonna need to break up the band for just a little while right after this meeting and our post-meeting skull session. Bob, I would like you to come to Florida with me to spend a little bit of time with the other team. They have a working theory we are running with, and I need you to find its Achilles heel. We need you to say why it won't work or convince the President it will. One of the two. We are approaching our commit time. If it's not gonna work, I need to know that sooner not later. Ann, your expertise is also welcome depending on what is going on here. But, Bob, your attendance is required. You won't need to bring anything because you won't be gone long enough or left alone enough to need anything except a nap on the flight back."

"OK, sounds like that was not for discussion, so what's next?" Bob asked.

"You got anything to eat up here? I need to soak up some of this twenty-five-dollars-a-cup coffee before it burns a hole in my stomach," Tom smiled at Ann as Bob and Dau looked at each other wondering what that meant. A few snacks and some discussion about how they might do the demonstration in the context of the summit and, before they knew it, they needed to head to the conference room and the Secretary General. Once the room was settled and the meeting began, it was clear that it would only produce *some* of the desired outcomes. The only member of the CCP delegation from the UN team present was not even a member of the team. It was, once again, the Chinese Ambassador to the UN.

The Secretary General exchanged greetings with those in the room, and he welcomed Tom and thanked him for rejoining their efforts but did not bust his chops about the unfortunate arrival situation. He went straight to the Ambo with visible disappointment, "Mr. Ambassador, I must ask. Have we done something wrong or somehow offended the members of the CCP delegation to our UN team? Since we left Australia, things have been both confusing and uncomfortable. And again, this afternoon, we have no representation from them. You are here in their stead. Can you please provide some insight, as we have much to discuss and decide today. And, with all due respect to you, Sir, you do not have the same expertise as those who would otherwise be in the room for these discussions."

"Mr. Secretary General, please accept my apologies. I am hopeful that we are on the cusp of resolving our personnel issues. This will enable us to rejoin the efforts appropriately staffed. I believe only one or two more days is all that will be needed."

"Sir, if I may ask, what are the staffing issues you are struggling with? Perhaps we have some suitable options that we could fill in for you, even if only temporarily while you pursue your solutions," Mr. Dau offered.

"That is most kind of you, Mr. Dau, but we are making some changes at the top of our organization, and I am afraid the expertise needed is quite unique," he replied, but Mr. Dau saw an opportunity he could not pass.

"Can you please be specific when you say top of your organization. Who do you mean?" Dau pressed.

"Sir, I am afraid due to some unforeseen circumstances we are replacing both General Chen and Mr. Wu. That is a hard task, especially on such short notice," the ambassador explained.

"Oh my. That is unfortunate. Do they know yet? When I met with them this morning, neither one mentioned their pending departure. I will miss working with both of these fine men. Can we still do the demonstration we discussed earlier today? It was such a good idea they brought us. Did they brief you on it before this meeting? Bob and I both thought it would be a wonderful encore to the two rainbow demonstrations," Dau asked. The look on the ambassador's face told Tom that was the last thing the Ambo expected to hear at this meeting. That was helpful.

"The idea you discussed with them this morning?" he paused, noticeably uncomfortable. "No, I am afraid they did not discuss their idea with me before this meeting. And no, I'm sorry but I don't believe either of them are aware of the pending changes. I am sure you understand how much discretion is needed when making such changes. Mr. Secretary, as I said, if you could indulge us a few more days that should be all we need."

"Of course. But I must insist that whoever is coming onto the effort be introduced and integrated expeditiously to ensure we can conduct another flawless demonstration. Not only will we have the world's media attention, but we will have key players from many nations here in person to see this firsthand in concert with the summit. If the other demonstrations were important, this one is vital. No mistakes, no excuses," the Secretary General agreed and warned the ambassador.

"Understood. Thank you, Mr. Secretary," he concluded.

The meeting wrapped up with a loose outline of how the UN's two events would be integrated but no timeline was agreed upon. There were still too many unknowns about the CCP team's compositions and which nations would be participating in the summit and at what level. Bob, Ann and Tom headed for the airport after a quick huddle with Mr. Dau to address the next few milestones in Thor's Craftsmen's two separate but collaborating efforts. There were lots of moving parts and lots of unknowns, for now.

CHAPTER SEVEN

PROGRESS AND SETBACKS

The flight on the now-familiar small jet taking them from New York to a small airfield in central Florida was long enough for Tom to thoroughly describe the concepts to Bob and Ann. While he could not explain the intricacies of the team's approach, Tom did an admirable job connecting the concepts being pursued. In the heart of that conversation, the steward approached the three and signaled for Tom to move to the front cabin. After a brief discussion with the pilots, the aircraft began a sweeping turn which signaled a change in direction, and likely their planned destination.

"Well, that was special" Tom began as he rejoined Bob and Ann in the comfortable seating to continue their discussion. "We need to make an unscheduled stop to pick up a few more guests. We are stopping in Norfolk, VA to pick up the Chairman and the SECDEF. They will be coming with us for the discussions and the resultant recommendation to the President. Seems we are quickly approaching a decision point and having us all in the room doing this eyeball-to-eyeball is the preferred approach. No pressure on you two really, just speak your mind. Seems you have a pretty good track record in doing that so far...*piece of cake.*"

"Tom, out of curiosity. If you had to pick one person in this group to put all your trust in, one person to make the call who would you trust to make it?" Ann asked.

"That is an unfair question, but you already know that. And you asked it anyway. If I had to go all in on one person, my money would be on Dutch. Your question was based on trust and I trust him to do the right thing without getting hung up on doing things right. Not that I don't trust the others but I trust him the most. That's for your ears and nobody else. Now I would like to be finished with this conversation and get back to the one we were having before, if that's all right with you?"

"Of course, and thanks, Tom. I appreciate your opinion and your candor," Ann offered as the conversation turned, as if in synch with the aircraft.

"So, if I understand this correctly, they are running historic data sets for the ground conditions to get the upper air conditions that existed during those for each of the principle atmospheric parameters? So, they are working solely with correlating knowns with knowns? And doing that for as many points as they can and then correlating these conditions. Is that right?" Bob asked.

"That is how I understand it," Tom concurred.

"That will take a tremendous amount of processing and time" Ann warned.

"They were given all we have which was more than they needed. Already have that portion done. They are working on integrating the historic with what it looks like from space, using current on-orbit commercial and military satellites. That is where yesterday's breakthrough came. I don't understand it really, but the data that makes each pixel in all these gazillion images gets tied to a value that equates to something that points to what is on the ground, and what it will be next. They synthesized this and it made sense to what was happening on the ground as it relates to what you can see from space. Andies says initializing the models in near real time lets you update the device inputs to get what you want to see next. And if you do it fast enough and often enough in each grid point it can translate to the next ones or stop. Makes *science sense* to him. He told me to think of it as a *self-licking ice cream cone*. I was a little insulted by that to be honest, but that's one of many reasons we want you popping into their party," Tom paused.

"Damn, that's smart!" Bob grinned. "They tested any of this yet? I mean the programming to do this can be simple enough but it has to be fast and constant for it to be applied on a large scale. That something they think will work...or do they already know it will work?"

"A little of both when I left yesterday. We will both know more once we get there and hear where they are now," Tom confessed. "I have to resist calling and checking in with these guys because it is a real disruption when I do. We get way more done when I leave them alone, until I can't. Tough to find the balance between my faith in them and my boss's faith in me given the timeline he gave us."

That was a lot for everyone to ponder. The aircraft descended for its approach into Norfolk. It didn't take long to get the two DVs and a few members of their security detail loaded up and now they were rolling back out for takeoff en route to Florida.

"Good to see you again Professor...Ann. How goes the UN effort?" the SECDEF said, once they had lifted off and the wheels were up.

"Honestly, we are at a bit of a standstill. The CCP delegation seems to be locked down and that has put the demonstration in a holding pattern. And the Secretary General's decision to have a summit in conjunction has everyone focused on who is coming to that discussion and who is not. So that has become the priority of everyone's focus right now. Who and when, not *what*," Bob summarized.

"The CCP delegation members are all being interrogated; that's why they aren't available. They are trying to figure out what happened to Chen and Wu and Zach. Everyone who was supposed to made it to New York except them. And they don't know where they are or why they are missing. Your team just added confusion to that mix at your UN meeting.

Their Ambo reported they were supposedly in the UN building yesterday meeting with you and Mr. Dau. That has them all spun up and, likely, bought us some more time. Thanks for that, I think. Time will tell," Fitz paused to gauge their reaction.

"You're welcome, I think. Time will tell," was all Bob could think to say. That drew a smile from everyone, as they continued to discuss what had happened since they were last together. And then the conversation turned to what was next and what they hoped to accomplish in Florida.

"You know an effort like this typically takes us many iterations of design and testing, both in labs and in the field. For this, we are likely going to end up going live without much—perhaps, without any—of that. To meet the POTUS' timeline, we are probably only going to get one shot at this. That needs to be a bullseye. So, any holes in this we need to find, fix, or adjust our direction. I am going to ask you both to be brutally candid in your assessments. That doesn't mean being *mean*, it means being *certain*. Can you do that for us?" the Chairman of the Joint Chiefs asked as he stared intently at Bob so he could see every bit of him when he responded.

"Yes Sir, I can and I will. We all have a lot riding on this," Bob assured him and Dutch saw that his body language matched his words.

"Good, thank you. And how about you ma'am?" he asked Ann.

"Yes, that goes for me as well. Ma'am, really, have I aged that much since this started?" she asked the four-star general only half-jokingly.

"That is commonly used by those of us in uniform as a term of respect, not a reflection of your age or appearance. I hope you will take it as such. That is how I intended it," he assured.

"That I can accept and feel much better about; thank you very much," she smiled and hoped someone would change the conversation for her. Tom, reading the room, readily obliged.

"We will be landing in about eighty minutes. How much time will we have on the ground before he gets there?" Tom asked the SECDEF.

"If everyone is on time, we might have an hour—two max, if *she* is coming along. After all, it is Florida, and they have lots of reasons to come to the state this time of year. We are a dark stop at the front end of a scheduled trip and speech in Miami. We should expect twenty minutes max given his itinerary. If it takes longer than that, it's because he doesn't like where we're going, and we'll need to rethink it anyway," Fitz concluded.

"Are you referring to the President? Will he be there?" Bob asked.

"You didn't tell him?" Fitz looked a little puzzled at Tom.

"Hadn't gotten to that part quite yet when we picked you guys up. Sorry Bob, and yes, the President will be there in person for this. He wants to see what we see; see who says it and how strongly they believe in it. You can only do so much decision-making over video conferencing. Big decisions, like this one, sometimes you gotta go with your gut. Best to do that eyeball-to-eyeball. Like you said, we all have a lot riding on this," Tom explained.

"Doesn't change anything for you two," Dutch chimed in. "You just do what you promised me earlier. Doesn't matter who is or isn't in the room. Facts are facts. *Opinions* vary. Differentiate between the two and say your peace...simple. Maybe not easy, but it is simple. Don't overthink this. As I recall, you have a mountain of money and ongoing immunity. If *you* can't speak your mind, not sure who can."

"When you put it that way General, it makes perfect sense to me," Ann smiled as she responded for both and was pleased to see Bob nodding in agreement.

"Since we don't really know if the CCP is aware that their RPVs are gone or who has them, does that change anything we have in the pipeline?" Fitz asked the group.

"I don't think it should," Dutch replied quickly. "First of all, we don't know that they don't know. Meaning they *might* know. Thinking they might not know is a whole lot of *squish*. The faster we get a global response capability, even if it is limited, the better positioned we are to repel or respond to actions from their regional systems. In addition to that, we need to remember that there could be other players that we don't see yet. We don't know if India was complicit in the events there. We don't know if the CCP has shared this with anyone else in the time they have had it. Entirely possible some other nations are working with them. What we don't know about all this will fill history books for centuries to come. What we do know, by comparison, could fit in a very small container."

"Tom, you've been unusually quiet. What do you think?" the SECDEF cajoled the National Security Advisor to the President.

"I agree with Dutch. But I also think we can and should put more pressure on them with the UN summit. We should schedule a series of CCP-led breakout sessions where they are on the hook to explain how their technology works and how it can be operated safely in both a centralized and decentralized manner. They should lead several of the key sessions. This will smoke out who else they have and keep them focused on their visible reputation ahead of their covert operations," Tom explained.

"I like that idea," Bob agreed. "We have what we believe are two of their key resources. Let's see how true that is by how much they resist, or how quickly they trot out some new experts. If need be, we can pick Chen and Wu's brains to see what kind of questions we could ask that might trip them up if they aren't the real deals. We could call Mr. Dau and put that in motion right now if that is what you want to do. I am pretty sure you have his number. If you would rather, I can make the call. I know my phone works in this plane most of the time, especially, in US airspace."

"Any objections?" Tom asked the group. "Seeing none, how about you make that call, Bob? Might be better coming from you than me given the circumstances and our new roles." And, with that, Bob picked up his phone and called his UN colleague and put that plan into motion. He returned his attention to the conversations inside the aircraft and reported that Mr. Dau would both put it into motion and inform the Secretary General. And he would do it, in that order. They liked working with Mr. Dau.

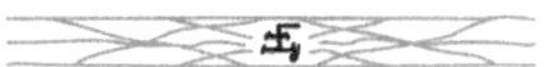

It wasn't long before the steward let them know they were beginning their descent into the small airfield, and it would not be long before they reached their destination. He also added that POTUS was wheels up and en route. Air Force One would be landing at their interim stop at MacDill Air Force Base outside of Tampa, where the President would transition to helicopter transport for his scheduled, and *unscheduled*, stops before continuing to Miami for the speech. Their time on the ground before he got there would be well under two hours.

"Can't wait to see the progress since my last visit. Seems like I was just here," Dutch said to Tom. "Hope they are ready. Do they know he's coming, or are you dropping it on them like you did the good Professor and Ann?"

"Frank is there. He knows. Not sure who he will have set up to brief, but it will be the right people. We lucked out getting him at the beginning of this. You have no idea. If you could have picked a team from everyone in the Air Force, you would probably have picked the guys you accidentally ended up with," Tom concluded.

"It's not luck Tom. It's Doc looking out for us," Bob smiled.

"If that's the case, let's hope he keeps it up. We still have a lot to do," Tom requested as they slowed to a soft touchdown and then the heavy application of brakes and reverse thrusters to keep the small jet safely on the short but well-maintained runway. They quickly deplaned and the group moved in unison to the open glass doors of the building that served as the operations building where Major General Lincoln was doing his best to close the distance and greet the group that was already ahead of him.

"Sorry, I wasn't in position to greet you. No excuse, just juggling chainsaws... which are all running...and I'm refueling two of them as I go. Hope you will forgive my tardiness," Frank offered the group.

"No worries, Frank. Got to have you earning that two-star pay now that you're wearing it. Congratulations, it's well deserved," Fitz eased the man's concern. He needed everyone on their A-game for this and he could see that Frank was carrying a disproportional amount of this effort.

"Thank you, Sir. I am wondering how you would each like to spend your time in advance of the President's arrival. We don't have all that much and I want to make sure we do all we can to get you what you need?" Frank offered the group as they continued walking.

"I would like to get some information from your weather and computer guys if that's possible. Tom explained the concept to me on the flight and, no offense, but he doesn't know the meteorology end of this the way I need to understand it to give an opinion. Is that doable?" Bob asked.

"Yes, Andies and Lessur are elbow deep in it. They are like kids in a candy store, but I don't think they have slept much the past few days so be ready for the over caffeinated version. Making history seems to keep them motivated," Frank obliged and pointed the professor in the right direction and he and Ann disappeared around the corner as they headed to the area where the weather team was working.

"Anyone else?" Frank asked.

"Let's find a place where the rest of us can talk privately for a few minutes. There are a few things I need to be clear on before we start," Dutch requested. Fitz, Dutch and Tom went into Frank's small office and closed the door as the security detail posted up outside the door and up the short hallway. They were used to being close to but not included in some of the nation's most sensitive conversations. It was part of the job, and they did not take it personally when they were asked to remain out of earshot. When they did hear something, whether they should have heard it or not, they knew the correct action was to allow the data to travel unimpeded in one ear to out the other, never to be recalled or spoken of again. What an enigma for these professionals; to have to un-know what they know they heard.

"Frank, between us, and before we start, I want your gut feeling on this. Give me a one-word response to this question. Will this idea produce the results we need?" Dutch asked.

"Probably," Frank said coolly, drawing a grin from Fitz and a frown from Tom and Dutch.

"You hedging your bets, Frank?" Dutch pressed the young flag officer.

"No Sir. I believe the concept is sound and it will work. Also, pretty confident we should be able to get the lift needed to fly these into space where we need them. What I am lacking is the confidence that the results we need are both consistent and understood to mean the same things around the room as they do to the commander in chief. That is why my answer was not a flat yes," Frank said very matter-of-factly.

"OK, let's unpack that by starting around the room. Where do you see gaps," Dutch pressed the conversation.

"We need an operational system to counter the existing regional systems. We could do that regionally, like we do with other weapon systems. To be efficient and effective, we are skipping that level of engagement to get to space and stand up a global capability. That provides tactical and strategic advantages. It also produces an offensive capability. That is a good deterrent, and it is also a formidable threat if we decide on first use operations. When we must make hard choices and tradeoffs in getting this done on this timeline, where do we lean in? Do defensive capabilities have priority, or is it the offensive capability that has to win out if we need to choose?" Frank was asking for guidance from his chain of command.

"That is a good question. Have you had to make those choices yet Frank, and if so, which did you choose?" Fitz flipped the script on him in true political fashion. Whether it was intentional or just curiosity was unclear.

"Not really...not yet. But I can see those decisions on the near horizon, especially if we have to produce a one-size-fits-all solution. By way of comparison, we have bombers, tankers, fighters, transports, intel platforms, fixed wing, tilt rotor, rotary wing, manned and unmanned aircraft because we have specific applications, mission needs and desired effects. We don't just have airplanes in the Air Force. You have asked us to build the equivalent of an *airplane*.

That won't be enough because we have already started bending metal and preparing orbit plans so we can decide what, when and how to launch satellites. We need to know where we can, can't, should and shouldn't put them and who will need to be able to control them once they are up. All these considerations need to be clearly known before we can move ahead. We are over the science hump of this effort, but I am still looking up the hill at who and how this is going to be operated. That drives all the rest, and I don't understand it yet. If someone else does, I need to know it to proceed properly. I wasn't hedging," Frank explained just one of the chainsaws he was juggling.

"I see your dilemma," Fitz sympathized. "Is this a DoD system, or State Department, or someone else. None of them are here Frank, so I gotta stick with it's got to be a DoD system. Defense or offense is just like a gun. It depends on the circumstance...who is using it and for what. By itself, it is both and neither. Put it where it best fits when the time comes, and we can sort the rest out later. We do that all the time; don't see why we can't do it here, too."

"Fair enough," Frank said calmly, and Tom took the opportunity to ask his question of the senior Defense Department leaders.

"Who do you intend to send to the UN summit on fielding this technology to the world? Will one of the two of you be there since it's a military system we are developing in secret, or will it be someone from State Department? Both? Neither? We can't double dip the UN demo team as our representatives to the summit, they are not policy makers. Has he decided how he is going to handle that yet? I have not heard if he has," Tom asked for a very specific reason.

"Don't know; we haven't landed on that one yet that I am aware of," Fitz replied honestly and when Tom turned to look at Dutch for his response, he was met with, "Don't look at me, I would get it from Fitz if I had it."

"OK then, let's land on that decision point before we leave here today if we can. That will help steer what Bob and Ann and their team do when they get back to New York," Tom requested.

"What else do you need cleared up inside this room, Frank?" Dutch asked the *Thor's Craftsmen* military leader.

"Zach, Wu and Chen. I am operating under the premise that is all in Tom's purview, but I need to know that neither of you have any expectations of me regarding them once our work here is complete," Frank added.

"They are not DoD problems, resources or responsibilities. That will be all Tom and no Frank," Dutch assured him.

"Understood. Thanks for the clarity. That should be all I need for now. I appreciate you taking the time to clear these things up for me. We should probably get over to make sure all is ready for his arrival. It won't be long." Frank was relieved and ready to move on to the next big task in his busy day, which was making sure all was ready for the POTUS arrival.

In the meantime, Bob and Ann had been busy listening to Chief Andies, Major Lessur and some other scientists describe the meteorological concepts and details they intended to apply in order to meet their tasked outcomes. It was interesting to Ann how they were able to move between tasks to prepare for the upcoming briefing to the President, continue their ongoing works, catch Bob and Ann up on past efforts and randomly discuss completely unrelated things like chow, upcoming ball games, and music. *This was a place where those with ADHD could thrive*, she thought, and perhaps that was the superpower this team had captured. And maybe that is why they were on this team? While she was considering that, the ten-minute warning came to them. He just landed. Whatever your position is for this, get to it.

"Welcome to Florida Sir!" Fitz shouted over the helicopter as he led the President toward the small group assembled for his arrival. They quickly walked into the building where the air was cooler, it was quieter and the water, snacks and restroom were all waiting for him. After a quick stop to *recycle some water* and take on some more, they were walking to the briefing room to get started. After all, this was an unscheduled and off-the-books stop so they had no time to waste. The room was called to attention as the President entered. Once he was seated, everyone else settled in and they got right to the tasks at hand. There were more people in the room for this than were typically in any other briefing. This seemed odd since it was a briefing to the President, but that is why they were all there. Nobody was sure where it would go or what he would ask so it was all hands. Bob and Ann sat with the weather and computer team. They could see some familiar faces in the room, including Chen, Wu, and Zach to name a few.

"OK, what do you have for me?" he asked the room, not sure who was leading the briefing.

It was Tom, who opened the discussion, "Good afternoon, Sir. We understand time is limited so we will hit the highlights, request some guidance, and take any questions or direction you might have regarding the on-demand weather program *Thor's Craftsmen*."

"So far this sounds like every other briefing except the name," he snarled at Tom. "Are we on schedule? You have a short timeline."

"Yes. And we may have some pad in that timeline if the CCP is unaware their RPVs have been compromised, but we are not counting on that. It appears the science is sufficiently worked out such that we have good confidence our approach will work from space in a low earth orbit," Tom began but was quickly interrupted.

"Sufficient and good confidence are not assuring words, Tom. They imply mediocrity and doubt. Is that where we are or are we somewhere north of that? I don't mean to be short or brash; you got three minutes to make me a believer. Can we do this?" he pushed.

"Yes Sir, in that case, I will pitch it to Major General Lincoln's team to explain the *it* that makes this do-able...Frank?" Tom said using seven seconds of the available three minutes. In typical fashion, Frank was up to the task and began.

"Mr. President. We now have the ability to sufficiently render the atmosphere from the earth's surface to the boundary with space. We can sufficiently represent the needed parameters in the present and future by fusing data, current observations from the earth and a wide variety of on-orbit imagers and profilers. We have learned from the CCP systems we captured, as well as, the expertise provided by Misters Chen, Wu and Zach how to integrate the weather modification systems into an overlapping grid. We can control the weather within each grid and create the conditions to hand off to the next grids based both on what it is and what we want to occur. This allows us to nest the systems areas and enable them to work with each other instead of against each other to produce the desired conditions.

"What this also enables is the ability to stabilize one area regardless of how many inputs might be added. Meaning, if the system is working in an integrated manner, the desired outcomes are spread across multiple devices creating a defense-in-depth against anomalies...even other devices with opposing inputs. Those inputs will be smoothed out by the overlapping areas of the other devices," Frank paused as the clock hit two minutes forty seconds. He wanted some time in reserve for a desperation pass if he needed one.

"Thank you, General, that is excellent. You specifically said the ability to…so we have this working now, right?" asked the President.

"It works on paper. It works in the computer models. It works in the simulators we built. What we don't have yet are enough satellites in the right places with the right hardware to make it work. We do have components being purchased, mocked up and readying for construction. We know how many we need, where we need to put them in order to cover the areas to ensure we have both capability and enough redundancy for a thirty percent failure rate," Frank added.

"That sounds like it will be a problem for the schedule we are on. Will it be?" POTUS asked.

"That depends on you, Sir," Frank said flatly.

"How's that?" he asked.

"We will need everything already on the launch pads reconfigured plus three more to put up the number of CubeSats we need to meet your timeline. If most get up by your initial date, we will have a decent capability. Get the rest of them up and it becomes robust. That order needs to come from you, Sir. I don't have any of those resources, and much of what is needed is not DoD."

"I will say one thing for you General Lincoln, you've got guts to put this back on me. But you are right, and you're right to do so. You did good with this one Fitz!" the President smiled. "Say I do everything you asked Frank. What part of this keeps you up at night? If it fails, where does it fail and why?"

"All of it keeps me up at night, Mr. President. None of us are sleeping much," Frank smiled at the man and pointed to those in the seats to make sure they were acknowledged for the work that he was representing to the leader of the free world. "We cannot have a bad launch. If we lose one payload or more, rebuilding, reprogramming and relaunching will be challenging. We bought or are making all there is to buy to make these.

You can thank Mr. Wu for the technical insights that enabled our guys to miniaturize these so that we can use CubeSats. The small packages on the RPVs were great. We can replicate those easy enough now, but we were able to miniaturize them without changing much and that brings the power demands down sufficiently so that space ops can be achieved."

"Thank you, Mr. Wu, that is excellent. It seems you will leave your mark on both the CCP and US systems. Seems several of you will carry that distinction. What do you think about this capability General Chen?" the President asked looking directly at the civilian-attired man.

"It is remarkable. We tried for years to get here and could not. This is an elegant solution which eluded us, until now," he stood as he responded.

"And why is that? What is different here that was so elusive to your efforts?" the President followed up.

"The meteorology solution. That innovation removed the roadblocks and created solution options that were never in our CCP discussions. That was the breakthrough we never made," he concluded then sat.

"Thank you. And who do we have to thank for that breakthrough?" the President asked.

"Sir, our entire weather team has built this out but it was Chief Andies who gave us the idea. Actually, he told us what to do and how to do it," Frank pointed in their direction.

"Thank you, Chief. That is some tall praise. Professor Mcleod, good to see you again. Have you had a chance to look at this weather breakthrough, yet?" the President asked.

"Yes, we discussed it prior to your arrival, Sir," Bob nodded.

"And, what do you think?"

"To be candid, Sir, I didn't get it at first. It's not something I would have ever come up with because it is so unorthodox, but it is perfectly applied to what we are trying to do. The math works. The data is available to initialize and run every window for every device. It is self-synchronizing and when it was run in the simulator using the historical climatological averages for all the available surface stations it worked and produced the intended weather for the downstream stations. The beauty of this is there are no super events. Meaning the big wind event in India could be detected and even prevented depending on the rules put into the model. It will work and it is *brilliant* in its simplicity. Sure wish I would have thought of it…maybe we could have avoided all of this," he added. "That's what I think."

"Fair enough; thanks Bob. Thanks Chief, and thanks weather team," the President moved on to close this out; his decision made.

"Fitz, let me know who you want me to call and clear the path for what you need and to get the launch support you need. All right everyone, a big thank you from me to you for what you have already done and what you will get done soon. I know you have a lot more to do so I will leave you to do it. Carry on!" he said as he got up and headed for the exit.

As they walked toward the sound of the already running helicopter, the President personally thanked Frank for the exceptional work on this to date, "I know I have given you in an impossible task, Frank, but I need you to keep doing the impossible. Keep asking *how*…not *if*. That goes for the rest of you as well. Like I said before, we get one shot at this."

"Sir, a quick question while we have you if I may?" Tom asked and continued as the POTUS nodded.

"The UN summit on how to roll this out. You saw the Secretary General announced that will be held in conjunction with the next demonstration. We put some more pressure on the CCP to do some briefings on how it works to smoke out their B-team players or see how deep their bench is to replace Chen and Wu. Wondering who you intend to have representing the US at that summit? We'll need to do some briefings and deconflictions. We don't have a lot of time and everyone is stretched pretty thin already."

"I hear you, Tom, and I know that was such a bush-league move. Not sure what else the Secretary General might try to pull at that damned summit. It's in New York and he will be there in person. Since he wants to be a big shot with a bunch of world leaders, so be it. I will attend to keep him in line and keep you guys focused on what I need you to do. I'll protect that if I need to while I'm there. Besides, my staff wants to set my schedule for me all the time. This will help remind them who decides what I am gonna do and when I'm gonna do it. Thanks for the question. Anything else?" he asked as he was putting on his sunglasses to exit the building and get on the awaiting helicopter.

"No Sir, that about covers it," Tom smiled and watched his boss as he bounded across the tarmac and up the few steps into the helicopter.

"Well, that went better than I expected," Dutch said to the group as the engines spooled up and the helicopter lurched forward as it gained altitude and airspeed in their effort to get the President as close to back on schedule as they could. The unexpected stop would be attributed to a minor mechanical issue.

Shortly after POTUS' departure, the small jet began rolling up the taxiway toward the building. Frank rounded up Bob and Ann to rejoin their traveling companions for a pending departure. As they climbed aboard, each was sitting in the same seats they had on their flight in as if it was expected. Bob and Ann sat down and looked at the three men who were each on their cell phones giving directions and listening intently. The door was buttoned up; the steward handed them a bottle of water and the plane began to taxi toward the runway. It occurred to them both that their small glimpse into the pace and magnitude of this level of work was plenty sufficient to let them know they did not want any more of it than was absolutely necessary. And it also made them appreciate those around them who did this all the time. *Better them than me* Ann smiled and closed her eyes while she could, unsure how many stops there would be between where she was and New York.

CHAPTER EIGHT

SOME SUMMIT

The aircraft touched down softly in DC, taxied, offloaded the SECDEF and the CJCS and, without delay, was rolling down the runway at National en route to New York. Well into their climb out, Tom decided this would be a good time to get into the specifics of what the UN team was going to need to deliver to keep these efforts synchronized. To Bob, it seemed like a lot of political jockeying with little payoff for their side of the ongoing effort which was to effectively field this technology to be used *by the many, for the many*. He was not shy about having this conversation with Tom as they had freely debated approaches in the past with mutual respect and collaborative outcomes. That is how they got this far together.

"It doesn't make sense to me to spend that much time to get such a short way down the road. It's motion for the illusion of progress with no real gains on getting this out there in a meaningful way," Bob posited.

"It's not about getting it *out there,* Bob, it's all about getting it *up there.* Getting this on-orbit is the main effort. It's already *out there.* I thought we were clear on that," Tom pressed.

"I guess what I failed to realize was the main effort is the only effort. I thought we had a primary and a secondary effort. That both were the policy objectives of the US; not that one was just a cover for the other. That the UN effort was just a distraction to keep the eyes off the main effort had not been put that plainly to me. Is that how it is, Tom?" Bob was agitated at the discussion, as the long day and lack of sleep were beginning to show.

"You could put it that way, yes, and you would not be wrong," Tom agreed.

"That is not what we signed up for, Tom! We chose to work on this part of the effort to finish what we started. That is not a charade to us. It is a stated objective that has not changed. It is why we came to the UN in the first place. What did I miss, and when did I miss it?" Bob's voice was getting louder as his frustration continued to build.

"I don't know that you missed anything, Professor. Maybe you only heard what you wanted to hear? Maybe your interpretation was different than the rest of ours? Maybe it's as simple as we are in agreement, but we are working on different timelines? Not sure, Bob. I can explain it to you but I can't *understand* it for you. We get this capability on orbit ASAP in order to mitigate the existing threat; establish a dominance that must be recognized in order to restore the balance of power. This enables us to set the conditions for the fair and equitable fielding and use for agreed-upon outcomes. How is that not what you understood from our previous discussions? I don't think anything has changed," Tom tried to explain but his patience was also wearing thin as the discussion progressed.

"Tom," Ann decided to interject to help de-escalate the discussion, "I think where you both are talking past each other is the sequence of activities and outcomes. At least that is how I see it. Your scenario has an operational US global weather on-demand system as a precursor and a needed lever to pull in order to be able to achieve the UN objectives. I want to believe they are complementary efforts that should be pursued concurrently. Why can't we also be working out the *who, when and how* this will be used? Discuss the best applications, potential benefits and locations of its use so, whether it's local, regional, or global systems that produce the desired conditions, there is a known framework in which to decide and operate? I don't see logic in these being sequential actions."

"Ann, I understand what you are saying. But from a national security perspective, parity is a disadvantage. The President is not looking for parity with the CCP, the Aussies, or anyone else for that matter. Sharing is caring, and I know that is why you brought this to the UN but right now the CCP can clean our clocks with this and that cannot be our going-in position any more than it can be our endgame. We need a decisive advantage, or we cannot drive the outcomes to meet our objectives," Tom tried again.

"That's the point Tom, our objectives," Bob focused in on the target. "You see *the* objective is not the same as the plural, objectives. When you say objectives, there seem to be many, and they are situational. They are transitory. They depend on who is in power at any given time. They depend on people who are elected, or appointed, or who pay the most, or whatever. But the stated objective, that is singular. That is what Doc wanted. That is the same thing Ann and I brought to the UN. That is what we agreed to when we signed onto this effort. That objective remains, to use this technology to help everyone better their situation. To reduce suffering, end hunger, all the things that make life better for anyone not there yet. I don't want to sound like a beauty pageant contestant Tom, but that is the objective as I understand...understood it. And, as I see it, that *can* be done concurrently. In fact, it should be done concurrently so what we are putting on-orbit supports that effort as opposed to undermining it when the next person in power changes the objectives simply because they can.

"Make no mistake, I don't want myself, my family or my country, or the world for that matter to be at the mercy of the CCP. That should not happen. But, when I flip that on its head, it sounds like you think if we replace CCP with US then it's all good? Myself, my family, my country and every other one out there should instead be at the mercy of the US government? I get how that is an improvement for us over the current situation, but how exactly does that change it for the rest of the world? I like to think that our government will act in a much more appropriate way than the CCP but it's still a government. Maybe that is the best approach, but maybe it's not. Isn't that what we are supposed to be talking about right now? Shouldn't we be looking at options for how to do that? Why is that not a prudent and appropriate concurrent action? That is the conversation this UN summit is supposed to advance."

"Power, Bob. It's that simple. Right now, we don't have it. When we do, we can set the conditions for Thor's Hammers' fair and equitable use. Until then, we are asking and hoping the CCP will do what we ask. That is not a good position. That is not a position the US can accept nor sustain. Right now, they can say no, if we think we should do something else instead. They activate their regional systems and what they say goes whether we like it or not. That's untenable," Tom concluded.

"I'm not saying they will, but what if they did come to the table? What if they agreed and we employ their systems as the initial capability for the UN effort instead of the US systems? Does that change anything?" Ann asked them both.

"It would change everything I know about the CCP and their stated goals. Do you really think they would agree to that? More importantly, do you think we should trust them to do it even if they agreed to?" Tom asked.

"No to both," Bob replied flatly. "Even if our President does what he has told us, do we think he is incapable of changing his mind? Do we think the next President will see things the same way this one does? I am not, repeat *not* suggesting we trust the CCP because I know we cannot. I am also not, repeat not, suggesting we stop what we are doing with the Thor's Craftsmen effort to get this on orbit. What I *am* saying, is we should pursue the UN discussions and that stated objective concurrently, not sequentially. To do anything else makes no sense to me," Bob concluded.

"Message received. I understand your position, but that does not change my gameplan or timing with what we need to do for the summit," Tom concluded. As the pilot let them know they were beginning their descent into New Your, Bob and Tom sat looking at each other neither really knowing if they had agreed…or agreed to disagree.

It was quiet the rest of the flight. Once they landed, the three walked through the terminal to the waiting cars. Tom climbed into one and quickly departed to wherever he needed to be next, and Bob and Ann climbed into a different one that took them to their hotel. It was a pretty short drive from LaGuardia to the UN headquarters and to the nearby hotel where they had their suite of rooms. Ann had texted both Steve and Betty when they landed and both were waiting at the hotel bar when they arrived ready to hear all about Bob and Ann's long day. Bob provided the short version since they were in a public place. His bad mood from his earlier conversations clearly showing.

"Well, that was not a very satisfying summary. I know it has been a long and stressful day for you two, but it sure seems like there is something you left out or something we should discuss upstairs. Sounds like you need to get somebody or something out of your system. Unless you two need to work something out...then never mind. Tell me to mind my business," Betty said what was on her mind, which was one of her many positive, but sometimes annoying, qualities. Steve looked on with a concerned father look as he waited for the reply, curious to see who it would come from.

"No, nothing like that. Sorry, it's the conversation with Tom on the flight back and I'm still processing it. So, I'd just as soon save that conversation until I've had some time to consider it, when I am not exhausted and hangry. I would much prefer to stop talking, stay here and eat something, listen to what you guys did today, and then get some sleep and start fresh tomorrow," Bob said.

"I have a better idea," Steve offered. "We literally, hung out all day talking, eating and wandering around. So how about the two of you order some food here, have them send it up to your room. Take yourselves and your drinks upstairs, unwind, eat and get some rest. We can meet upstairs or down here for breakfast; whatever works best for you two. Text us in the morning. Fresh start…fresh conversation. You choose the topic."

"I like that idea better," Ann added her support. "It's been quite the day. Come on Bob, I already know what I want to eat. Let's order and head up." And that is exactly what they did. The elevator ride up to their rooms was telling. Steve stood with Betty on his arm and her head leaning against his shoulder, as Ann stood beside them with Bob's arm around her waist and his head leaning against hers. He smiled proudly as he watched his daughter supporting her new partner just as he was. It made him feel good, despite the strain of the day. He knew they would drive on. *Nothing here a good night's sleep and another run at it can't fix* he thought as they exited the elevator and said goodnight.

It was later than he expected when his phone finally vibrated announcing the arrival of the text from his daughter. He sent a thumb's up response to the "our suite in half an hour?" message from Ann. And he smiled at Betty seeing the same message arrive on her phone as well. They weren't hiding the fact that they were together, but they weren't advertising it either. There was enough to focus on without making their relationship a distraction until it was asked about.

They arrived together, knocked and both walked into Bob and Ann's suite together. It was time for the conversation they didn't have last night. "Good morning. You guys hungry or have you already had breakfast?" Ann asked.

"Breakfast was hours ago; I'm already thinking about lunch," Steve responded. "But don't let us stop you two. Breakfast is the most important meal of the day according to someone we don't know but whose opinion we are supposed to care about. Betty, you need anything?"

"No, thank you. I'm good, but you two order up and I will make some more coffee for Steve and me. Then we can talk about whatever had your knickers in a knot last night Bob," Betty replied in that all too familiar tone that was telling not asking.

"You know, this new dynamic is both pleasing and terrifying to me," Bob confessed to them. "Betty as my colleague from work, my trusted employee and my surrogate mother-in-law at the same time kind of makes me want to have different conversations. Not sure if I am asking permission, telling you what to do or asking your opinion. I guess it's all of the above all at the same time. Cool, weird, and a little nerve-wracking, but I am getting used to the idea. Just gonna take me some time to grow into it," Bob started with his familiar smile and strained attempt at humor.

"Welcome to the party professor!" Betty began. "Seems like you are in a better headspace this morning. I hate to admit it but it looks like Steve had his one good idea for the month last night. Glad it worked out like we hoped." She shot a smile and batted her eyes at the man across the room who by now was rolling his eyes. Bob proceeded to summarize his conversation with Tom and solicited their collective opinions on the matter as they were not due at the UN until a meeting with Mr. Dau scheduled for later that afternoon, followed by a tag-up with the demonstration team.

"It's a matter of human nature," Steve said flatly. "*Absolute power corrupts absolutely* is what I've heard since I was a kid. What we are talking about here is the closest thing to that I have ever had to think about. You two were on the right course when you decided to make this technology so everyone knew about it and had it. Level the playing field so to speak. Proliferation —counterproliferation, that's just techno-speak for haves and have nots. All of that is just a measure of who has power and control, and who they have power and control over. Take that away; watch the value plummet. Once people have power or control, they generally are loathe to give it up. Governments are made up of people, so the same applies. Not sure anything in that regard has changed, or ever will."

"OK, with all that said and assuming it is still true, where does that put us?" Bob asked him.

"Same place we started. You find who you can you trust and what you can you trust them with? I can't answer that for you, but that's what you have to decide, or at least settle on the best bet," Steve continued as he sipped his coffee. "Tom is representing what he is paid to do. Advise the President on national security. That said, he doesn't have a wife, or kids, or whatever else right now. He has a job to do and it seems he is very good at it. But where you stand usually depends on where you sit. Would he see it the same way if someone else was signing his paycheck or bending his ear at the end of every single day of his existence questioning his every move and second guessing every decision he made? Not that anyone here does that. Just saying, he might see it differently if he had other considerations.

"Anyways, the point is that perspectives inform decisions. You can't know them all but the more you consider, the better informed your decision might be when the time comes to make it. Don't let Tom drive your action plan. He has one perspective and you just got mine. I'm sure you already got Ann's and, if not, you will. No doubt, you'll get Betty's too once I stop talking. Get Dau's this afternoon and as many others as you can. At the end of the day, you wrap that all into your decision calculus and let that help you decide what you can do with what is in your control. You are a meteorology professor; you did have to take calculus, didn't you?" Steve figured this was a good point in the conversation to get off his soapbox.

"Thanks for that perspective, Steve, and yes, I had to take a lot of calculus," Bob agreed.

"Good, because I never had to, got to, or *even* wanted to take calculus. Honestly, I don't even know what it is good for but I do know that decision calculus has less to do with math than it has to do with reading people. That means I just might be good at it even if I don't know much about math. People aren't numbers or equations and what you need to figure out is all about people and what they may or may not do. If math helps you do that, then use whatever you can to help you predict that." He stopped as a knock on the door signaled their breakfast and next round of coffees had arrived. The interruption paused the conversation and brought on the next topic.

An older gentleman greeted the group, announced the orders he was ferrying directly from the kitchen and began to distribute them. As he was going about his task, there was another knock on the door. Bob moved to open it and as he did, he was surprised to see a young man he did not recognize asking nervously, "Professor Mcleod? Bob Mcleod?"

Not seeing any of the ever-present but generally out of sight security detail that moved between their rooms, Bob's concern was heightened so he answered the question with one of his own, "And who might you be?"

With a little hesitation, he responded, "I am Special Agent Daniels, Sir. I work with Agent Miloc. He said you would know who he was." He paused and waited for Bob to decide what to do next.

"Yes, I know Miloc. What can I do for you?" Bob asked cautiously, and glanced quickly to his left to see where everyone else was in the room in case he had to react to the stranger at the door. He didn't see anyone except the older man posted up to his left, the coffee pot he had been holding earlier replaced by an ominous looking firearm trained at the wall exactly where Agent Daniels was standing on the opposite side.

"Can I see some ID agent Daniels? I think that will help things along for the both of us," Bob asked paying special attention to the man's hands as he reached into his jacket pocket from which he produced a very official folded leather wallet with a badge, picture of himself and lots of hard-to-reproduce emblems and graphics. As Bob examined it, a wave of relief began to sweep over him as he handed it to the gentleman to his left and invited Agent Daniels into the room in order to deliver whatever message he was carrying for his colleague, Miloc.

As Daniels entered the room, looking to see who Bob had handed his credentials to, the situation became clearer to the young agent. "Sorry to come up unannounced. I can see now that was probably not what you were expecting. That said, Sir, nobody challenged me and I strolled right up to your door. At least I knocked. Someone with different intentions may not have, and I wasn't sneaking in. If that is not ok, then I suggest you guys tighten up whatever you need to tighten up because I am not here to test your security."

"Why *are* you here?" Ann asked, trying to get the conversation back to whatever Miloc wanted communicated.

"Yes, Ma'am about that then. He wanted me to pass this along to Professor Mcleod, do you want to hear it privately or..."

Before he could provide another option, Bob interrupted him, "Thanks for the breakfast and the added comfort as I answered the door. Appreciate you looking out for us. I think we are good in here for now."

"Of course, Sir. Blessed day to you all," he said as he departed and closed the door behind him.

"Speak freely Agent Daniels. No secrets among us four," Bob assured him.

"Miloc said, before I start, to tell you Buck is doing great. Can you tell me what that means?" he asked.

"Doc's dog, well my dog now, or he was. Miloc's dog is named Buck. Sounds like he is doing great? The dog is great." Bob looked a bit puzzled at the question.

"Very well then, thanks. So, the message is we have apprehended the man who was on the doorbell video the night of the hit and run. Miloc is seeing to him personally which is why he did not deliver the message himself. That is the message. If you have anything for me to bring back to Miloc, I will, but beyond that I have nothing else," he paused.

"Thank you, Agent Daniels. And the message back to Miloc is the same. Thank him from all of us." Bob shook his hand, knowing from the young red headed agent's actions and words that he could provide no other details and led him to the door. "Thank you, Sir," the young man returned the courtesy. "And, seriously, your security guys need to step up their game. I made your guy inside the room moving to cover you well after the door was already open. If I was here for you and yours, he would have been on the floor right after you were without ever knowing how he got there. If you are really in any danger, you should make a call to whomever you need to call to square this away. If not, save some money because whatever this is costing you is not worth whatever you are paying." With that, he continued unabated down the hall toward the elevator. "See what I mean?" he added as the elevator door opened and he entered the empty car to descend to the lobby.

"Our tax dollars, Daniels. I will make that call," Bob shouted after him as the elevator doors were closing.

"Me too," the voice came from inside the elevator as the car began to move.

"More to that kid than meets the eye," Bob told the others as he rejoined them inside and closed the door behind him.

"That's exactly what I was saying before all this. It's about reading people, not just what they say to you. It's about what they do, what they are capable of, and what they are willing to do. Either when nobody is looking, or when everyone is looking. It's more art than science," Steve added. "I am glad they got the man responsible for your friend's death. I hope that brings you all some comfort." With that, he looked over at Betty and Ann who were in a hug, with tears already running down Betty's cheek.

"I don't believe in coincidence," Bob began. "Yesterday's conversation with Tom. This message from Miloc. Both right before the summit planning meeting this afternoon. It's pretty clear to me that someone is trying to tell me to simply accept what I already know but don't want to acknowledge. It is what it is Bob. Accept it and move on, I get it," he explained clearly to himself but it was cryptic for the others. "Shall we head to the UN for our meeting with Dau? I want to have some time to check in with the technology team and see if they are doing anything besides watching movies." With that, they finished their breakfasts, then their preparations, and made their way to the lobby and the waiting car which took them to the UN building.

The four of them made their way up to Mr. Dau's office where they shared updates to get everyone on the same page. "It is my understanding the President will be attending the summit personally. Not sure who else is coming with him, but he told us he would be here himself," Bob completed his sentence but reacted to the look on Mr. Dau's face. "When we were at the Thor's Craftsmen update, he told us there. I heard him say it, we both did," he said gesturing to Ann who was nodding in agreement.

"That is good...and that is bad. The Chinese team is stalling for time to name their new team leaders. The news the President is coming will support that due to the added security planning. If the US President is coming, then you can bet the CCP and others will want to have their top leaders here too, not some bureaucratic underling speaking for them.

"Why not keep the pressure on them by scheduling a demo the day before or the morning of the summit? Puts more pressure on them to commit, and move. We can always cancel or reschedule it, but having it out there presses them," Ann asked, then answered her own question.

"Tom relayed that your President does not want to do another demo on US soil. Especially in or near New York. Doesn't want an excuse for the CCP to activate or operate their regional system now that we know where it is. With Chen and Wu out of the picture for them, he doesn't want to risk them getting pressured into actually doing something, for an event or rehearsal for an event, that might endanger anyone up here. Makes more sense to me now that I know the rest of the story, in that *he* will be one of the ones up here and they don't want to risk an India-type event with POTUS and other world leaders at ground zero. Not sure we are going to change that position, not sure we would if we could," Dau concluded.

"OK then, looks like the demo team and its technology team continue to get paid to sit around and wait for the summit, or the results of the summit," Steve summarized. "What do we need to do for the summit, or to get ready for the summit?"

"Honestly, it's all logistics that our organization does regularly. Protocol, who is staying where, security deconfliction, food, beverages, seating charts ...all that is covered. I think the heavy lift is for us to come up with some operational recommendations for the policy makers. Maybe a few broad courses of action for them to consider, but really fleshed out as to what that would look like and how they would be implemented from a practical level not a theoretical one. You know, like specific events could look like this...an ongoing regional change would look like that. Command and control of these would need to be something like this or that. Who decides? Who pays for what? How and by whom are priorities established and disputes resolved?"

Dau was rambling a bit, but Bob interrupted him, "Not our problem. I mean it's our problem, but the attendees are the solution and no matter what the UN recommends there will be winners and losers. What possible construct keeps everyone happy? The US and China both get one vote, and the UN breaks the tie? What about everyone else? Everyone gets an equal vote, and then they trade votes among each other to get what they want? A vote becomes a commodity to be sold or traded for something else of value? What about the highest bidder? Whoever pays the most gets what they want. Then, instead of using the money on something else, we can use the money to build more Hammers, more regional capability and an on-orbit system. Make it a pay-to-play, self-funding system where the folks with the most money get to decide? Wait, that is what we already have now with the CCP and US programs right?" Bob was ranting and everyone was staring at him, concern on their faces, as Ann walked up to him and put her hand on his shoulder and pulled him in close for a hug to hide the tears coming down his cheeks.

"What have we done, Ann? What have we done and how do we fix it?" He quietly sobbed into her shoulder as they stood there, venting the questions that have been eating at him for some time, "How do we fix this?"

"You already did fix this, more than once Bob," Betty began. "Pull yourself together kid, give yourself some credit for crying out loud. Yeah, I said it and I meant it because you are literally *crying out loud*. Everyone knows about Thor's Hammer now and it's not a secret because of you. The CCP clandestine regional program is known because of you. The US has leapfrogged that and is on the cusp of putting a global capability on orbit because of what you did. You were just there a day ago helping that get done. Stop whining and just finish what you started. It's all but fixed already; just do what you have been doing and take it across the finish line. The hard parts over for goodness' sake. *Suck it up buttercup.* If it was easy, you wouldn't have been paid five billion dollars to do it. Well, technically, you were paid five billion to not do something...but that is beside the point. You already decided how to fix it, so just follow through and finish this."

"Yeah, ok. Wrong question then, Betty? How do we finish fixing this? Is that the right question?" Bob snapped at her.

"Now, you're getting closer to the right workspace, Bob. Yeah, ask the right questions and the answer is easy to find," she said calmly. "I can't tell you what to do, but I can give you my opinion *if* you want to hear it."

"Yes, I would. I would like to hear your opinion," Bob challenged her, but it was clear he was seeking counsel not a confrontation.

"Let the summit drive the course of action. Listen to who says what; read the room and decide based on what happens there. It's like Steve said, it's about people. This is about *these* people. Don't think it's up to you to solve it and present a solution to them. Talk with them and see what solutions make sense and which ones do not. Why do you think the solutions should be any different than the problem?"

"I don't understand what you mean by that?" Bob looked at her, puzzled at her question in the context in which it was asked.

"This technology was created by someone else. Then it was dropped in your lap and you struggled to learn about what it is and how to use it; made some money from it then dropped it in the UN's lap. So now it's their turn and they are doing the same thing just on a bigger scale. You can help them but it's no longer your problem; it's a UN problem and a UN solution to work out. They wanted to help and they are helping. You can help them or you can ignore it. You can walk away and they will still have the same challenge. You brought it to them but they wanted to keep it once you did. Let them lead; you help them do it. Your ego is in your way Bob; it's not yours to do anymore even if you want it to be. It's not. That's my opinion, do with it what you will."

The group all sat quietly for what seemed like a long time pondering what Betty had just said to Bob, until he finally broke the extended silence, "Thank you for your opinion, Betty and, for what it's worth, I see a lot of merit in what you said. I appreciate you caring enough about me to say it so plainly and help me see that point of view."

"I hate to break up the party, but I need to get a few things dialed in for the Secretary General before this meeting so, if you will excuse me? You are welcome to just hang out here until it starts as I won't be back before we begin," Dau said as he headed for the door. "See you all there."

It seemed like only a few minutes later that the meeting room was nearly full as the Secretary General, Mr. Dau and a few others came into the room, took their designated seats and brought the meeting to order. After discussing the purpose, timing, facilities and a rough schedule of events the conversation turned to the participants who had already RSVP'd for the first round of formal discussions about how to field this technology. The list of heads of state attending in person was long and impressive. The Presidents, Prime Ministers, Party Leaders and Dictators from nations large and small would be assembling in one spot for this summit in the United States. The protocol and security planning are going to be a nightmare for many of the UN staff who were already pleading for additional resources given the already long list of attendees.

This would indeed be some summit!

CHAPTER NINE

YES, IT WAS

The next couple of days were just brutal work at a frenzied pace for the UN staff pulling the summit together. The Secretary General got what he asked for but was seriously regretting his decision to put this level of meeting together on such a short timeline. The list of attendees included every top player in global strategic powerhouses, as well as, anyone who was not yet on that list but thought they should be. Scheduling primary discussions and breakout groups was proving most difficult for two reasons. The first reason was the topic of the breakout sessions would largely depend on some of the outcomes of the first few primary sessions. Secondarily came the issue of determining who should be pressed into a breakout session when their position and national representation should be included in the primary sessions.

There were not a lot of B-team players that could be delegated to a lesser meeting without offending or being perceived as throwing shade their way. The Secretary General was hoping to make some political hay with this summit but seemed frustrated with this embarrassment of riches. To exclude anyone from some of the topics at hand given their positions and status seemed to be the perfect storm for offending anyone and everyone regardless of the decisions needed to finalize the schedule.

Such are the problems of political leaders who find themselves in the spotlight at crucial times in history. The duality of choosing a path and position in hopes of being in charge at such historic moments is confounding given the pressures of rising to those very moments. Great leaders thrive in such times and lesser leaders shrink. It appeared shrinking was the current trend as the Secretary General chastised his staff time and again at each recommendation they made.

Finally, it was Mr. Dau who knew the time to finalize the agenda was long past. So, he decided to throw a lifeline to everyone in the room, "The opening session must be open to everyone, that we agreed upon. Once everyone is in place, we should really leave them there for the entire day. The posturing and comments, many of which will be scripted and read by the various leaders will take all day and we still won't get through them all. Everyone will be coming with ideas not on how to lead, but on how not to be left out. The biggest question that will drive the rest can only be answered by what the US and China say on day one. That will drive what we need to do on day two and three, or even *if* we will do anything meaningful on those days.

"I think it shows both foresight and respect to the positions of everyone attending to simply hold the primary open session for the duration of day one. Day two can simply be breakout sessions for framework and decision discussions, and day three can be held for operations and implementation. Don't even use the term breakout. Let the actual discussion be led by what happened the previous day. We aren't going to decide how to do this in three days. We are just laying the groundwork for subsequent discussions, assuming we even get that far without this breaking down before the end of day three."

As the Secretary General considered what he just heard, it was clear by the expression on his face that he saw the wisdom in it. "Mr. Dau, I believe there is merit in what you propose. The structure is topically sufficient, without pinning down any details or attendees. Candidly, it is the best idea I have heard thus far. If this is acceptable to the principles in the room, I am agreeable to that level of agenda being distributed to the summit primary contacts for each attendee. What say you all?" he asked as he looked around the room for their responses. Seeing indifference mixed with occasional nods in the affirmative, he proclaimed Mr. Dau's proposal as the decided action and dismissed the group to implement the direction he just provided. Creating or updating schedules, agendas, emails, meeting placards, directional signs, digital prints, flyers, graphics of all kinds were set in motion now that a decision had been made and the relieved staff set about their tasks.

Mr. Dau was used to carrying many of the decisions, staff direction and work that comes with being so close in position to the Secretary General. Everyone who ever has or currently holds a title of *deputy*-something, *vice*-something or *assistant*-something knows that accountability for failure is at the top. But that is just one level above them and, since *poop* rolls downhill, they are the first stop on that journey. It's always best to tighten the rigging before the storm, not during it. Dau was good at making things work out, despite the lack of foresight of others including his current boss. On his way back to his office Mr. Dau ran across Bob and Ann in the hallway, and it did not look like the encounter was accidental.

"Glad we caught you before your next crisis meeting, can we get a few minutes?" Bob asked as soon as he was close enough to be heard without yelling after one of the busiest men in the UN Headquarters right now.

"Of course, how can I help?" Mr. Dau asked. Upon hearing the question, it occurred to Bob at that moment that the question may very well be one of the most important questions one person could ask another. He made a mental note to file that thought away and consider it in his relationship with Ann, his role as team-lead for the UN technology team, his adjunct role with the *Thor's Craftsmen* exploitation team, and every other role he could think of having. *How can I help?* was the best question you could ever hope to be asked when trying to accomplish something. And Bob was particularly grateful to hear it right now.

"Fill in a few information gaps? Specifically with regard to schedule and tasks for us and the technology team? We are trying to determine what we need to do and by when, as well as, what we don't have to do and for how long…if you get my meaning?" Bob talked and walked, holding his fiancé's hand as they continued down the hallway toward the elevator.

"Good timing. We just decided and the agendas are being prepared. Short answers are nothing for the UN technology team as an entity for the entire three days of the summit, so that gives you a minimum of four days down even if they come back tasking the demo right after the summit, which is unlikely. So, my best guess is six days at least before anyone has enough details to provide any meaningful guidance or travel updates to the team regarding a next demonstration. Depending on how the US and China behave during the summit, the demonstration team, as we know it right now, may never get back on track unless the two big dogs play nice—or at least pretend to—for the summit and whatever post-summit actions are agreed to.

"That should leave you two free to participate in whatever capacity fits best in whatever Tom and your President need for their participation in the summit, or whatever else they need you to work on. If you get my meaning?" Mr. Dau parroted and smiled at Bob, who he truly did like.

"Thank you, that helps a lot and candidly is quite a relief to hear. What can I do to help?" Bob responded and decided to put into practice his new favorite question.

"To be equally candid, and hopefully not perceived as unkind to your offer, I just need time to do what I need to get done," Mr. Dau confided. "Not sure I can, even with your offer to help. I just need to grind out what needs doing. If you can run interference with Tom and the US team so I can focus on everyone else, I suppose that would be one less worry for me."

"We will do our best, but you know, as well as, I do that he shows up whenever and wherever with whomever. So, I'm not sure this is much more than a hope followed by an empty promise. But I will do my best to worry about Tom and the POTUS so you don't have to…until you have to." Bob tried to both help and bring a smile to his friend's face.

"Can't ask for or expect any more than that, thanks, Bob. You two take care. I'm sure I'll see you at the summit if not sooner. Call if you need something from me, or if there is something I need to know. That will be faster and easier than trying to find me or texting me. Lots to do and not enough time to do it. Same song, same chorus, new verse. See you in about a day!" And, with that, he walked into the stairwell and left them waiting for the elevator that seemed to be stopping on every floor except the one they were waiting on.

"Sounds like we have a little bit of free time tonight, at least from our UN commitments. How would you like to spend it?" Ann asked as they stood hoping for the elevator to arrive soon to transport them to the lobby and the exit.

"Honestly, I could use a long walk with you. I need to think through a few things, and I want your opinion without having to involve Steve and Betty just yet. You up for a stroll with your fiancé? There is so much security churning around this area right now, it may be the safest place on the planet for the next few days despite where it is?" Bob smiled and looked at Ann, thankful to have her with him for all this and thankful to hear the ding from the elevator finally arriving.

"Sure, count me in as long as you buy me dinner somewhere along the way. I listen better on a full stomach, and I think better when I am not thinking about when and where we are going to eat," she said truthfully.

"Deal. How about we walk until we get to a restaurant that looks or smells good, then we pop in and eat whenever you are ready?" Bob suggested as they rode the elevator, which stopped at every floor on the way down to the lobby.

"There is hope for you yet Professor; it appears you can be taught. I like that idea and am anxious to hear what you want to think through. As you already know, I do have an opinion on everything." She took his arm as they exited the elevator and made their way to the exit and out into the fresh air—well, as fresh as the air gets in New York—and started to walk.

While Ann texted Steve and Betty to let them know they were on their own for the rest of the evening, Bob explained their plan to the driver of the car that was waiting to take them back to the hotel. After a brief but futile effort to change Bob's mind, the driver radioed someone, left the keys in the car and climbed out to follow the couple along their chosen path. Bob had taken Special Agent Daniel's advice and made a call about their security detail at the hotel, and it had not fallen on deaf ears. Not only were some changes made at the hotel, but there was now more overt and visible security wherever they went. That was undoubtedly augmented by additional, not so visible, counterparts. While he still didn't think he needed to hire his own bodyguards, Bob was looking into the best way to provide that sort of protection for Ann, Betty and Steve for the times where they would not be in the same locations. That was not a matter of *if* it would be coming. It was more a matter of *when*. No amount of money was too much to ensure their safety although he seemed frugal in that regard when it came to himself.

As they walked along, it didn't take him long to open the conversation... toughest part first, "I have been struggling with the end game, Ann. I took Betty's advice to heart and will see what happens at the summit. The US and China both need to show some cards, but there is no telling what else or who else will do what. No point in worrying about all the what-ifs until we see it unfold in real time. That's not my struggle. No matter what happens, I am stuck with this same recurring outcome no matter who does what at the summit. It all lands in the same place when I look far enough down the road. No matter who has what agreement, what structure is in place, who pays for what and who decides what for whom, it all comes back to someone holding the levers over someone else. And if they change their mind or, if they get out of line, or are motivated to get paid so they don't get out of line it's still one over the other. All of these potential solutions just swap out who it is and what it is called. Someone gets to make the weather what they want it to be and someone else gets to hope they can benefit from that outcome while someone else is hoping they don't get hurt by it."

As she considered what Bob was describing, it occurred to Ann that he was also describing the way it is now. "Bob that future you just described is no different than how things are, I mean *were*, without Thor's Hammers. What I mean is, right now people don't know what the weather will be, just what the forecasters tell them it should be. So, people go on about their day hoping the forecast is correct, and the actions they took based on that forecast were sufficient for what they are trying to do. Similarly, other people are hoping, whether the forecast is right or wrong, that it doesn't do them any harm given what they could or couldn't do to prepare for the weather that was forecast. What is the difference in the two situations, if there is one? I don't see it from a practical standpoint?"

Bob pondered that statement as they continued walking, "From that perspective I have to agree with you, there really isn't much of a difference is there? So, what have we gained here, what does on-demand weather bring and what advantages are to be gained by its existence?"

"That Sir would be me giving you the answer to your homework. Are you sure you want me to tell you the answer this soon in our walk, or would you like some more time to come up with it on your own?" she asked, and Bob could not tell if she was serious or joking so he played along.

"Oh, please tell; I don't mind writing down and using your answer if it's correct," Bob told her.

"OK, I'm already hungry so this will be a short walk. The only difference between the past without Thor's Hammers and the futures with Thor's Hammers is certainty. A forecast is an educated prediction, it has some determinable level of confidence or certainty that is below 100%. With Thor's Hammer, one can act with a level of certainty that is near 100% given it performs without system defect or interference. It was a guess, now it's a certainty. We *know* the weather will be what we tell it to be, not we *think* it will be something. That's the difference. Feel free to copy my answer onto your paper and turn it in ahead of the rest of the class, if you want to impress the teacher, Professor." She smiled, took his hand and led him into the restaurant while signaling the maître d' *two for dinner*.

"I am not sure that is entirely fair," Bob protested. "I think you're right, though. I need to think on this, but you might be right."

"When you are finished thinking about it, you should conclude that I am right. In this instance, that would both be the correct response and the smart thing to do. In the meantime, would you like me to order for you so you can focus or do you want to do that for yourself?" she rubbed it in, enjoying the moment and trying to both lighten his burden and show that he could depend on her, no matter how large or small the issue. They were still growing into their relationship, and this was a moment for them.

"How about you order something for the both of us; I am trying to focus on this and find the flaw in your logic. This could take a minute," he played along. But it didn't feel like playing because the stakes were so high.

As they ate dinner, they continued discussing the logic and the different scenarios where the past and the possible futures intersected. Time after time, scenario after scenario and variable after variable until the check came…the only real difference boiled down to hoping versus knowing.

As they approached the entrance to the hotel Bob conceded the discussion and thanked Ann, "That was immensely helpful...not gonna lie. It seems that we may have landed on a bottom line to use as an anchor point for the Summit. Thank you, Ann." They strode through the lobby that was packed with people due to the proximity to the UN and the pending summit. No sooner than they entered the heads began to turn, the fingers pointed and the whispers and then questions came as the now-famous Professor Mcleod was recognized by those who were in New York tonight largely because of him. Strangers waved at them, tried to introduce themselves, asked for an autograph or a picture with the couple and generally made them act like the celebrities they had become. It was the first time they really encountered that type of response just for being present, but it served as a stark reminder that things were and would remain different for them from now on. The security detail assigned to them made it clear that it was time to go, and they weren't really asking at this point. That had become all too familiar recently and, while neither Bob nor Ann liked it, they certainly understood it especially right now. So up in the elevator they went and spent a quiet evening together, knowing they were both ready for one and that it might be the last one they would have for a while.

Bob and Ann stood in one of the many short lines outside the UN to pass through the initial screening for entrance to the on-demand weather modification policy summit. Given the plethora of attendees and limited space, Steve and Betty got to sit this one out. The pre-meetings Bob and Ann attended with the US delegation were peculiarly vague and proffered little in the way of insight or direction to the participants beyond the instructions to follow the President's lead. The security protecting the position and intent of his comments at the summit were as stringent as the physical security surrounding the structure housing the majority of key leaders of the free world, and many who live in places not counted among the free. While they marveled at the spectacle of it all, they were continually recognized and peppered with questions from those near them in line. Not a moment of quiet thoughtfulness to be had for the famous, and equally infamous, Professor Mcleod. When they finally cleared security and were making their way to the auditorium among the diverse and colorful crowd, Ann tugged on Bob's arm and nodded toward Tom who was approaching them as quickly as the crowd would allow.

"Nice to see you both made it into the circus tent," Tom greeted them.

"Nice to see you, Tom, how are we?" Ann asked.

"Hard to tell. The Chinese delegation did not acknowledge our invitation to meet ahead of or outside the summit. Not sure how to read that. I think we will find out today, hopefully. I just hate not knowing which way someone is leaning and, right now, I am not sure if they are in disarray or just pissed off at us," Tom confessed openly in the crowded lobby as he looked around. "Sorry, I will be smarter as the day progresses, I promise. If you don't mind, we have both of you sitting with me and a couple other members of the President's staff. No cabinet, nobody else, just us. He wants it clear that this is his train, and he is driving our position and our actions on this, and it has not been delegated to a *secretary of anything*. The world and the players will recognize him and you and nobody else should look familiar. That's the gameplan; follow his lead. Simple. Oh, and be prepared to be mind-numbingly bored with all the protocol stuff, important people like to remind people they are important, and to remind other important people how less important they are in the pecking order. You two ready?"

"OK, let's go," Bob said, as they fell in behind Tom and headed toward the very-deeply-orchestrated assigned seating.

They waited patiently as the auditorium filled from the edges inward toward the premiere seating where the big names would eventually sit amongst their colleagues from other nations. It seemed counterintuitive to have the leaders at desks without their attendees and trusted counselors adjacent to them, but the scurry in the walk spaces behind all these world leaders was near constant. As Bob, Ann, Tom and few others sat near the POTUS, it was interesting to see who, and how many people had bone-mics and earpieces allowing them to communicate with their national leaders directly despite not sitting next to them. It was equally interesting to see who was present but did not have one of these devices in their ears. Ann and Bob would be counted among them but were the only ones of the US delegates that were not equipped as such.

Tom was correct in that the introductions and protocol were boring, but they went quicker than either Bob or Ann expected. Shortly after the summit was through with all the formalities and pomposity, the Secretary General got right down to business. He explained, *quite concisely and impressively*, Bob thought, the context and concerns that brought them together. The objectives were to discuss and hear recommendations and concerns alike about how to effectively bring on-demand weather into the world's activities doing as much good as possible while also doing as little harm as possible. While some in the room had a substantial amount of time to consider these issues, the vast majority beyond the US and

China had spent considerably less time preparing and the discussions revealed that lack of preparedness.

As the various nations commented and postured for consideration of their priorities, both the lead nations in the UN effort sat patiently, watching, learning and waiting. Through most of the morning and into early afternoon the discussion was broad and brief but lacked the voice of either primary player until the President of the United States indicated he was ready to be recognized for comment. After several other attendees completed their remarks, the floor was his and he had the attention of all in attendance.

After greeting his colleagues and recognizing their UN hosts, he began to state the US position, "As you are aware, the United States has been involved with the UN weather efforts from the very first day. Our nation's delegate to the UN effort is in fact the very man who brought this technology to them in hopes to see us all addressing this very issue. As we are assembled today for that very purpose, Professor Mcleod's dream has become our collective reality. For that I would thank him, and I am glad to see he and his fiancée are both here with us today to participate personally in this history making meeting." He paused and gestured to acknowledge them as he continued speaking.

"You will also recall that, during our joint UN-US efforts to make the world aware of the potential of this new technology, our nation was accused of some dastardly deeds by our friends from China. I stand before you today and tell you plainly and unequivocally that the United States government did not steal this technology from the CCP, nor were we aware of any connection to China when we embarked on this journey with the UN. But I will also tell you that, since then I have learned and confirmed that the technology was indeed of Chinese origin." He paused for effect and let the translators catch up and made sure everyone had time to both understand and consider for a moment the admission and magnitude of the statement he had just made before he continued over the ever-increasing volume of the voices repeating and commenting on what he just said.

"We have confirmed that the Thor's Hammers weather-modification devices Professor Mcleod and his colleague Doctor Auster came to possess were of Chinese origins. While this was unknown to Professor Mcleod, it was known to Doctor Auster who was unable to communicate that to anyone prior to his untimely death. As a result, the ongoing Chinese on-demand weather modification efforts continued unbeknownst to Professor Mcleod. The CCP was equally unaware of Professor Mcleod's possession of their technology nor were they aware of his plans to reveal it to the UN until he had already done so. We are confident they were unaware of this because, had they known of Professor Mcleod's involvement, they would surely have killed him to recover their missing devices just as they had killed Doctor Auster for that purpose. It is only through fate and the power of good that we know these things and that Professor Mcleod was able to make this technology known to the world despite the best efforts of the CCP to keep it concealed."

With that the POTUS paused and waited quietly as the room erupted into a thousand conversations as the group made every effort to confirm they heard what they thought they just heard directly from the President of the United States. Bob looked accusingly at Tom and tried to fathom what was happening, why it was happening here and now, and what that might mean for him and Ann. There was an increasing mix of question, boos, howls and calls for explanation all growing in volume until the President spoke again and quieted the group as he did.

"The CCP claim that this is their technology and they are the experts in its application are both true. But that is because the very on-demand weather technology we are assembled here to discuss bringing into the world is not new at all. In fact, it is already out in the world. It is indeed Chinese, and while it is new to all of us it is *not* new to them. We now know they have possessed it and been using it discreetly for nearly ten years. We know all this; we have proof of all I have said today and we will share that proof. So, the questions we must consider today are what to do with this technology in this new context. Any discussion about on-demand weather modification in any other context would be disingenuous at best, deceitful and dangerous on its face, and potentially disastrous.

"My apologies for bringing this news to you in this way, but we have only recently been able to verify these concerns with certainty. I would have preferred to have delivered this news at a different time and under different circumstances. But, given the gravity of the issues, I saw no other option than to let you all know at the same time while we were here for this very purpose. I also wanted to provide a forum for my colleague from China to address you here on this issue in the spirit of the summit, which is intended for that exact purpose. It is why we are all here; to discuss and decide how to fairly and equitably field this technology for the benefit of mankind.

"It is my hope that the objective of this summit can remain the same, and we adjust our understanding to the current state of this technology. This will allow us to make informed decisions about how to proceed. With that, I would like to thank you for the opportunity to comment and am looking forward to a productive summit," he concluded and surveyed the chaos that quickly ensued as the Secretary General called for a thirty-minute break to discuss and consider what had just been revealed.

"Well, what do you think, Professor?" Tom asked.

"I don't know what to think. Was that the plan or did he call an audible after a morning of watching?" Bob asked.

"Maybe a little of both," Tom observed. "But we did table-top several alternatives, including this one. I wasn't sure which way he was gonna go when we walked in but he seemed to favor this one when we were discussing the options."

"Now what?" Ann asked. "What happens next? Did he just blow up the whole summit, or did he just put everyone in the express lane to finding a solution for a problem they don't know the magnitude of yet?"

"Yes," Tom responded. "Both...but what really matters is what the Chinese response is at the end of the half hour break we are on. You see, POTUS and the Chinese delegate are yelling at each other right now in several languages while I am standing here talking to the two of you. This part of the international power complex has very few direct witnesses. The principals, their personal security guys, a couple of translators and that's it. I will get to hear about it from each of them, but even advisors are outside the process when it gets to this point despite wearing an earpiece. Either he comes clean, denies it or storms out unwilling to dignify the ridiculous US accusations with response. My money is on one of the first two, the third could be perceived as weak or an admission of guilt by having nothing to say. If I had to say one way or the other, I go with they deny the bad stuff and own the good stuff and stall to see what we can prove and what was speculative."

"None of this is comforting, Tom...that you don't know, and you don't think either of them know either is not comforting," Bob complained.

"Not here to make you comfortable, Bob. This is all about people. Reading people, trying to predict what they will do and what they won't do when put in one position or another. It all depends. Right now, POTUS made his decision and his move. Next, all depends on the Chinese response...who makes it, when they make it, and what it is when they do. People can be hard to predict—like the weather—Professor. In fact, I don't see much difference in predicting the two. With people and with the weather you make careful observations, do as much analysis as you can, make some assumptions and follow some rules, then predict what they are gonna do and when they are gonna do it. Then you sit back and observe again to see if you were right or wrong. Maybe do some more analysis as to why it turned out that way. Then factor it in for next time...*rinse and repeat*. Predicting people and the weather, it's same process just different subject matter. What do you think about that, Ann?" Tom asked as he watched intently for POTUS to reappear somewhere as it seemed there was now a lot of chatter in everyone's earpieces.

"I see the logic, but I would much rather bet on a weather forecast than how someone will react to something of this magnitude. These are high stakes, Tom," she warned.

"You and me both sister; I would much rather be doing something else but alas here we are doing what needs to be done, where and when it needs doing. Isn't that the core of it all? Someone must do it. No matter what it was throughout history, someone did or didn't do what was needed to make a difference. It just so happens that this time, among others, it's ours to do. Here we are, so I guess people will write about what we did or did not do. And someone will write about what the Chinese did or didn't do in response to what we just did…and so on, and so on. Yes, I would much rather be doing something else but come on, how many people get to make history like this? You have a great seat for what others will only get to read about. Cost to sit here may be a little higher than they pay to read about it but, when people say *Bob Mcleod* a hundred years from now, they will still know who he was and why he was important. They will say that he was the one who led the *Storm Makers* who changed the world. Say *Tom*, and they will say *Tom who* and why are you asking? That's what I signed up for and how I prefer it, but I get a seat at a lot of historic events without having to attach my name to them. That works for me…and here he comes," Tom concluded.

The President of the United States and the UN Secretary General both walked out to their assigned seats and sat down as the meeting was called to order. It took several minutes for the conversations to break up, the attendees get back to their seats and the noise to settle down. In the meantime, nobody occupied the seat with the Chinese Flag and the national leader's name when the Secretary General began to speak.

"Ladies and gentlemen, thank you again for your attention. This has been quite a day, and we have heard some very difficult information. Each of us must struggle with and decide what to do with it all. To that end our Chinese colleagues have decided they will not participate in the remainder of the summit and are departing as we speak. They did ask that I read the following statement on their behalf, which I agreed to do for them.

It states the following:

"Colleagues, and people of the world you should know that some of what the President of the United States said today regarding the Thor's Hammers being of Chinese origin is true. And while we work out how Doctor Auster and Professor Mcleod came to possess our technology and our missing devices, we categorically deny any involvement in the Doctor's untimely passing. We apologize for the time spent and productivity lost in coming to this summit in good faith to discuss a worthy topic. The People's Republic of China will be happy to work directly with most of you on this very important technology as it applies to our shared national interests. Given the unfortunate events here today, we must depart this summit and abandon any assistance previously offered the UN on this effort. All of our future involvement in on-demand weather modification will be done through official diplomatic channels and considered official government actions to be carried out as such." A long pause followed before he again addressed the group.

"It would appear there is much to consider given what we have heard from both of these nations today. I have been informed by the President of the United States that additional information supporting his claims today will be made available through official State Department channels and White House press releases. Given all these developments. I would ask that you take some time over the next few days to familiarize yourself with the newly available information and consider how that impacts your interests and paths forward. To enable such reviews, we will be suspending our summit to a date uncertain when we will attempt to pick up the same topics once all the additional information has been adequately considered. Given the abrupt changes and scarcity of other support venues, please feel free to continue utilizing the facilities here should that simplify your efforts. The staff here will do its best to accommodate your needs. Thank you, ladies and gentlemen, with that we will adjourn." The Secretary General made his way directly out of the auditorium without the typical glad handing and conversations common to such proceedings. He had a lot of damage control to get to, and the longer it waited the worse it would be for him.

Tom looked at Bob and Ann, rolled his eyes and said, "Well like I said, it's about reading people. I would have lost that bet, so I am really wondering what was said down there. I guess it's time for me to go find out then start wargaming what's next for us. In the meantime, I suppose you know what I am going to say next? I mean you are the forecaster, right?"

"Not in the mood right now, Tom. What are you going to say next?" Bob braced for whatever it was.

"You and Ann, we need both of you for this. Be ready to spend some time back in Florida. I will have a car at your hotel for you at 0930. Pack light but plan on being there awhile. We need you on that effort full time now that we know the UN effort has no CCP component and the world has much to consider. Demo's are gonna be off the table for a while. We don't want to give the Chinese any pretense for the use or abuse of their regional systems. The best way to prevent another India-like catastrophe is to not have a demonstration for them to use for an intervention. The US will be pulling our support from that effort, as well, now that we know the CCP has already done so. All their efforts will now be through diplomatic channels. Good luck getting out of here. I am going to leave you to your own care as I need to catch up with him…Marine One and Air Force One are my rides. See you in Florida." And, with that, Tom made his way across the room and disappeared into the crowd. Bob and Ann did the same. They headed back to the hotel to pack and fill in Steve and Betty on what they missed, as if it wasn't all over the news already.

CHAPTER TEN

WHAT NOW?

The news from the summit dominated every news channel and every commentator had a different opinion on what the President had done and the potential impacts of those actions. Throughout the evening and, as promised earlier, more details were rolled out through the State Department and the White House. Bob and Ann were packed and ready to go, eating dinner with Steve and Betty as they listened intently to the news unfolding on the television in their suite.

"They are sure providing a lot of details in all of these releases. I am learning stuff I didn't know just watching the talking heads, and I was looking at the files they are quoting," Betty commented. "Why give them all of it up front?"

"My guess is to make sure everyone believes what the President said, without having to dig very deep to verify it themselves. It also puts the CCP on notice. It paints them into a corner and limits their options. And it keeps everyone looking at them while this is all unfolding. It puts them on defense *big time*, so they don't have much of an opportunity in the near term to go offensive with what they have," Steve offered. "That is my two cents worth."

"Yeah, but why on day one? Why do all this today instead of waiting to see what they were going to do or say during the summit?" Ann asked.

"He didn't want to let them say anything. They didn't start out with a statement at the beginning so that meant they were going to maintain the status quo as long as everyone else would let them—as long as nobody forced their hand. Inaction was their action; their play was to keep their head down. That is what he reacted to and why he acted today. It was clear by the afternoon that they weren't going to act, so he did," Bob explained. "That's how I see it."

"Well, that makes sense, which is what scares me. You are getting good at seeing and understanding all the politics and posturing that goes with these types of decisions. That makes me nervous," Betty said with concern on her voice as she gave him *that look.*

"I am a skilled observer and forecaster; those skills translate well from weather to people. Maybe Tom was right about there not being much difference if you put some effort into it." Bob considered the idea quietly while they listened to the news updates and continued eating. The updates kept coming with little indication that they would let up anytime soon. Already knowing much of what was being said and their morning departure growing ever closer, Bob and Ann decided to turn in for the night. They wished Betty and Steve a quiet next few days and promised to call them for anything they might be able to help with from a distance. The two departed down the hall as the security detail ensured all was in order. Things had changed for the better in regard to their hotel security detail after Bob's calls.

The next morning was almost too leisurely for the couple as they rose early, watched the news updates during breakfast and coffee before they found themselves in the elevator heading down to the car that Tom had arranged for them. But it was a madhouse when they stepped out of the elevator. Press, paparazzi, friendly and unfriendly questions and comments all being shouted at the same time in hopes of getting a sound bite or a picture of the two given the new context of their developing stories.

The security team earned both their reputations and their paychecks this morning as they quickly and effectively cleared a path and hurried the two through the crowd and into the waiting vehicle that was quickly buttoned up and rolling into traffic with throngs of disappointed people in their wake.

"That was a bit unexpected and *unfun*," Ann announced as they headed toward the airport.

"Sorry ma'am, but you probably ought to get used to that for a while," the voice boomed from the agent in the front passenger seat.

"Where we are going, I don't expect too much of that while we are there," Bob hoped out loud in response.

"Hope you're right Professor. We are here in case you are not," he replied and that was the last of the conversation until they arrived at the airport, which did not take very long. They made their way through the maze of people and checkpoints that finally ended in the waiting area of the private and charter gates which were becoming familiar to them. Without time to even settle in for a good wait, the two were led to the walkway where they could see the familiar aircraft waiting for them to board. As they climbed aboard, the steward greeted them by name and invited them to join Tom who was already aboard and on at least one of his phones. He smiled and gestured for them to sit in the spacious seats near him as he continued to listen, nod, and provide short and terse responses to whatever questions he was hearing come through the small earpiece, as he waved his phone around while he talked. This call seemed to be a little different than the countless ones they had witnessed since they met.

The aircraft door closed and they were already taxiing as Bob and Ann were settling into their seats. Tom's call ended abruptly and apparently not on a good note as Bob and Ann watched the phone fly across the aisle and impact the side of the nicely upholstered interior just about the same time that Tom began a string of four-letter words.

"He is not thinking clearly on this. What the hell is he thinking?" Tom had to finish his verbal venting, which was out of character for the otherwise cool and collected advisor to the President.

"At the risk of sounding stupid, is that a rhetorical question?" Ann asked, "And if not, it would help if we knew who *he* is."

"Sorry Ann, and Bob...my apologies," Tom responded, a little embarrassed by his outburst, especially after admitting that it was not rhetorical and *he* was the President.

 "He put the offense on the field at the summit. That move put the CCP on their heels. But he is telling them and the rest of the world just about everything we know. He thinks that will change the discussion once it finally happens if we control the narrative and the timeline. Not wrong, but he is not taking his foot off their throat to enable the conversation to begin," Tom paused, and instinctively looked around before he continued even though there was no need to worry about what he said on the aircraft everyone only half-jokingly referred to as his.

"To catch you up, just about half an hour before the President made his remarks at the UN summit yesterday, he got confirmation of something that helped drive his timeline. We initiated an offensive cyberattack on every one of their fielded regional systems. Hit them all at the same time and confirmed that they were all inoperable. Once he knew the cyber-attacks had successfully disabled their systems, which takes their weather attack off the table, he went all gas no brakes and has not let up since," Tom explained and was quickly interrupted before he was able to continue.

"What? What exactly does inoperable mean? How long does inoperable last?" a shocked Bob Mcleod asked.

"Good questions Professor. You are getting the hang of this. We hit them hard and don't think these systems can come back. They will need to replace the devices as well as the control systems. If they have any systems that were offline during the attack, we don't know about them. If they have any in reserve, spare parts or systems in production then whatever time it takes to get them finished and fielded is how long. We had good system knowledge from Chen and Wu that helped us know where to get in, and our guys know what to do once they are in. Took over the command node, sent instructions to each device that allowed free power to their key components and fried them all. Then the software eats everything on the command console controls and deletes the communications encryption codes. Even if anything survived that and they found a way to connect to each other the Thor's Hammers have no idea what they are being told to do and no ability to do it even if they could understand the incoming commands. It's triple dead," Tom wrapped up the explanation.

"You can do all that from a computer? And still have enough left to know it worked?" Ann asked, a little shocked, a little impressed and a little skeptical.

"I can't, but yes, we can. And we did," he confirmed with confidence.

"So, that all sounds like good news then. If their systems are inoperable, and from what you said potentially destroyed or unrecoverable. Why is that a bad thing? I must be missing something, or you must not be finished explaining why your phone got a flying lesson," Bob reasoned as Tom smiled, pleased with the Professor's continued insight.

"Yeah, that's not all of it yet. He decided the best offense should include being offensive. So, he called nearly thirty of the key party leaders to personally tell them that, not only have we taken down their regional systems, we have also confiscated and frozen all of the CCP leader's personal real estate and financial assets in the United States and any of our banks. Which turns out to be some pretty substantial holdings. Explained to each of them that it was a personal fine and penalty for using the on-demand weather modification systems on the United States and its citizenry.

"So, he is continuing to escalate from his UN announcements which were damning in themselves, but he still has more planned. That was me throwing my phone as I tried to remind him that not being able to change the weather like they could before is a loss in capability, but changing the weather is not the only weapon in their arsenal. They are a nuclear power for heaven's sake, and he is looking to start a civil war within the ruling party that has little chance of being exposed and explained to the average citizenry in time for it to do us any good."

As they listened to the concerns and explanations Tom had reasoned through for them but failed to sway the President with, it occurred to Ann that it was likely the President did not want the facts to get in the way of what he already decided he was going to do.

"So that is one side of it. What else have our colleagues in Florida done to assist in the effort? Just enable the cyber-attack or is there progress on the space-based version yet? Are we depending on the one regional system we have as being the sole survivor and thus providing an advantage?" Bob wondered as they continued to close the distance to assist the ongoing effort in Florida.

"You are both going to be duly impressed by this I think, but it's a big part of the frustration. To call it a hasty design and build would be a gross understatement, but we have a full production line running twenty-four-seven creating MicroSats with pee-wee sized Thor's Hammers," he began.

"What? You are already building them? How does that timeline pencil out?" Ann said in disbelief. He raised his hands and gestured so he could continue his update, knowing Tom would likely answer her questions as he continued his explanation.

"They bench tested the design and went straight to initial production, then ramped up a full line as the parts rolled in. They added capacity and staff to outpace the supply line, which hasn't happened yet. Once there were enough on hand, they...OK, well, we skipped all the regular testing and configuration protocols and kept making them as fast as we could." Tom seemed like he was confessing to the couple.

"That sounds risky. Not having a full test protocol and a really wrung out control system yet," Ann's concern showing and growing.

"Yes, I agree risky all right. But not as risky as when we put them on orbit without doing any of that either. Yes, I said they are already on orbit," Tom agreed, and braced for the response he knew he was about to get.

"What do you mean they are already on orbit?" Bob was shocked.

"Yesterday, one launch from Vandenburg and one from Cape Canaveral. We replaced the planned onboard payloads and had west coast and east coast launches as fast as we could. They are now building out the remaining parts as fast as they come in and loading the rockets as they go for the next two space shots. As soon as they reconfigure the launch pads and get these rockets fueled, they will go again with the same payloads of whatever we have on hand. That is one of the reasons we need you both in Florida. We need you two to help us ops check these things already up there and see if we have what we hope we have, and if they do what we need them to do."

"How is that even possible, on that timeline? I find that very hard to believe, Tom," Ann said skeptically, being intimately familiar with the technology development process.

"Best and brightest, Ann. There is no, *NO*. Whatever they need, whoever they need it from...drop everything you are doing and find a way to do it, and don't stop until it's done. That was the direction across the board straight from POTUS. Combine that with Frank Lincoln...that's how it is not only possible but it's real. But it's not finished. We don't even know if it will work now that some of it's up there. They are establishing communications, stabilizing power systems, orbits, timing—all that space operations stuff that needs doing before the satellite is allowed to operate. What is up there should be ready in a day or so. Everything is on a greased rail, and nobody is sleeping until it's up and working. All hands-on deck and that is where the operational testing needs you two. We need a test plan that both checks out what we need from the devices and the system at the same time, without tipping what we are doing, or at least not revealing how capable or incapable it is...or will be. And we need to do that part just as fast as we did everything else.

"That is the primary reason for the in-your-face, public campaign against the CCP right up front. We need as much of their attention on addressing their position and credibility on the world stage as possible, leaving little or none to concern themselves with all of our flurries of activity. At least until we have achieved our objective. Knocking the UN demonstrations off the list of things to worry about provided two advantages. It got you back on the main effort without all the distractions that came with that, and it just sped up the timeline on the inevitable failure of the UN effort. Same outcomes, just much faster getting there," Tom explained.

"OK Tom, I see the logic but am about to lose my shit unless you give me a straight answer right now," Bob fumed.

"It would help if I knew the question, Bob," Tom responded coolly.

"Why was the UN effort destined to be an inevitable failure?" Bob chose his words carefully, ensuring he phrased the question precisely as Tom had said it just seconds ago.

"Because he was never going to let it get far enough to succeed," Tom said matter-of-factly, then paused for effect before he continued answering the question on the table. "He couldn't let the UN decide what and how to use this technology. That would give them power beyond their charter and far beyond their ability given their pathetic performance over their decades of existence. It made a good cover story, but it was never going to be a reality. When the Secretary General sprung the summit on everyone instead of just doing another demonstration, that set into motion a whole new timeline. The only way to get where we needed to be was by blowing up the Chinese efforts, both figuratively and literally. But he won't take his foot off the gas to provide a viable off-ramp for the CCP to get off this train. We want them to see the futility of their position and do some or most of what we tell them we need. We don't want them backed into a corner so far that they decide the best option is to shoot their way out, so we don't do to them what they were already doing to us. That is why my phone got a flying lesson."

Ann interrupted the dialogue, hoping Bob would take the extra time to think before he spoke next, "Tom, what do we know the CCP is doing now, and what do we think the CCP is going to do that has you and the President at odds? What advice from his National Security Advisor is the chief decision maker not responding to?"

"The short answer, Ann, is still long. We know that, by snatching both Chen and Wu, we created more than confusion in their program. It was so compartmented, that we took out two consecutive primary links and that broke their continuity for a bit. Once they re-established that line, which they have, their effort was to figure who best to re-integrate into the UN demonstration team effort. Not for the purposes of succeeding in the UN objective, but to finish the job they started in India. To discredit it. The headlines would read:

> Even with the help and expertise from the CCP's best experts, the UN's lack of expertise and unwillingness to heed the wise counsel of the CCP led to yet another disaster. As a result, the CCP cannot in good faith continue collaborating with the UN.

"They are willing, however, to work unilaterally with individual nations who seek assistance with this technology, but it must be outside of any UN activity.

"You see, Ann and Bob, their gameplan never included the success of the UN effort either. They left the UN effort yesterday proffering that same option, but it was under very different conditions than they would have set. So, in the end either the US or China—perhaps now both— were never going to let the UN achieve their stated objective. He—rather *we*—put the offense on the field first, and that probably saved some lives compared to the Chinese version of how the UN effort would have failed. But it also pushed the already *impossible timeline* to a new level. It sucks, but not as much as it could have sucked." Tom nodded up and down as he let this all sink in.

"So, if you both had the same intended outcome, what is the difference between us and them?" Bob challenged Tom.

"Me and the President?" Tom asked.

"No, Tom. The US and China. Both wanted the same thing, for what appears to be the same reason. So, what is the difference between the two? What difference does it make if all that is different is who has the lever to pull over the other one? It's still someone over someone else." Bob's frustration showed, and Ann didn't wait for this to escalate between the two men, she answered for Tom.

"I know this is upsetting Bob, I am upset about it too. But we live in the greatest country in the world, despite its flaws. We won the lottery being born and raised here. Compare that freedom and opportunity guaranteed to everyone to those living in China, and the freedoms and opportunities to choose for themselves the average citizen there does not have. At its core, that is a huge difference and that is enough all by itself." Ann's comment was calm, reassuring and heartfelt. As soon as she finished speaking the words, she could see by the expression on Bob's face that they hit the mark she was aiming for with her fiancé.

"I know you are right Ann, and I apologize Tom. But this is a lot to process all at once and my ego and feelings are literally in play right now more than I think they have ever been in my entire life. And a big part of that is that it feels like the President, and you, Tom, played me. Played both Ann and me and I am not alright with that. I'm pissed about it, and I am sitting on an airplane with you flying to Florida where you want me to help you finish doing precisely what you lied to me about. How am I supposed to feel about that, Tom? How would you feel?" Bob spit each word out painfully as he tried to both control his emotions and process all this new information.

"I wouldn't feel about it, Bob. And you can't either. You don't get the luxury of feeling while we are all thinking and doing. That's right Bob, feeling is a nice-to-do activity right now, but doesn't matter to the outcome.

The must-do at this moment in history is the *thinking* you need to do to help us get this in the hands of the greatest nation in the history of the world, instead of an oppressive communist regime. That is how you are supposed to think about this Bob, and I don't really care how that makes you feel. But if I must placate your feelings, then you should feel good about doing your part to enable that outcome. But do us all a favor and feel that after we are finished thinking and doing. Not now. Not while we are doing it. Not while we are hoping it works. Not while we are breaking it in. Not at all until we are finished with all this do I want you or anyone else to be concerned with how you feel about this. I need 100% of your energy focused on *thinking* about it. That's how we all should be feeling about this Bob."

It was then the steward stepped into the heated exchange offering a small basket holding a variety of chilled brown bottles with colorful labels, some of them not in English. "Might I suggest the Porter? It, like the conversation, is heavy and just a little bitter, but the alcohol content is the highest. It tastes best just a little below room temperature. So, it should be about right. I have more in the back if needed." Everyone appreciated the timing and the artful suggestion, and all three reached for one of the bottles. He who serves, serves best when he knows what to serve and when. Steward was such an understated job title for anyone in this organization.

"I am not sure what else you want me to say, or what else you want to know Bob. Ann? What else do you want to know that we haven't already covered?" Tom asked as he smiled and nodded in appreciation as he took a drink of the dark and heavy beer staring at it and waiting for either of them to respond.

Bob broke the silence, as they all appreciated the beer now in small glasses in their hands. "So, what is the new success-criteria, Tom? That's what Frank always laid out for us...*success looks like this*, he would say. Tell us what success looks like now that we are where we are."

"It doesn't look much different than it did before," he began. "We have some version of a global operational capability on orbit. We hope it has the ability to counter other threats making them less—or not—impactful on our nation's operations. It is primarily defensive, but as with almost every technology out there it can be employed in offensive operations under the right conditions if needed."

Before he could finish, Bob interrupted, "What would that look like Tom? What are some examples of the offensive operations, or conditions that might trigger such operations? What do we need to be able to do? Is that the same list as what we would want to be able to do?"

"Fair enough. As an example, if someone initiated some on-demand weather event from their machine to damage or destroy a US resource, say a particular crop, or a facility or a shipping lane or whatever interest that might be. If we know who it is, or what they are planning, we could defend against that effort with our own weather event or counter condition, so the intended impact on us is never achieved."

"Or," Bob began, "we could send an event to destroy their facility, or base of operations. Instead of airplanes with bombs, or missiles we could just send an F4 tornado and blame it on mother nature...or, send a CAT 5 Hurricane and pitch a fit about the impact global warming is having on that coast line. We could do that to right?" Bob asked.

"Yes, Bob I suppose so. But everyone knows this technology is out there, so imagine the uproar when those events occur. It would be just as easy to blame someone, especially us, for those now," Tom countered.

"Yes, but plausible denial would be just as easy right now. It wasn't us; it may very well be a natural event? Maybe someone else has chosen to use their version of this technology to create that event? We don't do those types of things, it's against our laws? Our policies? How do you prove we didn't do something without proving it was in fact someone else. Until you prove who it is, you can't really prove who it wasn't when it comes to this, right?" Bob had given this a lot of thought recently, and he was ready for this discussion.

"I suppose your logic is sound, but what is your point, Bob?"

"The point, Tom, is there is a transparency requirement here that your plan does not seem to acknowledge. Without addressing that, there is no differentiating between defensive and offensive uses. Except what the US decides to reveal, a government narrative, on a government timeline about a government operation and a government ascribed outcome. It's an echo chamber without transparency. And with transparency you can't achieve a legitimate differentiation between US-initiated actions and responses to the actions of others without revealing the classified methods and techniques of those collections and actions. That classified stuff is what you need to ensure the safety and success of US-initiated operations. It's still a catch twenty-two, so you gotta pick whichever one is more important because I don't think you can have both. You can't get both on the path you are on now."

Tom pondered the dilemma the Professor had laid out before him as he sipped the beer, and motioned for the steward to bring some more for the group. He sat quietly, as the glasses were refilled with more porter. "I am gonna need something to help soak some of this up, do you have any pretzels back there?" Tom asked, already knowing the answer but buying some time and a distraction as he continued to ponder Bob's questions. He thanked the steward and took some pretzels then offered some to Bob and Ann, who both took a handful and waited for Tom to resume the conversation.

"You are describing essentially every classified thing we have, the way we do it for everything else that is sensitive, Bob. Why would we do it differently for this?" Tom asked.

"How can you not?" Bob asked. "If we are going to answer questions with questions, we aren't going to get very far in this discussion Tom. How do you give the world any confidence that any and every weather event that was injurious was *not* a US offensive weather operation? Just tell them it wasn't us, and they have to trust that to be true? I will give you a hint about the difference from other offensive operations. The kinetics are typically discoverable. A bomb, missile, bullet all physical and they fragment or leave some residue or whatever clue as to what it was, and where it came from. Radars, satellites, cameras all provide clues or proof of what it was, where it came from and generally you can get a good idea of who did it. That is not the case with the weather, Tom. Was it natural or not is the first question. If it can be known that it was not natural, then how do we prove who did or didn't do it with this technology and who already has it?"

"We found the CCP systems and traced 'em back to them. That is how we got here. We do it the same way," Tom said smugly.

"We were only able to trace what we found back to the CCP because they were the only ones who had it, Tom," Bob declared. "But you are forgetting that they used it successfully on us for years without us even knowing it existed. Now we know. The world knows. They know we have it. They know the UN has it, and that means just about anyone willing to pay enough can also have it. And that means that this transparency issue is a widespread problem not just a US problem. So, if we need an offensive and defensive capability because anything bad could be natural, or it could be anyone who has obtained this technology, the only way to rule out the US as the culprit is to have a hundred percent transparent operation so people can see who it wasn't. That will allow them to focus on who it was. Then decide what to do about it," Bob re-explained what he tried unsuccessfully to communicate earlier.

"OK, Bob so if I buy your logic which I am not saying I do just yet, where does that leave us? What are our options, and which is the least bad one if we can't do what we really want to do?" Tom wondered.

"You have to change your success criteria if you find that you cannot achieve the outcome previously stated," Bob said just short of disparagingly to Tom. "You can't get what you want, Tom. Not now, not with what has already happened. You must redefine what success looks like and settle for what you need, but it has to be achievable."

"Bob you are making my head hurt with this, but I have not spent as much time on this specific thought as it seems you have. You have been in this from the beginning, at least as far back as anyone on our team has been. You have seen all there is to see with this, and you have gained some pretty good national and international insights along the way. What would you do or, more specifically, what would you have us do? What now, Professor? If you were the President, what would you do if you had to decide what to do with what you know right now?" Tom was sincerely interested in hearing Bob's response as well as his rationale behind it.

"I wouldn't decide just yet," Bob said plainly. "We don't know what the CCP is going to do, or when. We don't know what nations, if any, will approach China in an effort to align themselves under that banner hoping it will provide them some safety or advantage. For that matter, we don't know how many allies or other nations will want to cozy up to the US for the same reason. It may very well be that the President has forced every nation to pick a side in what may quickly escalate into a global family feud over this technology and what to do next. If the UN is not going to host a summit to have those conversations, somebody better do it soon or it won't matter much. But I do know that the dilemma I posed earlier is not one that is coming eventually. It is already here, and the President may have painted us all in a box whether intentional or not. Whatever weather events happen from now on, if they have a negative impact on someone then we better be prepared to be blamed for it.

"We smoked the CCP capability, but if we didn't get every bit of it, we better be able to get the rest ASAP or be ready to prove it wasn't us who used their technology to make bad things happen to someone. The UN has one of their own systems and the US has our Thor's Hammers and the functioning CCP regional systems we captured. I don't know if the Aussies kept or copied what was grabbed down there. And we don't know, or at least I don't know if the CCP shared this with any others before we found theirs. So, the cat is out of the bag and, if you thought nuclear counterproliferation was difficult, this will be far more challenging. I built some of them with parts I bought off the internet, and since then it's gotten easier not harder."

"OK Professor Optimist, where does that leave us? What now?" Tom asked once again.

"I don't know, Tom. Let's see where they are, and what they have accomplished in Florida and go from there. That will fill in some blanks, and maybe we will have some information about the CCP or others that will start to fill in some of the missing pieces. Wasn't it the President who said we only get one shot at this? I want to take my time, breath, and slowly squeeze this trigger. I don't want to take this shot until we absolutely have to shoot."

"I can live with that," Tom conceded. "In the meantime, I need to give your words some thought. And I need to make some calls before we land. Can I borrow, your phone?"

CHAPTER ELEVEN

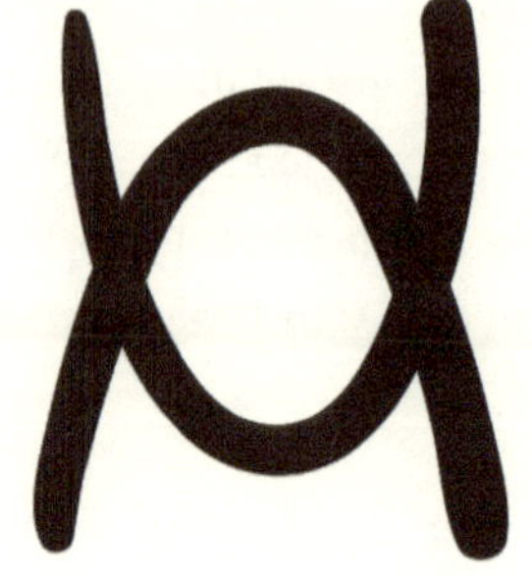

NO "T" IN CAN'T

The small jet landed at the private airfield in Florida, taxied to the nearest hangar and the passengers disembarked and walked into a windowless cinderblock building. There was no one there to greet them, nor was there anyone there to hinder their movements once they arrived. The few people they encountered were moving from place to place with purpose and the sense of urgency was palpable. Ann, Bob and Tom walked together until they saw Major General Lincoln passing instructions and pointing to some unknown point on the ceiling, in the sky, or in space to help illustrate the point he was making to the dozen or so people huddled around him and hanging on every word of his instructions. He was focused and so were they as the trio settled in behind him and waited patiently for him to finish. As he did so, it was Tom who spoke in order to get his attention before he was consumed by the next task on his mental list.

"You look like shit, Frank!" was his opening line as the man turned around to greet the familiar voice.

"Awesome! That was the look I was going for. Finally, I accomplished a lifelong goal. So nice of you to wrap up your sight-seeing trip in the Big Apple and come to the Sunshine State to join in the real work Tom. I see you brought along the A-team to make up for your lackluster abilities.

Hello Ann, Professor, it is good to see you both." Frank forced an unconvincing smile which prompted Ann to move across the gap and give the man what looked to be a needed hug. As she did so, she whispered into Frank's ear so only he could hear her words.

"You do look like shit Frank! What can we do to help?" And with that he broke into a quiet laugh as he answered. "Where to begin, Ann, where to begin? How about we go to what I am calling my office to decide that. Some coffee and information so none of us are wasting any of the time we already don't have enough of?"

"Lead the way, Sir," Ann directed and turned to Bob and Tom "Come on boys, the General could use our help. Everything else can wait." She took Frank's arm and walked with him down the hallway as her travelling companions looked at each other, shrugged and fell in step behind them. The coffee was already made, and Ann reached for some cups and began pouring before the others had even indicated if they wanted some. She knew they all needed it and began to pass around the cups as they all turned to the business at hand.

"I think it will be best to start with where you are with the Craftsmen effort, what is done and what remains to do?" Tom suggested "The rest of what we are bringing is contextual more than actionable at this point."

"OK," Frank began, "We had two successful launches. So far, we have over ninety percent success rate for bringing the CubeSats to life. A few failures and a few more to get through before they are all PMC. Sorry, *partly mission capable*. We have these arranged in a coarsely gridded network that we will continue to gap fill with the subsequent launches. That is unprecedented speed and volume, but we've had every resource we've needed. It's amazing what you can accomplish when you have the nation's resources at your disposal and you don't care who gets the credit...or who gets the bill," Frank said with a smirk that revealed the truth behind the key limitations to most big government programs. Most government programs *do* care, usually too much, about who gets the credit. Less about who gets the bill because ultimately it comes from the taxpayers.

"The production group is building CubeSats as quickly as they can get all the parts *space-ready*. The launch teams are loading the payloads and prepping the lift for another two launches. We expect those will happen in two days, three as a schedule option if it's needed or worth the wait. What we really need to do, and where I want you two to help, is to make a system check to see if these things are really going to work together the way we think they will. And we have been directed to do that in a very clandestine way. Not in the traditional sense of clandestine, but in a very different and benign direct-action, live operation in plain sight of the entire world…no pressure, no diamonds, right? Once again, we have been given the only two things we need, a plan and not enough time." Frank paused, to let their facial expressions catch up with their brains, and when he saw Bob's forehead scrunch and his eyebrows begin to move toward each other he continued.

"We have a pretty eclectic team working on that aspect of it already. I have to say, again catching you guys up, that Chen, Wu and Zach have all participated and made meaningful contributions to these efforts. We have a shadow team reviewing them after the fact, videos of everything they are involved in, but they have been shooting straight with us from the get-go. We would not be this far without them and I hope that cooperation continues, but I intend to continue this trust-but-verify approach with them indefinitely. It's the nature of this effort," Frank added. "Questions so far?"

"You said a coarse network; what does that look like?" Ann asked.

"We have low earth orbit coverage and believe the initial network will be enough to sufficiently cover the equatorial band out to about fifty degrees north and south. That covers most of the population and active agriculture in both hemispheres. The next launches will extend that to the poles and provide a second mesh of coverage across the board, filling in gaps and providing the redundancy. This design was based on the timeline. We are pushing everything into the first shots because that was the guidance. We may not get another chance at this. On top of that, we will have broken the bank on parts and equipment this way. There simply aren't enough pieces out there right now to do any more than we are already doing and, when we are done, it will be quite a while before we can generate enough parts to do more even if we needed to. Let's hope we won't need to," Frank explained.

"Given all that, what is it you need to test in order to know if the next launch is a GO or there is a reason to stop and adjust the second round?" Bob asked. "Assuming what you say about parts is such a factor, if we launched a problem in round one and repeat that in round two then it will be a long time before we can fix it. You can't go get these things, fix them and then put them back up there."

"That's a fact Bob. We can't. What we need to test are three primary things. We need to know that this nested, networked handoff to the next closest CubeSat is gonna work in real space and real atmosphere as well as it does in the lab during testing. And we need to know that, when they are talking and handing off based on conditions, the onboard devices are sufficiently located and powered to generate the conditions needed to get the desired effects and move them along in the flow to have them relating to each other. The big thing—the final test—is making sure this upside-down meteorology is going to translate to the surface conditions that we are hoping they produce at any given time and location. And we need to do that on a global scale, not just a region or a specific spot on a map. Simple enough? And if it doesn't work, we must shut it down and make it all stop so nobody gets *un-alived* because of what we are doing. Do no harm; hide in plain sight; take no credit; and take no blame for anything weather related until we can control it all. How do we test that, and make sure it works?"

"That's all? What do you have planned for tomorrow then?" Bob asked sarcastically.

"That has been our pace here since we started this effort, Bob. Welcome to the party. That's why I look like shit. This is not New York. If you haven't already, you better take your 'T' out of can't and put it in the dumpster out back with all the rest of them. If you are incapable of doing that, then stay away from my team," he said politely, but in all seriousness. "Nobody is entitled to be part of this effort, not even you. Carry your weight like everyone else or step off and stay out of the way."

There was a long pause, and for the first time since this began Bob considered taking the off-ramp that Frank had laid out for him. After all, he had already done a lot, more than his fair share in bringing out on-demand weather for everyone. His name would be in the history books no matter what happened next. And he was still rightfully, in his opinion, pissed at Tom and the President for lying to him about the UN effort. They are the ones who put him on a bogus path to keep up appearances while all this effort in Florida was going on behind the scenes. At that point, the switch in his mind flipped, and it all became clear for him. I am the only one accountable for my actions, not them. They let me do what I wanted, they gave me a choice and I chose to work on the UN effort and not this one. That was my decision not theirs. Maybe they left out some details about how far it would go, but it needed to continue from Australia, and it did until just yesterday when it became clear that action was needed. That was what happened, but it was not the only thing that could have happened. Self-pity and hurt feelings are luxuries, their own self-indulgence at a time when there was no time. It was clear to Bob what had to come next when Ann declared for both of them.

"You have two sets of fresh eyes, ears and ideas. Point us in the right direction, Frank. We're both all-in from the start, no changing that now." She looked over and was glad to see Bob smiling and nodding up and down in agreement.

"I have some ideas. Do you still have Andies and Lessur working on the weather parts of this?" she asked.

"Understatement, but yes. Andies is the heavy lifter on that team, and while I am sure he will appreciate the help, don't lose sight of the fact that you are joining them, not the other way around," Frank cautioned.

"I hear both what you are saying, and what you are not saying, Frank. We got this; we can work with that," Bob agreed. "What else do we need to cover?"

"Nothing right now, but I think once you get integrated it might be helpful to take a run at Wu and Chen, in that order, to see if there is something you can ask them that we didn't consider yet. They are good resources, but the right question at the right time might make them great resources on this, especially Wu given the scientific nature of his work and what we need soonest."

"OK, and what about Zach?" Bob followed.

"Helpful, but still reserved. I think he is holding back, but seeing as other people are contributing enough to keep things on pace my sense is he is waiting for an opportunity, a mic-drop moment so he can reach Tom's *enough* threshold. Could be wrong, but I try hard not to be," Frank smirked, waiting for the next question as he felt the coffee kick in.

"I might be able to get a sense of that since we have more of a past than anyone else he knows here. He might trust me more than the rest of you," Ann offered.

"And he might try to exploit that for the very same reason," Tom cautioned and immediately regretted saying that out loud upon seeing the look on Ann's face as she responded in the same tone as Tom's comment.

"And if you don't think I know that, then you haven't been paying attention. The one I need to recalibrate my trust meter on is not Zach," she shot back.

"Yeah, so I had that coming. Sorry Ann. It's not you who needed to hear that, it was me who needed to say it to get it out of my head so I could move on to the next problem that is mine to solve," Tom apologized and she asked her follow up question.

"And what might that be? What will you be doing Tom?"

"I have to convince the President to adjust his current course. And get a new phone. It might take a stack of new phones knowing how he is once he gets something in his head and makes a decision. He falls in love with the plan a little too much, a little too often. Appreciate if you keep that in this room so I don't have to lose any more of my integrity by denying I said that," Tom tried to begin his fence-mending with Ann and Bob with a little humor and a nod of the hat by giving them something they otherwise would not have been in a position to hear. It might come in handy later or it might not, but his gesture was appreciated.

"As much as I have enjoyed this little reunion, I think it's time we all get to doing it instead of talking about it. If you need something you don't have, let me know what it is. It seems my primary job is removing roadblocks and getting things for other people. I am pretty much a glorified valet and waiter in a flight suit. I will do my best to get your orders correct." Frank's self-deprecation was one of the tools in his kit that made him both approachable and insightful. He put himself in your place, and tried to put you in his so you felt like you were working with him not for him. Both in principle and in practice, he believed that his job as a leader was to get you what you needed in order to succeed. Be that direction, information, equipment, people, access or whatever; he would organize, train and equip you for success. With Frank you succeeded or failed as a team. Success was yours, but failure on the rare occasions that it happened, that was his and his alone. He was the right man to lead the *Thor's Craftsmen* program.

With that they went their separate ways, and it only took a few minutes for Bob and Ann to find their way to the small workspace where Chief Andies, Major Lessur and about six others were deep into their discussion around some computer screens, and lots of charts, graphs and stacks of who-knows-what else that seemed related to the ongoing effort.

"What can we do to help?" Bob said loud enough to cause everyone in that discussion to turn and see who was asking.

"Put this genie back in the bottle, Professor, so we can have a little more time to figure it all out? We have the time machine right over there; building that was easier than what we are doing right now," Andies only half joked as the two new arrivals joined the crowded workspace while he introduced them to the group assembled to build out the test plan.

"Yes Pete, if it's Frank Lincoln who is asking, the answer is still, *Yes and what else can I do for you this time.* I know he's a two-star and you're a four star, but this is from POTUS himself." General Charles, paused to let the voice on the other end of the line object in a way four-star's do privately but not publicly. "Pete, it's not that I don't care; it's that it doesn't matter whether I care or not," he began and then paused as the Commander of all things Space was not hearing the message the Chairman was sending. "Pete, you just have to do it. It's that simple. Make it happen. If you can't do that, say so right now and I will give Lincoln your stars and you can retire with his. I don't want to fight with you over this but make me and you will lose. I am still blocking for Lincoln. He has the ball and the President called the play. There is only one acceptable outcome and anyone who impedes that gets rolled over. That's straight from the Commander in Chief and SECDEF has a pen in his hand to clean house of anyone who wants to defy that order. I've known you a long time and I don't want that for you. So, don't put me in a position where I have to pick between my friend and my duty. I love you man but you know how that will have to go. This is one you want to be part of helping succeed and not be on the other side of."

Another pause and the call concluded with a thanks, and I'm buying the next time we link up. Dutch had been taking and making a lot of these calls in the last couple of weeks, and they were weighing heavily on him. Not for the conflicts and damage to some of his relationships or reputation, but for the fallout that Frank would likely receive. Right now, the name Frank Lincoln was notorious—not famous—for what was being asked. In the long run as things are revealed, people will have their aha moments, but right now there is a disruption in the operations of the force and that disruption has a name and the highest sponsors in the nation. Bullseye on that guy.

The Chairman was still thinking about the call he just ended, when his executive officer poked his head into the office, "The SECDEF is here to see you."

"I didn't know he was on my calendar. He's not, is he?" Dutch said.

"No Sir, shall I show him in?"

"Of course, if he needs to see me let's have him," the Chairman instructed. While it is a subtlety of the office, the Chairman has no operational command authority over any military units. He is the principle military advisor to both the SECDEF and the POTUS. The Chain of Command does not include the Chairman, so while he can communicate the instructions of the top two leaders of the US military to his friend Pete, they both knew Dutch had no direct authority to order him to take any actions.

The SECDEF strolled into the office, warmly greeted the Chairman and took a seat. "Dutch, I just got off the phone with Tom. He's concerned about the CCP response to the President's actions yesterday. More specifically, the lack of an outward response thus far. So am I, and I know you are too. The intel community stuff gets so filtered by the time it gets to me I don't know what to believe about what they are telling me or what to wonder they aren't telling me. What do you know, and more importantly what do you think?"

"Today, Fitz, I don't know that there is any distinction between what I know and what I think. They have not changed their military posture that we can tell, nor have they issued any public statements in official channels about what the President said yesterday. While the chatter and intercepts are all still very much alive, it seems they are doing a pretty good job of keeping us from hearing or seeing whatever discussions they are having and any related actions they might be taking. We know they play the long game, and this is one of those times that inaction might be their best action…for them I mean." The Chairman's choice of words was very deliberate.

"Why do you think that?" he asked. After all he was seeking counsel not giving direction.

"A couple of reasons," he began, "First reason is first impression they leave with the rest of the world about the accusations and evidence we have been spilling into the media. That first impression needs to set up the actions they plan on taking next. So, if they come out with a denial and try to wave this off as nothing more than an information operation or US and UN propaganda, then we know whatever response they plan will be low key with a high degree of deniability.

"On the other hand, if they come out with an admission but with their version of the truth, then it becomes a race between our version and theirs. It sets up a binary option and that means pick a side because we are both gonna throw down not back down. My money is on the latter because they have already claimed the technology as their own as part of the UN initiative. POTUS yesterday just told the world that we agree with China that this was their technology but here is the rest of the story. They are experts because they have been using it on all of us for almost a decade, and here is the proof. Either way, the long game says don't start too many fights, but never walk away from one. That's what I think?"

"That aligns with Tom's concern too," Fitz agreed, "…but POTUS wants to grind them on it either way. It's under his skin and he sees it as an abject failure for us, and they need to pay a high price for what they have done to us already. Hell, I had to convince him not to take kinetic action already and, his words, *settle for that soft cyber-attack to take out their capability.* He wanted to obliterate every device with a cruise missile for heaven's sake. The collateral damage alone where these things were all situated would have been immense. Small price for them to pay for the blood and treasure they have stolen from us with this technology. The only thing that changed his mind was me convincing him the average citizen did not do this, but they would be the ones who paid with their lives by the hundreds if we went kinetic instead of cyber. That heat was just enough to convince him to change direction, but he is convinced now more than ever that there is a debt still needing to be collected."

"I don't disagree with the concept of the debt needing to be repaid, but we need to make sure we keep him focused on who needs to repay it, and how it gets collected," Dutch admitted. "What do you think you want that to look like, Fitz?"

"Well, I don't think we want this to escalate into throwing nukes at each other so we better think of something else that will satisfy POTUS without bullying the CCP so hard that a global thermonuclear exchange sounds like an attractive option to the alternative," the SECDEF dramatized for effect, but it was only a little bit. "I am not sure what that is yet, but we better figure it out fast and convince him to like our plan better than the path he seems to be on now. I know we can do it, but I don't know if we have enough to time to do it."

"Sure, we do, Fitz. That's what they pay us to do, and that's what we do. We find a way," Dutch assured him.

"Well, the good news is there are a lot of people from the summit still here meeting in the building. The bad news is they are almost exclusively the people who were not able to fly out already and most of what they are doing is trying to arrange their travel or give their ambassadors instructions on their nation's response to yesterday's shit show," Mr. Dau explained to the UN Secretary General, who was pacing across his office like a caged cat being guarded by a watchdog.

"That man, he infuriates me. Whenever he can, he pokes me in the eye. This though, this was not a poke in the eye, this was a beheading. A public execution of our efforts and did he have the brass to look me in the eye and let me know it was coming? No. He stood up, got everyone's attention then lopped off our heads in our own house. I don't see a way to recover from this with both the CCP and—because of their misdeeds—

now the US pulling out of our efforts. We now get to do one of two very unattractive jobs. Either we align with one of these two nations and alienate the other or we stand by until whatever happens between them gets resolved and help sweep up the broken glass. Unbelievable. We went from being in the world's spotlight to holding the flashlight so everyone can walk safely to the exits. Damn that man," he fumed.

"And to add insult to injury, if we are to believe the press versions of the US evidence, they highlighted as one of their examples of China using this technology for financial gain a UN led humanitarian relief effort. In response to a Typhoon in Malaysia, the China and UN led response to provide, food, water and shelter to those impacted by the devastation resulted in big profits for a couple of companies that won big contracts. Guess who has controlling interest in those companies? I'm sorry, did you say the CCP? That's right, Mr. Dau. And did you say those same companies provided substantial contributions to the UN and the UN Secretary General above and beyond what the collaboration efforts cost us? It looks like kickbacks and, while they weren't, that doesn't matter. Actual or perceived, it's the language and threshold for conflict. One is as bad as the other, but when it's both! That is hard to come back from."

"Just because it's hard to do, doesn't mean we can't." Mr. Dau in his attempt to console his boss did exactly the opposite.

"Wake up, Dau. I mean *really* man, get your feet back on the ground where the rest of us must live every day," the Secretary General lashed out. "From this one example, our entire involvement in this gets called into question from the very beginning. The demonstrations, Mcleod's choice to bring it to us, even Doctor Auster's death by the hand of the Chinese …it calls into question whether or not the UN was in on this with the CCP from the very beginning."

"Were you?" Dau asked his boss plainly, and that drew a venomous response that was not completely undeserved.

"No, Mr. Dau I was not. Were you?" he fired back.

"No, Mr. Secretary I was not. Now that we have that important discussion out of the way, I suggest we consider and decide on what our least bad option might be so we can get off our hands and begin some damage control. Are you ready for that yet, or do you need some more time to fume over things from yesterday that we cannot undo without taking some action that gets us back into the news cycle."

"Yes, I can do that. Thank you, Mr. Dau, shall we begin again?" and with that they took another run at their meeting.

The phone rang three times before Steve got to it, and when he looked at the caller ID he quickly spoke in response to the ringing.

"Hi Ann, how are you?" As he listened to her, he pretended not to see Betty motioning for him to put the call on speaker so she could hear both sides of the conversation. After what seemed like a long time listening, as Steve began to speak, Betty's phone began to ring. She could see it was Bob, so she picked up and walked briskly into the other room so neither would talk over the other's calls.

After several minutes Steve began to catch on as he could vaguely hear Bob's voice in the background. "Are you and Bob literally in the same place, Ann?"

"Maybe…" she smiled big enough that he could hear it through the word coming across the phone. "Look, Dad, it is pretty stressful here right now and we wanted to give you guys your privacy even if you were together. We did not want to assume, or put any extra pressure or expectations on you two. After all, you are two individuals with your own responsibilities and…" Steve cut her off.

"Cut the crap; you had your fun; now tell me what else you need."

"OK Dad, it's just that simple. Bob is in fact on the phone with Betty and is letting her know which of the books or files she needs to find and bring to us down here. You are her travel companion, second set of eyes, trusted security guy, all those long lists of things you do behind the scenes; you are right there too. But you gotta step it up and double time getting those things here ASAP.

"Tom has already sent the plane back to get you, so as soon as you can get to the airport, the sooner you can get here," she paused then filled in some more gaps. "Same airport, same terminal, same loading area as the last time you and Betty were there, and it should be the same airplane and the same crew. If it's not, then call me before you load up. Any change from before, or anything that does not feel right, you call me."

"I can do that," Steve assured her. "Now, I am going to throw a few things into my backpack and help Betty with whatever...however much it is we need to bring, and we will be on our way to the airport. I will let you know once we are taxiing; no need to bother you until I know we are on our way. Love you too sweetheart, see you soon. Good luck with things on your end." He hung up and walked across the suite, and looked in on Betty who was still deeply involved in her call with Bob.

She was bounding around the room with the phone between her cheek and the top of her shoulder, looking for and in boxes and folders for the items Bob was describing through the phone to her. She was both focused and smooth in her movements, so Steve decided to let her do her thing without interruption from an offer to help that he knew she would decline. So, he left briefly to go stuff his backpack with a few essential that would keep him equipped for at least twice as long as he expected to be gone, then made his way back to where Betty was still methodically adding to the small stack of documents and thumb drives in the center of the bed.

She waved for him to come in, and when he did, she said, "Here hold this please," as she put the call on speaker and the phone in Steve's hand.

"And the last ones I should need, are the recipe books. There is the paper one Doc had, the thumb drive that has all of his stuff, and the thumb drive that I got from the church. That should be it, Betty. You have them all now?" Bob asked.

"Yes, I have them all Bob. And Steve just joined us, I put the call on speaker so he can hear us," she said and winked at him.

"Good, hi Steve," Bob greeted him and continued, "I'm glad you are there. Do you remember the items we left in your care at that spot we dug a hole?" he asked cryptically, but sufficiently to describe the vault they built in Steve's shop.

"I will likely remember that adventure forever, Bob," he affirmed. "Do you want all the thumb drives where we left them, or do you need Betty to make copies before we leave for the airport? We're good; right now everything we had there is right where we left it."

"Good, thank you," Bob replied. "OK Betty, I think that's it for me. Steve has the plan from Ann, you bring what I asked about and that will be a huge help. Be careful, stay safe."

"I can do that," she assured him. "We will see you soon."

CHAPTER TWELVE

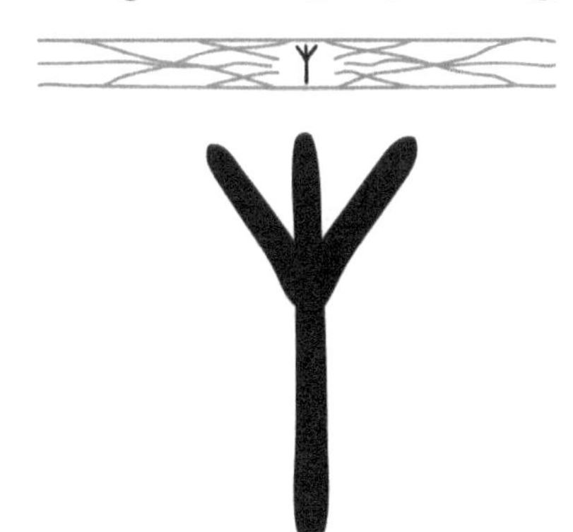

TESTING, TESTING 1-2-3

Ann and Bob had passed along their instructions to Steve and Betty to bring the recipe books and some key files with them to Florida but they still had plenty to keep themselves busy. They understood the key components that Chief Andies wanted to test and why, but the team assembled had very limited experience using the devices. This experience was further challenged with the changes in components, power, and application of these modified systems being employed from space to impact conditions on the ground. Having Bob and Mr. Wu available and all in for this test plan made its success plausible, but it did not make it likely. What did make it likely was having a composite team of intellectuals, theorists and operators with practical experience and knowledge working together with all the resources they needed. That is what gave this a chance to succeed.

"But that is too subtle, Bob. It could be natural, or it could be us and we won't be able to tell the difference. We won't know if it's working as intended, or if the environment is simply doing what it does." Major Lessur was simply not buying into Professor Mcleod's idea for a low-key hide-in-plain-sight test parameter.

"Ron, that's precisely why it will work and not a reason why it won't. The variable we control for the test is not the what, it's the when and the where. Behind the cold front we will have the temps rise but they will be slower than the forecast and normal occurrence would be…but just a little slower. We will incrementally keep that slow pace, so we know it's us. And to make sure the model runs don't adjust too well to our slower pace, we will offset that pace by keeping the warm sector just a little further south than it should be, and then adjust it a little further north. It will be a little frustrating for the forecasters, and the models will be off a little bit, but not enough to trigger any kind of anomaly report or bust review. We'll know it's working when the warm sector is a little off, and then changes again when and where we tell it too," Bob explained.

As he did, he noticed the smile on Mr. Wu's face as he began to speak, "Yes, professor that is very similar to the testing we conducted in our program. It is also, I believe, the way Doc Auster caught on to us although it took him years to do so. Regardless of what we choose to use as a test plan, it does concern me that fooling the masses will be simpler than getting a test past the teams who have been doing the same things for many years. They know what to look for, and what they have done, so indicators will not be viewed by them the same as they are by others. Having said that, I do believe this is still the approach that has the greatest probability for success because it will be the hardest for them to confirm even if they do—as you say—sniff it out.

"If my former colleagues are acting true to form, they will be far more concerned with addressing the political and media aspects of the problems the US President gave them. You see, whether intended or not, your President gave them three immediate problems that are far more time sensitive than watching the weather. The first was taking out the operational systems, that is a big hit and repairing or replacing them will take concerted efforts and much time. But the other two problems are more important to them than regaining their operational systems. They need to explain to those many senior party leaders who were not aware of this program that it is indeed real and that the accusations are true. This will be a big deal, and it will delay their reactions because they must do this before they can agree on and implement a response to the accusations and evidence against them. The time to test is now, the sooner the better if we are to stay undetected."

Looking around the group there was nothing but support and validation for the gameplan on the table, so they pressed ahead developing the details and the timing. The recipe for temperature changes was one of— if not *the*—simplest to enter and monitor because it was such a basic parameter that drove or was impacted by meteorological events and changes. It was widely and accurately measured as one of the key components of every weather observation, so the data was as rich as any across the spectrum of recorded weather data either live or historic.

But picking and monitoring the temperature changes to occur for the testing was the simple part. Integrating that into the basic algorithm developed to hand the subtle changes to the various sensors is what was the primary target of the testing. They needed to demonstrate the on-orbit constellation could receive directions from the ground control node and then execute those instructions across the nested platforms to deliver the desired outcomes at the time and place as tasked. That required a whole different test plan, and there was a whole different group doing that, now that the weather piece had been communicated to them by Chief Andies.

Major General Chen was walking toward the group of weather experts when he recognized that both Bob and Ann had rejoined the ongoing efforts. Whatever business he was coming over to attend to was put on hold as he greeted Ann first and then Bob and asked for a moment of their time for a sidebar conversation.

"It is good to see you both here. I saw the news. They keep us well informed as we work. I am sorry for you both that the UN effort appears—well, seems to be—indefinitely delayed," he paused, hoping to gain some insights from their response.

"Delayed is a polite word for terminated, I fear. Not sure there is a path for that effort to be resumed until the success of this effort and the CCP response are determined. Even if it does resume, I am afraid it will be without Ann and me. Too much baggage for the two of us to be anything other than a liability for any UN effort on this technology going forward."

Bob appreciated the courtesy Chen showed him but they both knew it was just that.

"I fear your assessment is correct, Professor. I see the same things you see on that matter. And, perhaps, I might have some insights on another matter that might be even more unique to my perspective. Do you have a moment that I might share them with the two of you?" Chen asked Bob while he was looking at Ann to make sure she was included in the conversation and the response.

"Of course, what is it General?" Bob agreed. Ann nodded smiling as he began on cue.

"This testing is very fast. The on-orbit versions were not rigorously tested, nor the design vetted in a typical manner before going onto the spacecraft. The feats are immense and the speed in which they have been accomplished is quite amazing. Seeing it would have been quite thrilling but, being a part of it, I must admit has been an incredibly fun and satisfying experience. I am almost ashamed to say that out loud, but the science and the process once the politics are removed is nothing short of amazing. Well, there I go again, the politics are never really removed. It just morphs, and I wanted to tell you both that being a part of this process has helped me understand, I think, why you did what you did," he paused and nodded.

"And what specifically did we do, that you believe you now understand?" Ann asked him politely but curiously.

"Ahh, yes. I meant that you turned over the Thor's Hammers to the UN rather than keeping them for yourselves. You could have been rich beyond your wildest dreams had you kept them. But you did not, and for that you should be commended. While I on the other hand was a key leader in my nation and party's efforts to use this for our own gain at the expense of others. You two were not. And what I see here, while marvelous to behold, seems to me quite like what I was doing in China but simply under a different flag. So, I was hoping to ask you, now that you have returned from the UN to help with this effort, why? Can you help me see your greater good here, and not just the political expediency of my own current situation to keep me and my family safe?"

"That is a heavy question, but the answer I think is simple. I need to finish what I started, and if I am *not* here to help and influence this effort then I am leaving the outcome to others. I simply cannot do that; *we* cannot do that." Bob looked at Ann, "You see Chen, this may not be the path we chose to get this technology in the hands of the world to make it a better place, but this is the path where that is happening. So here we are."

"I suppose it can be that simple if we let it be. That is a good perspective, Professor, and it is my wish for you both that you can keep it. And now back to the task at hand. The test plan for the handoffs and the networked systems is going to take a little coding but the team seems to think it won't be very complicated and, if there is some kind of failure that it will be easy to detect, stop, contain and recover from. In short, they all like it, so your team's ideas are supported and in the works already. I know others will communicate that in the correct channels, but I wanted to pass that along myself when I saw you had returned. And to congratulate you on another good idea. Keep them coming Professor; please keep them coming. The voice of reason is needed now more than ever as I fear the President intends to extract his pound of flesh from the CCP many times over. This may cloud his perspective, and it may threaten your goals as well. Thank you for the discussion; it is nice to have you both here. As you can imagine, the number of friendly faces I encounter here are very few." With that, he turned and headed back down the hallway.

"That was both nice, and weirdly, cryptic?" Bob observed.

"Yeah, same. But he did not say anything I haven't thought to myself dozens of times. Well, except for the part where you keep having good ideas. Are you going to tell him those all come from me, or you just wanna keep taking credit?" Ann joked as she poked Bob in the ribs hard enough to make him wince in pain. "Ahh, what's the matter Bob you can't stop the mean little girl from picking on you? Come on, let's go a couple of rounds and see what you got?"

"What has gotten into you?" he asked as she was bouncing around him with her closed fists up around her face in a protective position looking like she was more interested in punching him than defending herself.

"Coffee has kicked in. Plus, not sure if it was his intention or not but Chen just inspired another great idea that you are gonna get to take credit for once we do it," she said as she continued dancing around Bob, bobbing and weaving as she moved.

"Yeah, and what's that?" Bob played along.

"Plausible denial," she smiled.

"What does that mean?" Bob asked and Ann stopped, dropped her hands back to her waist and looked disappointed.

"Plausible denial is when something happens…"

She stopped as Bob said, "I know what plausible denial means. What I don't know is what you mean when you say we have it, or what we need it for."

"Yeah, you do, it just takes you longer to get there than it takes me. Don't worry, I will wait for you. Always do, and so far, you haven't disappointed me. Now let's get back to the group, we have more work to do." She moved back across to where the rest of the team was addressing the timing and sequencing of how to complete the temperature change test procedures.

Steve and Betty completed the familiar route to the airport and waited to board their *charter flight* to Florida. As had been their previous experience they didn't have to wait long before they were instructed toward the doors that took them down the small walkway and out to the aircraft that was already in position and ready to whisk them to sunnier, warmer climes. Once aboard, they recognized the steward who, of course, knew them by name and offered them a beverage as they settled into their seats. Steve texted Ann that they were on their way and moments later the two, with their boxes of files and bag of thumb drives, were lifting off to deliver the precious cargo to the point of need at the small airfield in Florida. The flight was uneventful and so was the landing except it was much sooner than expected.

As Steve and Betty began to concern themselves with the change in travel plans, the steward appeared to inform them of the interim stop. "It seems we are diverting to D.C. to pick up some additional passengers. I trust you won't mind travelling with them, in fact you may have already met. If not, I am sure you will find him great company. I typically find him happy to divert his attention from his duties to some other topics while he is traveling, especially when there are people as interesting as you two on board."

"May I ask who we will be joining our flight? Him or them?" Betty inquired.

"Of course, I am sorry. General Charles, the Chairman of the Joint Chiefs of Staff, will be joining us and travelling to the same destination. And whatever of his security detail that is needed will also be boarding. It won't be long before we land, so if you will excuse me?" Then he moved to the back of the plane to attend to one of the many things that required the man's attention.

"I think I would remember meeting him, pretty sure I haven't." Steve told Betty, who replied the same. "Seen him but have not been introduced. This should be fun. I wonder why he is going to Florida. I mean, I imagine it's the same reason we are going, but I wonder what he needs to do or decide, or what is happening that has us and him there at the same time."

"I guess we are about to find out," Steve said as the two could hear the landing gear come down. They looked out the darkly tinted windows to see some of the Washington D.C. landmarks whiz by as they approached the touchdown point on the runway at National. They taxied, stopped, opened the doors, and closed them almost as quickly as they opened.

General Charles and two men who clearly were his security detail bounded aboard and quickly took a seat as the aircraft was already moving back toward the taxiway and the waiting active runway.

As the man whom they recognized but was not in a military uniform turned toward them, he greeted the two and introduced himself.

"Hi, my name is Dutch, Dutch Charles. Thanks for letting me catch a ride with you, sorry to slow you down," he apologized as the two just stared at him. "And you are Steve and Betty, is that right?"

"Yes, I am Steve, and this is Betty," he stammered a bit.

"Good, glad I got that one right. Would have been a might embarrassing if I got the two of you mixed up." The general tried to brighten the mood, but couldn't help himself, and asked another question.

"So, what takes you to Nicaragua?" he asked inquisitively but with a big grin as the look of shock on both their faces let him know he needed to dial it back just a little.

"I'm kidding, we're not going there. And I already know what brings you to Florida. It's the same thing that brings me there. Some pretty amazing technology, isn't it? I understand you have been working with Bob for a long time. I have grown to like that guy. Should I like him, Betty?" he asked, not betraying if he was serious or messing with her again but knowing it was a little of both.

"If you're a smart General, then, yes, you should like him. If you're one of those political hacks in a uniform, then you probably shouldn't. I'm pretty sure you are the former, or I would have heard about it from Bob already." Betty decided it was time for her to reset the tone of the conversation although she wasn't really sure why she felt that way.

"Fair enough. I try to understand the politics of the situation and the decisions to be made but not to be motivated or influenced by them. That is for the politicians and their appointees. I get to be—rather I need to be—apolitical. I like to think I do a pretty good job at that part anyway," the Chairman replied in candor.

"Good, then you should like both Bob and Ann. For that matter, you might like Steve and me too," she smiled. "Can I get you anything? Or, I guess I mean get him to get you anything. I forget this is not my place, but they do take good care of us when we are traveling on this plane."

'I'll have what you are having Betty. You seem like a pretty good judge of what is appropriate for the situation," he complimented her.

"OK then, I could use a drink. I hope you like your bourbon neat. That is how Steve and I like it." She motioned for the steward to bring three of the beverages he already knew was their choice, as she continued speaking, "I assume your security detail doesn't drink on the job and, if they do, they don't while I'm here."

"You are right either way about the security detail, and yes, neat is how I like my bourbon as well. Seems we just might have a lot in common," Dutch said.

"We'll see General, we'll see. It's still a long way to Florida, we got time to figure that out before we get there. Unless you need to get on the phone, radio, video conference or whatever," she pushed a little.

"No, let's figure it all out before we get there," he agreed.

And so began a long conversation where the three of them talked about things such as where they were from, where they lived, what they liked to do and what they did not like to do. They discussed a good number of things from their personal lives as well as their introductions to this new and vexing on-demand weather modification that brought them together on this flight to Florida. They talked about Bob and Ann, and how they came together and what they hoped to do with the UN effort, and how that seemed to morph into the ongoing efforts they were traveling towards at a little over five hundred miles per hour. At that point Betty thought it was as good a time as any to see if she was reading the man well, or if this was something more nefarious than it seemed.

"So, General Charles can I ask you a very direct question?" She leaned into the space between the seats as she spoke.

"Sure Betty, go ahead."

"How do you think this all plays out?" She was more vague than direct for a reason.

"By this, do you mean our efforts to get this technology on orbit?" he sought to clarify before he answered.

"No, Dutch that is already happening and I know that will happen. It's almost there already. By it, I mean what happens after this is on orbit and the US has an operational global ability. What's next? How does it play out with China and all the others? How do you see it playing out?" She tried again to learn his view.

"That's the big question we all have now, isn't it? You see, it very much depends on what the CCP and the others do along the way just as much as it matters what we do and when we make it known." He paused more briefly than he planned as Betty rolled her eyes and yawned, shaking her head from side to side.

"OK, you wanna hear what I hope happens, or what I think will happen?" the Chairman asked.

Before he could take another breath, Steve answered for them, "Yes. General, we want to hear them both. And if they are different, then we also want to hear why. If that is something, you are willing to tell us."

"Right, let's leave the politics to the politicians then, shall we?" he began, as Steve and Betty both nodded in agreement. So, he continued, "What I hope happens is the US and China decide an arms race is both expensive and unwinnable for either side. Mutually assured destruction is not an attractive future for most people when you ask them if they would prefer that or something else. So, I would hope the leaders of the two nations with this technology could come to some agreement on how to proceed with its employment and its use...and by whom and on what timetable.

"What I think will happen is not that. I think the two national leaders will both dig in their heels and puff out their chests. Both will demand the other back down and neither of them will. Brinksmanship becomes an ego contest which becomes a political liability if they back down, and an escalation of tensions when neither of them do. For someone to win, the other has to lose and neither of them is willing to take that offramp because losing in the global geopolitical landscape is easy to do but very hard to come back from. I don't think either one of them is capable of backing down at this point, and that is extremely concerning. It is very dangerous if there is no offramp for people to take after all the chest thumping. I can advise him as long as he is willing to listen, and I can say the same things until I am blue in the face. But, when he has his mind set on a particular outcome, he is all transmit and no receive. I believe that is where we are right now with the President and, while I can hope, I don't see him changing his mind from the path we are on currently.

"That is why I am on this flight with the two of you. So that we can have this very conversation. You see, we are the supporting cast. We counsel, we advise those who are the stars of this operation. I advise the POTUS and the SECDEF. The two of you advise Bob and Ann. And advising others...that is our primary role in this. They may not listen, and in that case, we need to understand the issues, and their calculus in coming to conclusions. I am hoping that you might see if you can get Bob and Ann on the side of collaboration with the rest of us. Hoping we can convince the Commander and Chief to de-escalate the situation instead of escalating it."

"So how do we pull that off?" Betty asked.

"Any number of ways really. Depends on the issue and the timing. But, if we are all leaning in the same direction, when the moment comes the action can be effective if it's swift. Right now, just trying to understand who is leaning in which direction," he concluded, needing to draw a line between discussing and encouraging any particular action.

"We are leaning in the same direction, Dutch. Seems we're good on that. Now how about you let me process all this while I take a little nap before we get there. I am an old lady and need a little beauty sleep, or at least a beauty doze before we touch down."

"Of course," the Chairman agreed. "I could use a little of that myself and let this bourbon help me into a power nap. Sweet dreams y'all. See you soon."

It seemed like only a few moments had passed when the steward began bustling around making enough noise to alert but not startle the passengers as he prepared for the rapid descent into the small airfield. They collected their thoughts and the few belongings that remained unsecured from the earlier portion of the flight. A smooth touchdown on the runway followed by a hard but brief brake to slow the craft and make the turn onto the taxiway that took them to the main building that everyone recognized from their previous trips to the same spot. The pilot shut down the engines, switched to auxiliary power, then opened the doors allowing the warm humid air to rush into the cabin. They grabbed their belongings, and each took a box or two and were on their way into the flight line operations building that also served to house some of the *Thor's Craftsmen* teams.

"OK, let's get after it," Dutch smiled. "We have a lot to do, and nobody seems to have enough time to even meet and greet us. Their schedule must be a little tighter than I expected."

Ann was the first to see the three coming into the work area schlepping the boxes Bob had requested they bring, and she was surprised to see the Chairman in between Betty and Steve as heavily laden with boxes as they were. She quickly alerted Bob and Ron Lessur of the new arrivals. She could see the blood draining from the weather officer's face when he realized the CJCS was not met upon his arrival, and they were hauling boxes of papers to their underlings to boot. He grabbed a couple from the team and rushed over to relieve them of their boxes as he apologized while doing so. As Ron took the boxes from Betty and the others relieved Dutch and Steve, he first apologized then greeted and offered to lead them to Bob and then go find Major General Lincoln. But the CJCS had a different plan in mind.

"Thank you, Major. But I know you all are laboring on a near impossible task. What I'd rather do is hang with Betty and Steve and help get these files and ideas integrated into your test plan if that's ok. That alone gets me most of what I am here for anyway. That OK with you? If having me in the room will make your teammates nervous or otherwise cramp your style, then no offense taken from me. We could do things the more formal way, if you think they would prefer that," Dutch offered.

"You're the Chairman, whatever you prefer Sir," Ron agreed.

"Thank you, but that does not answer my question," he smiled and waited.

"No Sir, it did not, did it? Sorry General. If everyone gets to speak freely and doesn't need to filter for what the brass or elected and appointed officials might find offensive, then it should be fine. If not, then perhaps we should consider the more traditional path. There is already enough stress at everyone's level on this project. No offense intended, Sir, but that's my opinion. And if that's okay with you, I think it best they hear it directly from your mouth from the git go." Ron took a deep breath, waiting for the response and hoping it was the one he wanted and not the one he expected from the senior military advisor to the commander in chief.

"I can see why Frank speaks highly of you, Son. That is exactly what I wanted to hear, let's get started shall we?" He moved past the young major and made his way toward Bob who was already digging into one of the boxes that Betty had not surrendered until she personally handed it to her boss and friend. After grabbing the bag of thumb drives he was looking for, Bob turned and nearly ran into the CJCS still clad in his civilian attire.

No matter how he dressed, the Chairman was still a large, imposing human presence in whatever room he occupied but his smile, when he used it, was warm and somehow comforting. Without a word it told people that he was approachable, and he was one you wanted on your side of whatever the issue was. That was comforting because, when he wasn't smiling, it was pretty evident that you did not want him on the other side of whatever you were doing at the time. After a short summary of the conversation he just had with Ron, Bob called the team together for a quick update and task apportionment now that the items he requested had arrived.

"All right everyone, listen up," he began as everyone on their team settled into the small area. "First of all, thanks to Betty and Steve for bringing the files from New York. We now have what we need to wrap this up. Next, a quick welcome to General Charles, Chairman of the Joint Chiefs of Staff, who will be joining us in our work this morning. It's all-hands-on-deck for this effort I am told, and we got some pretty capable hands to help us out today. General, welcome."

"Thanks Professor, and thanks to all of you. Thanks for letting me work with you this morning. Please promise me two things. First that you will not do anything different because I'm here. Say what you think, do what you do, don't pull any punches or change anything because I am here. Two, remember if you need it, it's possible. My job is to make sure you have what you need to do what it is we asked you to do. No job too big, no job too small." He nodded back to Bob, about the same time a voice from the side of the group responded loud enough for everyone to hear. "Let's wrap up our test plan so we can get the actual testing done."

"That's the spirit, let's hear it," Dutch responded, and with that Bob began to fill in the remaining gaps for the group as the CJCS drifted toward the back of the group joining Steve and Betty so as not to be a distraction for the main effort. Bob provided a quick summary and related tasks.

"The computer guys and the space ops guys report that the CubeSats are settling into their assigned orbital positions in the grid and most of them are communicating with their adjacent cousin systems. Cousins are those within two to three layers of each system which are the ones they listen to, and the ones they talk to. The groups of cousins overlap, but they are insulated and isolated from the ones further upstream and downstream. This is both a security feature for the overall system protection and a capacity issue for the Thor's Hammers, so the power and weather modification do not get out of hand before we can both identify any anomaly and take actions to address it.

"Our immediate task is to assign a wave of small temperature changes to a random set of cousin groupings and proliferate those changes through the entire network and monitor that they are all performing as expected. We need to ensure these changes are discrete enough that they don't raise any eyebrows. The good news is we need to get this done yesterday. The results of our test will be the go/no-go for either loading the remaining CubeSats onto the spacecraft for launch or figuring out why they aren't working and reprogram or rebuild them to correct the problem.

"What I need from you guys is to split the test into eight mini tests that we can run through concurrently. Think of it like a shotgun start of a golf tournament. Everyone starts at a different hole and plays them all instead of everyone starting at hole number one and finishing at eighteen. It will go a lot faster, and everyone gets to play the entire course. Make sense?"

After nods, a series of questions, assigning regions, and discussing the collaboration, integration and coding, timeline review and final quality control, it seemed like the tasks were apportioned for each to break off and begin once the *questions and alibis* were completed. The timeline was aggressive but very doable given their approach.

"How many of us do you need to monitor the performance and the results?" one of the scientists asked.

"All of us. We succeed as a team, or we fail as a team," Bob began. "I, for one, would like to see the look on every one of your faces when this does exactly what we expect it to do. I think, our victory should be savored by all of us. That said, if you'd rather grab a nap or some quiet time, self-care or whatever, that's your call. I am sure we will have enough to cover whatever comes up in real time," Bob responded. "Anything else? Seeing none, let's go make this happen."

Dutch looked over at Steve who was smiling approvingly at Bob's response, and he quietly provided his own, "You know, Steve, some people get it and some people don't. Your guy Bob, sure seems to get it. It was not very long ago he had no idea that people, things, efforts like this even existed. Not only is he surviving in this new and stressful environment, but he is also growing, learning, thriving and shaping it. Trust me when I say you could do a whole lot worse as sons-in-law go."

Steve looked over at the General and smiled, "Yes sir, and trust me when I say I know. Yes, that much I do know."

CHAPTER THIRTEEN

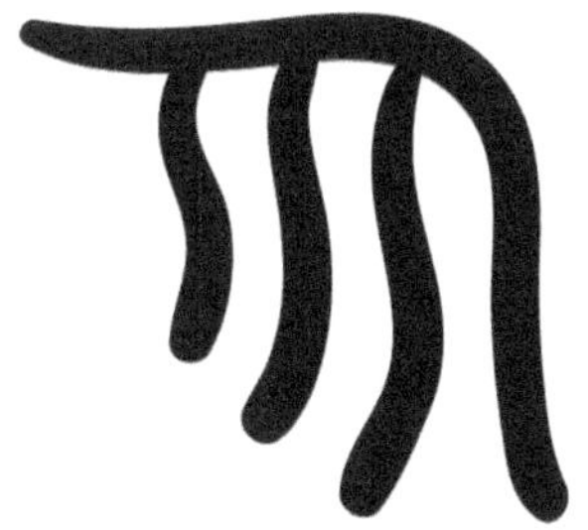

PROOF AND PUDDING

The day had been a long one, but the short nap on the flight down had helped him keep his edge. Despite the nearly impossible schedule and the complexity of the issues he needed to both understand and predict, General Charles could hold court on any topic in almost any company. The man never forgot a face, name, place, issue, fact, action or failure and he did so with the same measured competence regardless of the pressure of the situation. And this was just another in a long string of situations that turned out better than it otherwise would have because of his involvement.

He walked up behind Frank and tapped him on the shoulder as he ended the call he was on and was readying to make the next one. A little startled by the touch and a lot surprised when he saw who was doing the tapping.

"General Charles, Sir. Sorry I didn't know you were coming, let alone that you were here," Frank began but was cut off by the Chairman's smile and his calm voice that complemented his open hand facing the young two-star in a calming motion to stop.

"Frank, stop. You didn't know I was coming because I didn't tell anyone, didn't want to disrupt your work. In fact, that is why I am here. I'm here to help. And before you start to wonder what that really means, I want you to rest easy…you are doing everything *right*. That's the problem and what I am here to help with. You see we put you in an impossible situation and you're getting it done, just like we asked. But now it's crunch time and you need to focus. I am here to help you do that, to help you bring it home. And I do that by being here for a couple of days and staying out of your way but giving you more time," the CJCS paused.

Frank considered that and asked, "Schedule changing or something else?"

"No such luck, but nice try," Dutch began. "Schedule is the same. I know you don't have the luxury of concerning yourself with entertaining the notion of wondering how many people you have pissed off since we put you on this one-hundred-mile-an-hour train, so I will save you the brain cells. The list of who you haven't pissed off yet only has four names left on it, and that's OK from a mission perspective, but not a Frank's-career perspective. Again, clearly that is not what you worry about and, for that, I am thankful but that is partly why I am here. To take that heat off you down the home stretch and put it where it belongs...on me. I am hoping to carry most of it out the door with me when all this is done. I am retiring. People can dump on me as I head out but you can decide what you want to do next for yourself with a little less fire on your neck.

"That is part of it, but the most important part is you get a break by telling me what you need, when you need it and where. I will make it happen for you so you can focus on getting these test results and then doing what needs doing to get this second lift into space and filling in the gaps on orbit. I work for you now, so whomever you were about to call next, just give me the name, number and what you need and keep 'em coming. I will take it from here." Dutch held out his hand and could see the relief had already swept across the tired man's face as he smiled in agreement.

"Thank you, Sir, really. That means a lot. But, with all due respect, I need to make this next call myself. It's my daughter's birthday, and I haven't been able to talk to her yet." Frank was serious, and his face showed it.

"Take all the time you need, but first point me to a place I can drop my stuff and settle in a little so I can make good on my promise. I don't expect to be sleeping much so don't worry about a bed or a room, just a spot I can curl up in if I need to. I know we have a lot to do, so point me in the right direction." Frank pointed him to a corner in his makeshift office as he turned his attention to the most important call he would make all day. As he was wrapping up the call with his daughter, Frank was interrupted again by the four-star tapping him on the shoulder again and motioning for him to hand over the phone. Of course, that is what he did.

"Hello young lady, happy birthday," he said warmly. "You're very welcome. And I want to extend my personal apology that your dad is not home for your birthday. That is my fault, and I am truly sorry for that, but it is because your dad is the only person I trust to get this very important job we are doing finished in time to make a big difference for all of us. The President and the Secretary of Defense personally picked your dad, by name, to do this job and I am here to help him. My job is the Chairman of the Joint Chiefs and, right now, I am working for your dad on this job. It is really, really important work because, if he could, he would be there for your big day. He can't this time, but don't be upset with him. Be proud of him instead, ok? You can be upset with me because I am the one who needs to keep him here for a while longer. Sure, he is right here and yes, I will put him on," and with that he handed the phone back to Frank and shrugged his shoulders.

"Yes, that really was General Charles," Frank assured her. "Ok, I will ask him. Of course, and me too. Love you and happy birthday. See you soon," and with that he ended the call and turned to the General.

"Thank you, sir, that was very kind I really appreciate it. But she is a skeptic. Trust but verify, you know the kind, right? Would you mind a quick *selfie*? So, I can show her later it was really you; that was her ask."

"Smart kid, of course. Hang on." After a minute they both leaned in for the photo with the Chairman holding a piece of paper with *happy birthday* written on it. "Surprised she knew my name; it won't be hard to find a picture to compare this one to for verification, right? What's next?" The CJCS was happy to give something back to the man and his family who had already given so much to this effort from the beginning.

"Right now, we need to get the space lift loading plan dialed in. Space Command is really churning over these back-to-back launches," he began.

"Yeah, well good news. I did that before I got here and, to be honest, that was the call that made it clear to me I needed to come down. Those wheels are already in motion. What next?" Dutch challenged.

"I really need to check in with the communications and ops teams on their testing. It started off pretty positive, and I don't want to jynx it, but it was looking promising. You wanna tag along and listen in? If we need something fast it will come from those guys so that is your next target area anyway, as far as I am concerned," Frank reasoned.

"I'm following your lead, let's go," Dutch agreed and they headed off to see how operations were doing with the CubeSat initialization and integration. Next stop was to check in with the group that was collaborating with the team out in Colorado who were talking to and driving all these small satellites. While they could not actually control the constellation of CubeSats from their small work area tucked neatly away in one of the many military training areas in Florida they could maintain a continuous live audio, video and computer feed with those who were. With Frank in uniform his entrance into the workspace was noted but Dutch, still being in civilian attire, was able to blend into the background just enough to present as another grey beard technical expert on something or another. As he watched and listened, he could not help but appreciate the irony that he could go unrecognized in this setting when only a few minutes ago he was surprised that Frank's teenage daughter knew his name and his voice. He decided to keep his mouth shut for that very reason.

They had been testing the satellites' abilities to talk to each other and hand off simple instructions to their cousins down the line. The results were as successful as they could be and the group was demonstrating this for

Major General Lincoln who was quickly immersed in the discussion. Dutch knew Frank's background was not in space operations but you could not tell that by the ongoing discussions. He was asking the right questions and he was using the right terminology so there was little lost in the jargon or translation between the operators, the technicians and the decision makers. That impressed the Chairman, and he was seeing a prime example of what being a general officer was intended to provide. Frank was a problem solver who knew how to think, how to lead and how to produce the required outcomes regardless of the subject matter. He was not a technician with a depth of subject matter expertise that was far deeper than his breadth of experience who was promoted primarily to lead other technicians. And he was not one who was promoted because of who he knew, where he graduated from or what type of airplane he flew or how many badges and tabs he wore. Each service has its own favored tribes whose sons and daughters get further along than others, but it was clear to Dutch that the Air Force got it right with this man even if it whiffed on some of the others.

"So, what happens when we drop the second-lift birds into the gaps? How do these first ones who are now connected know to talk and listen to the new guys dropping in between?" Frank asked.

The voice from Colorado boomed over the speaker, "They are proximity linked based on an authentication code. We tell them, who to listen to and who to talk to, based on a radio frequency identification and a specific encryption code that has to match the send and receive modules. Think of it as space-based walkie talkies with encryption keys. They must be on the correct randomly selected frequency within their operating bands, and be using the right coder-decoders. Same concept as having 12 walkie talkies in the same room but the only ones that can listen and hear each other are the ones you key up the right way."

"OK but, how do we tell them. And who is the *we* that decides which ones talk and listen to which other ones," Frank continued.

"We do that based on position, that is the easy part. Once the second lift birds hit their intended orbit positions, and their comms are confirmed for both transmit and receive then we connect them into the network and introduce them to their neighbors, establish their roles relative to each other. Meaning who they transmit and hand off to and who they receive and take direction from. This can be in any direction because the tasks are transactional from bird to bird, but the result and impacts of these are cumulative to produce the desired, I mean the *programmed* conditions. Still tracking with me, Sir?" he paused.

"Yes, you're making perfect sense. That should scare us both," Frank encouraged the space systems operator on the other end of the call.

"Not that part, Sir, but this is the part that should scare us both. When we expand the existing constellation, we have to open up the existing crypto keys to let the new birds join in. Not a big deal if we got to do that all at once but we can't do it that way. We need to open each grouping individually to let the new birds into their cousin roles individually. That means for a few seconds that particular cluster is unsecured while the new bird is brought in and we have to do each new one individually. It's not ideal, but it is so fast that it should not be a substantial risk either. That said, it only takes one or two of these integration actions to fail and create a gap or new hole in the network. Not because of a lack of coverage, but because of a lack of ability to talk to each other for the birds providing that area's coverage."

He paused again, then picked up where he left off, "Technically we do this a lot and rarely have any issues. But last year bringing on a new bird we encountered some jamming precisely when we did a similar cutover. There were no known or perceivable electromagnet storms that could have caused that to occur but there was also nothing tangible to convince us it was a deliberate attack on our system either. If I'm betting your paycheck on one being the more likely cause than the other, I bet it all on a deliberate attack. And it worked. So, it is my belief that we need to keep a lid on when we intend to do this cutover."

"Absolutely agree with you on that. We know the CCP has ramped up all their surveillance systems, and likely everyone who can has a heightened threat condition and is keeping eyes, ears and sniffers fully engaged. How soon can you be ready to take the next round of CubeSats into the existing coverage?" Frank asked.

"A day or so. We should be FMC on all our systems by then, so we will easily be ready before you can get them in position for us to do our thing." His statement was met with nodding heads in Colorado and Florida.

"Sounds good. I am going to hold you to it, because we are about an hour out from our go/no-go call for loading the second lift. General Charles, do you have any questions for us, Sir?" Frank offered the opportunity to the Chairman, as many heads were turning and looking for anyone who resembled the big man whom they believed Frank was referring.

"Thanks Frank, just one question. What can I do to help?" he asked the group, but nobody could really specify any action or widget they needed but hadn't already covered.

"Looks like we are good here sir; how about we go and see how the weather technology team has progressed with their temperature test?" Frank invited as Dutch was already walking towards him eager to move on to the next success and thanking those closest to him as he did. As they walked off, the whispers and sighs of relief kicked into high gear as those in the room and on the other end of the call made sure to spread the word that the Chairman was on-site in Florida. As much as it may have been a quiet start in-house, his presence was no longer a secret nor was it meant to be.

"Frank, I saw General Chen in the group but he didn't say anything. What has his involvement been like?" Dutch asked.

"He's been a good contributor. He responds when asked, and speaks up with relevant input when he's not asked. We are both feeling our way through this, but it's not easy. He has a handler from the agency constantly hovering so that contributes to the idea that he is a part of the team, but not really on the team. Gotta be a struggle for him since he's only here because we put him in a position to pick his least bad option." Frank sympathized with the man, Chen, but not with the soldier that was Chen.

"Mind if I stop and chat with him? Consider it a professional courtesy and see what he has to say?" the Chairman asked.

"Your show, your call," Frank responded, and then realized that was not how the Chairman saw it at this point, so he corrected himself. "Sure General, I think that might be helpful to get his perspective if he can deliver it directly to you instead of it being filtered or reported. I think that is a good idea."

"Good. Follow my lead," the CJCS instructed and headed toward Chen and greeted him. "General Chen, how are you?"

"Fine Sir, I am treated very well, and my family is safe. That very likely would not be the case had I remained in China. Thank you, General," he replied, recognizing Dutch despite his attire, and in his calming demeanor continued the conversation.

"That's good, but we both know we put you in that bad situation. I don't expect any forgiveness for that, nor do I think you would have done things all that differently had our roles been reversed. I know to say this is difficult for you is a gross understatement. I am hoping we might have a very candid conversation about this effort, would that be alright with you?"

"Of course, what would you like to discuss?" Chen complied.

"First, the terms of our conversation. I am asking for your gut check candor, no polite formalities, no coy phrasing, no politically correct bullshit. I am looking for straight truths, man-to-man. For that, I am willing to do the same. What we say stays right here, you, me and Frank." He looked over at the agency handler who was hovering nearby, not quite close enough to hear their already deliberately soft voices and looking for an opportunity to close in and or be invited into the conversation. Instead, he was provided a very clear and deliberate personal invitation from the CJCS to get lost.

Both visually and verbally. He reluctantly moved across the workspaces where he could still see his charge but was not within earshot of what was being said.

"I will go first, if you agree to those terms and don't mind," Dutch began and continued as Chen nodded in agreement. "I am concerned that once we get this capability on orbit that my government will take swift action to demonstrate it to China. We both understand, peace through strength but I am concerned this will escalate quickly beyond that. There has been little response yet regarding the allegations from the UN summit. Do you think the people in power right now, who I am sure are preparing both a verbal defense and a kinetic response if they feel backed into a corner, are more inclined to employ one or the other? What would be the deciding factors here?"

"That is a big ask General; one might feel like a traitor to provide that information in this situation." Chen paused and let it sink in but seeing no inclination for the Chairman to pull it back or rephrase the question, Chen decided to continue since they both agreed to the same terms and appeared would abide by them.

"Back them into a corner without some face-saving option, thin as it may be, would likely make them shoot their way out. If they decide to do that, it likely won't be a measured response. It will be a response that ensures they can leave that corner at the time and in the direction of their choosing.

"They know there is no denying the evidence you have already. They know by now that you have Wu and me and they undoubtedly believe we have provided you everything we know. The best they can hope to do in the court of global opinion is to be forgiven. That is not a position they will find comfortable. That presumes they have done something wrong which needs to be forgiven, and that is the dilemma. In their minds and, for the perception of the people, simply being wrong and doing wrong is unforgiveable. That is their threshold and being hypocritical is certainly nothing new to them, but needing international forgiveness would provide a need for something that, even if granted internationally, would not be possible to grant nationally. General, I am afraid that there is no decision to be made as far as what they will do next. The real questions are what it will look like and when will it occur. That is what I think the actions at the UN have put into motion in my home country. I have considered this and said so before. I appreciate the opportunity to say it again to you in person but I still fear it may be a paradox in the minds of the party leaders. They, too, find themselves in a position where they must choose the least bad option. It would be nice if you guys could come up with a good option to put into these situations, occasionally. It would make it a little easier for those of us who find themselves having to choose." He tried to find an opportunity to establish some rapport with the four-star advisor to the President.

"Yeah, that is what I was afraid you were gonna say. So, with all this going on—putting this technology on orbit—and assuming it works, how do we keep the worst things from happening? How do we give them the room to take a least bad option as opposed to a full-blown throw down?" Dutch asked. "Mutually assured destruction is a pretty permanent solution to a temporary problem."

"You are assuming this effort will work but what if it doesn't? Or what if it does, but there are some unintended consequences, and this on-orbit global ability doesn't work exactly as it was expected to? That might change the dynamic sufficiently to provide a way out of the corner that does not include a shooting war," Chen offered.

"I thought we agreed not be coy General, what do you mean?" Dutch held him to account.

"Yes, well this effort is very impressive, but the timeline has forced so much as you say *corner cutting* and skipping normal procedures and steps that the probability that it is successful are extremely low. No offense Frank, but they set you up to fail. They hope you won't, but they must expect that you will. That is the only explanation for your President's announcement at the UN—beg pardon—*our* President's announcement. He is preparing in anticipation of having to grind the CCP in the unlikely event that it works or maintain the initiative if it does not. The President and the CCP are now both in the same position. Now they both need a face-saving way out or they need to be able to win a shooting war. You de-escalate for both by succeeding in this effort, but in such a way that it does not endanger either. That is what the benevolent illusion of the UN effort offered, but with that now off the table it needs a surrogate. I am not sure what that is, but we don't have a lot of time to find it and, if we don't find it soon, it won't really matter."

"Thank you General, this is the conversation I was hoping to have. If you were running this operation, what would you do differently to ensure it succeeded?" Dutch continued as Frank listened attentively, sensing correctly that his presences was as note taker and witness and not participant.

"Please, as I have explained to Frank and the others, Sir, please call me Chen. I am no longer a General, and in my mind, I failed in my duties to keep that title, so it stings every time I hear it. That said what I would change first and foremost is the timeline. It is unreasonable and the root cause of all the other things that are not happening but should. Chief among them is the frequency and depth of the testing. It is madness to put arguably the greatest technology ever developed on-orbit for global deployment without testing and proving repeatedly that every aspect of it works as intended. Much of this is being tested upon deployment or post deployment, and that is unsafe at best and reckless at worst," Chen scolded them both. "But I understand that is beyond your control thus far. Find something wrong and, perhaps, it comes more into your control?"

"Perhaps, and perhaps it also pushes that same controller closer to seeing the probability of an anticipated outcome as even more likely. That could speed up a path down that course of action and be an unintended consequence of a well-intended effort," Dutch countered.

"Now who is being coy, General?" Chen challenged the CJCS on their agreement, and both men smiled.

"Forgive me, I've been in this job too long. I have delayed my retirement once for this effort, and I fear I will get asked to do that again if the situation continues to escalate. I have fish to catch, and other things to do with my family just as we all hope to someday. Perhaps our families can meet in some fun activity when this is all done?" Dutch offered.

"I would like that and I am confident they would as well. For now, we must put all our attention into this effort succeeding so the President can see the situation from a different threat lens. I am not sure that success changes how the CCP will see it for the better but, candidly, that is a secondary concern. If the President does not have *Thor's Craftsmen* as a real option, it won't matter what the CCP thinks about this technology because they will be looking at other weapons as the primary tool and this only as an enabler," Chen concluded.

"You make good points Chen and thank you for the conversation. Now let's all get back to work to make this a reality, despite how unlikely some think that might be. They don't know what I know about this group; there is no *if*, there is only *when*. Thank you, and I am looking forward to going fishing with you," Dutch said as he motioned to Frank and both began to walk toward the workspace where the technology team was busy with their temperature testing efforts.

"That was helpful. Glad he felt a willingness to speak freely, whatever you are doing with him Frank, keep doing it," Dutch directed as they walked toward the team that was now keenly aware that Frank and the Chairman were coming for a check in.

"How does it look?" Frank asked as the two walked up.

Chief Andies took it upon himself to begin the response to the team, "If you are actively testing or monitoring, keep your heads down, eyes peeled and focus on what you are doing. You can listen with one ear while you are doing what needs doing. If you can't do that, then I will fill you in on what you missed later. Right now, if you screw up this test, I will personally see to it that you never have to worry about testing anything ever again. Stay focused, what we are doing right now is what we came to do, so do it right!" He then turned to the two generals and asked, "What can I do for you, General? Depending on your perspective, the timing of your visit is either perfect or whatever the opposite of perfect is in General-speak?"

"Shit, Chief. In General-speak, the opposite of perfect is *shit*. Thank you for what you are doing, and thanks to your team. The last thing we want to do is get in the way. That includes you Chief, if that is what your team needs to focus on. I am sure you have the same demands on you, and I don't want to be in the way of that," Dutch affirmed.

"Thank you, Sir, and, *yes*, I have a lot on my plate right now that I should be focusing on and none of it includes polite conversation with anyone. Will that be all, Sir?" Andies asked as Frank smiled and shook his head, but the Chairman was not to be excused.

"No Chief, that is not all. Is Mr. Wu over there integral to your testing or do you think a five-minute conversation with me would be low impact to your efforts?" Dutch asked.

"Yes Sir, that is Mr. Wu. And if you can keep him out of my hair for five minutes, I will be grateful. If you can do it for the next half hour, I will buy you both steak dinners. That I don't have an advanced degree in meteorology is not something he has been able to get over. Don't get me wrong, he's been very helpful but cannot seem to understand why I am not working for him on this effort instead of the other way around. Take him for as long as you need him."

"Thanks Chief, keep up the good work and finish strong!" Dutch said and stepped toward Mr. Wu, nodding to get his attention as Frank followed alongside.

"Good to see you again Mr. Wu, what do you think of the testing so far?" Frank began the conversation and waited to see if Wu recognized his companion, which he did.

"It is good General Frank and I hope it will stay good for the Chairman. Hello General Charles, I hope you find our work satisfactory so far." Wu was as politically savvy as he was technically adept.

"Good, that's good to hear. And how are you doing, Mr. Wu? I mean, with all this, it must be a challenging situation for you," Dutch began.

"Yes, yes this is quite an uncertain time I find myself and my family working through. As for the work, this is quite different than how we did things in China," he agreed.

"How so?" Dutch bit on the opening Wu dangled in front of him.

"The speed of the work is much faster than is safe for such a technology. The testing is very broad and—how do you say it?—*hand-waving* important milestones on through the process without really evaluating them thoroughly. And, if I may say, having an enlisted man leading the effort is most unusual although I find Chief Andies is not at all like the Chinese enlisted men that I have worked with. Those are the biggest differences but, if you would like, I will elaborate on those or provide more examples." Wu paused, waiting for Dutch to provide guidance. That was insightful in itself as it was clear from his previous engagements with Frank, as well as, this one, that he thought little of the military writ large but seemed to have no problem pandering to senior military leaders.

"That is interesting, Mr. Wu. I would like to explore your concerns about testing so, if you don't mind elaborating a bit, that might be very helpful. I am sure Frank here won't mind if you voice your concerns openly. After all he cannot fix a problem he doesn't know he has, right?" Dutch requested.

"Of course, General, and with no disrespect to General Frank who has been given an impossible deadline. But this technology, while sound, is being applied in a way that has never been done before, on newly modified hardware and software, and in a meteorological way that has only been tested and proven meaningfully in a lab but not in the real world. One of these things alone would be very risky, but to do them all at the same time is not safe. It is dangerous. These things should be done by seasoned scientists and not ambitious operations people."

"So, if you had the same deadlines as Frank, what would you do differently Mr. Wu, to make it safer and less dangerous?" Dutch asked, curious and hoping to gain some insights to the CCP process that he didn't already know.

"I would do several things, but the most important would be to test the other weather parameters before I loaded the remaining systems into the space craft," Wu began. "If something is not right, there is no fixing it once they are launched. And if something is not right, they must all be unloaded, fixed and then reloaded. That will foul any chances of meeting the deadline I understand we are targeting. How would you respond if you launch all of these systems and the only parameter that can be changed successfully is the temperature? And how will we know that is not the case before we launch the second group if we don't test other parameters? We really should test the rest of them, and I know that will delay somewhat. More testing, a lot more testing is prudent but even a little more testing is vital to knowing what will happen as opposed to hoping it will happen. After all, this is science and it can all be known but it cannot all be demonstrated with certainty without testing first," Wu paused.

"So, you are worried about it not working right. How come? Besides not testing it before it goes is there something in the methodology of the Thor's Hammers or the meteorology that gives you pause or perhaps something else?" Dutch continued.

"Yes, all of it. We know what our devices, sorry the CCP devices, do to the atmosphere from the ground and from the air but nobody has really tested what they do from that high up, from space. We saw only slight variations between the ground placed systems and the airborne ones, but there were some differences. Mostly in moisture content and the sort, but we have no plans to test any of that before load and launch. We have only one ongoing test that this upside-down weather of Andies' will work, and we only test temperature. It is not enough. I understand you are rightly worried that the CCP is monitoring and will likely detect anomalies related to additional test. I helped alert you to and design the tests to lessen those risks. But the risk calculations are all very impacted by the timeline, and I fear that may be a fatal flaw," Wu confided.

"I understand, yet the President gave us the deadline and that is not going to change. If anything, he is likely to speed it up not slow it down. What would you test in the remaining time after the temperature test but before the pending launch?" Dutch asked.

"That is a very short amount of time General, too short for any meaningful and substantive checks but a similar pressure change could perhaps be done if we replicate the temperature test. If the temperature test was compromised, doing the same thing with very minor pressure changes would likely confirm for whomever was monitoring that something was amiss. Contrarily, if the temperature test is wholly successful and undetected, the risk of doing the same for pressure would be lessened, and without another test to be detected it could still be declared an anomaly." Wu considered what he proposed after he said it, rather than before.

"What do you think, Frank? Is that doable or too much to put into the mix at this late stage knowing the schedule doesn't change?" Dutch was thinking out loud.

"We talked at length about this General when we built out the test plan. For lots of science reasons, Chief and Professor Mcleod having heard all the discussion determined that no matter what we tested or the results, they would be either inconclusive because of their subtly right after the temperature post-test stabilization period, or they would have to be so substantial that detection was near certain. The way the devices work independently and when networked is the same no matter what parameters we program. So, if it works for one it *should* work for all and vice-versa. So, we put all our eggs in one basket with the design parameters of the ongoing temperature test. Like you said, we didn't get to change the schedule. Do that for us and maybe we come to a different conclusion, but it won't change the underlying facts around the operations of the systems just the confidence in how they will perform…or won't perform," Frank added for their consideration, and then invited Wu to comment on what was just said.

"I agree with General Frank's conclusions. Change the timeline Mr. Chairman so we can do the needed testing. Don't change the timeline, and the risk increases exponentially. That puts the fate of this entire effort on Chief Andies' upside-down idea working just as well, or just as poorly on everything as it does on the temperature. That is a big risk, and I hope he is right in his calculations but I don't have the same confidence in his work as you all seem to have."

"Fair enough, Mr. Wu and thank you for your candor. This has been very helpful for me. I should let you get back to your work, and we must resume ours." The Chairman decided to terminate this conversation in exchange for the next one. They did not reach the steak dinner threshold, but far exceeded the five minutes the Chief needed to simply be grateful.

"I need some time with Mcleod and Zack. It doesn't have to be now, Frank, but it needs to be soon," Dutch explained. "If you have something you need to attend to, don't let me stop you. If you have another fifteen minutes, it will be good for you to hear this discussion too. After it, we will have some tough decisions to make and I don't want to paraphrase what I heard. I need you to hear it for yourself."

"No time is a good time, so let's do it now. If something goes to shit, they will find me; they know how," Frank said resigned to finish what they started.

"Good, I am following you." Dutch looked around to see which way they might be headed. Frank led him outside into the warm humid air and across some rough pavement and into another maze of hallways, rooms and poorly lit makeshift work areas until he found Bob and Ann huddled over some computer monitors. They greeted each other and within a few minutes Zach and a couple of his security monitors joined them, curious about why he was summoned to what looked like a high-level discussion given the company he found himself among. After a few minutes of niceties, the Chairman asked for everyone's full attention and their candor.

"You all have been immersed in this effort, and you all have a lot of experience in research and development, and with this specific technology. More than most, but this is nothing to play with. We all know this is not a game, but I am going to ask you to do something you might perceive as game-like. I can assure you it is anything but. I am going to ask you one question, and I need you to immediately respond with either a thumbs up for yes, or a thumbs down for no. Can you each do that for me?" Dutch asked, and looked around to see everyone nodding in agreement.

"All right then, once I am done asking the question I want your gut level response immediately, not looking around or at anyone else. There is no right answer, this is an opinion question. Ready...once this is on orbit will it work?" the CJCS asked the four people in the circle, and looked quickly at their hands and saw all four had their thumbs in the same direction. Four thumbs up.

"OK then. Thank you, now I am going to ask you all the same follow up question, but this time I want you to each write down your answer. Again, immediately after I ask it, your gut response a word or phrase max five seconds. Write it and push it into the middle. Will you do that for me?" All agreed and found something to write on and with, and when they were ready the Chairman asked the following question, "*If* this technology fails, why does it fail?"

After a few seconds everyone had met the Chairman's conditions and there were four pieces of paper with a few words on them lying together in a small pile. He reached in and separated them enough to see the words written on them.

"The people using it," was the first one he read. "The President" was the next, "Power and greed", and finally "Human nature." In a matter of seconds, they had all reached the same assessments for both the fielding of the technology as well as the results of its operation. It took them less time to read the assembled responses than it did to write them, but consensus was the same as unanimous.

"All right, that seems to be a sad consensus," Dutch said, "and the last question I have for you I will ask you to answer out loud."

"How do we keep it from failing like that? Everyone willing to answer can, I don't care about the order." As they looked around, Zach decided to seize the opportunity and go first.

"Make sure this President is not the one who gets to operate or specify outcomes without other checks and balances in place. Lots of transparency on its use or every one of those answers is a guaranteed outcome, and not a prediction. I have seen every side of the man in my past role, and I promise there are sides none of you have seen. Why do you think Tom has been so scarce lately? It's not because he has great faith in you all; it's because he is up to his ass in prepping what his boss is going to do with this once he thinks it's good enough to use. I can make this case with shocking examples to support every one of your answers, and you know which one was mine," Zach shared his opinion without hesitation.

Ann followed with this, "People are the reason every tool or technology has ever failed. In one hand it's a tool; in another it's a weapon. Rocks, guns, food, water, weather. It's not the technology, it's how it's used."

Frank did not want to have the last word, he thought that should be Bob's, so he went next, "Absolute power corrupts absolutely. This is as close to that as humans have ever come."

He left it at that and looked over at Professor Mcleod, who opened with, "That leaves me still holding the problem General Chen left me with earlier. What's the difference if we are doing this for CCP or the US, same outcome just under a different flag. I struggled with that, still am. But I think the difference is us, the people having this conversation. Would this be the same conversation in the CCP? We know the answer to that question is *no* because they have had a decade to change something they have not. We are having this conversation, but in a fraction of the time they had to consider options and act. And maybe some who expressed dissenting opinions met a horrible fate, but that too continues to this day.

"They killed Doc Auster to ensure they could maintain the course they were on, so even ten years later they made the same decisions. They had power, they were making money, and they were willing to kill their own and our innocent citizens to keep it. That is the nature of some people, and the need to keep power and maintain stability is the nature of every government. It seems there are people we can put our trust in, but in practice I have not seen that same trust earned by the governments that presume to represent those individuals. That is my struggle. That is why I took it to the UN initially. I love my country, I think it's the best one on the planet; really, I do. But I don't know if any government in history, present or future can be trusted with this. That is a hard, hard truth and I just don't know the answer, General," Bob concluded, looking flummoxed at the Chairman.

"Me neither, Bob. And thank you all for the candor. I know we have lots yet to do, and I don't know if this is the best place to leave this discussion, but it is where I am going to have to leave it. I have a meeting in a few minutes, and I am not looking forward to it. I suppose on this, time will tell. The proof is in the pudding, as they say. Let's hope the testing concludes successfully and we get these next lifts loaded and on orbit. That will give us the ability to work on the next tasks which are all associated with your written responses. I really hope you all are right about one of your answers and wrong about the other. And in case you are wondering about where I stand in all of this, I can assure you we have unanimous consent. Thank you for sharing what you think, it has been very helpful for me, both as a person and as the Chairman. Now if you will excuse me, I really can't be late for this one." Dutch headed off on his own as the four others stood there wondering silently what to do with all of that, and what to say next.

"All right...that will go down as one of the weirdest meetings I have ever attended. But if there is nothing else you need from me, I was in the middle of a good movie and am really curious how it ends so I am gonna get back to it. Let me know how the temperature test turns out will you?" Zach asked as he turned and walked away from the group. Then they all headed back to check in on the temperature testing which they had been away from for longer than any of them felt comfortable

CHAPTER FOURTEEN

SEND IT

The Chairman found a quiet spot in Frank's office and waited impatiently for the communications Sergeant to connect the right wires, boxes and crypto keys so General Charles could join the secure video conference with the others who were largely attending in person at the White House. Dutch was thankful that she finished the connections a few minutes before the meeting was to begin so he could compose his thoughts before he delivered them. It was always risky to think and speak on the fly and given the circumstances he knew it would be foolhardy to do so right now given what was at stake. It didn't help that what he was thinking was certainly going to be unpopular no matter how he phrased it. *So why struggle with it, just do it,* he concluded, as the President walked into camera view and seated himself so they could begin.

"All right, sorry I am late, but a lot of people are wanting to know what we are or aren't going to do. Candidly, so am I. So, let's figure that out here and now, shall we?" the POTUS began and motioned to Secretary Fitzgerald to kick things off. "Fitz, what do you got?"

"Sir, the Chinese aren't talking much on their typical communications channels, but they keep increasing their readiness postures across all services and systems. The message is getting out, and while they are making it hard for us to hear about it, they are making it easy for us to see it.

"I have not had any contact from my Chinese counterpart and back-channel sources aren't talking either. He has not responded to my calls. The embassy guys and the military advisory groups are just as tight-lipped right now. The only trickles that are coming into us are the standard state department and political advisory statements which all refer questions to the CCP. They aren't talking about anything besides how disappointed they are about the UN collaboration ending, and their ongoing internal discussions regarding the CCP's options for using their on-demand weather modification technology.

"For our own efforts, the Thor's Craftsmen project is making substantial gains. They are on the tail end of testing and we should know soon if the second space lift will go up in a few days or, if they will need more time, due to some test results. Dutch is on site down there and on the call if you have anything specific you want him to address," the SECDEF offered and paused for the POTUS's response.

"Thanks Fitz. Dutch, what do we need to know that we don't already know?"

"Mr. President, from what I have seen, we have a basic IOC, Initial Operating Capability, for the constellation of birds but the weather modification ability is still being tested so no on-line capability yet. Should have preliminary results in a few hours, and that will drive the lock-and-load timeline for the CubeSats with the weather devices for the second round of rockets. I have to say from what I have seen thus far; this group is making it happen. Once we get the second lift loaded and launched, we ops check it all, and go from there. If I was a betting man, and you know I am, I would bet on this testing being successful and the most likely timeline from what I see here is another week and half to two weeks and we will know what is and what is not functioning on orbit. Not sure where we get these people, but damn glad they are here and getting it done," Dutch reported.

"Good Dutch, thanks. That is good news. Go ahead and start loading the next lift and get them up as fast as possible. I'm a betting man too, and if you are betting on the testing working, then I will assume it did unless I hear otherwise. In the meantime, let's save a day or more and get the rest of what we have available assembled and loaded up so we can shoot these things into space as soon as the doors close, and the boosters are full."

"With all due respect, Mr. President, that was not what my advice was intended to convey, Sir. While I have confidence, that's not the same as me recommending it. That's a lot of risk and it's not yet prudent. Any minor modification or small amount of retesting to ensure valid results will cost days. And it's still a couple of days before we know with certainty that these CubeSats are good to go and ready to load even with no modifications. We can't pull them back once we send them up."

"Thanks Dutch, I got that. I need you to start loading and get them up there as soon as they are loaded. Once they are up and filling in the gaps, then you can test them to your heart's content, and maybe you can even operate them while carefully recording the results and call it live ops testing. Like you said, we got the best people making this happen, so make it happen," he concluded.

"Sir, this is already a lightning-fast effort but a couple of days to dial in and make sure…" Dutch stopped when he recognized the President's hand was elevated. Both he and the President were speaking at the same time.

"I didn't stutter Dutch, I said load 'em as is and send 'em. Pack them all in there and get them into space where we need them," the President ordered, and while he recognized the CJCS's sage advice and position, he was not about to tap the brakes on anything they were considering, regardless of who was asking. "SEND IT General Charles. Clear enough?"

"Yes, Sir. Crystal. Will put it in motion," Dutch confirmed with the tone of his voice clearly indicating his dissent with the decision along with his confirmation that he understood the order and would carry it out.

"Good. Thank you. Now what are we expecting the CCP to do once they decide to get off their asses?" POTUS advanced the discussion, but the CJCS was still fuming over the previous discussion and direction. And that didn't change as he recognized the voice responding to the question as Tom's. The National Security Advisor was in the room with the President and had a detailed list of bad news about what the CCP was already doing, and what they would likely do next. In a nutshell, it appeared they were preparing for a shooting war, and they appeared to be posturing for both initiating hostilities and defending against them. In these cases, it is difficult to discern preparations as being intended for offensive or defensive operations, but there are subtleties to be seen by those in the know and Tom was one whose job it was to be in the know.

"It looks like they are readying for a *trigger*, some actual or perceived action they can point to as *the* provocation that pushed them into taking offensive operations. But I have no doubt they intend to go on the offensive. What remains to be seen is when, and what story they will use to justify it. Candidly, they already have three such events they could play right now. The first is they could claim we stole it and took it to the UN without them. The second is announcing that we actually stole one of their regional airborne systems and then destroyed the rest of them. And the third is you calling them out at the UN summit. In their eyes they could maintain that they have shown restraint already but must act in defense of *our* aggression. We need to keep our version of the facts out in front on the global stage, and we need to remain convincing because there is a plausible counter discussion to be had if they go there," Tom explained and then paused for reactions and direction, but he was a bit surprised at the reaction and from whom it came.

"Why would that perspective not be publicly supportable if they claim any or all of them?" Fitz asked, and quickly followed before anyone could respond. "I mean the actual harm here is all about what they have done in the past. We should be focusing on demonstrating that past harm they did to us, and to the world in the years they had this technology and hid it. They used it against people around the world. Lied about what caused these events and drove national policies, inflicted damage costing fortunes and pushed opinions in the direction they wanted based on the covert application of this on-demand weather technology. I think this is one of those situations where we need to stare intently into the metaphoric rear-view mirror and glance up at the windshield to make sure we don't run into anything instead of the other way around.

"If we focus on a shooting war, the reason we entered it becomes a footnote in the history books while we all focus on trying to win a war…or how not lose one. In fact, this could very well be the next phase of their long game plan. Consider it. They have been using this technology for a decade and plotting out its course. We have been discovering and reacting from day one on this, and we still are right now. If you think the CCP assumed that we would never find out then you don't know them. They hoped we wouldn't, but I promise the CCP I know would have prepared for *when* we did find out not just hope we wouldn't. They have consistently shown us things to look at and focus on while they were busy doing something else that they did not want us to know about or pay attention to. Do you think it's possible they are doing the same thing now with the big military preparations? If they are showing everyone that, what are they hoping we aren't seeing or looking at? Who is following the money, their money? Are they consolidating assets? Selling them off? What is happening there? When has it ever been about anything other than power and money for these guys? Why would we expect that to change? When we freeze their assets or lock up their resources that is what their *trigger* will be. That will be us escalating to economic warfare, inflicting harm on their civilians by freezing their leader's personal assets, which incidentally are comingled with Party assets for that exact reason. An attack on them or their assets, is an attack on China and the people of China. Not acceptable for them.

"They don't want a financially or politically expensive war any more than we do. They are willing to put their citizens on the battlefields and lose them in droves, far more willing to do that than put their own positions of power and fortunes at risk. So, the relief valve for this has far less to do with who has what militarily. It has to do with who is willing to blink financially and politically. This is not about territory, technology, culture, citizenry or ideology at this point. Nope. Right now, this is about saving face and saving fortunes. That is the currency they are dealing in, and it would appear that is the same currency we are dealing in, as well. So, where is the win-win in those terms? That is what we need to understand, and that is where we should be focusing our attentions." Fitz, sat back down and waited to see what kind of incoming fire his remarks would bring.

"That sounds a lot like a man who does not want to have to do what he is being paid to do," the President pushed back on his SECDEF. "I know you are no coward Fitz, but we are running headlong into World War three here and you want me to take a knee? After what they have done to this country, you want us to back down? Maybe you aren't the right man for this job given what is happening right in front of us." The POTUS's words were intended to be harsh, and they hit their mark.

"Maybe not. I serve at your leisure, Mr. President. So, you can send me packing whenever you choose. But I am the right man in the right place at the right time for this exact conversation. You have *not* finished what you started at the UN. You have *not* publicly provided numerous examples conclusively proving what they did, and how they did it. You have *not* offered an acceptable consequence for their actions, a sufficient level of accountability for their *past* behavior. You have *not* given them an off-ramp to consider, or counter. You had a mic-drop moment, and the press is dribbling out examples of things that appear to be—or that certainly indicate—you were correct, but there is no litany of smoking guns that provides irrefutable proof of what they did. Mic-drop insults, backed by little more than our own press passing reports that are speculative at best, look to everyone like a throw-down because they are. *We* need to finish that chapter before *they* start shooting because we have not given them an alternative to consider. Without that, we can be pretty sure what is coming. And at this point, I am not convinced that is not your preferred option, Sir."

You could hear the oxygen leaving the room as the SECDEF concluded and the POTUS' face reddened. "That is some kind of gall, Fitz, some kind of gall to accuse me of wanting a war where we can be sure many people will die. On both sides. That would make me a piece of shit who worries more about elections, power and money than my own countrymen and even theirs for that matter. That would make me just like them. That would make us just like them. The gall to suggest that, to think that," he fumed as he paced back and forth quietly considering his next words before he spoke them. He stopped in front of his SECDEF and leaned into him, making eye contact as he inhaled to say what he decided needed to be said.

"Screw you for suggesting I would prefer that or somehow want that eventuality for any reason. But thank you for helping me see that is how they might be seeing our actions and that they might consider an alternate way out if we present them one. That is an idea we will need to consider more immediately and in depth so we can decide what to do with it and what plans to alter. That said, we will do that without you, Fitz. Thank you for your years of dedicated service to your nation, and for your loyal support to me and my administration…right up until today.

"You are excused to go write up your resignation. I will reluctantly accept it before the end of the day when I will announce on your replacement. Best wishes Fitz for you and for all of us in these difficult times ahead. We will need clear minds to navigate this turmoil and I understand how yours might not be aligned with what must be done in these dangerous times. That will be all." And with that, the President of the United States pointed his Secretary of Defense to the exit of the White House situation room for what would likely be the last time.

Secretary Fitzgerald stood up, shook his head slightly and popped a salute to the Commander in Chief, who reluctantly returned it and then watched as the disappointed and, now *un-appointed,* SECDEF walked through the exit.

"Well, that was a very uncomfortable situation I am sorry you all had to see," the President offered to those in the room and still on the line. "Now, we should probably take a few minutes to make sure we are all still on the same page. First and foremost, Tom would you please see to it the agency and DOJ expedite the forensics on some of these cases so we can have some ironclad examples of what the CCP did. I want something solid, but I want to be able to release it with a statement from me directly within twenty-four hours."

"Yes, Sir. We have some already. I will get some more added in and have something ready for you tomorrow," Tom confirmed.

"Good, thank you," the President said now pleased to have regained his composure and having re-established what he considered a tone of compliance within the meeting.

"General Charles, my previous directions remain unchanged. Are we clear?" he asked.

"Yes, Mr. President. I am very clear on the direction you have given me and the actions which I must take," the Chairman confirmed.

"Good. Everyone else, do whatever these two need from you to carry out their actions. You are all excused, I have to decide on a new SECDEF," he said and walked out.

Bob was pleased with how well the temperature test had proceeded. Everything he was responsible for addressing had performed as intended, and he was pleasantly surprised at how well the weather changes were flowing through the network. The atmospheric changes were very precise, and the handoffs between the CubeSats and their cousins to enable the designated changes to flow from one system to the other were much smoother and natural than the professor expected. It seems Chief Andies and Mr. Wu were both remarkably good at what they were doing despite their natural friction. The thing that Bob was struggling with was the encryption keys that were needed to enter the commands that would dictate what parameters would be met.

The teams had modernized the input coding for the on-orbit Thor's Hammers and rendered them quite distinct from the versions Bob was used to using. They had completely abandoned the idea of using recipes for desired outcomes for a more simplified and direct command screen that was laid out by specific parameters and desired events. So, you could change the temperature or atmospheric pressure within a finite set of parameters, or you could allow the system to regulate those in order to produce a specific event such as a wind gust, or a rain shower at a specified location and time. There was a *within-identified-norms* menu screen, which allowed the operator to select atmospheric conditions or phenomena that were within the climatological norms for a location or larger geographic area. The command screen indicated that the subtle temperature change testing was being controlled and monitored.

Beyond that, was an advanced user screen which required a completely different set of bona fides to access and another one to operate, or input commands. This is the one that contained the selections for significant variations from normal conditions. This included the menu selections that could call up such conditions as tornados, high winds, gusts, hurricanes, heavy rain or snowfall, extreme heat or cold, and every other impactful meteorological condition that would inflict damage or discomfort on the intended target location. Bob and the team had, of course, tested the access to those commands menus and ensured they operated all the way up to *GO* but, given the low-key nature of the testing, there was no way outside the lab to verify these substantial events would form up when commanded or behave and subside as commanded.

That was a great leap in faith that everyone involved with the *Thor's Craftsmen* program understood, but it was the one thing they all worried about no matter their role in the program. For now, they were incrementally, sequentially and diligently testing out the system from the foundation through its initial operations and, so far, everything they tested was working as intended. The hope was that would continue throughout the systems as they put them through their paces, all in good time. That said, everyone also recognized that *hope* is not a course of action. The familiar phrase, which had become a military mantra over the past couple of decades was perhaps as true as it had ever been given the potentially catastrophic events that could occur with even the quirkiest of malfunctions of on-demand weather technology. But Bob could not wonder about these things right now, he was struggling to get the access codes correct so he would not be locked out again for too many incorrect attempts to access the operations menu with the correct passwords.

"Hey Chief, would you please look over my shoulder on this? I am on my third attempt and these twenty-seven-character passwords are simply kicking my ass without enough coffee. Why don't we just use something we will all remember like pASSwords1234567890ALLsuck! That would be easy to remember and hard to hack, right?"

"No Professor, sorry but I used that one already so it would be easy to hack since we both already thought of it," the Chief responded, only half-jokingly as Bob wondered if he really had come up with the same one.

 "Seriously though, I understand the security access and all that as far as keeping unauthorized users out but why make it so hard for authorized users to get in and use it? Especially if we need to do so in a hurry," Bob asked, sincerely wondering about what appeared to be a common practice across the program.

"It's another distinction without a difference, Bob. If you make it easier for the authorized users, you cannot help but make it easier for unauthorized users to get in, as well. It's not a complicated concept to grasp once you are sufficiently caffeinated," Andies replied as he handed Bob a cup of lukewarm coffee from the pot that had been turned off an hour ago. "Here, see if this helps."

"Thanks." He took the cup and winced as he swallowed the bitter brew and continued the discussion, "So, right now we are testing what is on-orbit. We all have access to the systems to ensure they are talking and working together as they are supposed to. Once that is done—the testing I mean—what happens then? Who operates it, and what do they need to do so? Who controls, or watches or changes who gets to do what? How will that work?"

"Depends. I mean the mechanics don't really depend on much because that is just encryption and coding. Who gets to do what, who has access and when is something that I suppose is still being worked out by folks well above my paygrade. Imagine they will let us know when we need to know. Seems that is the way these programs tend to work," Andies observed, which was one of his greatest skills. He was an exceptional observer which is one of the reasons he was such an exceptional forecaster.

"And now you are in...the coffee must have helped. Once you're finished walking through the event screen options to make sure they're all functioning, let me know. We can then go through the failsafe menus together. Remember, that takes two security keys to get into?" he added.

Bob was still fuzzy on all the computer options available in the updated menus, so he asked the Chief for some clarification, "So, when we do that, can you refresh me on what all that includes? I mean I know it allows us to terminate an out of parameter order, but I don't really understand what else is in there and what it takes to employ it."

"Sure, but it isn't much more than that. It's an over-ride that shows you all the pending commands and event orders and lets you cancel them or let them continue. Think of it like your network printer Bob, when you have a bunch of pending print jobs and yours is a rush. You can pause them and put yours through first as a priority, or you can cancel one, some or all of them. That's about all there really is to it, conceptually, but I will show you how to do it when we are in there," Andies agreed.

"Sounds simple enough. I know how network printers work even without enough coffee," Bob smiled and took another sip from his cup.

"Fair enough," Bob agreed and got back to his testing. After a while of putting it through the myriad of menu options and combinations, all of which reminded him of the various ways weather could be used to inflict harm on people, events, or places Bob said he was ready for Chief Andies to help him though the failsafe testing screens. As they logged into the next layer of menus, Bob noticed the much different layout of the screen and the options presented so he commented on them.

"This doesn't look scientific at all, Chief," the Professor noted.

"Nope, sure does not. Because it's not science at this level, Bob. It's pure operations if we must go in here and start giving commands. These are the *do-this-don't-do-that* screens. This is where we tell it to stop it right now, or to send it, and send it fast. If you are in here, it's because you no longer have a reserved seat at the kid's table. There won't be a lot of time to think or debate, consider or wonder how did that go again? This is designed to be idiot proof even under the most stressful conditions, which is what whoever is in here will be enduring. Think of it as what Mr. Wu would have wanted to have during the UN demonstration in Australia. If he had one of these in Australia for their airborne systems to help him through what we did to him, we probably wouldn't have succeeded and we wouldn't be here today," Andies opined.

"That makes a lot of sense. So how does it work?" Bob asked.

"There are three modes in the first screen that help populate your drop-down menus for the events that need to be addressed. First is an event mode, if you are looking to shut down, stop or initiate something on a specific spot. You can either terminate an ongoing event by location, or you can initiate one. See here? Just go through the screens to find your spot and your event and hit the big red X or the big green check mark.

"You can do the same thing by region. You use the cursor to draw the area of concern. Then it's the same idea. Pick from existing jobs or start a new one and tell it what priority to give it. Red X or green check mark.

"The last one is a bit more complex because it also includes intruder detection options. So, if we get hacked or if someone who is not authorized gains access, there are some fail safes that make sure nobody can do too much damage even if they do get in where they don't belong. It also protects us from *gomers* who are allowed to be in but don't remember their training. Don't be a *gomer,* Professor," the Chief cautioned.

"I will try not to but, remember Chief, you are the one training me so I will always have a viable excuse for my shortcomings," Bob nodded as the Chief shrugged his shoulders in tacit agreement and continued.

"So, this works in a couple of ways, but different events can trigger it. First is your *go-to*, the wrong password too many times. That triggers a lock out. Once a lockout occurs, there can't be a new input or command triggered until new-user authentication occurs. I will get to that, so hold your questions please. If you are in and working, and you put in a command sequence that is outside your approved input authorization, same thing. So, like right now, we are doing minor temperature changes from the operations screen. Normal stuff. If you tried to send a hurricane to a specific location, that is well outside the use-case permissions you have with your user bona fides so that would also trigger a lock out. You with me so far?"

The Chief paused and waited for confirmation. Once the Professor nodded and agreed, Andies continued, "OK, good. So once a lockout is triggered there are a couple of options to resolve it. The first thing that happens, no matter what the trigger, is an alert goes to the command screen to let the operators know of a violation event. Then a similar notification is sent to each of the cousin CubeSats for wherever the violation command was initiated. When that happens, the cousins all suspend any ongoing commands and retrograde their areas to the normal climatology for that area and time. That makes sure things don't get out of control, and it makes sure that there are not any whipsaw condition changes from different inputs. It goes to *normal* and stays there until a new verification sequence is received before it can move off to respond to a new command," Chief explained.

"So, I like the insurance policy, and I understand the gradual default back to climatological average as the reset conditions. But I am not sure I understand the sequence or timing of the resets to get there or back out of there. Especially if we are in a hurry or stressed to respond to something that is ongoing, that sounds like it is on an entirely different tempo than emergency response?" Bob questioned the now-smiling E9.

"Good, then you do get it," the Chief nodded. "What sets the tempo, and the corrections are the keypad inputs. An unauthorized access triggers a reset with a randomly generated password sent to the operator, and that must be uploaded to the primary CubeSat and its cousins in a specific amount of time to restore the system. The time can be set by the operations chief console to reflect the threat condition, or the violation response as needed. The cypher is a randomly sized string of randomly selected and sequenced letters, numbers and symbols that is encrypted and sent through a random communications path to each CubeSat. The good news is it is pretty hack proof; the bad news is it is pretty hack proof. So, this all happens at every whatever number of minutes is selected until the system is reset and the authorized operators resume control of the system.

That means if we are locked out, or there is a breach our own system cannot be hijacked and used against us. It goes to *climo* until we provide the proper authentication to regain control. If one node gets blown up, we do it from another system control node on the network, which we can access from any computer really, if we put in the right codes. Physically it is safe because it is networked and can be accessed remotely, and it's operationally safe because it defaults until it is authenticated, even if that takes a while. They might find a way to take our proverbial weather gun from us and even point it at us, but they won't be able to use it on us."

"That makes sense, but not by looking at the screens in front of me, Chief," Bob complained.

"OK, so click there. See the authentication screen? That is where you put in your credentials. Go ahead, put in the wrong ones so you can see it here first, because I am sure you will see it again," he encouraged Bob, who complied, and the blinking screen came alive and more urgently demanded additional input from the operator. "Right, now you get another chance to get it right, but in this big event screen you only get two opportunities…read that as *one* mistake Bob. Put it in wrong again, we might as well test what we are here to test," Andies instructed and Bob cautiously complied.

"OK Bob, you got it wrong twice, well done, Gomer. Now the system has locked you out, sent a notification to the command console, a notification to the device you were trying to communicate with as well as all of its cousins. You need to reach out to the command node, if they haven't already called you to find out what the heck is wrong with you. In this case that is my console, where I will find an updated command sequence and the crypto key to unlock your mistake as long as I can put in my correct controller authentication code. And that looks like this." The Chief skillfully clicked and typed and clicked some more and within a few seconds he had cleared the errors, recovered the system and put things right enough to get Bob another chance at putting in the correct user ID and password for the ongoing testing.

"Good, that worked like it was supposed to. You are more trained than you were when we started. You're good enough for now, Professor, I have some more stuff I need to grind through before General Lincoln, and probably the Chairman get back for an update." The Chief was telling Bob that was all the time he had for him, and, in this case, the training and testing was all Bob needed to kill both birds with the same stone.

"Yep, thanks Andies that was super helpful, I think I got it but if I screw it up it's gonna all be on my trainer." Bob smiled as the Chief walked away with his hand held high...his middle finger extended above the rest. "Gotta love these Air Force weather guys," Bob said as he turned and almost ran into Frank and the Chairman.

"Sorry Generals, I didn't really see you coming in behind me. Everything ok?" Bob stammered.

"Not really Professor, but if you will come with me, I would just as soon explain this once," Dutch requested, to which Bob agreed and fell in step alongside Frank as they followed him down the hall. It didn't take long to get the couple of others into the room so the CJCS could say what he needed to communicate to the group.

"Listen up. I just got out of a meeting with the President and am here to communicate his orders. We are to commence loading the rest of the Thor's Hammers into both the east and west coast space lifts and get them on-orbit ASAP. I have already had the discussion about testing, risk reduction, supply limitations and decision prudence and the orders are as I have communicated them to you. Every assembled operational system gets loaded into one of those two rockets and we launch them as soon as they are loaded, fueled and in the right position to light them up. Fill 'em up and send 'em as soon as they are loaded. And that means whatever systems are ready in hours not days. Is that clear enough, or do you need me to clarify any of it for you?" The Chairmans' voice was clear and sharp but had an edge to it that was not typical of his conversations earlier in the day.

"Seeing none, please get to it and let me know if there is anything you need that I can help with. Frank, a minute please?" he said and waved everyone off in an informal but clear dismissal to go do what needed doing.

"Yes Sir?" Major General Lincoln asked, his concern visible across his already tired face.

"In that same meeting that I received his direction on this, he sent Fitz packing. The POTUS fired the SECDEF so by end of the day we will both be hearing about his replacement. Fitz got sent off not for what he said, but for what he insinuated about the President wanting a fight with China and putting us on that path by not giving them an out. I don't know if he was right or not but I never saw POTUS that lit up with a member of the cabinet. So, I have to believe the nerve he hit was a live one. He was out two minutes after he said it to go write up his resignation. You need to know that and you need to keep your head on swivel. If he is willing to do that to Fitz, then it makes me wonder if he was right. You know we are a means to an end; we are active-duty officers, so we come and go...expendable. I just didn't expect this level of expendability from him. Extra vigilance is now called for," Dutch said, with a sorrow in his voice that Frank had never heard before.

CHAPTER FIFTEEN

NOW YOU'VE DONE IT

To the world the global news cycle was divided into two main categories: what was going on with respect to every aspect of on-demand weather modification and everything else. The President of the United States held a news conference with very little lead time, and appeared with the Vice President, the Secretary of State and the, until now, Deputy Secretary of Defense to announce that Deputy was no longer in his title. Given the out-of-the-blue announcement and that Secretary Fitzgerald was not standing among them, it was clear to many that his departure was directed. That was the POTUS's intent, and the announcement clearly indicated that was the case.

It seemed both unfortunate and unnecessary given the state of uncertainty that existed regarding the next steps for China and their ongoing military readiness increases. Again, the President appeared to be intentionally making his intentions unclear which could only serve to confound and concern the CCP. Their established lines of communication and relationship with Fitz were knowns, but now those too were uncertainties. The US had introduced another variable into the equation at an inopportune time. While the Deputy Defense Secretary was known in these circles, there were many more unknowns than if the same conversations were being held with Fitz, the man whom they had been dealing with for several years now and known for much longer.

The *new guy* would have to spend some time learning and growing into his new role, and of course prove to his boss that he made the right choice. What that would look like for the CCP was now seeming to have been made deliberately unclear with Fitzgerald's removal. And the optics seem to indicate that he did something to trigger his sudden removal. *What was that?* they wondered, as did many of those watching the new Secretary of Defense express his appreciation to the President for the faith in his abilities to take on this prestigious and vital national role. He promised to do everything in his power to accomplish what was being asked, to defend the nation he loved and to represent those who stand in the breach every day to protect her and her citizens' interests at home and across the globe.

It was a sufficiently righteous speech that checked all the boxes, used the right buzzwords, thanked the right people and promised the right things. The man didn't get to this position by only being someone's mouthpiece, but he was certainly comfortable enough in that role when he needed to be, and this was one of those times. That did not sit very well with General Dutch Charles, the Chairman of the Joint Chiefs of Staff whose position requires working hand-in-hand with the SECDEF. Dutch was already not a fan of the Deputy, and that he was tapped to replace Fitz in a manner that would tarnish his reputation did not sit well with the Chairman. The *new guy* was not new to Dutch and this was adding insult to injury as far as he was concerned. To say he was unhappy with the decision would be a substantial understatement, but Dutch also knew that, at these levels of government, professionalism and courtesy were critical to success. Much could be done behind closed doors but, when facing the public, it had to be a united front and seamless implementation of decisions made. Just like at home, you can fight like brothers with the doors closed but you stand on the porch shoulder to shoulder to protect what is yours from others intending to do any of you harm.

Steve and Betty came into the office together not knowing it was already in use by the General because he was sitting in the corner with the television on. The commentators were providing opinions on the big story of the day, and seeing if they could connect it to their list of other big stories about weather modification, the UN summit ultimatum, the CCP actions and potential plans, and how the rest of the world could respond to the myriad of possible actions either might take.

"Sorry General, did not see you over there. We can go and leave you to your…" Steve offered but was cut off mid-sentence.

"No, Steve, Betty…don't be silly. Come on in. Your timing is perfect actually, I don't need to be alone right now anyway. My mind might take me to places I don't want to—well don't *get* to—go," Dutch confided.

"I am sorry to hear about Secretary Fitzgerald. He seemed like a good man. We didn't spend a lot of time with him but, when we did, he seemed like one of the good guys," Betty offered seeing that Dutch was struggling.

"Yeah. Yeah, he was—well *is*—one of the good ones," he smiled.

"And the new one? You don't seem very happy about this new guy. I've only seen him on TV occasionally; never met the man. What do you think of the President's pick?" Steve asked.

"Mom told me, *if you can't say something nice then zip it skippy.* Now seems like a pretty good time for me to follow that advice, if you know what I mean?" he replied.

"Of course, sorry General I can see that was not a question I should have asked as it puts you in a bad position. I understand and, candidly, that is kind of what I was expecting to hear about this guy. Well, I hope he turns out to be more of an asset than a liability," Steve apologized.

"Time will tell. As with most things, time will tell," Dutch offered. "Now what have you two been up to and what can I do to help—either what you need or what you've seen that needs some help?"

"Not much really, to be honest. It looks like we should be asking you that question really. We could use something to make us feel more useful and you look like you could use some kind of help, but I don't want to offend you by saying any more." Betty tried to give a supportive look that was not to be confused with one of derision or judgement.

"To be honest, I could use some advice. Who better to give advice to a seasoned operator than a couple of seasoned operators? How about a cup of coffee and some opinions; would you do that for me?" the Chairman asked.

"Of course. We got on the same page coming down here; no problem seeing if we still are, or touching base to make sure we still are," Betty agreed to the request for both of them.

They sat and talked for the better part of half an hour, sipping coffee and *what-iffing* a variety of hypothetical situations and decision points. He called it a sandbox for developing potential courses of action and Steve called it talking things through, but Betty called it just doing what friends do for friends. And while all three of them were correct, it was clear that the conversations they had on the flight down had laid a fast but strong foundation for some weighty discussions that would influence the CJCS's views on one of the most important issues in the world and how he would advise the President of the United States on that vital issue. It's what friends do for friends; it's what Dutch and Fitz had done so many times but, until this very moment, he hadn't recognized that for what it was. It was also then and there that Dutch Charles chalked that up to a lesson learned and a mistake he would not make again.

As if on cue, Ann joined them in Frank's office, "Hope I'm not interrupting, but I was looking for the two of you. I can come back later if you need some time to finish up."

"No, Ann, please join us," the Chairman insisted. "I would like your perspective on something we have been discussing if you wouldn't mind."

"OK, if I am free to give my opinion, I am pretty willing to do that on almost anything when asked. What's the topic?" she agreed.

"End states, Ann. Specifically the end state of what we are doing here. Is this something you would be willing to offer your opinion on? I mean beyond the discussions we already had or, perhaps, a continuation of those discussions? Hypotheticals only, of course. We are deliberating prospective responses to various potentialities and such."

"OK, pretty vague but OK, I'll give my opinion. What's the hypothetical?" she asked and the General looped her into the ongoing discussion.

"OK, the not-hypothetical baseline is we are currently loading all of the remaining CubeSats into the launch vehicles in California and Florida. Everything that can be assembled, programmed and loaded safely will be finished in time to button up the rockets and launch them as soon as that's done. The Cape launch will be early tomorrow, and the Vandenburg launch will be later the same day, as soon as, we get the right position to lift off. The President gave that order earlier today. That was in the same meeting where he relieved Secretary Fitzgerald from his position as SECDEF," he paused to make sure Ann got all the foundational information he intended to convey.

"Yes, I heard. There is a lot of secrecy here but it's pretty hard to keep a secret. Especially when everyone here is jumping through hoops to accomplish what you just explained. I am sorry about Fitz, I like him. Thought he was doing a good job, too," she confirmed.

"He was. That is what got him relieved, I am afraid," Dutch added but Ann quickly interrupted him.

"Pardon me if this is an insensitive question, but do you think he is likely to do the same to you? I mean you are doing a good job, too. Frank is literally a miracle worker; do you think you guys might be next?" she jumped ahead.

"Hard to say, really. But realistically, I don't see that happening to either of us until after we have the capability launched. If that goes well, then it makes sense to keep us all on it through testing. When it comes to operationalizing or turning over the launched and tested system, then I will change my answer. If we are going, that is when he should—pardon me—that would be when it would make the most sense to remove us if that was determined the most prudent action. That, of course, depends on what the CCP does in the meantime. It also depends on what POTUS and the new SECDEF do with respect to the CCP in that same timeframe. And those are the hypotheticals I would like to hear your thoughts on." He smiled, and Ann nodded in agreement as Steve and Betty listened to what had become a dialogue rather than a group discussion.

"Assuming we get a reasonably capable system on orbit and it works such that we have confidence in its performance, how do you think it will be operated? What decisions, decision-makers and utility do you think will go into its use or operation, Ann? *Thor's Craftsmen* program is a success. Now what?" he posited for her consideration.

"It's a military-led program now. I don't see that changing. It will be a crucial national system for the US to pursue its national interests. Just like it was for China when we got involved with it. The difference is we didn't know about their capability and, while you guys might hope they don't know about our on-orbit capability, it's very different. We didn't know they had *any* ability to modify the weather and they used that on us, and others. Now, they know we know they had it, and they also know we have everything they had. They will expect we will have even more at some point. They will also expect we will use it on them, either to get even for the past or to shape the future. They will correctly predict we will use it on them for both retribution and to meter power and resources in the future. That means it will stay a military system. It was always going to be that way from the very beginning. I can see that now but I was more hopeful earlier. Actually, I was far more naïve earlier but that is clear to see in hindsight. That is my opinion, General, and it will be tough to change it at this point," Ann concluded.

"Thank you, Ann, and would you clarify for me if you mean it will be tough to change your opinion? Or did you mean it would be tough to change the outcome that you think is coming?" Dutch followed up.

"I don't see a distinction really," she answered unemotionally.

"What if there were? What if the premise was changed to not having an operational military system? Would that be something you might also opine on?" he asked carefully and, when she nodded, he continued.

"In our earlier discussions, several key concerns were raised about the speed of development and fielding, the lack of testing and even the confidence in those who might be operating or controlling the system once in place. Suppose, for the sake of discussion, hypothetically speaking of course, that a perfect storm of those conditions was to impact our system and it was not ready for prime time for some period. With low to no confidence what might that look like?" Dutch asked.

"Not very different really, just worse outcomes. I see the people in play right now would still direct its use and hope for the best. The President seems bent on getting this on orbit for the actual or perceived threat of using it on the CCP like they did on us. Even if the on-orbit systems weren't working well—or at all for that matter—they would revert to the regional airborne systems or put individual systems out there and do it one device at a time. The genie is out of the bottle, Dutch. We can't put it back in. That's why we went to the UN after Bob made the deal with the President for the billions. Bob didn't trust him then; he doesn't trust him now. The on-orbit systems work, or they don't. That doesn't much change the landscape of the technology being out there now. It just impacts the scale and proximity it can be employed. In the end, it's a technology that enables power, influence and resources and somehow those always end up in the hands of governments instead of their people."

"Damn, that is cynical, Ann," Steve chimed in, "realistic and probably correct but pretty cynical."

"Who do you think I learned that from, Dad? Like we said before, it's human nature. That's my opinion, General Charles. It's inevitably a military system operated in government interests by people who may or may not legitimately represent those interests. At this point, that is the only perceptible difference between the US leading this or the CCP. We are the free country who represents individual choice, freedom and our personal happiness as opposed to the collective happiness however the government defines that. At least for now, that is the hope. Time will tell," Ann paused.

"Thank you again for your opinion, Ann. What if I were to tell you with certainty that was not a predetermined outcome. That your opinion is still as likely to be incorrect as it is to be correct?" Dutch asked.

"As likely? Fifty-fifty? I'd say I don't see that as being realistic at all. But I much prefer those odds over the ones I see now. Again, my opinion." She smirked sarcastically but was hoping the Chairman might continue down the road she had already spent considerable time traveling down earlier.

"Again, hypothetically, if you could do something to even the playing field to fifty-fifty would you be inclined to do something that might produce those odds?" he asked her and watched closely at how she answered when she did.

"Depends on what it is. The ends don't justify the means, and if the means are something that make me as bad as the people we are worrying about then, no, I would not be inclined to do so." She was really feeling tested at this point, and starting to worry about who was implying what.

"That is what I was hoping to hear, thank you. If there was a way to put the proverbial genie back in the bottle, would you do that? Or would you prefer a world with this technology, imperfectly employed as it turns out to be over a world without it?" Dutch seemed to be landing on a point.

"Knowing what I know now, and knowing what I expect will happen. I would much prefer this all went away over what I expect would or could happen with it now. I think I'd prefer a world where nobody had it over a world where some have it and some don't. What a pity that is, when I hear myself say that out loud it makes me sad," she concluded.

"Thank you all for your opinions on this. It may very well have been the most important hour I spent today. It has shaped my thinking in a very beneficial way, and for that I thank you. If you will indulge me, I may at some point in the future refer rather cryptically to this conversation. I hope, if that time ever comes, that you recall it as favorably as I do. Thank you, and if you will excuse me, I have some space-lift things I need to address, and the time is shorter than ever." He thanked them and departed urgently to address whatever was pressing for his attention.

"Was that weird or is it just me?" Ann asked Steve and Betty, who both responded at the same time, "Just you." The three laughed and then continued talking about what Ann missed before she joined them. With that, it made much more sense to her, and it appeared that her answers were aligned with the earlier conclusions.

"Now you've done it, Ann. You went and put us all on the same page by independently verifying what we were thinking earlier," Betty smiled. "Do you think Bob will see it the same way you do?"

"He usually does, but it takes him longer to get there. I think it's all the weather stuff he knows that clouds his thinking. Pun intended just for you, Dad," she smiled and high-fived Steve for the bad joke.

"That's my girl. Speaking of Bob, we probably should go check in on the testing and the load-out to see what kind of help he and Andies need," Steve said, and the three started the short walk to their work area. As they walked up, it was not the typical dispersed flurry of activity. Frank was holding court with the technology team who was busy providing input and taking actions as the discussion was fast, precise, concise but also very broad as they were finalizing the actions needed for finishing and loading the systems. This was no time to interrupt and the three joined in silently and listened intently for actions they could take and contributions they could make.

The next several hours seemed to pass in minutes. Hasty actions, calls, emails and computer commands were all punctuated by brief infusions of caffeine, sugar, jerky and whatever else could be used to infuse some small level of fuel or boost for those pushing to get everything loaded in time for the launch windows at the two sites. It was a flurry of activity with Dutch, Frank, and occasionally Bob on calls, video conferences and follow up meetings and updates. The surge of activity resulted in them meeting the tail end of the east coast launch window. This was punctuated by a brief but jubilant cheer at lift off followed immediately by a resumption of activity to make sure the west coast launch window was met as well. Which they did. Once that success was also jubilantly recognized, the leadership team of the *Thor's Craftsmen* program was called into their de facto briefing area for another secure video tele-conference. This one included a lot more of the on-site team members by design and, when the encrypted screen finally lit up, it did so with the seal of the President of the United States, who was ready to greet the group as they joined a larger meeting that was already in progress.

"Welcome to our team in Florida who are now joining us," POTUS began as applause from the others on the VTC could be plainly heard. "General Charles, I trust you are there somewhere...Dutch?"

"Yes Sir, still here," CJCS responded loudly from the side of the group as it appeared on the screen.

"Congratulations General Charles, General Lincoln and the whole team there in Florida. Both launches have been confirmed; you've done it. I gave you a seemingly impossible task, with an arguably impossible timeline and you've accomplished both. Now you've done it all right! You have set a new bar of excellence that others will now be measured by. You have succeeded in a spectacular manner and for that I am profoundly grateful, and I wanted you all to hear that from me directly. You should be rightfully proud of the work you have done, the contributions you have made to this program, to your organizations, the nation and, in fact, to the world. This work is historic, the impacts will also be historic and at the same time vital to the future.

"That said, your work is not complete. Though we are close, we must finish strong. We must test and integrate the new on-orbit systems into the existing network and get this thing up and running as an operational system. I know that will take a little more time. I am asking that you catch your breath, take a short break, and then transition to operations as quickly and successfully as you got these things up there to protect us all. *Finish strong* is the catch phrase for the tail end of our *Thor's Craftsmen* effort. If we all do that, we can have this operational and get back to our families and our lives knowing we did our part to field perhaps the greatest technology known to man and, on a scale, never done before.

"Once again, I thank you for what you have done and thank you in advance for what you are about to do. I beseech you to finish strong!" With that the President applauded the Florida group as did the others. He then waved and the screen went blank.

"All right, everyone you heard the man," Dutch said to the group in his *outside voice* which succeeded in getting everyone's attention. "Finish strong for us means we start transitioning to IOC procedures and continue lighting up these birds, getting them into their correct spots and making sure they can talk to us and we can talk to them. Once that is sufficiently demonstrated we will commence the operational testing to make sure the on-board systems are performing properly. If you need a break for a nap, a shower or a hot meal, now is the time. If you can get all three, then you probably don't understand why we are here. Thanks everyone. You've done it, now you get to do it again!" the Chairman concluded as the team cheered and clapped on their way to get it done.

Bob, Ann, Steve and Betty began their walk to get something to eat, feeling good about what they had just accomplished at the same time anticipating the upcoming surge of operational testing of the newly launched systems that should round out the existing network.

"I do want to go over the ops testing plan one more time, Bob, to discuss the changes we are integrating from the lessons learned by the first systems tests," Ann stated very matter-of-factly.

"I don't remember reviewing changes to the test plan. When did those come through? I must have missed them but that doesn't surprise me. I am running on fumes," Bob confessed.

"They haven't yet. You missed them because you were busy and you are exhausted. I'll fill you in on what you already know but need to hear again. There's time, and the changes are minor. It won't be difficult at all," she assured him as they arrived at the food line, met with greetings and congratulations from those already in line ahead of them as well as those who arrived behind them. It felt good to succeed, it would feel better on a full stomach and another cup of coffee.

CHAPTER SIXTEEN

MEANING WHAT?

The screen went blank, disconnecting the *Thor's Craftsmen* team in Florida from the broader meeting. The President continued now that he was confident the distant team was clear and would not be hearing the rest of the meeting.

"Tom, have we heard any more either formally or backchannel from the CCP after our west coast launch?" POTUS asked his National Security Advisor.

"Nothing publicly, but privately we have received several inquiries regarding our intentions for these two unscheduled launches. They can see all the CubeSats we put up, and they will see soon enough that these are going to be more of the same type of craft and that they are filling in gaps among other similar birds. It's unclear if they know what these are or what they are capable of. Right now, they represent a new and urgent something, a something that the US was not openly talking about. Put that in the context of what has been front and center on everyone's mind across the globe and the task is really to convince people it is not related to weather modification technology. The ongoing assumption is that it's something to control the weather, or some way to counter it. The CCP is hoping for some indication or clarification on which one it is. They are looking for something to help guide their next moves," Tom paused.

"Meaning what, Tom?" POTUS asked him curtly.

"Meaning it appears they are increasingly less subtle about asking for us to indicate our intentions. The longer they don't hear plainly from us, the more they will have to assume we are preparing offensive operations. They will continue their preparations. Metaphorically speaking Sir, they have pointed out that they have their turn signal on and are looking for an exit from the road they are on. We can tell them which one we would like them to take or we can stay silent in which case they will either pick their own exit or simply turn off the signal and stay on the road they are on. That's what it means Mr. President. It's our action, and inaction is its own action."

Tom stopped, looked around the room with contempt at those anxiously squirming in their seats, obviously freshly chilled to the thought of speaking their minds given what happened to Fitz. The new SECDEF was especially uninterested in doing anything but listening to the others as he was still coming to grips with his new position and the circumstances which put him there. It's hard to give sage military counsel to the Commander in Chief when you aren't inclined to speak on a topic of vital military importance as a course of action is being decided. Whether this was what the President wanted or not, this was the outcome and a direct consequence from his previous actions.

"What do you think they want to hear Tom, and what would they do with it if they heard it?" *Now that was one of the smartest questions the man could have asked,* Tom thought as he considered how best to respond and guide the President toward a de-escalation plan that everyone seemed interested in hearing about but were unwilling to start.

"I would start with, we won't tell the truth about you and your past if you don't lie about us and the future," Tom began.

"Meaning what, Tom?" POTUS asked impatiently.

"We make good on your UN promise to expose them, but we pull punches when we do it. We can let the world know the CCP had it for some time and, while they were researching and testing there were examples where they created events that—well—got out of hand and had substantial impacts but weren't deliberate acts against us. New technology often has issues, this was no exception. Similar to the unfortunate UN wind event in India. As a result, China, in an effort to prevent a repeat of some of their earlier problems, agreed to come clean. That is why they confessed to the technology being theirs and their level of experience with it. Once they understood the level of confusion regarding the timeline and evolution of this technology, which was laid bare at the UN with the President's speech, the two sides quietly came together in a series of bilateral meetings to understand the evolution and create a common understanding so both can move forward with a safe and stable application of this capability.

"They won't call us out for stealing and destroying their advanced regional systems leaving them vulnerable to our offensive operations with an advanced technology we don't really understand but are willing to use despite knowing the impacts in order to prevent it being used on us. They won't blame us for any and every weather-related event that has a negative impact on someone or something. That is what I think they want to hear.

"What do I think they will do with that if they hear it was the second half of your question, Sir, and the second half of my answer is this. I think, with that getting into the news cycle and becoming known, they will use that opportunity to de-escalate militarily. They will provide a version of each set of events that makes them look more victim than perpetrator, but they will also not be attacking us while they do their own damage control. I don't think it changes anything long term in the sense that we will remain peer competitors with opposite ideologies. It won't make us friends and allies, but it avoids a showdown right now, and for who knows how many decades beyond that," Tom concluded.

"So, they want us to blink, so they can take an offramp to regroup, refit and come at us later when they are better prepared to win, at a time and a place of their choosing? Why does that sound a lot like capitulation to me? And why would I choose that instead of throwing down now and taking away their ability to come back for us later? How does that improve our national security posture, Tom?" POTUS pushed again, his blood pressure up at what seemed to be another run at his apparently favored course of action.

"It moves things to the right, Sir. It avoids a near term fight where both sides can escalate sufficiently to assure the other's destruction including nuclear exchanges and, if that doesn't do it now, we can do weather warfare. We both have the ability to literally send hurricanes, tornadoes, hailstorms, blizzards, floods and whatever else at each other until ultimately, if we are lucky enough to survive all of those things, we find ourselves right back where we are in today's meeting with the same objectives of de-escalating and finding a win-win. If we can find that now, instead of after countless people die and fortunes are spent, then that to me is a national security victory, Mr. President. Some can win more than others and still call it a win-win. Same goes for a win-lose or a lose-lose, they are never even splits." Tom concluded with, "That is my perspective for your consideration, Mr. President." He recalled that he was looking for a job when this one found him and he was sure he could find another one if this conversation earned him a walk down Fitz's path.

"That is a lot to unpack, Tom, but I can see the wisdom in exploring that course of action. Do you think your counterparts are able to get the CCP anywhere near that potential alignment of our efforts should I be willing to entertain such a notion?" POTUS asked.

"Yes...yes, I do. I can say with certainty they would consider something like this because they brought much of the idea to us. Something like this is what they are looking for. They don't want to lose their fortunes and families any more than we do," Tom offered.

"I see. Not to be callous but I do not intend to walk down a road like this being led by some middleman bureaucrats on either side who may not translate nuanced words or intentions precisely. If he is serious about pursuing a version of this, then get the word back that I want this to be a sit down, just him and me. And it needs to be done here in DC. Not a neutral site, not an objective third party nation ya'da ya'da. He asks to come here, in person, and talk to me about this in my house. When he asks, I will say yes. If he doesn't ask, I will know his true intentions and take actions accordingly. So, get the word back to him, first action is on him and whether he takes that first action or not has meaning."

"Yes Sir, I will put that in motion directly upon the conclusion of our meeting today," Tom agreed and his response indicated he understood what he was to do from the President's direction.

"In that case, we are concluded Tom. The rest of you get this on orbit system wrung out ASAP. We are gonna need to do something with it as soon as we know the CCP response. Go make this happen, history will judge how well we did it." POTUS ended the meeting, the screens went blank, and the rooms began to empty. Except for Tom who was instructed to hold fast as the other principles departed the Situation Room. The President strode up to Tom, put his arm around his shoulder and smiled as he leaned in and softly spoke into his ear.

"You troop lead me like that again in a crowd of my key staff and you will never again see the light of day. Now together we are going to finish this weather thing with CCP, and I hope to God you can pull off this win-win you say they are open to. But if you can't get him to ask within the day, then we fire both barrels of their past events and what they did to us into the press. We will publicly embarrass the shit out of them, and then blast them all to hell as soon as they look at us cross-eyed for exposing their dirty past. That can be part of your message delivery if you think it will help. Meaning this all ends very soon, Tom. One way or another, this ends very soon. Clear enough?" he asked as he clapped the top of his shoulder as he stood straight, still broadly smiling.

"Crystal clear Sir," Tom confirmed while the distance between them increased rapidly as the President walked out and Tom stood flat footed watching the leader of the free world move on to his next task.

"Now don't take this the wrong way, Bob, but I don't understand how running the same test on these as we ran on the ones before can be a bad thing," Frank protested. "I mean we know how it behaved previously. We add in the new CubeSats, the primes and their cousins talk, do their hand offs and we watch it ripple through the system just like before."

"That is precisely the problem with that approach Frank. It's just like before," Bob said as if that alone should be enough to make his point.

"Meaning what exactly Bob? Why is that the problem?" he pressed.

"Meaning we won't really be able to tell whether this is just the previous test working again along the same handoffs. We need to confirm that each and every one of the CubeSats that are supposed to be doing something, or confirming they have nothing to do, actually do that in the sequence of commands. That means we don't really have a conclusive test if we use or do the same thing. Get it?" Bob explained, a little exacerbated but trying to be patient with the pilot.

"OK, I see your point. Doesn't mean I agree with it, but I see it. So, what do you suggest given the short timeline and the continued direction that testing be benign and discrete at the worst, and undetected at the best?" Frank needed to make some decisions and he wanted to do this testing criteria planning with them, not to them.

"Wind is another one that can be objectively measured and very precisely deviated by direction or speed to be easily hidden in plain sight throughout the entire system without raising too many flags. We can put surface wind conditions through the system and track them with precision. It's as easy as doing it with temperatures and it gives us more options to vary the commands. Winds have always been the round two plan for that reason. So, I don't understand why this has become a big deal or who is making the case to do temps again, but changing it now is not smart in my opinion." Bob was tired but understood this was a marathon and he had prepared for it, so he wasn't so tired that he was delusional or missing anything big yet. At least that is what he thought.

"General Chen thought it might be prudent to expedite the testing given what the President is pushing Tom to talk to the CCP. It's getting to be crunch-time and the margins are getting slimmer. That's why the revisit, Bob. For what it's worth, Wu and Chief Andies are in the same camp you are. I already asked them before I came to you. I wanted independent recommendations not a team position or anyone being influenced by group think. Sorry, Professor. I was not looking to undermine your position I was looking to ensure collective scientific objectivity," Frank quasi-apologized and quasi-rationalized his actions.

"Careful, you are starting to sound more like a General and less like a friend who is also a Colonel," Bob said and regretted saying it before he had even finished the sentence.

"Well, Bob, I am sorry you feel that way, but a lot has changed for the both of us since then. Rest assured, I still consider you a friend and I value that friend's opinion. Always have, always will. So, let's do the wind parameter and get started with it. I am hearing it should only be another couple of hours, maybe less before we have the rest of the birds in position and shortly after, the rest of the position controllers, power shields and comms should all be fired up. How soon can you start flowing that wind test through the system? And what do you need that you don't already have to make that happen?" Frank added.

"Sorry Frank, that didn't come out quite the way I wanted it to. We can start as soon as you give the word. That is what we were planning on testing, so we are ready. The temperature test would have been the change, and we would have needed another eight to ten hours to transition to that. What I need is for you, or anyone else to *not* change our test plan this late in the game. It may sound simple, but it's not easy to change it now," Bob offered in response, although it felt like it fell well short of what he should have said.

"OK then let's lock it in and get it going as soon as I give you the green light. Trust me when I say I know there is a lot of pressure on you right now, and trust me when I tell you there is a lot on me, too. Once this is done and we can take a deep breath, I think a steak and a few beers will help us make all this right after the fact. In the meantime, let's focus on finishing what we need to finish. I'm good if you are," Frank suggested as he was almost to the exit.

"That sounds good to me, Frank. We're good. Like Dutch said, let's finish strong," Bob agreed as he turned to head over to finalize the preparations with Chief Andies and the rest of the technology and weather team. It took a while to load the commands and the monitoring scripts to the control module but they were ready well before Frank gave the greenlight to send the test sequences. For all the hurry up that went into the preparations, now was the wait part. That did not provide comfort to anyone on the team. What it did provide was an opportunity for everyone to wonder and worry if they did everything they were supposed to do, or if they didn't do something they should have, or forgot something they shouldn't have forgotten. The wait stage puts everyone on edge. It's not fun, and it's not for the faint of heart.

When the call came in and Chief Andies heard General Lincoln's voice on the other end tell him he was cleared to commence the testing you could hear a collective exhale from the team. The Chief echoed the General's clearance to proceed while confirming what he heard and informing the team at the same time. This was common practice. That is when your anxiety transforms to adrenalin fueled excitement. Right or wrong, that transition point where you shift from wait to go is like an emotional catapult.

"It's *go-time* folks. We are cleared to commence the testing sequence. Professor Mcleod, would you do the honors, Sir? The command screen like we trained, Bob, authenticate then *let 'er rip tater chip!*" Andies smiled the smile of equal parts excitement, relief, concern and outright fear.

"No, Chief, that twenty-seven-character password is not my friend today. If it's all the same, I'll pass on the test launch. Maybe I could raincheck for next time and give it a go for the initial operational commands if we are still here for those. That be OK with you Andies?" Bob requested.

"Fine by me, I got you. How about I sign in, get us to the ready screen and then let Mr. Wu hit the go-button on the test? What say you, Mr. Wu? I kinda still owe you one from before. You want to launch the test sequence?" The Chief extended an olive branch.

"Thank you Chief Andies. Sure, why not? It's a big deal and I would like to have a part in putting this new chapter of our project into operation. Symbolic as it is, I appreciate you offering me the privilege," Wu agreed and recognized this as another step toward integrating into his new life even though it was not of his choosing...well, not initially.

"Ready when you are Wu. Mash the green checkmark and our test will begin," the Chief directed and, when Wu did as he was instructed, the cheers went up from those around him. The test sequence coding began uploading to the control system and the network of satellites that would now be the make or break of the on-orbit weather on-demand strategy of the US. They would all know soon enough whether the system was performing as they had hoped while they monitored the surface wind direction and speed.

Ann held Bob's hand tightly as they watched the many screens with scripts of code flashing past faster than it could be read by those looking at it. The myriad of displays indicating direction and speed at key ground observing stations were translated into a series of green, yellow or red lights strung around the globe. Each one indicating whether or not the expected wind conditions were actually what occurred at the stations as the testing worked its way through the MicroSats in the network and translated the commands into conditions on the earth's surface. When the green light came on the first spot it meant the command was successfully received by the satellite. The command was translated and communicated to the weather modification module and the module executed the appropriate sequence, then passed action to the cousin systems it needed to advance the tasking. Green was good. Yellow meant, there was a system issue, and the action was being tried again. After ten failed attempts the system would terminate the pending action and the light would turn red. Red meant it wasn't going to happen from that command, and the action would need to be resent if it still needed to be done to meet the tasking. It was simple to follow, simple to interpret but not easy to watch during operational testing. All green, no red was what everyone hoped to see during testing, and it was what everyone would expect to see during operations.

"Green is good," Mr. Wu commented nervously, as he was the least comfortable with the sustained silence while the testing was underway.

"Yes, green is good," Bob assured him. "So, what do you think of this Mr. Wu? Seeing the technology, you worked on for years evolve from the surface operations to airborne regional systems, and now to a space-based global capability. You have seen this from its early stages to the most advanced. That must be satisfying, at least from a scientific perspective."

"It is, Professor. Seeing something evolve; advance if you will. It is not unlike watching your child grow. You do what you can to help it develop; to reach its potential. That is very much how it is with this, Bob. Sometimes it goes fast; sometimes it goes slow; sometimes it hurts; sometimes it makes you swell with pride. Today, for me, is all those things. I am happy to see the technology advance. I am curiously nervous about how it will be used, who will be using it and what they will use it for. Time will tell. It is as you say, a bitter but sweet feeling, Professor. Bitterly sweet," he nodded.

"Fair enough, and I completely understand that perspective. Like you, I did not see this as being the desired outcome when I began to work with this technology. Clearly our involvement with and understanding of the technology were very different, but I find us strangely ending up in the same spot with similar perspectives at this moment. Quite different but very similarly convergent paths that put us side by side today for this test," Bob acknowledged.

"Perhaps more similar beginnings than you might imagine Bob," Wu corrected him, which he rarely missed an opportunity to do once presented. "Like you, I was exposed to this technology and first utilized it in its ground portable configuration. I was not part of the team that created the technology. Much like you, I was brought in shortly after that to help determine what to do with it and how to do it. Our journeys are more similar than you acknowledged. I want this test to be successful just as you do. I think we both want to see this used for what it was intended. Controlling the weather is a tool as you told me earlier; it is no better or worse than the persons using that tool. I hope it is good people using this. In the past you might say there were bad people using it, and maybe you would be right. Maybe I was a bad person among bad people. But we were using it to gain power and resources. This, too, was a recent conversation we had here, perhaps the people here who will use it now are better people than those who did similar things before. Time will tell," Wu concluded and noticed the Chairman joining the growing audience as they congregated around the test team, anxious to learn the results.

You would think that most folks would be getting something to eat, a shower, a nap or whatever nicety they had gone without during their extended work to get to this point. That is largely not how these things work. When you put your hard work, best ideas, sweat equity, and max efforts into an intensely focused effort across an unrealistically short timeline, you do what you can to see it through. You want to see how it turns out. You need to see how it goes. If you did it right, you need to see that it works like it is supposed to. If you are really a team, then you succeed or fail as a team. You are on the field when the game ends, you don't read about the final score or hear it from you team mates when they come into the locker room after you get out of the shower. So it was for *Thor's Craftsmen*. They were assembling all around the test team to cheer, sigh or curse together at the test results. This was the scorecard for their collective efforts and virtual presence was actual absence. If folks could be there, they were.

It was a bit challenging for the test team to stay focused with so many of their colleagues looking over their shoulders, but focused they stayed. As the clock ticked-and-tocked, the wind directions and speed that were supposed to occur kept occurring. The green lights kept coming, and the occasional yellow light blinked for a while but eventually turned green. Chief Andies, reached for the phone but he felt the hand on his arm gently push it back down. He looked over his shoulder to see Major General Lincoln standing over him, pulling his hand back as he released the Chief's arm, "Tell me in person, Chief."

"The test is finished, General. The winds have migrated through the system and touched most, if not all, of the CubeSats. It's green enough Sir, green enough," the Chief smiled.

"Meaning what Chief? What does green enough mean?" General Charles, who was standing next to Frank asked.

"Green enough General means you now have an operational global on-demand weather modification system that is capable of controlling the winds across the globe. We have not yet tested the rest of the parameters or conditions, and many of the big events you won't want us to test, but the wind test passed with flying colors. Pun intended Sir; more greens than you can fit in your salad, Sir. IT WORKS!" The last two words were deliberately loud and intended to inform those waiting for the results. The cheers were incredibly loud as the collective celebration was an emotional release representing hard work, personal sacrifice and a devotion to duty that is hard to describe unless you have experienced it.

"Congratulations Frank. You did it. You all did it." Dutch slapped the two-star on the back. "By damn, you did it. You go congratulate your team, take a victory lap with them and thank them. I will be on your heels, doing the same thing in a minute. I need to send a text to SECDEF and let him know we hit our milestone, and he can inform POTUS. That's his role not mine, and I expect someone will wake him up to make sure he is aware."

"Will do Sir. You don't have to tell me twice. This was worthy work, and they need to know we appreciate that they successfully did what we asked them to do and I for one appreciate it. I am confident that list will grow as time goes on," Frank agreed and turned to slap Major Lessur on the shoulder and start making good on what the Chairman directed him to do.

Dutch pressed the letters to create a very simple message in his phone to send to the new SECDEF's phone. It simply said, "IOC Achieved." Then Dutch proceeded to greet, congratulate and thank the people in the room for what they did to make this national capability a reality. Several minutes later, his phone vibrated in his pocket, and he read the response from the SECDEF. It too was brief, and Dutch read the words on the screen. "Great, see you tomorrow. More to do." *Meaning what?* he wondered as he continued working the room to thank whoever he could.

.

CHAPTER SEVENTEEN

GET IT BACK

The good news traveled fast through those who had the right clearance and the need to know that *Thor's Craftsmen* had achieved initial operating capability. You would think that would take some of the pressure off, but the reality was quite the opposite. The team was now preparing for another inundation of DVs. Some indicated the President himself might also be among them for another update. Good work gets more work it seemed, but they were all ready for a break not another surge. Major General Lincoln was simply running on fumes, but advancing through IOC to have an operational system was the next and, perhaps, most important phase of this program. Rationally, what does everything to this point even matter if the system doesn't do what you need it to do now that it is up in space? He knew that from a personal health perspective that he could not continue at this pace indefinitely, but he rationalized that, in another week or two, things would calm down a bit. He also knew that was wishful thinking, but it was all he could muster at this point. He didn't have the time nor the energy to think anything else.

He had managed to get several power naps in the past few days, but the poor diet, lack of exercise, and excessive amounts of caffeine could only sustain even the best of men for so long. It was showing on him and, while he knew it, he didn't really know the extent that others could see it.

"Congratulations Frank you did it, and you look like shit by the way!" Tom exclaimed as he strode into the office not realizing, nor caring that the 2-star was on his phone.

As he dropped his gear and made himself at home in the General's work space, Frank ended the call and responded, "Didn't I literally just see you in the Oval with the President when we hit IOC? What are you doing here?"

"Frank, that was hours ago! If you haven't already taken your victory lap it might be too late now," he began. "The old man and a crew of heavy hitters, cabinet members and the like, will be descending on us in the morning to see this in action. They want to better understand what it can do, and what they can do with it. Confidence levels, countermeasures, level of difficulty, all the things so they have a better idea of how they can or will be able to use it. What the vulnerabilities are, how to factor it into their negotiating position with the CCP. Dog and pony with a decision flavor for who, what and when. They are on a greased rail with this, and I cannot slow them down despite my best efforts.

"I have him considering a course of action that provides some off-ramps, but he insists on pursuing these concurrently with his current course. If one doesn't work, the other moves to the front. I don't think he has decided which is which yet. That is a big part of this visit and why it is so fast and well attended." Tom paused, as he realized Frank was two shades paler than when he walked in. "You OK buddy?"

"No, Tom. Not OK." Frank took a deep breath knowing he was about to shoot the messenger, but he was simply unable to check his fire. It was one of the few times in his career the man had exceeded his threshold for cool, calm and collected under pressure. "We just did the impossible. We're all exhausted, but still need to wring this out and make sure it works like it should. We *don't know* if it will all work yet. We *think* it will, but knowing will take some time and a lot of work left to make sure. And you want us to assist in a premature policy discussion with POTUS and his top brass to tell them what? Tell them we don't know yet about 150 times? How about we save everyone the trip and us a lot of headaches?

"I'll type it up, copy and paste *not sure yet* as many times as I need to and send it myself if that will help. I need you to do your job, Tom, and control the situation so I can do mine. Consecutive miracles Tom, that is what you are asking of us. Start managing expectations and get us some realistic timelines or we will all be explaining the disasters that came from not having them. Do that and you can count me in, don't do that and you can count me out. I don't have that much left in my tank, Tom. I just don't have that much left," he ended softly and realized he was standing up in Tom's face and far across the line any reasonable man would allow being crossed without reacting.

"Holy shit, Frank, you *are* human! I was really beginning to wonder," Tom smiled to de-escalate the conversation, a lot. "Look, I know you are correct, but that doesn't make you right. The CCP keeps readying their forces and POTUS is worried they are going to start shooting before we are ready to respond. That might happen, but I don't think it will if we lean in and whisper what they are hoping we might say. High risk, no decisions yet on either side and the longer we wait the more paranoid each side will get. Paranoia is bad for either side but it's likely catastrophic if it's on both sides. We gotta make a difference on one or the other. My best play is we influence our side. This on-orbit stuff works…then he has confidence in his own way out. It doesn't work…then paranoia spikes and options plummet. It is what it is, but we need to show them what it is.

"Do the best you can, that's all anyone can ask. That is what I am asking. If you can't do that tell me now and point me to Dutch because he will end up doing his job and yours which I know he would be OK with if it comes to that. I'll let you make the call but make it now General Lincoln." He cocked his head and waited for a response and hoped to hear the one he was pretty certain was coming…but he needed to hear it.

"Copy that Mr. National Security Advisor. I will make it happen. And I'm sorry I lost my shit Tom, really unprofessional, really sorry." He waited as he owned his mistake and regretted making it.

"Don't sweat it. I understand. No pressure, no diamonds, right?" Tom conceded and while he appreciated the apology, he knew there were more important things to be doing than this right now.

"I expect to start this discussion and walk-through in about four hours. Can we walk about 15-25 people in and around at the same time and still have room for your folks to keep doing what they need to do?" he asked.

"If I say no, will it matter?" Frank asked half sarcastically and half seriously.

"Not really," Tom smiled and appreciated the return to what he considered their *normal*. The Frank that Tom knew from the UN effort was back, and that was encouraging. That was when General Charles joined them.

"Tom," he greeted him. "This can't be good. When will they be here, and is he coming in person?"

"A few hours, and yes. Frank and I were just getting started on the prep. He wants a pointy-talkie to inform himself and some of the cabinet and principals on what it can do. He needs to bake this into his decision calculus with the CCP and time is running short. You know the deal, Dutch. He's gotta see it and feel it to really hear what it tells him. He goes with his gut as much as his brain, sometimes instead of his brain but it has gotten him this far. Let's help him get this one right too, shall we?" Tom requested.

"Assuming the SECDEF will be with him? I never hear from that guy directly. I suppose I know what to read into that. I have been trying to retire anyway so why not now? With Fitz out, it makes sense to make another change. Gonna put you on the spot, Tom, and not apologize for it. Will that also be one of their topics while they are here?" Dutch asked.

"If it is, I haven't heard anyone talking about it, so I doubt it. Pretty sure they would ask my opinion if they were considering replacing you. That is unless, of course, we are both going at the same time. Haven't heard anything like that either, so how about we focus on this new on-orbit global weather modification system we just fielded. Let's stack up some more victories instead of worrying about a defeat. For what it's worth, I spoke with Fitz, and he sends his regards. Asked me to pass along his best, and a request; please finish what we started," Tom added.

"OK then, thanks. Let's do just that. What do you need from me?" Dutch asked and Frank did not hesitate in his response.

"Sir, if we could divide and conquer that would be a great help. If I can focus on the system and ask you to focus on the converging brass? I will pull hard with the crew here to be ready to talk about what they are doing with respect to the integration of the new birds and focus on what that will enable. If you want to lead the gaggle and guide the discussion, I will make sure we have the right people talking to answer whatever questions they have. Does that work for you?"

"Yeah, Frank. I can do that, and I appreciate you taking the hard part. No, I mean it works to our strengths. We can do this. He has some tough decisions to make on short order. Our job is to give him the information he needs to make them. If we keep it that simple, it will be that simple." Dutch patted his shoulder, and suggested he get started. Frank didn't need to be told twice and he was out the door and headed to put some of this into motion. He was still unhappy with himself for losing his composure with Tom, but he also knew that, at this level of responsibility, that was one of the only places he could. Senior leaders vent to, with, and on each other because to do that in front of subordinates was not acceptable under any circumstance. While it was not good form to vent too far up the chain, Frank knew in hindsight that Tom would not make a big deal of it but that was not the point. Frank didn't choose to do that; he simply was not able to stop it from happening and that was so very much not Frank that it shook him. He promised himself that would not happen again, not with Tom or anyone else. Lesson learned.

"Hi Bob. I need a minute please," Frank greeted Bob who had his head buried in a bank of computer monitors as he was discussing some weather something or another with several members of his team.

"Sure Frank, excuse me please." Bob was in a better than usual mood as he stepped away from the ongoing discussion. "What's up?"

"Can you grab up your primaries and meet in about ten minutes? I want to do an update with a bigger group, and I only want to do it once. Can we do it here?" he asked.

"Sure," Bob agreed. "It's your show; whatever you need we're still working for you, boss."

"Good. Thanks. See you in about ten minutes," Frank said and made the rounds to the other sections and folks quickly began assembling for the mysterious impromptu meeting with General Lincoln. Bob was surprised at how quickly and how many people apparently considered themselves primary members of the various teams, but it was good to see everyone coming together for a few minutes even if the purpose was unclear. Then it occurred to Bob and he wondered if this was the beginning of the end. Was the program transitioning to a new phase which meant *out with the old and in with new* already? Bob knew that would happen sometime soon but he didn't anticipate it this quickly. An intense chill of worry came over him with that thought because he knew they weren't ready just yet. He wasn't ready...soon but not yet.

Looking around Bob saw the faces that helped bring this new era into existence from what was nothing more than a well-resourced challenge a couple of weeks ago. Ann, Chief Andies, Major Lessur and Mr. Wu were here with him. He could see the other technical team leads and was pleasantly surprised to see both Chen and Zach among the others assembled. Frank began with a thank you to all present for what they have already done before he dropped the other shoe, "We continue expediting our system integration, calibration and evaluation to get to an operational acceptance level of confidence where we can declare this system live and hopefully get to full operational capability, FOC as we call it. We don't have a traditional set of system specs to measure FOC against, so it is kind of up to us to decide what that looks like. So, I appreciate your expertise in your areas in making these subjective calls.

"That said, we are going to get some help in making our assessments. And that begins in just a couple of hours. We will be getting some augmentation for our test efforts, but not the kind you might be thinking. The President of the United States, and some of his cabinet, key leaders and policy makers are converging on us as we speak to see two things. The first of those is what our system looks like now that we have the birds, comms and systems in place and talking to each other. The second thing they will be seeing is what it can do, how to operate it, and how it can be employed as well as defended against."

He paused to let the moans, murmurs, looks around the room and other responses pass through the room for about ten seconds and then continued before the negativity could take a foot hold, "I know that is not what we need right now, but it is what they need and they need it now. And that is why we are here, to deliver what they need," Frank paused and he was surprised to see Dutch in the back of the group, even more surprised to see the look of pride on his face. Clearly, he still believed he had put the right man in the right place for this job. Frank was glad to see that look and was happier that the Chairman was not in the office with him and Tom just a little while earlier because the look on his face would have been much different had he been there.

"I don't yet have a sense of how this visit will unfold, what details they will want to drill down on, or who they will want to talk with so go with the flow. Our primary task is to continue to ops check our stuff and stay on task. However much they want to see or talk about won't be worth anything if the system doesn't work when they call upon it." He paused and looked around as the shifting shoulders and fidgeting indicated folks had questions but there was little appetite to ask them. That suited Frank for now, so he wrapped up, "So, we play it by ear. If asked a question, answer it. We are the experts not them. Be professional but be candid. I would rather under promise and over deliver than do the opposite. Now get back to it, and we will see you again soon, like it or not with a crowd of VIPs."

"Frank, one question please?" Ann asked as he was departing but before he got away. Frank stopped, greeted her and came back around to take her question which she asked as soon as he was in earshot. "When will we wrap this effort up here? Meaning how much longer do you think Bob and I will be needed to help with whatever needs to happen next? I mean, we do have a wedding to plan and Dad and Betty are feeling a bit cooped up and underutilized."

"I really don't know, Ann. I just don't have any insight to that yet," Frank said candidly and was a little surprised with her follow up.

"But you would tell me, if you did? You would, wouldn't you, Frank?" she worried aloud.

"Of course. I have always been straight with you and Bob. I don't know, Ann, but I will let you know when I know. That will have to be good enough for now because it's all I got. Anything else?" he asked her.

"No, that was it. Thanks Frank. I will make sure you know our wedding date once we set one. Which sounds like it won't be until after you guys decide what is gonna happen. It's hard for me to fathom how anything gets done with such little planning ahead, but with us it always seems to work out like it should. That takes extra effort from all of us," she stirred the pot, but just a little as Frank shot a glance behind him and said just loud enough for her to hear the words, "Can't wait for the wedding. Better be an open bar!" And then he strode off to attend to the next thousand tasks that needed to be done before POTUS's arrival.

"What was that all about?" Bob asked her.

"We still have some time, but I don't think it's much. He was telling the truth; he doesn't know when they pull the plug on us and send us home. That said, we also have no idea how much time that is either. POTUS isn't exactly your biggest fan and the new SECDEF is an unknown as far as we are concerned. It wouldn't surprise me at all if they told us to pack up and leave on one of the airplanes with them. They don't need us to finish the testing or to use the system, and they have some depth on their bench already. We are not crucial to either effort. We do improve the coolness ratio for the operation but that alone is not enough to keep us around for the rest of it. I think that means the time to act is gonna be ASAP…meaning *As Soon As POTUS*. ASAP, get it?" She smiled and groaned in anticipation of the yuk-yuk-ending to her bad pun.

"I want you to be wrong, Ann, but I don't think you are," Bob confided.

"If I had a dollar for every time I heard that," she smiled. "Seriously, you better give some thought to this and do a couple of dry runs to make sure you can do it live if you decide to do it and get the opportunity," Ann suggested.

"Again, you are probably right. I may only have one shot at this and, if I miss it, I may never get it another. I am feeling a little queasy. I think I'm gonna take a break and go chill out for a little bit and see if that helps. I will want to be sharp when they get here," Bob admitted.

"You need anything let me know. Otherwise, I will stay here and hold the fort down so you can focus," Ann directed.

"Thanks, I'm good. See you in a while. Like Frank said, we will just be flexible. That's good advice, I think we should take it," Bob suggested as he walked over, kissed Ann on the lips and then headed off to wherever breaks and chilling were likely to be available for Professors needing to struggle with some heavy deliberations.

He found a quiet spot outside between two of the buildings. There was little foot traffic, and he was pretty confident once he sat down with his back against the wall and his eyes closed that nobody would bother him unless it was important. He let his mind wander back to the gravel roads that he drove to check the traplines for Doc Auster. That seemed like a lifetime ago in experiences but, in *time* it was not long ago. Bob wasn't entirely sure how Doc got the Thor's Hammers, and neither Chen nor Wu had any certainty beyond what they heard from some of their colleagues. What Bob was certain about was Doc was dead and wouldn't be if not for having figured this out. Bob was sad about that but also determined to not meet the same fate. Waiting to see who did what, was not an acceptable plan of action for Professor Mcleod—not in his past and certainly not now. It was time to take matters into his own hands, especially since he had Ann to consider now. There were other reasons but, at best, they were all in a battle for a distant second priority far behind her.

It was still a little surprising to Bob how simple this might be when it's all said and done. He had learned a lot while here working on this program, and from a lot of different people. But there were a few things that stuck with him and putting them all together seemed like it was all somehow orchestrated to bring him exactly what he needed. Yes, it may very well be divine intervention, it may be fate, karma, dumb luck or just teamwork dropping all he needed to see the path forward as clearly as if it were a paved road stretching out ahead of him. Nobody besides Ann knew what he was contemplating and nobody else needed to know. In this instance he didn't need any help, in fact his success if he chose to pull this off depended on not having any help. It was elegant in its simplicity and seemed doable without putting anyone at risk. In fact, it could very well eliminate the vast majority of risk from the unknown future they faced.

That seemed like hyperbole to Bob but the more he considered it the more Ann had convinced him that she was right about this too. *Plausible denial* she kept saying was how every other politician operated, and it would absolutely work for Bob in this scenario. She knew it would, and she knew he could do it. She had faith in him, even if he didn't have the same faith in himself. Ann also knew the system of systems type of architecture being utilized for this constellation where sensors, satellites, encryption, communications packages, command and control nodes, system operations command sequences all talk to and listen to each other. No single system is more important than another. They succeed as a team, or they fail as a team. People could learn a lot from that mindset Bob thought, as he heard the faint roar of aircraft engines approaching. How long had he been out here he wondered; they are already here. With that Bob rose up off the ground, watched the aircraft land and taxi to parking and open the doors. He recognized several of the people waiting to deplane down the metal stairs as they were being rolled up to the side of the shiny plane with the very distinctive logo on it. *Showtime*, he thought to himself walking toward the door to the building that held his team and said aloud, "All right Doc, let's see if we can get it back."

Ann met him at the door, and asked him, "You good?"

"Never better Ann, never better. I hope we get a chance to show the President and his team what this thing can do, after all that's why they are here according to Frank," Bob smiled. "Should be an interesting time Ann, I hope everything works as advertised. We all need a fully operational system."

Dutch had done what he could to recommend a sequence of events and a path of travel through the operation but, as with most plans, it did not last long given the majority of people milling about were very senior staff members used to giving direction not following it. That is, until the President decided for all of them.

"Dutch, I want to be really clear about the tone and tenor of this walk through. We are here to see this thing working, and make sure we are ready to use it for whatever purpose we need it. The CCP is still amping up their military posture. I don't know how much more ready they can get or need to be, but they sure seem ready enough to do something right now." He looked around until he found Tom, and then called him out.

"Tom...I tried what you suggested earlier. They don't seem very interested, or at least they don't want us to think they are interested. Might just be posturing for a better negotiated settlement but might be that I pissed them off so much it doesn't matter what I say or do. They need to make me pay for what I said and did. So right now, we are not perceptibly closer to any solution nor is any outcome more favored than another. So, gentlemen, let's go see what this can do and make some decisions shall we?" He took a couple of steps toward his CJCS intending to fall in behind him as he led the way, but Dutch didn't move.

"All due respect Mr. President, you do recall that we are still doing Cal-Val on the whole system. We just got the augmentation birds in place and online. We did a temperature change test using the initial birds, and a wind check using both old and new ones. They both went around the globe, but beyond that we have only done a few other local changes, two regionals and the rest are ongoing tests. We are still a week at least from testing and checking everything sufficiently to call this system FOC," he reminded the President.

"Yes, Dutch I do recall. I recall from the previous time you told me. That was the same time I told you that I understood there was some risk involved and that was fine. Time the CCP does or does not give us is the driver here, not your test schedules," he scolded.

"Not my test schedules, Sir. The system takes time to operate, and we probably shouldn't be doing any destructive weather events anywhere near any populated areas until we have this all wrung out and know it works like it should, or at least we know that it works well enough," Dutch countered.

"Not saying you're wrong Dutch, just saying it is what it is. We may or may not have that time. That has been a consistent message, and the CCP's silence is not a good indicator. That's where we are. Now let's go see what we came here to see." He stepped out in front of his CJCS. As they walked, the group followed in behind them and spread out around the group so they could see the assembled team and their computer monitors.

"Frank, good to see you again. Congratulations on getting this up and running," POTUS acknowledged him as the group began to wiggle and squirm for a good vantage point in the tight space. "Professor Mcleod, I see you are still an integral part of this effort. As we have already paid you handsomely for your services, I suppose that is appropriate. Shall we get started? I trust you have good news for us all." The tone had just been set for the day and it was clearly not intended to be talking about stuff, he was here to see it.

"Mr. President," Bob began a bit shakily, "what we are doing right now is checking to make sure the weather modification hardware and software modules on each of the newest satellites are capable of producing the needed parameter changes across the spectrum of weather conditions they are expected to produce."

Before he could continue, POTUS interrupted, "That sounds like it is going to be tedious and take a long time Professor."

"Yes Sir, it will be both. That said. We have already done a low-key wind event across the integrated system, and it produced remarkably successful results. As we…"

Again, POTUS interrupted him with a statement, "Not why we are here today, Bob. I am going to need you to step up the testing, and I came prepared to help. Here is what I would like to hear about and what we are here to do. I'm going to sit next to you and together we are going to use this system to change the weather in some specific ways of my choosing. You, and whoever you need to help you, are going to give me some instructions so I can make the changes myself. Then my people on the ground are going to report back to me what they see. Simple enough, Professor?" He paused and waited for Bob to acknowledge his instructions.

"Yes, simple enough to understand. That said, it might be risky given that we are just starting the…"

Again, he was interrupted, "Yes, Bob. General Charles has dutifully and thoroughly advised me of the risk. I intend to make sure we don't blow up any underground natural gas storage areas with our test today, Bob, unlike what may or may not have happened in your earlier testing events that I was not involved in. Safety first Professor, do no harm. I get it. Here you go, let's start with these." And the President handed him a yellow post-it note with a bunch of numbers written on it in his own handwriting.

"What is this Sir?" Bob asked.

"Latitude and longitude coordinates, Bob. That is where our first event of the day will need to occur. What I am looking to do is to make it cloud up over that spot with some thick clouds as soon as we can. I don't want the Chinese satellite that will pass over it in a couple of hours to see what we are moving in or out of that spot. Show me how to make that happen and let's see this thing in action. What do you say team? Let's do some live testing and you can get your test results as we go. Maybe it will help save you all some time and trouble by providing some insights by doing these events together today," he encouraged, but the tone indicated clearly that was an instruction and not a request.

"OK then. Clouds we can do from the primary screen. Do you want me to take you there and then hand off or do you want to start making entries now?" Bob sought clarification to ensure he stayed within the POTUS's clearly thought-out agenda for the day.

"Tell me where to click and walk me through it. We will do this just like we were in an airplane. Do you fly, Bob? Well, it works like this: I have the stick and I will tell you when I want you to take it. Then you will tell me you have it and I will confirm you have it. Then I will let go of it. Right now, I have the stick. Get me to the primary screen," he instructed the technology team leader as others looked on uncomfortably. After getting him settled in, orientated and briefed on what they were going to see, Bob began a series of instructions that got them to the primary screen where the desired event could be manually entered or digitally uploaded so the software scripts describing complex timing or sequencing could be used without the risk of a last-minute data entry error at the operator screen.

The President moved through the selection menu, picked a thick layer of cirrostratus clouds to come in high above the location and then a second layer of altostratus clouds to come in shortly after and below the first. This would enable his observers to see both events occur and confirm that their location was indeed cloud covered and obscured from overhead visible imaging sensors. The gap between the two cloud layers would also make it more difficult for infrared sensors to discern some objects on the ground. Once that input was entered, he confirmed the request via a review screen very similar to verifying the items in your digital shopping cart. The final screen was the big green checkmark or the big red X. Clicking on the check mark, the President took a phone out of his pocket, typed and sent a short text message then put the phone away.

"OK. My folks will reach out and tell me when they see that happen, or not. How do we tell from the system?" he asked Bob, who deferred to Chief Andies who explained the details of the summary screen within the system but was cut off before he could describe the global network of satellite imagery, radars, surface and upper air observations that fed into the complex data bases of each nation and how they were shared.

"I get it, Chief; it ties into the rest of everything weather and beyond. Thanks. Can we keep this window open while we move to another task or do we need to close it out and move on, then come back to it?" POTUS asked Andies.

"Yes. It can do either, or both, Sir," he answered what he thought the question meant.

"Thanks. OK Professor, here is the next one," he said handing Bob a green post-it note from his pocket with a similar string of numbers on it. "This time we are going to make some surface winds along the coast kick up the surf and swamp a few boats tied up along a pier at these coordinates. Not the entire shoreline, just along this marina. Same screens Bob?" POTUS asked, and Bob nodded in agreement.

"Good, let's see if I remember what we just did?" POTUS challenged himself loud enough for the others to hear and he correctly navigated the screens just as they had done previously. When he entered the coordinates from the green note, now stuck to the frame of the monitor so he could see it better, the map indicated the point was on a lake shore in interior China. And the President grinned as he explained to the group that is where the Communist Chinese party leader keeps his extravagant houseboat which is frequently used for both business and personal outings on the large lake. With Bob looking over his shoulder and checking his inputs, they arrived at the green checkmark and the red X. Again, the green checkmark was selected and the on-demand weather instruction was sent through the communications links into space where the new constellation of satellites would parse the ones and zeros into commands for the various pieces on the MicroSats to send the needed impulses and energy streams toward the earth in order to begin the sequence of atmospheric events that would produce the desired conditions on the surface at the designated place and time. It was remarkable. It was real, and it was currently in use by the elected leader of the US. An historic moment, which the President marked by sending another text message on the phone from his pocket.

"OK, enough playing around," the President said as he pulled a red sticky note from his pocket. "Some of you have already had the pleasure of seeing and creating a tornado with these Thor's Hammers. Sadly, I have not, which makes me feel a little left out really. As I recall, Dutch, Frank, Bob, and the Air Force weather guys on your team were all at the isolation facility when you guys did one right there. Kinda bold, maybe even reckless by OSHA standards but I get the dramatic effect you were going for. We won't be near that danger close to anything or anyone. We will do our tornado on a missile test range where there isn't anything that hasn't already been blown up at least a few times. My observers will be in the blast bunker not outside watching in the rain. Safety first. Let's make a tornado, shall we? Specifically, an EF3."

POTUS's instructions, requests and tone all appeared to be deeply vindictive toward Bob but, if he was trying to get a reaction, it wasn't working. It felt to those in the room like he was a child taking away and playing with another's favorite toy simply because he knew he could. It distracted from what they were really there to do, but he was the President and even on a bad day, he was still their boss.

"That Sir, we cannot do from the primary screen. Any event or entry that exceeds normal, or climatological conditions requires us to go to the event screen which requires an advanced user credential. To get there you need to click here, then here, select credentials then I should probably take the stick, so I can type in my user identification and passwords," Bob suggested.

"Nonsense, just tell me what they are, and I will type them. It's not rocket science—well not really—from where I sit right now," he joked as the nervous laughter subsided. "After all, I probably have a higher level of clearance than most of the people here so let's have it. You can change your password after I leave if it will make you feel better, Bob."

"Of course, Mr. President, but both are rather lengthy and there are security features," he cautioned.

"Yep," the President typed as Bob provided him the lengthy user identification string that was unique to him. Once he was finished typing, Bob then provided the twenty-seven-character password which the President dutifully typed in as they went. Selecting continue to event screen, produced an error message indicating *User Authentication Error. Access to this portion of the system denied.*

"That's not what I expected to see next. Let's try that again, Bob," the President grumbled. Bob protested at this point, but again was cut off. "User ID again, Bob," POTUS said tersely, but it was Chief Andie's voice that came out next.

"Mr. President the system failsafe will lock us out after only two failed attempts at this screen. It is designed to keep unauthorized users from being able to access or produce a damaging event. Once locked out, there is a time sequence and recovery process to regenerate new bona fides and an updated lock-out for that user until it is cleared back in by numerous other security account holders. It's a lengthy process, Sir, to recover the..."

This time POTUS interrupted the Chief in mid-sentence, "I know how security layers work Chief, thank you. Professor, if you please let's try this again, shall we?" he pressed and Bob complied.

Once again, Bob spoke his user ID and password as the POTUS typed and confirmed it, expecting to be on his way to creating an EF3 tornado. But that is not what happened next. The screen did not take him into the events selection window, instead it began blinking the words *System lock-out enabled. User authentication failure. All access DISABLED.*

And that, compounded by the perpetual beeping alarm that accompanied the blinking screen, elevated the blood pressure of everyone in the room especially the *man with the stick.* The President looked at Bob, then at Chief Andies, then at Frank, and then Dutch and calmly said to them, "I am giving you the controls. Take the controls please and get the system back online. Get it back!"

With that he stood up and said, "Well I suppose this would be a good time to take a short break everyone, while our experts resolve our login problems and get us back to business."

There was a buzz of conversation, the staff was scurrying around, and the visitors were all looking around, not sure where to go or what to do, or what taking a break even looked like here. Everyone looked concerned given the tone of the session so far, and now this. Everyone that is, expect Professor Mcleod and his fiancée.

CHAPTER EIGHTEEN

IT WORKS

The short break got everything but shorter as the team held several sidebar conversations while the group of distinguished visitors waited patiently...at first. It became evident to those who were watching that the first, most obvious solutions were not working. Bob knew that trying his user ID and password would not work since that is the one the President tried to use when the lock-out occurred. Frank tried to use his and while he got into the event selections screen, it was disabled and would not allow him to select any event from the various options lists. He could not get any further into the system, but he could get back out. Several others tried but all had the same result. They were able to access the menu screen and see what was there, but none could get their passwords to allow for selecting any event or navigating any further in the system.

A bit flummoxed and looking to manage the expectations of the important collection of national leaders, General Charles suggested they break into a couple of small groups to see other portions of the system. This would also, and more importantly give whoever might have an idea how to resolve this an opportunity to talk it out without having a bunch of DVs looking over their shoulders and tapping their feet impatiently. In the meantime, the President received a text and let everyone know the cloud cover had indeed moved in over the first target. The upper-level clouds moved in first, followed closely by a dense lower layer of clouds that obscured from the ground anything above it. Similarly, when the satellite ascended in its polar orbit and passed the site in its collection window, all it could take photos of were the tops of the clouds that weren't supposed to be there.

"Well, that is nice to hear. It works, at least that one did. How are we doing on unlocking this thing?" POTUS asked trying to add at least some encouragement to the situation.

"Still working on it, but it still has us locked out," Dutch reported.

"Well, more good news, this time from China. Seems there was a fair amount of wind at a certain marina and several boats were damaged from the unexpected wind and waves. Some large houseboats among them. Seems that worked, too. Testing seems to be going pretty well. I am anxious to resume, Dutch. What's the hold up? Can't be that hard to reset a password, can it? I mean that's all they should have to do; right? We do this same thing on military systems everywhere; this delay is not making a lot of sense and we have a timetable we are trying to keep for our friends waiting for a tornado at the range. How about you go check with Frank and see where we are while Tom and the rest of us start to dial in our options? I like what I am seeing so far."

POTUS indeed wanted to get on with the testing and was anxious for an update, but Dutch could hear in the words and by his assigned task that his counsel was not vital to the conversation he would be missing while he was chasing down an update. That was simple enough to interpret he thought as the Chairman found Frank and the group of people having what appeared to be a vibrant conversation about their ongoing obstacle.

"Have we figured it out yet?" Dutch asked the now very large group of *Thor's Craftsmen* team members as he walked up. With his arrival the conversation all but stopped as everyone looked at the CJCS with what could only be described as disbelief.

"Don't stop talking on my account. That is, unless you are stopping on my account. Why do I feel like you may have figured this out? Let's have it then, what do you think it might be," Dutch urged them to speak what their faces already revealed.

"Good news is we know what happened," Frank began. "Bad news is we think we also know how it happened." He paused for a moment, bracing himself for what he was going to say next and the look on Dutch's face meant he needed to continue and not sugar coat this.

"First problem was putting Bob's authorization code into the system incorrectly. It's a twenty-seven-digit sequence and we confirmed that is what triggered a lock out," Frank began but Dutch was clearly impatient and looking for the bottom-line up front.

"Yep, we all saw that happen, Frank. And we saw who did it," Dutch confirmed and then looked over at Bob and asked pointedly for all to hear. "Did you give him the right one, or the wrong one, Professor?"

Bob, and just about everyone else, was surprised at the question but anxiously awaited the answer from the man who had regularly been struggling with entering his bona fides throughout the testing.

"I gave the President my user ID and password, General. In fact, I was relieved that he was typing them in. As you may recall, I have had a few less than proud moments doing that myself earlier in the program," Bob responded and continued talking. "Yes, I gave him the right ones. I can't speak for what he heard me say, or what he typed but I told him the right things General. I gave him the same information I used earlier to get me in. It worked when I did it myself."

"Thank you, Professor; had to ask," Dutch nodded and looked back to Frank to continue. "What else General Lincoln?"

"Seems during the preparations for the short notice visit, and my guidance regarding this visit likely have some bearing on what happened. For that, I will take responsibility, Sir. Here is what I believe happened, and where our recovery efforts will require some follow up discussion," Frank warned before he continued.

"Knowing we would be continuing our Cal-Eval during the visit but not knowing what the DVs would want to see or do, we made some preparations to ensure we could show them whatever they wanted to see. One of those preparations involved the security and encryption scripts. As you heard, Professor Mcleod and some of our other leads have been challenged by our operations access codes. Knowing the two-failure lockout rule is hard coded, and for good reason, we did *not* want anyone doing operations testing or someone doing the briefing getting us all locked out during these concurrent actions. It can be more than a little intimidating entering all that information each time with POTUS, SECDEF, yourself and others watching and waiting while you do so."

"Get to the point Frank," Dutch directed.

"To account for the likelihood of such mistakes—be they nerves or too many hands in the system at the same time—we adjusted the failsafe system for today's events. The intent was to ensure that, should we have a two-attempt authentication failure or other anomaly, it would still trigger a lockout, but it would not escalate through the system to be resolved by a higher system authority on the normal timeline. This way the two next-level authorities needed to reset or reinstate the person who was locked out would have more time to do so. It seemed like a prudent adjustment given the attendees and those who would be doing the talking and the showing. Again, taking some of the nerves and exhaustion out of play for several hours today and it would also extend the time allowed to correct a mistake should one occur. To make that happen, we reset the time value for the encryption generator that synchronizes the event access menus with the operators based on their approved permissions," he explained.

"I hope you are getting to the point of all this soon, Frank." Dutch knew it had to be bad if the setup from Frank was this detailed, but he was not prepared for just how bad this was about to get.

"So, the encryption screen allows us to set the timing of the randomly generated encryption keys that enable the command sequences to be securely uploaded to the satellites. That encryption and associated decryption is how the selections made in the events screen become securely encoded commands that are communicated to the birds and the subsystems that do the weather making and changing. That input prompt, the one the operator sees, is labeled Cryptologic Authentication Time Limit. Not wanting to work against a running clock to get everyone in place to fix a problem we knew we'd very likely to face today, this entry was made as zero. That zero was intended to represent no time limit, so we could work and recover if needed without fear of escalating the failsafe sequences. Time to get it right and prevent the system from timing out if we did not. If someone got something wrong, the next level authority could take as much time as they needed to reset passwords or authorize access without being on the threat condition related timers. You will recall, the failsafe system is designed to prevent unauthorized access, protect against any under-duress commands, a hostile overrun of the operations centers, on-site threats, etc." Frank paused long enough to take a deep breath and it looked like Dutch was about to lose his mind when Ann's voice came from the sideline to contribute directly into Frank's explanation.

"I entered zero. But a zero, in this case, as it turns, out does *not* mean no time limit, so now you can take as long as you need. What *authentication time limit* means and what that number zero that I put in actually represents is the amount of time between authentication attempts before a new crypto sequence is generated and must be used to unlock and move further into the recovery sequence. General, I put in a zero and that seems to have us now in an endless encryption refresh loop. The system is generating and expecting authentication of new encryption keys with zero seconds between them, and no time to input one even if we knew the right one. We are locked out, don't know the key to get back in, and even if we knew it, we don't have any time to use it to get back in. And we don't know what, if anything, can be done to get back in. It—I mean the input menu— looked like it meant something different than it does, and I don't know what I can do to change it. I can't go back in time, and I don't know how to fix it," she concluded and the group was similarly vexed. Nobody had any ideas to share, a solution was not obvious, and it did not feel good.

"I just heard you say we are locked out. And we literally have no way to get back in because the randomly generated crypto is being regenerated instantaneously so there is no way to know what it is because literally as soon as it becomes the answer it is changed to a new answer. And even if we knew what the answer was at a split-second point in time, we don't have the time nor opportunity to put it in fast enough to use it. And there is no failsafe in the failsafe to otherwise stop the loop. Please tell me I got this wrong, or some smart software coders put in a backdoor or something like that which will save us from this," Dutch hoped.

"No, this system was specifically designed to keep out people who should not be there, good guys and bad guys, either external or internal. In this case, it locked out the good guys, and the President himself was at the controls when that happened. Sorry General, but that appears to be the situation. I don't know how we get back in. That will take some follow up, but I am sadly confident if we can get back in that it won't be anytime soon," Frank concluded.

"Assuming that is the case, and we can't get back in, what does this failsafe condition do about the weather? Can we hack into all these on-orbit weather changing systems individually without going through our internal control system? Or is there no telling what they will do on their own so now we gotta blow them all out of their orbits to prevent who-knows-what from happening?" Dutch asked, and it was Bob who opted to respond to that question to take Frank and Ann out of their hotseats.

"Failsafe defaults to climatology, General. When the lockout triggers the failsafe action, the on-orbit systems all go into what is essentially a safety mode to ensure there is no unauthorized use of the system to do harm, or to provide an advantage through anomalies either good or bad. The system stabilizes and normalizes the weather in the designated areas by employing the weather systems to generate and sustain the typical weather for that time and location until they receive new commands from an authorized system user. What that means for us, right now anyways, is we won't be able to use the system to generate any weather changes while it's in this mode. It also means—and this is important—that anyone else who might have a system that they use to impact the weather outside of normal conditions will trigger our system's countermeasures to keep conditions within climatological norms. It won't let us or anyone else generate conditions above or below the climatological normal range," Bob concluded.

"You are telling me that, for now anyway, all the weather around the world is gonna be safely held within climatological norms until we figure this out? No extremes, good or bad?" Dutch wanted confirmation, and he got it from Bob.

"Yes, Sir," Bob affirmed for the Chairman. "We are indefinitely locked out of our own system because we cannot create and use the keys. While this lock-out persists, the on-orbit system will maintain and sustain a balance between individual site and regional climatological conditions to prevent any intended or unintended consequences. The weather will remain what is considered normal as long as the system remains in lock down or failsafe. Even naturally triggered conditions that might otherwise become significant events will be corrected to keep them within climo ranges. While it may not be doing what we want it to do right now, it is doing exactly what it was told to do."

"Great, thanks for that. Let's go tell the President the good news, and the bad news. The system is working," Dutch said sarcastically pointing at Frank and Bob, and he didn't really care who else came or who didn't.

Frank and Bob looked at each other and followed behind the Chairman as he started back toward the waiting POTUS and senior staff. You could hear a pin drop and, by the sound of it, nobody else seemed anxious to join them, well almost none. Bob felt a hand take his as Ann fell into step alongside as they walked three-abreast behind the Chairman.

"I'm the one who entered the zero, it wouldn't be right for any of you to be held accountable for something I did. I remember hearing more than once since we got here, *we succeed as a team, or we fail as a team*. Well, I am not sure which one this is or if it's both, but I do know I'm the teammate who entered the zero," Ann stated. She wasn't asking if she could or should be part of the coming discussion; she was telling them she was going to be whether they wanted her there or not.

"Good. Dutch is back, can we get on with it now? Is it back up and running?" POTUS asked as the four of them joined the assembled discussion.

"No, Sir. Bottom-line up-front, Mr. President. We are locked out of the system indefinitely and that just might be a permanent condition. The failsafe protocols will use the on-orbit system to keep the weather—all the weather everywhere—within climatological averages until we can get back in and regain control of the system's event scheduler. That is if we *can* get back in, Sir," Dutch summarized for everyone who looked on in disbelief at what they thought they just heard the CJCS say.

"I hope I heard you incorrectly, General Charles. What I thought you said," POTUS began but was cut off mid-sentence by his senior military advisor who completed the sentence for him.

"Is exactly what you heard me say, Mr. President. We are locked out, everyone is locked out and the system is designed for, and seems capable of, keeping the global weather just normal for as long as we are locked out," Dutch said to drive home the point.

"Just how in the hell does that happen?" he fumed.

"You entered the wrong user ID and password, twice. That triggered a failsafe sequence Bob tried to describe which prevents any unauthorized operations from being scheduled through the command screens. That began the failsafe sequence that got us where we are," Dutch again summarized, the details could all come later.

"So, this is my fault. Is that what you are telling me?" The President shot back at the Chairman, in what appeared to be an escalation into a discussion that was not really about the problem at hand.

"Not what I said, Mr. President; not what I meant either. It's nobody's fault per se. It is a series of events, that have culminated in an unintended consequence," Dutch corrected, the man who pressed for more.

"Explain what that means," he demanded.

"We pressed a team to do the impossible, and they did it. They took a technology with world-ending potential and, in an unprecedented manner and timeline, put it on orbit. They made it work, despite the pressures on them. And it does work. It is still working. The problem with such endeavors is sometimes the consecutive miracles land in an unanticipated direction. That appears to be the case here. The randomly generated encryption and decryption keys that are needed to unlock and regain control of the system from its failsafe are in a loop. They are changing the encryption keys as soon as they are making them, and we have no way to know what the codes are or time to enter them even if we did. We can't get in, but that also means nobody else can either. It's on autopilot until we can figure this out, if we can figure it out," Dutch stopped on those words so they could sink in.

"What do you mean *if?*" POTUS demanded.

"Not sure there is a way to *un-randomize* a randomly updated set of random characters that is instantaneously updated as soon as it is created from a previously randomly created set of twenty-seven. The permutations appear to be infinite. We may never get back in. The failsafe appears to be working as designed, but not as intended. That is the meaning of *if,* Sir." Dutch concluded.

"Accidental, or intentional General? How did this happen?" he demanded.

"Both, Sir. With all due respect, this system is doing exactly what we told it to do. That might not be what we wanted it to do, but it doesn't know what we meant, it only does what it is directed by the ones and zeros that are the computer code. Accidental input still prompts intentional actions, and intentional inputs also seem to prompt accidental outcomes. In this instance it appears we have a convergence of both," Dutch suggested as he worded that response carefully so he might be spared long enough for more of this discussion.

"And it began with me having the controls, with me signing in, rather trying unsuccessfully to get signed in. And that makes me a link in this chain of events in several places now, doesn't it? Makes me no less to blame for this circumstance than anyone else who may have also been involved. Both? That is rich, really, I don't know what to do with this. All right folks, lots to think about right now and I am going to need a moment to digest and reflect on what we just heard. Everybody take fifteen minutes and walk this dog down your respective paths and see what it might mean. Then let's get back together and talk it out. I am going to do the same. See you in fifteen minutes." And with that, the President left the room, taking nobody with him except the secret service agents who were ever present.

He didn't ask for anyone to come with him, and nobody followed the President out of the room. They all stood there looking around, not really knowing what to do or what to think. Tom was the first to say what was on his mind, although it may not have been on anyone else's.

"What happens if we just shut it all down and bring it back up? Can we do a hard reset, like I have to do with my computer? Will that make the prompts come back up and give us a shot to get in?" he asked, grasping at some idea that maybe hadn't been discussed.

Frank responded for the group, "We tried a variety of restarts and resets, Tom. All gave us the same result. We can get as far as the log-in sequences but can't get past any of them. We don't have permission to be in our own system anymore. Failed attempts take it into failsafe, then failsafe needs us to authenticate to get out. We don't have any valid user ID and password information as they were all changed as a security function of failsafe protocols. The system administrators who need to validate or reset these can't get to theirs either because the encryption is continuously updating. In short, we're screwed and likely, hopelessly so," Frank conceded, but Tom was not a quitter.

"How did it work during testing of the first birds?" he persisted.

"It worked fine. The failsafe performed correctly in the breach testing, and the recovery protocols were all fleshed out and they worked too. We were up and down, in and out at every level without issue. But we did not change the time steps from the standard setting for those tests," Frank replied.

"So why change them on this go around? Why now, and who decided?" The national security advisor was looking for something to grab on to.

"I decided," Frank said. "Ann came and asked me about taking a little pressure off Bob and the team because the two-time rule was a challenge for them, and we didn't want to muck up the works with the crowd of VIPs...which is what we ended up doing anyway. It was a good idea so I said yes. And here we are," Frank owned the decision.

"OK. Who made the change, and when?" he continued.

"Ann made the change. I think about an hour before we started, I didn't green light the idea much before then. We had a lot of plates spinning when you all decided to drop in on us, and the short notice just added to the fun." Frank decided he would speed up the discussion. "Bob has locked himself out at least a dozen times since they got here. Some people don't have all the talents for passwords that DoD does, Tom."

"Yeah. Right now, our talents need to be focused on lemonade. We better figure out how to make some out of this truckload of lemons, Frank. While we are doing that, we need to figure out how to spin this to the CCP and the rest of the world. We are either inept, or reckless, or we could be both. Whatever we decide, we need to understand what that looks like and how long it will last, and what we can do about it. There is always something we can do. We need to find that, and soon. The old man just wrecked the Party Chairman's houseboat. The clock is ticking, and I am pretty confident he won't think it was an act of nature. POTUS came down here like a peacock, strutting and ready to put on a show for the world with your new toy. That is now off the table but that little parlor trick was the starting gun as far as the CCP goes. We need to resolve this for him."

As Frank was considering Tom's comments, he noticed the voices in the room were louder and more plentiful as the discussions were underway in earnest. As he looked around, he saw Dutch talking with the new SECDEF and the SECSTATE. Hoping he would not get pulled into that conversation, Frank decided to hold some court of his own. He collected up the members of the UN team who were also here, pulling in Bob, Ann, Andies, Lessur, Chen, Wu and Zach and a few others from communications for this specific conversation. They posted up along the only stretch of wall that did not have a lot of people on it and addressed the group.

"Assuming everyone knows the situation we find ourselves in?" As they all nodded in the affirmative, it was Chen who spoke first.

"It is unfortunate but should not be a surprise given the speed and limited testing. If I were doing the summary review, that would be a causal finding," he offered, but that is not where Frank was heading with this group.

"I agree with you on that Chen, but that is not my focus right now. I need to do some speed thinking and too many people make it too slow. Stick with me please. We don't have a lot of time," he urged them. "When we were playing cat and mouse in India, for the UN testing. What was it about our operation that enabled you to thwart our efforts? What was vital to your success in pulling off the wind event?"

"We let you think what you wanted to think. We showed you what you wanted to find and put it where you could see it and hear it with systems you trusted," Chen admitted. "We kept you busy with something you expected to see so you wouldn't see what we were busy with."

"Exactly. And it still worked, even when we knew to defend against it. We couldn't help ourselves. Zach, same with you, how did they snatch you up over there when you knew you were being hunted?" Frank continued.

"Ask Mr. Wu, he is the one who rolled me up into a tourist bus and took me to a copycat underground bunker across the border in China," he said, half admirably and half still holding a grudge.

"Fair enough, Wu?" Frank encouraged. "What was key to rolling up Zach."

"He has a predictable nature," Wu began. "But not how you might think. We paid him a good sum of money for access and that was, as you say, transactional. But what I am speaking of is his need to know. He needs to know how things happen, what they can do, how they will turn out. He has an impatient curiosity. I knew he would want to take the Thor's Hammers on his own adventure. It was not enough that he had access to the best R&D minds, and unlimited resources. I waited and watched. When he committed to experimenting in India, it was easy after that. He never got to use them, never made any effort to sell them or copy them. He was the perfect scapegoat because he was true to who he was, and we knew who he was through our past efforts. Please do not be angry with me Mr. Zach, I am still quite the admirer of you and your work."

"Thank you, Mr. Wu." Frank hesitated but asked Zach, "Why did you agree to help us on this effort? You could have told Tom no."

"Tom is hard to say no to, especially when no includes being disappeared. That said, I helped because this is some historic shit and I wanted to be a part of it and see how it turned out. I have had a front row seat to a lot of great technologies, some have been brought into the light and some have not. I have met a lot of interesting people along the way as well. Looking around, I count you among some of the most interesting given the circumstances. Fascinating stories, all of you. Candidly, that's really the best I can come up with. Self-preservation and a fear of missing out."

"Thank you for your candor, Zach, and remind me to buy you a few beers and continue this conversation when we have more time," Frank added. "Bob and Ann, and I am sorry, but I need to hear your team thoughts about this. Biggest hope and worst fear about this technology when you decided to take it to the UN?"

"Biggest hope was that we could do what Doc Auster couldn't," Bob began. "Biggest fear was that we couldn't."

"And what was that, that Doc couldn't do?" Frank asked.

"Get Thor's Hammers out there where everyone could benefit from them. He wanted to make his wife proud…I guess that became my goal along the way, as well," Bob smiled and cast a glance at Ann who took that as a sign to give her response.

"Worst fear was that this got weaponized and used against people who could not defend against it," Ann said, "…and biggest hope was to have something good come from it. I didn't—still don't—care what that *good* looks like as long as we leave it better than we found it."

"Lessur and Andies, we have been together on this since before we knew it was a this. Meteorologically, what's your take on the impact of our current situation? Don't pull any punches," Frank requested.

"It sucks!" Chief Andies began. "We were on the precipice of achieving global on-demand weather from space. We would have controlled the weather, at every point on the planet at any time of our choosing. You want it; we dial it up. While that would be a real pain in the ass, Sir, it would be awesome. As a bonus, we could essentially mandate compliance. Gives peace through strength a whole new dimension. A little coercive perhaps, but still. On the other hand, I am a little disappointed. It looks like forecasting the weather will be a lot easier if we can't figure out how to undo this. Conditions always within the climo won't be hard to predict. I might need to find a new gig with Tom," he concluded and looked to Major Lessur to wrap up.

"General Lincoln, Chief Andies and I have a little different perspective on this. A forecast is a prediction of what might happen. With the failsafe implemented and maybe indefinitely, that means we don't have to predict the weather in the future we will *know* the weather in the future. Climo is what is typical for a site or region. We know what that is, we provided the global climatological data set that it uses. It's not a prediction anymore. We can plan and act with near certainty based on that data. It's almost as good as controlling the weather and, in some ways, it may very well be better," Ron paused, wondering if he had gone too far astray for Frank's objective.

"How is this better, Ron?" Frank asked, because he recognized the major was onto something.

"The human variables are removed, for now. The action and response sequences are moot. The system will counter them all to keep the weather within the natural ranges. Extremes are gone. Without what we have going on right now, they would still exist and need to be predicted, countered, or accepted. This way, no more extremes. They can no longer happen, statistically the anomalies have been eliminated, whether natural or man-made," Ron said, matter-of-factly.

"Elaborate please, I don't see how," Chen requested.

Ron had everyone's attention including some of the others in the room who began to listen to the explanation from the young man who elaborated for the growing group, "Failsafe keeps the conditions within climatological norms, which are simple averages. Easy example...the climo tables for the average high temperature for a location are statistical means. So, if the average high temp for the month is seventy degrees, that is derived from raw data where maybe half the days are eighty and half are sixty and none or maybe a few are seventy. Mathematically, the seventy-degree average is rarely the actual high temp of the day, but it is the average of the range. So, if the climo says the average high temp is seventy, and failsafe will use that…then the eighty- and sixty-degree days are gonna lose out to seventy across the board. Apply that same logic to winds, pressure, and the rest so things like the extreme low pressures with strong hurricanes will never happen. Can't get there with the math. Climo in this case, means certainty, and moderation.

"That would be a pretty good system if we designed it that way. To get there by accident or circumstance is—well—I would call it a fortunate accident. It's amazing really. I will probably need to join Chief Andies in looking for something else to do for a living if this becomes our new normal because my forecast accuracy will be extraordinary, but irrelevant. Everyone else will know the same thing I know. No art, no science just read the climatology tables, rinse and repeat."

"Thank you all. That is exactly what I needed." As Frank turned around, his epiphany in full view on his face, he was shocked to see that everyone in the room had been drawn to their discussion. They had all heard what Ron had explained and they seemed to understand, at least on the face of it, that the situation was at least salvageable and, perhaps, even beneficial. It was then that he saw POTUS standing among them, nodding his head in acknowledgement. It took Frank a little longer than the allotted time to walk his dog down the path to see where it led him, but it provided an opportunity and some options for a path forward that others seemed to be willing to consider. That seemed to include the President. *Trust the process* is what Frank reminded himself before they began. Now he was confident that advice was worth its weight in gold. He tossed out a silent thanks to whomever he heard it from, whenever and wherever he'd heard it. Funny how life's events shape the future with or without your understanding or approval. It really does work.

NOW WHAT?

For the national leaders, their trip to see the *Thor's Craftsmen* team in Florida turned out nothing like they expected. As they prepared for their departure and return to DC, the courses of action were now narrowed to a few, and they would continue to work them out en route back to their offices inside the beltway. Well, some of them would. The stay-behinds would continue trying to come up with a way to get back into the now seemingly autonomous system that was normalizing moderate seasonal weather conditions across the planet. This new problem was creating nearly ideal seasonal conditions for everyone, everywhere. Unless the access issues were resolved, this would continue through seasonal transitions without big storms, floods, droughts, blizzards, tornadoes, hurricanes, etc. but still allow for showers, thunderstorms, wet and dry seasons and the like.

General Dutch Charles was one of the stay-behinds tasked with trying to figure this out and regain control of the system. That decision was a clearly intended signal from the new SECDEF and POTUS that it was time for someone new to assume the role of their senior military advisor. That suited Dutch since he had already delayed his announced retirement at the request of Fitz and this President. With Fitz gone and now these two unceremoniously icing him out of key discussions, Dutch was happy to give them what they wanted but were too pusillanimous to request. As he processed what had taken place here over the past few weeks, he couldn't help but laugh a little. He looked forward to wrapping things up as well as they could under the circumstances. Tom popped in on his way out to the aircraft that was already loaded and waiting for him so they could depart.

"Dutch, I hope you can find a way back into the system. But, if you can't, I'm not sure how big a hurry you will need to be in to get back to DC," Tom said apologetically. He liked Dutch and he already felt bad about Fitz.

"Won't matter either way, Tom. We both know that's a decision already made, it's just timing now. I am not optimistic that we will get it back, so he is going to have to plan for that being the most likely outcome. Check in with me and Frank in a few hours for a SITREP, we will have a follow up to the recommendations you are considering by then. For what it's worth, I think Frank's idea has merit. You should consider it the primary course of action. Give him some other throw away options and push this one. It's the only one that makes sense given where we are, and it makes him look good across the board. What politician doesn't want that?"

"All right, I will see how this pans out. I'd much prefer another option to consider. I would also much prefer that you be there to discuss it with all of us on the way back to DC," Tom agreed.

"Yeah, well *wish* in one hand…" Dutch replied but did not finish the instructions. "We will do what we can here, you do what you can in the air. Talk later; good luck Tom. And thanks, it's been my pleasure."

"Same General…same." Tom popped a crisp and sincerely respectful salute to General Charles then wheeled around and headed in a trot to the waiting aircraft. As he climbed up the stairs and bounded aboard, the door was closed quickly behind him, the stairs pulled away. The large aircraft taxied toward the runway and was airborne a few minutes later. The mood on the climbing aircraft was somber and contemplative as the senior leaders wrestled with options that all seemed to end up with far more cons than pros.

They were getting frustrated when Tom suggested they reconsider the idea Frank had pitched them a short time earlier, "General Lincoln's approach still seems to be the frontrunner, despite the somewhat hard-to-take first step. It should de-escalate their current posture and gives a new flavor to peace through strength. We should consider a few variations on that theme and see where that gets us."

"Come on Tom, you too? Do you really think those guys know more about the geo-political landscape than all the minds assembled here?" POTUS asked accusingly.

"I know the logic is sound. I know Chen and Wu were both deep inside their decision-makers processes and they both see merit in it. The UN won't balk. You might even get the Secretary General to support it publicly. You get to claim benevolence and, more importantly, you get to claim the moral high ground both at home and abroad without having to share it with anyone else. And, just as importantly, you get to claim that you did it personally. Whether you disclose that it was accidental or not is your call," Tom chided just a bit, knowing he should be walking on eggshells with the topic but unable to muster the required concern given his recent farewell with Dutch.

"You think calling the Party Chairman, and apologizing for the condition of his houseboat is a good start? Then tell him that was just to make sure he knows that what comes next is an olive branch that I want him to take and embrace with great enthusiasm. Show him our on-orbit system and promise that we won't use it again, on him or anyone else, as long as he agrees on my terms. Non-negotiable and a one-time offer. You think he will bite? Do you know him better than I do? I think he tells me to pound sand, Tom," POTUS contemplated.

"He might, but he will at a minimum challenge the sincerity of your offer. It's not what they would do nor what they did, when they had the technology," Tom agreed. "You give an ultimatum. They agree to stand down the military buildup, reduce the alert and readiness posture and embrace a meteorological stalemate. We will put our space-based system in stasis…on ice indefinitely. Get them to agree to do the same for any remaining site or regional systems in exchange for mothballing our freshly launched and operational space-based global ability.

"We can tell them, with precision, what the weather will be for the interim, we can use that to convince them we can do what we say. We don't want to wreck every houseboat, naval vessel, aircraft or missile base to prove a point. We tell them, if it ever comes out of the acceptable range that we give them, they let us know so we can resolve it. As long as they aren't behaving militarily, we will help them economically, socially, and environmentally. This sells itself boss, it just does," Tom paused. "If we figure out how to get back in and control the system that's a bonus. If we don't, nobody needs to know. If everyone does what they agreed to do, nobody will know except the group we have today. It's better than coming completely clean and giving them cause to consider acting in who-knows-what manner before we figure out what we can salvage from all of this."

"There is a lot that can go wrong with this approach, Tom," POTUS countered. "First and foremost is they push back, or counter with some other test of our capability that we can't pass."

"True. And I can think of a lot of other things that can go wrong with this as well. That said, I stand by the idea that they are looking for an off-ramp that helps them save face. They *want* an off-ramp and this gives them a viable one that legitimately puts our skin in the game in a, seemingly, equitable way. They can claim a great negotiated win from their buildup. Then get back to working on their portfolios and lining their pockets. After all, in the end, that is ultimately what they care most about. They can stop spending their treasure on military chest thumping to deter a foreign power with designs on their interests and focus internally. And you all get to do the same thing." That sounded worse than Tom wanted it to, but he couldn't pull it back and re-say what he just said.

"Careful Tom, you're my advisor not my judge," The President warned, but continued before Tom could respond, "That said, I see what you mean. What you meant to say, that is. How does the UN piece fit, and what do we need it for anyway? You know the Secretary General is still beyond pissed at me."

"Yes, that's true. But put him in the same category of getting a win from his current loss. The UN gets the role of third-party monitor...honest broker for the US and China agreement. It adds both credibility and transparency to your offer but, in reality, for us, it's nothing more than ceremonial since the system is going to do what it does if we don't get back in. It also provides a platform for implied mediation between two superpowers so both appear to be coming to the table for a brokered settlement instead of escalating to a shooting war. It's the perfect *out* that lets both you and the party leadership appear to win through the internal national lenses that judge their leaders," Tom explained. "In the end both of you get to say the other gave up more. They blinked and backed down without the appearance of doing that themselves. A game of chicken where everyone wins; that's a good outcome."

"Maybe, but this on-orbit system cost us billions of dollars," the SECDEF challenged them. "How do we explain all that? Not to mention the five billion that Mcleod got in the first place. What do we have to show for all that expense?"

"You've got a system that will moderate the weather around the globe. You have a negotiated, indefinite peace with our closest geopolitical rival, a global reputation for benevolence and a great re-election campaign. What else do you want?" Tom pushed back.

"I see your points, Tom. If we don't get the system back before we get to DC, then let's put it in motion unless anyone around the table has a better idea. If you do, I want to hear it and hear it now," POTUS directed as he looked around at the key staff who all seemed to have nothing to add, despite the several minutes of awkward silence they all endured. "Well, that is kind of tragic really. I want you to pull Lincoln out of whatever he was doing before this and get him to DC where his insights can get to me and I can get to him. Make him DNI or something, three or four stars whatever it takes, but I want him in on however this rolls out, and I want him close. It's his bright idea. He's gonna have to see it through and make sure it plays out like he imagined it would. Just don't let him retire. If he's a civilian I can't reassign him to DC."

That was not a playful suggestion. This President didn't do that very often and today of all days was not one of those rare occasions. He was serious, and the SECDEF took him at his word knowing that would take some doing. Frank would soon be headed to DC for a new adventure that was simply a continuation of this current one. Tom was not sure if that would make him happier or madder that Bob Mcleod somehow pulled him into all this with his Thor's Hammer experimentation. *It is what it is*, Tom thought. They can figure that out on their own because he had his own problems right now, not the least of which was the best way to get the CCP leader on the phone with the President to talk about his houseboat, and some related topics.

First, he decided hoping-against-hope that checking in with Dutch and Frank might put some other options into play, so he made the call, "Hi Dutch, it's Tom. Please tell me something good," he pleaded.

"OK. This will be a short call. Nothing has changed since you left. Anything else I can do for you?" the Chairman asked as Frank looked on a little surprised at the tone in his voice while wondering who was on the other end of the call.

"Sorry to hear that," Tom confided. "Do you have a minute for an update from this end?"

"As much time as you need," he relented.

"I think he is going with Frank's suggestion. There wasn't a better one for consideration from this group," Tom began.

"Not surprised, and I didn't come up with a better one from here either," Dutch admitted. "What else?"

"You might want to give Frank a head's up. His idea so he should expect a call soon to move to DC to see it to fruition. *By-name* from the top. Inner circle assignment still TBD, but it's coming. So, if you get a chance, give him a quick survival course on your lessons learned on how to live with the wolves." Tom was going out on a limb with this one, but he liked Frank and knew Dutch would arm him with some important survival tips. Frank would do well no matter what, but he would do much better with some keen insights and good advice from someone who had been there, done that and then some.

"Poor bastard…I'll do as you requested," Dutch smiled, knowing that was a good thing despite how he may be feeling about his own situation.

"Thanks. I want him well prepared. I have the sense we will be seeing a lot of each other up here. Do you have any confidence in our chances of getting this system back? What do you know, and what does your gut tell you?" Tom asked.

"Short some miracle, I'd say slim to none. They tell me that picking the winning lottery numbers and then picking a random lottery to play them in would be infinitely more likely than getting the right log in. Then we'd have to figure out how to put it into the system just to try to guess at a new password. My gut says this thing runs until it falls out of the sky, Tom. Peace, out! *Done-ski* my friend. Get your miracle workers on it. Let me know how they do because we're screwed down here. We'll keep trying for a while but it looks futile at best. I hope Major Lessur's assessment is a good one. We see it normalizing and, if that continues, well maybe that is how this was always supposed to work out. Maybe that was the big plan all along," Dutch conceded.

"Maybe that was someone's plan, but it wasn't POTUS's plan. I doubt very seriously it was the CCP's plan, and I know it wasn't the UN's plan. Is there something you aren't telling me, Dutch?" Tom asked. There had been something in his tone that made Tom ask the Chairman directly.

"There are lots of things I don't tell you Tom but nothing you need to know about this. Nothing to tell. We'll keep looking, maybe something will shake out, but I wouldn't bet on it," Dutch wrapped up, but there was something hollow in his promise and Tom could sense there was something unsaid in the Chairman's response. Someday he might learn what, if anything, that was but he could tell that day was not today.

"All right then, thank you General Charles. Thank you, Sir," and the line went dead.

"That was Tom," Dutch said to Frank as he put his phone away.

"So, I gathered," Frank affirmed. "Anything, I can do?"

"In fact, there is. Sit down and pay attention, I need to pass a few things along before you get your new assignment." The four-star began, and after about a half an hour of *good talk* they headed down the hall to check on the progress of those trying to find a way back into their creation. The walk was kind of surreal for Frank who was still processing the new information he just received. DC was a nice place to visit but he wasn't a big fan of living there. That said, there was much to consider although most of it was beyond his control. Certainly, it was beyond the time horizon of the tasks and problems that required his attention right now. They were both surprised to see the previously assembled group still very much intact and trying mightily to come up with options to restore their access.

"Make any progress?" the CJCS asked a bit cavalierly as they walked up.

"Yes, Sir. We know what hasn't worked so far. That reduces the options for things we want to try or try again," Chief Andies said as he stretched his neck and made it pop as he moved it in a circular motion.

"At that rate, Chief, when do you expect to be back into the control node?" the Chairman asked re-inserting a serious tone into the conversation where he was seeking a serious response, although he believed he already knew the answer.

"Sorry Sir. No, we have had no success and, candidly, we have run out of new things to try so we are re-trying things we have already done. I think we are making it worse when we do that, not better. It sucks General. We don't know how to make it un-suck," the weatherman admitted.

"Understood Chief, understood," he assured both the man and the group around him. That group included Bob and Ann whom he addressed directly.

"You know, the two of you are responsible for most of this," Dutch began, and the entire group braced for what they thought was going to be a brutal verbal beat down. But those people didn't know Dutch Charles.

"Without the two of you, none of this would have happened. I don't mean getting locked into a failsafe loop...although that is true, too. What I mean is that the two of you had the brass to step into the breach of history and bring this technology to the UN so it would help everyone. And now, *in the strangest twist of fate*, that has come to fruition. Perhaps not how you imagined it, but seemingly our reality, nonetheless. I respect the courage and conviction it took to do that. Had you been lesser people, that would not have happened and we wouldn't be here. Thank you and, while I'm at it, I guess I should also thank you both for having the President doing the input that locked us out and brought us to the new normal of *knowing* the weather instead of *predicting* what could happen.

"Accidental or deliberate, doesn't really matter does it? The President's input was wrong, and *his wrong* it will always be, if we don't find a way back in." He was staring at Betty and Steve who were standing sheepishly on the fringe of the group which is where they felt included but out of the way. The wry smile on Betty's face was subtle but discernable, and the nod he returned to her was the same. "I guess we need to figure out what that means going forward. If we can't think of a way in right now, then let's shift our focus for a bit. I would like you all to think about what we *can* do, instead of beating ourselves over what we *can't* do.

"Please shift your focus to what we can and should do to make sure this constellation stays operational and status quo for as long as possible.

What do we need to finish up to make sure we get as much life out of this as we can? That may give us some new perspective for how to get back in, but we must include all the actions needed to ensure the failsafe operation is sustainable for as long as possible. If it turns out we cannot get this back, we need to make sure nobody else can get it either. More importantly, we need to make sure the parts we need to work stay working so it can do what we want it to do…which is keep producing the moderate ranges of the climo for as long as possible. That is the defensive application of this on-orbit system. If that stops working, then we go back to device-on-device, regional-on-regional systems in conflict and another race to space for a replacement global system.

"So how do we make our system as tamper proof as possible while we are extending the lifecycle of our brand-new system for as long as we can?" he asked the system experts.

A bit surprisingly, Mr. Wu was the first to reply to the Chairman's question, "General, most importantly but perhaps opposite from your inclinations, would be to sever the communications up-link from the ground stations to the satellites."

"And what would that accomplish, Mr. Wu?" Dutch asked.

"If you are conceding control of the system to the failsafe, then severing the connection ensures there are no malfunctions, unauthorized commands or glitches communicated to the birds, intentionally or accidentally. That assures stasis, minimum power consumption and positioning. Essentially it freezes it in time, and its output is assured as long as the power lasts. These each have solar panels so that could be indefinitely."

"He is right," Major Lessur affirmed. "The location climo is already onboard the birds and tied to their orbitally determined positions. Even if they get out of position over time, they are looking down and can tell where they are and align the locations with the appropriate climo. They talk with their cousin systems so they will continue to collaborate to keep producing the weather within the acceptable ranges."

"So, we break it to fix it? That's the Army way. I do see the logic in your approach. What else do we need to think about?" he asked the team.

"How will it respond to unexpected outages, or holes in the coverage?" Ann asked no one in particular. "We have robust and redundant coverage, but what about a bird that fails, gets hit with space debris, or shot up...or whatever? What happens?"

"The birds will adjust locations over time to fill the gaps. It's designed as a self-healing mesh. Not sure how many it will need to do the globe, but the original design was three systems and one on-orbit spare. We have exponentially more than that up there, meaning we would have to lose most of them to get out of minimum coverage. We won't be using multiple systems to produce substantial catastrophic events at different locations, so the redundancy is substantial," Frank offered. He knew his systems, their capabilities and limitations, as well as, how to effectively employ them. This one was no different, but that impressed and even surprised the Chairman just a little. Then he remembered why he picked him for this job and chuckled to himself for being right yet again. There weren't any more good ideas forthcoming and the silence was getting awkward as the what-we-can-do list was short and all pointed directly at what they still could not do with their fledgling system.

"Frank, please develop the action plan to do what was suggested. Build it but do *not*, I repeat *do not* implement it," Dutch said sternly. "Not until I get the green light from POTUS and not until you all have exhausted every reasonable option to get this back online. Call who you need to call; talk to who you need to talk to. If there is a way, I want you to find it," he instructed. He then invited Bob, Ann, Steve and Betty to adjourn with him into a small office which he had set up in order to give Frank some of the privacy he needed to do his work without tripping over each other.

They followed and, once inside, he closed the door and looked them up and down as if inspecting their uniforms as he addressed them collectively, "I don't want any of you to say anything, I just want you to listen until I am finished. Can we agree on those rules?" They all nodded in agreement.

"There are three things in this world that I know to be true. My experience in DC and serving my country for so long have shown me time and again that one of them matters more than the other two." He stopped and faced them all, exposing a slight but unmistakable smirk before he continued.

"There is *what you think*, there is *what you know* and there is *what you can prove*. The most important of these is the latter. It's *what you can prove*. So, let's review, shall we? I think we were all of like mind and on the same page on the flight down here. I know Ann changed the time setting on the crypto, and I know you approached Frank with the suggestion, and he approved your idea. I know Ann claimed to have not understood what a zero would do, and I know that could be either true or false.

"I also know the President was typing whatever input triggered the lockout. I know Bob told him what to type. I know Bob could have told him either the correct, or the incorrect information to type. I also know POTUS could have typed it correctly or he could have typed it incorrectly, *twice*. I know the President put himself in the seat but I also know that Bob struggled with passwords, and whether POTUS or Bob was typing the same outcome could have occurred.

"I think it's entirely possible those things are connected. The two of you are central to these events and I think this doesn't happen without both of your actions taken together. I also think two heads are better than one, and in this case two couples with smart heads are better than just one…Steve and Betty. I think it's entirely possible that these results were not entirely accidental.

"But what can I prove? That's the key here," he methodically continued, "I can prove there was not sufficient schedule or opportunity to adequately test these systems and features to ensure they were fully understood and functional. I can prove each of you were asked to be here to be part of this effort. I can prove none of you asked to work on this effort. I can prove you all asked for and were given other assignments of your own choosing. I can prove there were opportunities for others to completely change the course of events that likely would have produced a completely different outcome had they acted differently. Frank could have said *no* to Ann's request. POTUS could have typed correctly, or heard better what was said, or had someone else do it. I could have given different directions or orders. There is sufficient cause for doubt, sufficient plausible denial across the board that I cannot prove anything beyond what we can take at face value about what happened here in front of everyone. They all saw the same things we saw.

"I expect the four of you to be smart enough, disciplined enough, and patriotic enough to keep it that way. What everyone saw and heard is the only version of what you talk about, and that is all. Full stop. You don't expand or elaborate on anything. You don't rationalize your thoughts or actions. You don't remember anything new or forget anything that everyone else saw. You don't talk about how it made you feel. You simply recount what was observed, what has already been said and discussed in the larger groups where everyone saw and heard the same thing. You don't need to talk to anyone about what you did here. That is what the *Thor's Craftsmen* Non-Disclosure Agreements require. That is what they are for and that is what you will say and do and, more importantly, what you *won't* say and what you *won't* do.

"It doesn't matter what anyone thinks, what they insinuate or even accuse you or anyone else of doing...or not doing. Even if they know or think they know something else. So what? Everyone can have an opinion or know a piece of something without knowing the entire thing. That is how DC works, nothing new there. The only thing that matters is what *they* can prove...and what *you* can prove. You can *prove* exactly what happened because everyone saw and heard the same thing. It stays that way. The only way it doesn't stay that way is if one of you four changes it. And, to be clear, if one of you change it, you change it for all of you. Plausible denial is enough, until it isn't. Let the facts be the facts and let the facts as they are stay the facts. If you had intention, motive, or opportunity to influence the events and eventual outcome here to what ultimately did happen then you are no different than everyone else working on this program. Don't do or say anything to jeopardize that same-as-everyone-else status you still have. We all contributed in our own ways to this program…to its outcome, and *that* we can prove. That is enough to keep you all safe if that's all there is. So, make sure that's all there is. Are you clear on this?"

The four of them were darting looks back and forth, knowing full well what the CJCS was saying, as well as what he was not saying. And based on what they knew from the flight down, he was assuring them he would be doing exactly as he was instructing them to do. After all, retirement was supposed to be less worries, not more worries.

Bob responded for the group, "I think we know what you mean, and we will prove it by doing as you say. Now what?"

They all smiled a knowing smile, lips pursed and with no words until Steve broke the silence, "How about a drink, I know I could use one, and I think you all could to. Anyone want to *prove* me right?"

A nervous laughter broke out. His assessment was spot on so they filed out of the small office and headed to the one spot on the facility where they could get a drink near the dining hall. After draining his glass and a little bit of small talk about anything but what they had just covered, Dutch excused himself from the group to go check on a few more things and then make some calls that he was not really looking forward to making.

Once he had the confirmations he needed from the teams on the ground, he rounded up Frank and the two of them got on the phone, made some calls and waited patiently for the SECDEF to get the President lined up for an update.

It was not what he wanted to hear, but it was the news that he had come to grips with the longer he pondered it. After grasping at some straws to see how far and wide the team had looked for solutions, POTUS reluctantly agreed that it was the same conclusion the separate teams he had working on their problem had also come to. You don't go to all this effort and expense and throw in the towel without a second, third or fourth opinion. On this it was unanimous, they weren't getting back in and the best course of action was to protect what they had in the configuration they had now.

"All right Dutch, dial it in, then cut it off. We deployed it but, if we can't have it on call, make sure nobody else can either. Once that's done, figure out what you need to monitor it. Then start breaking it down and sending people home. Seems like a lot of expense and effort just to mess up a houseboat—That's me sulking—I am getting over it and I have a meeting with the CCP leader in a few hours where we will see if General Lincoln's theory pans out. I hope it does, because, if not...well... I sure hope it pans out," he paused and the line went dead.

Frank looked at the Chairman, raised his eyebrows and asked, "Now what?"

"We wrap it up like we just discussed. We go to DC. I retire, you get moved in and start a new job," he smiled.

CHAPTER TWENTY

OFF-RAMPS

To the world watching and the press assembled at the UN building, the announcement that the United States, China and the UN had brokered an agreement regarding the on-demand weather modification technology had monopolized the headlines and news cycle for the past twelve hours. Uncharacteristically, there were no leaks, no talking points, and no advanced copies of what would be revealed at the joint press conference which would begin in about an hour. What was obvious was the level of security in and around the UN and the airports in the past twenty-four hours. There was well founded speculation that the two national leaders would both be attending in person.

Mr. Dau and the Secretary General had not been seen outside the building for the past couple of days nor were they available for comment beyond their earlier announcement to a hungry press. That was because they had not left the building since taking the call from the President of the United States. It seemed there was a meaningful role for the UN in fielding their previously demonstrated technology after all. That role however depended on an unprecedented level of collaboration between the two nations who had both made very public and potentially damaging claims against each other regarding the origins and the application of this technology that was new to the world but seemed not to be new to either of them.

To move forward in a positive and convincing manner required both countries to take a couple of steps backwards. The President and US surrogates would need to walk back their earlier claims as a misunderstanding of the conditions and the context of the CCP actions and intentions. For their part, the CCP would similarly concede that it was reasonable to interpret what the US saw in the way they did. Just as it was reasonable for the CCP to have misinterpreted the circumstances which led to their own inaccurate claims that the US had stolen the technology from them. After considerable candid and open-minded discussions, under the skillful moderation of the UN senior leadership, the two nations came to a common understanding of the facts. The missing information provided to both sides by the UN facilitators resulted in clarity of actions and intent. This accomplishment proved to be a great relief to both nations and provided the opportunity to recalibrate their understandings and come to a common belief on the best path forward. That path was to be revealed today.

While some would find this hard to believe, others would see it as the hopeful new foundation for collaboration between the two global powers. The rationale, circumstances and motive behind it would not be completely revealed but there was no mistaking the two had agreed to an arrangement that both were sufficiently content to implement. The rest was the same political theater, national spin, media taglines, bottom lines and flexes that played into any other day. The biggest difference between this and any other topic was there was something in it for everyone, not just them. That alone made this historic. Their agreement could impact everyone in a positive way. *Win-win-wins* are hard to come by in international politics.

The notion that two nations, with the UN negotiating for everyone else, would decide what would happen for everyone was anything but normal. They could, and would, claim that the global tension and military escalation between the two nations needed immediate action to de-escalate sufficiently to satisfy their national governing bodies in order to prevent the hawks on both sides from initiating hostilities to gain the upper hand in what seemed inevitable. In doing so, there was not sufficient time for alternative courses of action, but bringing in the UN was an agreed upon solution space to provide a voice for the nations not at the sensitive discussions.

After all, this was at its foundation a dispute between the US and China based on what they each thought they knew. The deficiencies in their existing intelligence apparatuses on both sides revealed vulnerabilities they did not want exposed any further than was needed between the two primaries to correct them on both sides. National security being what it is, means it can be used as cover for literally anything and that seems to work regardless of the political composition of the nation.

For this to work, there would be three sides to the story. The press conference was designed to provide that narrative and support it with a visual that would be broadcast around the world, played over and over again, and analyzed by all sides to either support or refute the validity of what was going to occur here today. There would be the US side of the story, the PRC and thus CCP side of story...both vehemently partisan. And there would be the UN side of the story. The neutral, objective arbiter of the truth and mediator of the misinformed conflict that nearly escalated into what many described and feared as World War III. The leaders of each would be the only ones to speak and the only ones to respond to questions if they chose to do so. This was intended to remove any doubt about the level of understanding, commitment and agreement being announced and carried forward. All three understood and committed to a *buck-stops-here-*level of responsibility and accountability for what was to occur. That is what was needed for it to succeed and that is what they agreed to provide.

Their supporting cast was equally important. The President would be flanked by this Cabinet members, and on the other side would be the same including the CCP Chairman and top leaders. The UN Secretary General would be accompanied by Mr. Dau and the key leaders of the *Thor's Journeymen* demonstration effort from both sides. This would show the world that both sides were represented by their decision-makers, as well as, honest brokers who know what did and did not happen along the way during the UN weather modification activities. This was perhaps one of the most delicate portions of the negotiations between them. After all, this is where the majority of the uncertainty existed between the nations and now where the animosity was high.

General Chen, Mr. Wu and Zach would be perceived by most as those who were CCP participants in the UN demonstrations. Those in the know on both sides knew, since Australia, that was not the case. Professor Mcleod and fiancée Ann would be seen as UN loyalists albeit from the US. The National Security Advisor, Major General Lincoln, Major Lessur and Chief Andies would all represent the US side of the UN team despite their recent vital roles in the *Thor's Craftsmen* efforts. This was image over content, style over substance and theater rather than debate to support the narrative. While this was not uncommon, it was new to most of those who were being brought back together for this instance of what was far too familiar for some other participants.

The small group that included Tom, Frank, Chen, Wu, Zach, Bob, Ann Ron, Andies, Steve and Betty had left Florida the day prior on Tom's plane and were sequestered in their own rooms at Fort Hamilton since their arrival. They had no phones but were able to watch the news unfolding on their TVs so were aware of what was coming but not yet of their involvement, or lack thereof. That would come on the shuttle ride to the UN after they were appropriately attired in the garments delivered to their rooms earlier. They were each told prior to their departure that their work on the *Thor's Craftsmen* program was not yet complete, but that they would not be returning to the Florida facility. On the flight up, they were given little additional information beyond instructions not to talk to others or each other about their work. Get some rest and await the next briefing where they would be provided updates and any additional guidance on their release from the program.

Bob and Ann were allowed to share a room despite the recommendation from the security officer, but Steve and Betty were not. That is until Betty decided that arrangement would not be suitable to her. So, despite operational concerns from the officer in charge, once Tom intervened on her behalf the arrangements were altered to meet her request. None of them were particularly comfortable with the lack of information and the waiting but, after the grueling schedule of the recent past, they did welcome the opportunity to rest and reset.

No one was used to failing but they couldn't help but feel like they had in this case. Despite their best sustained efforts, they were unable to regain access to the on-orbit weather modification satellites, either individually or as a constellation. Their failsafe was indeed that and it performed flawlessly. Funny how computers do precisely what you tell them to and not what you want them to do…but in this case nobody was laughing about it. As designed and programmed, the lockout took the conditions for all the bird's operating areas to a climatological normal condition and waited for new instructions which never appeared. The systems dutifully maintained the normal weather for every region, and it seems it would continue to do so until new instructions arrived, whenever that might occur. In this case, those instructions had no way to be successfully sent, received or implemented. They put the system in place, and it works, but it still felt to them like they failed—well—at least, to most of them.

Bob and Ann had a slightly different perspective, and that perspective was shared by Betty and Steve although they all knew better than to talk about it. Especially not while they were holed up in a quiet room on a small military post in New York, as close to the UN as they could get. Chances were, if someone was going to bug a room, with or without permission, it would be one of these. But that didn't mean they weren't thinking about the situation, what had happened and what was coming next. While none of them believed anyone knew for sure the details of what began the sequence of events when the President triggered the lockout, there were certainly those who thought it was no accident. They could think what they wanted, but Dutch's speech had been burned into all of their heads and proving anything would be a tall task as long as they did what he compelled them to consider. Still there was an element of fear of the unknown that each of the four felt, especially given their knowledge that those who thought it was not an accident were more right than wrong.

Finally, a knock came on each of their doors by a messenger who delivered notification that they should get dressed in their delivered attire and be ready to go in one hour. They would be escorted to the departure area where the group would travel together to their destination. That could only mean one thing. They were going to be at the UN somewhere for the press conference. If that was the case, it likely meant they were going to be seen there and likely seen together. That provided hope and fear, and the variations on what could come from that were infinite. So, in the meantime, they got ready and waited patiently, and impatiently for their next movement. This was military style personified, *hurry up and wait,* which is exactly what they had been doing since their arrival.

The knocks came and each of them were escorted to the assembly area, arriving nearly concurrently, and were loaded onto a very unremarkable shuttle with tinted windows. Once loaded they quickly departed. There was a three-person civilian attired security detail in addition to the driver, who was clearly skilled in things beyond driving a shuttle, and Tom, who was instructing the driver about something before he addressed the group.

"Hi everyone, and might I say you all look great. Thanks for taking this seriously. You are all going to be in the spotlight today and people will be seeing you around the world whether you want to be seen or not. That is, and please take no offense by this, all but Steve and Betty who will be allowed to take up your favorite positions along the edge of the support staff if that suits you both?"

"Fine by me," Steve agreed, as Betty at the same time exhaled audibly, "Thank God, yes. Me too."

"Very good then. For the rest of you, though, we are getting the UN demonstration team back together for the press conference. The faces familiar to some, and identifiable to anyone who wants to compare the tapes from previous locations will get to see the same mugs from before assembled today for the press conference. The good news is you will have a front row seat to an historic event. I guess you have already had that for some time now that I think about it. Well, you will get to see this specific historic event. But make no mistake about this, we are sitting at the kids table for this, and we are to be seen but not heard. Not a single word from any of us. We don't have a speaking part, and we won't do anything to draw attention to ourselves and take it away from those who are at the adult table saying what they are there to say. Is everyone picking up what I am laying down? Are we crystal clear on this?" Tom paused.

The vertical nods from all were a clear indication that everyone understood the instructions, but that was not going to be enough for today.

"OK, that's a good start but I need clear confirmation from each of you that you both understand my instructions *and* that you will comply with them. It's a formality, but I need you each to affirm please," he said pleasantly, but it was clear that he would not continue until he had what he needed. Around the shuttle everyone responded in the affirmative and, once that was complete, Chen asked what was on everyone's mind.

"What is it we are going to be doing, or seeing today, Tom? And, for Mr. Wu, Zach and myself, what is gained by putting us in the public light to confirm beyond doubt that we are alive and well but *not* in China?"

"Lots to unpack there so let me start with the easiest first. We will all be seated at the UN staff table with the Secretary General, Mr. Dau and a few others to hear the US and PRC explain their new UN brokered agreement. That is what you have seen on the news and that is where we will be. Having the three of you there, along with a couple of hand selected Special Colonels who will be sitting there as well, will show the PRC and CCP have their UN representatives along, as well as, the US's…that would be the rest of us, including myself. Your families will know you are alive and well," he concluded.

"So, too, will those who wonder what happened to us. They will know we are alive and well in New York today. That will jeopardize us and the families who stayed behind," Chen protested.

"That might be true…might not be. Depends on who keeps their word. One of the agreed upon conditions for this meeting was the promise that you all, and your families will be safe and off limits for any action or retribution for what may or may not have happened along the way here. They agree, and this agreement is in writing and is signed. That's the best we could do, Chen, I hope it is enough," Tom explained.

"It might be enough; it might not be enough. Time will tell and the consequences of breaking that deal will decide for us all. Thank you, Tom," Chen surrendered to his thoughts about the most likely outcomes.

"Can you give us some insights as to what we are going to hear today, Tom? I'm afraid I don't have a good poker face, and I don't want to look as shocked as I fear I might be at some of the things we might hear today," Bob asked for himself and the others he knew were also wondering the same thing.

"I can give you the takeaways, but the details, or what they will say beneath the main points? I have no idea. Whatever they are, your reaction needs to be that is exactly what happened and how you recall it," he began. "While that might be hard to do, that is the task of the day for all of us. Support the narrative. Be flexible and, above all, be convincing. You are going to hear both nation's leaders acknowledge previous misconceptions and misunderstanding that led to accusations they now understand to be unsubstantiated. To avoid additional strains and to reduce risks of future misunderstandings the UN will resume the role of implementing and operating all fielded on-demand weather modification systems. They have assumed that role today and have control of *all* such systems from both the US and China."

Tom paused and let that sink in to those in the shuttle who, collectively, had some of the most detailed and comprehensive knowledge of the entire saga of Thor's Hammers from beginning to present. They considered the potential holes in the story, the potential outcomes in the future if someone were to disclose more details or if the technology failed, or a myriad of other potential things that could unravel this narrative. Slowly but surely a degree of confidence in the possibility of this succeeding began to take root amongst the group.

"If nobody pushes for anything outside of climo then the UN is good to go? But, if something goes wrong in the future, it's on the UN's watch. And over time, what really happened to us can be the exact same cover story the UN uses to explain why they cannot initiate any events outside the climo range…because that part is true. That's the negotiated agreement between the three, to stay within climo for everyone's benefit? That's today's announcement, Tom?" Major Lessur, asked him directly.

"If not that, it will be some version of that approach Ron, yes," Tom ceded, glad to see the Major had caught on quickly.

"Are there any parts of the history of how we got here that get changed, Tom? Does anyone's credibility take a hit, specifically mine, or Doc Auster's?" Bob asked.

"Not that I am aware of," Tom said candidly, "…but I am not the one doing the talking today. Doc discovered the technology, but the context in which it was being used in the US was not clearly understood by all. But that misunderstanding is now cleared up. You got it the way you got it, and it's all clean from there. It's what happened."

"Except for the part where the innocent people in India were killed in an effort to discredit the UN effort," Bob contested, as that event still weighed heavily on him.

"Again, context and intent. It is unfortunate that something went wrong with either the demonstration equipment or the CCP equipment being used to monitor or counter the UN systems. Not working together and collaborating produced a catastrophic event. That must be prevented from ever happening, which is why the UN will operate the system on behalf of every nation's interests. This is the outcome the summit should have produced but did not. It is unfortunate that the two primary nations that could have enabled that outcome were instrumental in it not coming about. We have fixed that now and we are here today to ensure that agreement is cemented in history and lives up to the potential it offers."

"You sure you're not the one speaking today? Maybe you should be, Tom. Sounds like you got this dialed in and down pat." Frank asked, in what first sounded like a compliment but could have been taken another way.

"I'm sure, but I have heard it all enough now that I very well could deliver it if called upon," Tom assured them. "But remember, I will be sitting at the *seen-but-not-heard* UN table with all of you."

"That is all well and good, but who is actually going to be doing *what* with the on-orbit system? Are we really turning it over to the UN? Chief Andies asked. "I mean that sounds like a risky path forward given the nature of this system and all the sensitive infrastructure needed to just ensure we're sustaining the status quo. To maintain the failsafe climo, the constellation still needs to be up and running…the CubeSats on orbit and all."

"Yeah, well you have a point," Tom smiled. "I mean we have no control of the systems, including their maneuverability, so all we can do is monitor their location and see that they are still communicating with each other, and performing as needed. Sounds like some pretty good duty for someone with the right clearance and expertise to me. How about you Chief, sound like good duty to you?" Tom offered.

"Maybe for someone but it sounds boring as shit to me, Tom. If you are inferring that might be in my future, that's a hard pass from me if I have any say in the matter. And, since I have over twenty years in and am retirement eligible, every day for me is a decision on whether I stay or go," Andies provided his perspective despite this not being the time nor place for this type of discussion…yet there they were having it anyway.

"Figured as much, but thought I tease it and see. When we wrap all this up, I'd love to talk to you about a next gig, because I think I have something else that is right up your alley. That is a discussion for another time. Back to the task at hand. We are getting pretty close, any other questions before we get there, and *hurry up and wait* again for the protocol folks to usher us to the right spot at the right time?" Tom concluded.

"I have a question, Tom," Zach asked. "What happens after this press conference, assuming all goes as planned?"

"Well, in a perfect world Zach, we all get to go on our merry way. That will look different for each of you but, depending on how this goes, we will hopefully be done with the *Thor's Craftsmen* commitments. Everything will become a transition and that means out with the old and in with the new. New program, if there even is one—we close the books on this one."

"I like the sound of that. So, let's see to it that everything goes as planned, shall we?" Zach suggested for all to get behind, as he had much that might be gained from that outcome.

It was not long after that they approached the now familiar entrance to the UN Headquarters building. The security detail did their thing and oversaw the orderly exit from the shuttle and quick walk into the security screening area which many of the group had become familiar with from their previous visits. The heavily tinted windows on the shuttle shielded them from the throngs of people and paparazzi assembled along the route and near the entrance, but the press already in the briefing area waited anxiously for those approaching. The flashes and shouts were impossible to miss even though there was glass, distance and doorways between them all. This was clearly already a spectacle and it promised to be even greater as the day wore on and the event began.

They passed through the security check points; the number of armed guards was staggeringly higher than any of them had seen previously. Clearly it was a better to have them and not need them as opposed to needing them and not having them was the strategy being employed today. You could hear various people passing by and radio calls mentioning the National Guard being in position and on standby if needed. There was a lot of power and importance being packed into a small space. It was more about preparations for the response to the news they intended to deliver than to protect those delivering it.

The group was staged in a small meeting room near the main briefing chambers. They could see that members of the US and PRC senior leadership teams were assembled nearby and also sequestered in small groups isolated from the others. Bob could see the CJCS standing with the SECDEF, SECSTATE and DHS Secretary all standing and chatting, waiting patiently for the call: *get ready and take your seats*. It was then that Bob also noticed another familiar face walking toward them. It was Father Gannon, smiling as he approached the group.

"This is a pleasant surprise. Hi, Father it's good to see you," Ann greeted him ahead of the rest of the group.

"When Mr. Dau asked me to come and be part of this, I could not refuse. It's good to see you all," he said, looking around at Bob, Ann, Betty and Steve. "It's nice to see you and good to be here with you again. I can only imagine what it's been like for you all."

"Honestly, Kevin, I don't think you can. It doesn't seem real but it's good to see you. It reminds me that all this is real and why we came here in the first place. I'm glad you're here. This is an historic day and it's only fitting that we all see it together. No thundersnow today though, ok?" Bob nodded, and it was then they got the signal and instructions to take their seats. The press conference would begin shortly.

The first any of the group seated in the UN staff area saw the Secretary General or Mr. Dau was when they approached the two remaining empty chairs in the center section of the DV area labeled UN. It was deliberate that the PRC and US sections flanked the central section that both divided and brought together the other two. It was also deliberate that the event was being held at the neutral location of the UN Headquarters. The symbolism was consistent throughout. Every detail was considered and decided with the intent of supporting that theme. This was all about wins for everyone, a few draws for China and the US but no losses. There were to be no losing moments today, implied or intended.

As Professor Mcleod sat waiting for the principals to arrive, he could not help but think about Doc Auster and their days at the University. It seemed so long ago considering all that had happened, although, in actual time, it wasn't all that far in the past. This all happened very fast compared to the rest of the events in Bob's life and, regardless of how today turned out, he knew the lady sitting next to him right now was proud of him. He now understood how that single hope could have motivated his former boss and colleague to work tirelessly on something, even if he chose to do it alone. Doc's wish to make his wife proud seemed to be coming true. At the same time, Bob was being granted the same but not because of a wish he made himself. It was perhaps the best outcome of the circumstances he inherited from Doc—their ability to live vicariously through each other's actions, past and present.

Bob was confident that Doc had made his wife proud and by extension enabled those assembled here today to finish what he had started. There was no way Doc could have done this alone. It was also impossible for those here today to have accomplished what they did without Doc. With that thought fresh on his mind, the room quieted as two men walked to their assigned national seating sections and took their seats at the table with one microphone. Each section was pie shaped with the three men seated only a few feet apart so they could all be kept in camera view regardless of who was speaking. They were backed up with a wedge-shaped group of representatives behind them. If you were in this seating area there was no place to hide from the cameras. It was showtime and, like it or not, everyone was *on*.

The Secretary General began and welcomed his esteemed colleagues from both nations and explained why they were there. He outlined the events that brought them to be there and generally reviewed, at a very high level, the events that had occurred before the summit that never took place after the President's remarks. The Secretary General then glossed over what he called a series of misunderstandings that resulted in an escalation of military tensions while concurrently all but eliminating effective communication between the two nations. Through persistent UN diplomatic efforts with both countries, they were able to re-establish communications and clear up the misunderstandings on both sides. This series of events highlighted the immediate need for a structure and process to be in place to prevent this from recurring as they continued to resolve their existing differences. Since they were on a roll, so to speak, they carried the discussion to its natural conclusion and are assembled here to collectively present it to the world.

The Secretary General laid it out for the world just as Tom had done on the shuttle on the way over. He stated that between the two nations, there were individual operations, as well as, surface and airborne regional systems, and limited on-orbit systems all able to trigger on-demand weather events. He explained that both nations believed that they were the only two who possess such systems, and that both had turned over all of their systems to the custody and operational control of the UN prior to the commencement of this press conference. It was at this point both leaders read identical statements, acknowledging and apologizing for past misunderstandings and affirming the turnover of all their operational and test systems to the UN. They each ended by declaring that they would provide the needed technical support for the UN to effectively carry out their new mission of maintaining the global weather within climatological normal ranges for all locations across the globe.

Once these were complete, the Secretary General promised more information would be forthcoming soon and ended the press conference without taking any questions. This was more of a press covered announcement, than a press conference, but it was a big announcement. Not taking questions allowed both nation's leaders to stay on task such that the only sound clip for the media to run would be each of them saying identical things. For their own national audiences, that meant they got the best of the other guy. The UN could carry the weather discussions from here on out and the other two leaders could get back to the business of running their countries and finding whatever strategic advantage could be gained under the new normal of knowing with certainty what the weather would be, and more importantly, what it would not be on any given day.

"That was pretty anti-climactic," Betty said as the group stood up and the volume in the room rose simultaneously as those hearing this for the first time began to discuss what just happened.

"That was the plan. I think we can call that a success. Now let's get you all out of here before anyone can do anything to change that," Tom said. "Please follow me out. We will head back to the same spot we came in and grab the same shuttle back. "Father Gannon, good to see you again." Mr. Dau and the Secretary General had already departed along with the heads of state from both nations. As instructed, they all fell in step behind Tom and headed for the exit, careful to stay quiet and together. For a few minutes they waited, smiled and waved but said nothing until the shuttle pulled up and they were loaded up and pulling away from the crowd and flashing cameras.

"If I never come back here that will suit me fine. I am not a big fan of New York," Steve said unapologetically. "But I'd be happy to have any of you pop in for a visit if you're in my neck of the woods. I think I will be staying there for a good while after all of this is done."

"It looks like we are just about at that point now Steve. We can get you set up and, on your way, once we get back," Tom announced. "In fact, that goes for the rest of you as well. That will be the next order of business once we get back. Get into something more comfortable than suits and class-A uniforms and get packed. I will pop in on each of you to discuss your destinations. Be thinking about what you think or want that to be." With that realization, the trip back went a lot faster than the trip there. The mood was lighter and the thoughts and discussions were polar opposite in tone and tenor from those just a few hours earlier.

CHAPTER TWENTY-ONE

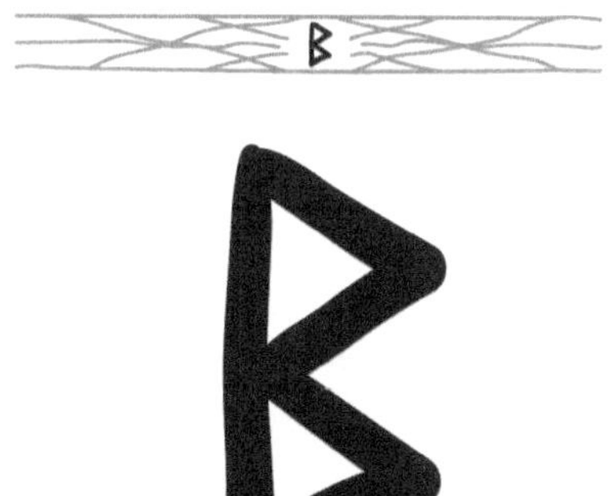

ENCORES

The shuttle pulled through the gate unimpeded and went directly to the billeting area where it stopped to disembark the passengers who had just been a part of the historic announcement. They were not allowed to loiter and were escorted directly to their rooms to change clothes and prepare for departure, as soon as, possible. There would be no chances taken that any one of them would wander off to accidently—or deliberately —come in contact with or comment on the biggest story in the world. Dutifully and nervously excited at the prospect of being done with all this they all followed instructions and then waited patiently for their respective visits from Tom or whoever was going to knock on their door.

Tom chose to do the easiest ones first. He had been on the phone for the past hour, flipping from the tasks at hand of getting everyone out of here and responding to the results of the press conference. By all accounts, so far it had produced the desired outcomes and the responses were positive thus far. The President had been busy calling the leaders of the US's closest allies to fill them in on the reasons the PRC would not negotiate with anyone else but the US and UN and how he had their interests in mind as he negotiated the deal he made. The press coverage was positive, and the sound bites were landing favorably as predicted. *So far, so good* he thought as he knocked on Frank's door.

"Hey buddy; you good?" he asked as he walked into the room and looked around not surprised to see he was packed and ready.

"Yes, ready to get home," Frank replied.

"Yeah, you're gonna have to get the family ready to move to DC, huh? I suppose we will still be running into each other regularly, but I will be glad it's not all about weather stuff. I learned more about millibars and isotachs since we met than I ever wanted or needed to know," Tom smiled as he waited for a wisecrack in response.

"I suppose. DC is not my favorite, especially with a teenager...but duty calls. Right now, I am looking forward to just getting back to my family, my own bed and a schedule that actually has time to get into both. Lessur, Andies and I are all traveling back together, right?" Frank requested.

"If that's where they want to go, yes. Let's go find out, shall we? Grab your bags and let's go. I'm not your porter," Tom said and led the way out the door, kindly leaving it open so Frank could follow. They knocked on Major Lessur's door and went in. He too was ready to go and, by go, he meant back to his post citing similar reasons Frank had just moments earlier. This had been a great adventure but he was ready to be home for a while and knew that feeling would be mutual as soon as he walked through the door. That could not come soon enough. The trio proceeded to Chief Andie's room and found him sitting on the edge of the bed, with the door open and waiting for them.

"Took you long enough," he complained. "Not sure where you all are going but hopefully someone can get me back home. I need to sleep for three days and the only place I know to do that safely is my own house."

"We have consensus then. Everyone going to the same place for the same reasons. Let's go. I have a van waiting for you guys out front, and a plane ready to go as soon as you get there," Tom said. "You didn't think some of that forecasting skill would rub off on me? As much time as I have spent bailing you guys out, I'd think you'd have already made me an honorary weatherman. Dare to dream; maybe someday." He turned and led the way to the van, helped them load their gear into it and gave the driver specific instructions on where to take them, what to tell the gate guards and which aircraft in which spot he was to deliver the three men in his charge. "All right then, thanks guys. It's been *real*, and it's been *fun*…and mostly *real-fun* this go-round. I am confident our paths will cross again. Till then, good luck, and safe travels. Go get some rest." He closed the door and slapped the side of the van twice sending it on its way as he strode back toward the billeting rooms.

Chen opened the door after the first knock and, when Tom entered, he opened with, "I am hoping to rejoin my family, Tom, and I am hoping we can make a fresh start somewhere out west. Is that possible, or is there still more for me to do on this?"

"Did you have spot in mind?" Tom asked.

"Eugene, Oregon. It's a college town, and my wife and I would like to open a small restaurant so we can feed and hang out with the young folks. Help us learn and adjust, share some of our good culture and disappear into the fabric of America," Chen proposed.

"Sounds like a good plan. I want to thank you for keeping your word. We put you in a bad spot and you did what you said you'd do despite the circumstances. You kept your word and I will do the same. Eugene Oregon, OK then," Tom agreed.

"Thank you, Tom. I knew you would. I am experienced enough to know that you cannot trust governments, but you can trust people. When governments become untrustworthy, it is because those in positions of power are not to be trusted and vice versa, as you say."

"Thanks Chen, let's get you to Oregon," Tom said and led him to the waiting car. Again, he provided instructions to the driver and sent them on their way after warning Chen that he would likely pop in to see if the food is any good next time he finds himself in Eugene.

"I promise, you will not be disappointed," Chen assured him.

"I have no doubt, Chen. You have not disappointed me since we met," Tom said as the car drove off. *OK Mr. Wu, what are we to do with you?* Tom amused himself, thinking how we would never tire of those little rhymes. Small pleasures in life; funny how that works.

"Mr. Tom, please come in," Wu invited as Tom stepped in and closed the door. "Is it so, that my family and I can go to a location of our choosing?"

"Yes Wu, but it needs to be in the US. That is not something I can change," Tom cautioned.

"Of course, I understand. I am hopeful that my family and I can go to Silicon Valley in California. There could be work for me, school for my children, and community for my wife. It will not be the same as home, but we will be able to assimilate and find a happy medium between what we left behind and what we have to look ahead to. Can we do that please?" He was almost begging.

"Of course, Wu. You did what we asked, and we will now do what you ask. You understand that you cannot work on this technology? You cannot talk about it, or anything you had to do with it before you got here or since you have been here. You understand that right?" Tom wanted to be certain and know that he was also crystal clear on what we required of him.

"Yes, Tom I understand but I know what I know and my understanding and experience will help me regardless of what I am working on," Wu correctly clarified.

"That you do and that it will. Very well, then, Mr. Wu let's get you to California, shall we?" Tom encouraged as they walked to the parked car waiting for its passenger and instructions from Tom. With Mr. Wu on his way, Tom went back to pull the three musketeers plus one into a discussion about what they wanted to do next. He knocked on Bob and Ann's door, and when it opened was not too surprised to see Steve and Betty also sitting in the room with their bags talking with Ann.

"OK, this will make it easier I suppose. Have you decided where you want to go and what you want to do or do you need more time?" Tom asked as he joined them in the already cramped room.

"That depends," Bob began. "I have a lot of files to load and we all have personal items in our rooms at the hotel. I am getting the impression you want us out of New York, as soon as, possible. A lot of people already know that is where we have been staying."

"Yeah, about that," Tom interrupted. "With everything going on today, I might have forgotten to mention that I took the liberty of having everything collected from those rooms moved to our evidence storage area. Now that sounds worse than it is, so let me explain before you get upset with me.

"Knowing what was coming, and that, as you correctly pointed out, lots of people know where you have been staying, I didn't want to risk having a run in with some ambitious journalist or extremist deciding now would be a good time to do whatever. The evidence area is guarded, secured, and everything was inventoried as it went out as a preventive measure. It's not evidence as you might define it formally. This way we can ship it to wherever you want it sent and be confident that it is safe until then. And while I was at it, I paid the bill for the entire time of your stay. That alone was one expensive gesture. They must have figured you were a billionaire or something because they were gouging you, *big time*. Full transparency, I made them reduce the cost to the government rate for the rooms so if you intended to use that expense as a tax write off you don't get to anymore," Tom paused, as he read the room. "OK I'm done. Even if you were to go there, it would be pointless, and you don't have a room to go to anymore."

"OK, Tom, that's understandable. But everything that left that room better find its way back to me. You know Betty keeps and tracks all that, so you are on notice. She sets the gold standard for knowing what is where and what is missing."

"So noted. Can we get back to the main point here, which is where do I need to get you guys to? For all practical purposes, we are done for a while, and I need to get you guys on your way into obscurity as soon as possible. Ready to go home?" Tom continued.

"Isn't that the first place, or at least one of the first places someone looking to ask us questions would start?" Ann began. "Seriously, Tom, you must be tired if that's the best you can do."

"I am tired," he agreed playfully.

"Alaska, Tom," Ann declared. "Speaking for the four of us, we would all like to go to Alaska. Generically speaking, this is the best time of year in Alaska for fishing. We want to go on a fishing trip to Alaska. It will take several weeks, since we want to fish for rainbow trout, salmon, Dolly Vardan and graylings. Remote private cabins, along the rivers. Boats in and out will be fine, depending on which rivers we end up on."

"And halibut, and crab," Steve added. "It wouldn't be right to go all that way this time of year and not pay some attention to the rest of them, too. Deeper water, different boats, and likely we might see a few whales while we are out. *Gotta* give the halibut some love while we are there. Wouldn't be right not to include them," he smiled as he passed to the, until now, quiet Betty.

"Yes, I agree with Steve. Wouldn't be right to go all that way and not give them their due. In fact, since we are already up there, I don't know how I could forgive myself if I didn't take just a little more time to go see Denali. I mean we'll be almost right there. We can drive, or hike or whatever but I just don't see how we don't go there for at least a little while after traveling all that way. And if we go on this trip, think about how much time and trouble we save by not having to make a second trip to go back and see it then. The carbon footprint will be cut in half if we don't fly back up a second time. Yes, we definitely need to do Denali while we are there."

"You guys are too much. You have more money than you know what to do with and you are going to have me finance a month-long Alaskan excursion for the four of you?" Tom shook his head smiling. "It makes perfect sense, though. In a month people may be a lot less interested in talking to you about what happened today. And a month in the remote confines of Alaska you should be able to get your stories about all this as straight as an arrow.

"You want us to work out the detailed itinerary or do you want to do it on your flights to Anchorage?" Tom relented.

"I think we will work it out and email it to you as we go. Just keep a tab open for us. Probably best we are not too predictable for those who are persistently looking for us," Ann instructed. You could count on her to think three steps ahead and prepare for contingencies.

"What about after the fishing trip and Denali? What then?" Tom persisted.

"From there we will head back home, at least what is home for now, back to the houses near the University. Mine and Betty's. We will take it from there," Bob began. "I am sure that, while we are in Alaska, we will have plenty of time to plan our wedding, consider and decide what is next for us. After all, as you reminded me, I do have a few dollars saved up so we can take our time figuring this all out. We might even have to discuss a double wedding if this trip is long enough."

"Don't get ahead of yourself champ," Betty scolded. "Are we gonna keep talking about this or are you gonna get us on a plane to Anchorage, Tom? Can we shop along the way, I don't think my Florida bag is going to be appropriate for Alaska?"

"Lots of shopping along the way and once you get there, Betty. And yes, let's get you all on a plane to Anchorage. It's a good plan, expensive but good. I was kind of expecting a Mediterranean Cruise or something more extravagant," Tom admitted.

"That's on the table?" Betty asked.

"Not anymore," Tom smiled and began to pick up her bags. He may not be Frank's porter, but he was unhesitant in being hers. "I was expecting you would want to travel together so I have a van waiting. Shall we?"

"Not just yet, if you don't mind, Tom. Just another minute if we can?" Bob requested of the man holding Betty's bags.

"Sure, what is it, Professor?" Tom asked dropping the bags on the floor.

"On behalf of all of us, I want to say thank you. Not just for today, but for everything. This has been a crazy ride for all of us. And, while you weren't with us early on, ever since it got into the complicated and dangerous venues we found ourselves in, you were there for us. I think you sincerely cared about not only what we were doing but also about those of us who were doing it. I mean you put yourself at risk to get us out of India. You found a polite way to protect Betty from undue risk and you replaced the lax security detail at the hotel just to name a few. You got Frank and his guys promoted, rightfully so for what they did but it took *you* doing it. There is a lot of *walk-the-talk* where you are concerned and that means something to me...to us. Thank you for all that. In a world where people aren't what they appear to be, you always did what you said you would do when it came to us. And I want to acknowledge that and thank you for it. You helped me and you helped me protect my family when I couldn't. I appreciate that; we all do. Our door will always be open to you. Thank you."

"*Takk*...It has been my pleasure, Bob. Now let's get you all out of here, I still have more work to do." Tom reached for the bags.

"What does *Takk* mean, Tom?" Bob asked as he watched Tom roll his eyes.

"That is Norwegian for Thanks, Bob. For a college professor, and the guy nicknamed *Thor's Apprentice* with *Thor's Hammers, Thor's Journeymen,* and *Thor's Craftsmen* all under his belt you should at least know the Norwegian essentials like please and thank you. Can we go now, *Ville du vært så snill?*" Tom requested.

"I hope that means please," Bob smiled as he followed them out to the waiting van. They loaded up; the driver acknowledged the instructions and affirmed the location of the waiting private jet that would carry the four out of New York.

"I expect an invite to the wedding or weddings. Whatever you decide. Safe travels and I hope the fish are biting. Good luck," Tom said as he headed back toward billeting to visit the last room on his list. He knocked on the door, and Zach opened it slowly and invited Tom in. The security detail continued at their designated post outside the door.

"Hello, Zach. Have you made your decision?" Tom asked.

"Before I answer, I have to know have you made yours yet? It will impact my answer," Zach paused, waiting to hear his response.

"Made my decision? Which one?" Tom asked cautiously.

"When we first met, you said my future depended on whether or not I did enough. Did I do enough, Tom? Enough to disappear to the place of my choosing? If I am breathing when I disappear, it is a different answer than if I am disappearing to a place that I am not. That is the decision I am waiting to hear about," Zach explained without really needing to, as he was certain Tom recalled their conversation as vividly as he did. One did not get as far as they both have without that capacity and they both knew it. Each was jockeying for position. They also both knew that.

"Yeah, Zach. The way this turned out you did enough or perhaps, just as importantly, you didn't do anything to prevent the needed outcomes from occurring. You are almost home my friend; I just need to know where you want home to be and to agree on what is and isn't OK once you get there," Tom said, as his curiosity was about to be satisfied.

"How about the Maldives? I think the weather there is ideal for my bursitis," Zach suggested.

"How about some place that has an extradition treaty with the US just to keep us all true to our word? Can we try one of those places that might be just as suitable for your bursitis?" Tom countered with a smirk.

"OK, how about Belize? That sounds like a happy medium that can adequately meet both of our needs without losing too much of what is important to either of us," Zach began. "Extradition is possible if needed; the weather is nice; there are beautiful beaches. I can live comfortably on my savings and the reasonably generous stipend I will be receiving from the US government for my continued cooperation for either doing or not doing anything related to any of those advanced research projects including this one. And it's not too far for us to visit from time to time should the need arise. But I have to be breathing and I have to keep breathing for this deal, Tom. Do we have an agreement, then? Can we shake on it?" Zach offered.

"Sounds good to me. In fact, I am a little envious but *yeah*, you did enough. Belize will work and we have a deal that we can shake on," Tom agreed and extended his hand to Zach who happily accepted and shook it vigorously.

"Good then. Thank you, Tom. Shall we get going? I am excited to get to Belize. Never been there but heard really good things and I'm excited to get on with this new chapter in my life." He picked up his bags and they walked down to the car waiting to take him to the airport and start his TSA adventures en route to Belize without a valid passport. That would take some doing for Tom who now needed to expedite getting Zach's suspended passport reinstated. With his bag loaded, Zach climbed into the car as Tom gave instructions to the driver and his companion in the front seat.

"Am I really going to get to Belize, Tom? Please be honest with me. I've been in this game a while; I know sometimes we have to do what needs to be done," Zach asked.

"Yes Zach. But for an act of God, a commercial plane crash or some other event I cannot foresee, you have my word you are on your way to

Belize," Tom assured him, looking him straight in the eye and nodding with conviction. There was no need to lie, either way, and Zach was convinced the man was telling the truth.

"Good and thank you Tom for being honest with me along the way. I consider that a professional courtesy. Not that I earned it in any way, but that says a lot about you and your character. You treated me fairly even though you didn't need to. That is more than many others in your position would have done. In fact, more than many others have done, including our boss. Thanks Tom. See you later." Zach waved and leaned back waiting for the driver to depart.

Tom stood up, but hesitated long enough to process Zach's farewell, "What makes you think you will see me later Zach?"

"F35, MQ-1, X-47, MQ-8." Zach said flatly.

"I don't get it?" Tom confessed.

"What do these all have in common Tom?" Zach asked playfully.

"They are all US air assets," Tom replied. "So what?"

"Good, what else do they have in common?" Zach pressed.

"They all fly and do important stuff for us. Speed this up for me Zach," Tom demanded.

"Yes, but these along with many other things I have not mentioned have identical twins in the PRC military. Copied from US systems that the Chinese somehow developed the exact same systems at nearly the same time but fielded shortly after we fielded ours. Funny how that seems to happen over and over again huh?" Zach teased.

"Yes, the theft of intellectual property, especially military and profitable capabilities is something we all seem to think they are very proficient at. You could add Humvees, Javelin missiles, M-4 rifles and a bunch of other stuff to your aviation list. So what?" Tom stopped as Zach interrupted.

"If you were to add Thor's Hammer to that long list of curiously similar capabilities, who would you think they may have stolen that from? I'm off to Belize for now, but I am sure I'll be seeing you again, Tom. Let's go driver, we have a plane to catch," Zach commanded.

Tom nodded and waved the driver on. After all he had made a deal with Zach and Tom was a man of his word. He also knew where to find him if he needed his help unwrapping the surprise gift he had just been given.

EPILOGUE

Zach was enjoying the morning sun as he sat in the comfortable chair enjoying the warm sand and cool morning breeze on the beach in Belize. He was well settled into his nice three-bedroom oceanside bungalow with a comfortable wrap around porch. He had a great spot, close enough for him to walk to a few restaurants, bars, and a small store to get the essentials without having to drive. He was far enough from the tourists and the congestion to not be bothered by them but close enough to conveniently get into the middle of it all when he was so inclined. But what he enjoyed more than any of that, was the stretch of beach at his backdoor.

It was beautiful, never crowded and convenient. He could walk off his back deck and in a couple of minutes cross the warm sand and put his feet, or all of him, in the water. It was as liberating as anything he'd ever experienced. After years of working—well actually living and working in a covert underground government advanced research and development facility for months at time without seeing sunlight, this was the exact opposite of that. He had fresh sea air, twenty-four-seven. Sunshine or shade on a whim, and the smells of the sea surrounded him in a calm that can be described but never really understood until actually experienced first-hand. It was similar to describing a color to someone who could not see; it fell short despite the best efforts of the person describing it.

He had found his spot and, in his mind, he had earned it. It was comfortable and it was inspiring. As much as he enjoyed it, he also needed to be engaged in something he considered meaningful and that provided him a sense of purpose. This morning those things came together for him, as he sat on the beach sipping his morning coffee. He decided to embark on something he hadn't done before but knew he could do given his previous jobs and personal experience. He opened his laptop and began writing chapter one of a fictional story, with a working title of *The Weather's Tamed*. After writing the story and listening to some friends as he sought their opinions about his ongoing efforts, he renamed his work *Thor's Apprentice*.

Symbology

Dawn, break-through, awareness

Magic, mystery, feminine

Decompose

Mirage

Disruption, confession, loss, change

Power, authority, strength

Endurance, lasting energy

Protection, shield, sanctuary

Fusion

Reduction of gold to powder through heat

Growth, beginnings, liberation

Revelation, knowledge, creativity, inspiration

Heat, visibility reduced by smoke

Space, the stars, safe travels

Heavy thunderstorm with snow

Thunderstorm, discovery

Joy, success, peace, fellowship

Wet fog

Lightning

Zodiacal light

Note to my Readers

Thor's Craftsmen shows us how on-demand weather modification is the same as any other tool. In the right hands and used for the right purpose, it can provide amazing benefits. Alternatively, in the wrong hands or used for the wrong purpose, it can produce devastating results; sometimes intended, and sometimes unintended.

General Chen told Tom, "I am experienced enough to know that you cannot trust governments but you can trust people." Bob Mcleod trusted a lot of people, and for good reason. But in the end, he and Ann decided that no matter how well intended their efforts were, trusting the government, any government with the technology was high risk at best. You can decide for yourself whether you think they duped the President into entering the wrong password or if it was his own error…we will likely never know for sure. But, in the end, it doesn't really matter. You may also think the team gave up too easily on getting the system back. When your intelligent system randomly selects the passwords in milliseconds and reassigns them just as fast…you get the results you asked for even if they weren't intended. Artificial intelligence is based on actual instructions. As we say in our family, you can choose your own actions but not your own consequences. And that's how it happened with the on-orbit system. The long-term impacts of the weather without extremes is just as interesting to contemplate as the weather we understand with its outlier extreme events. While it might be nice for a while to have stable climatological norms across the planet, what might that do to plants and animals? The planet has gone through five ice ages and the idea of man-made impacts to the climate are at all significant are still new. Let's hope Bob Mcleod's fictional success to stabilize the weather does more good than harm in the years to come.

It has been a great pleasure working on this trilogy with Rip at Bohannon Hall Press. Without his efforts, this story would have never made it off my desk. I enjoyed the opportunities to collaborate on the covers and artwork with my daughter, Emelia. Her work inspires me, and I am proud to have her works throughout this series.

A special thanks to all the readers who spent some time and treasure on *Thor's Apprentice* and kept coming back for more. I didn't plan a trilogy when I started this effort; blame or thank Rip for that. Because of my reader's responses and encouragement, I continued with *Thor's Journeymen* and now *Thor's Craftsmen*. And while this story is wrapped up, I am considering following up on another daughter's suggestion. She was curious if Bob and Ann would have any children, and what they would be when they grew up…and what 25 years of weather all being the same might produce. That made me wonder what the rest of the characters might look like in that same time frame. I haven't decided if I want to take on another writing project but, if I do, the working title for that one might be *Thor's Legacies*. Time will tell.